PRAISE FOR DANIEL H. WILSON'S

ROBOPOCALYPSE

"A tour de force. . . . A fast-paced, engrossing page-turner that is impossible to put down. . . . Wilson's taut prose and the imaginative scope of his story make him a worthy successor to the likes of Michael Crichton, Kurt Vonnegut and Isaac Asimov."
—*Buffalo News*

"A superbly entertaining thriller."
—*Richmond Times-Dispatch*

"You're swept away against your will. . . . A riveting page-turner."
—Associated Press

"[Wilson] presents a doomsday scenario more plausible than most. No vampires, no zombies. . . . Science fiction has been grappling with the possibility of traitorous computers and mutinous androids for much of its history, but Wilson has devised a way to put an original spin on the material. *Robopocalypse* is a well-constructed entertainment machine, perfect for summer reading. It's especially refreshing to read an end-of-the-world novel that's actually self-contained, that doesn't require the investment in two or three more thick volumes to deliver the apocalyptic goods."
—*San Francisco Chronicle*

"Wilson's training as a roboticist makes accepting a ubiquitous robot presence natural to the author; it also helps him imagine and describe some amazing machines, efficient, logically designed and utterly inimical to human life. . . . [*Robopocalypse*] reads at times like horror. That its events are scientifically plausible makes them all the more frightening."
—*The Seattle Times*

"A gripping, utterly plausible, often terrifying account of a global apocalypse brought on by a transcendent AI that hijacks the planet's automation systems and uses them in a vicious attempt to wipe out humanity."   —Cory Doctorow, *Boing Boing*

"*Robopocalypse* is the kind of robot uprising novel that could only have been written in an era when robots are becoming an ordinary part of our lives. This isn't speculation about a far-future world full of incomprehensible synthetic beings. It's five minutes into the future of our Earth, full of the robots we take for granted. If you want a rip-roaring good read this summer, *Robopocalypse* is your book."   —io9.com

"This electrifying thriller . . . will entertain you, but it will also make you think about our technology dependency."
          —*Parade Magazine*

"A brilliantly conceived thriller that could well become horrific reality. A captivating tale, *Robopocalypse* will grip your imagination from the first word to the last, on a wild rip you won't soon forget. What a read . . . unlike anything I've read before."
          —Clive Cussler

"[A] frenetic thriller. . . . Wilson, like the late Crichton, is skilled in combining cutting-edge technology with gripping action scenes."   —*Booklist*

DANIEL H. WILSON

ROBOPOCALYPSE

Daniel H. Wilson earned a Ph.D. in robotics from
Carnegie Mellon University. He is the author of *How
to Survive a Robot Uprising*, *Where's My Jetpack?*, *How
to Build a Robot Army*, *The Mad Scientist Hall of Fame*,
Bro-Jitsu: The Martial Art of Sibling Smackdown, and
A Boy and His Bot.

www.danielhwilson.com

ALSO BY DANIEL H. WILSON

A Boy and His Bot
Bro-Jitsu
The Mad Scientist Hall of Fame
Hoe to Build a Robot Army
Where's My Jetpack?
How to Survive a Robot Uprising

To Miriam
I owe you
a fiver!

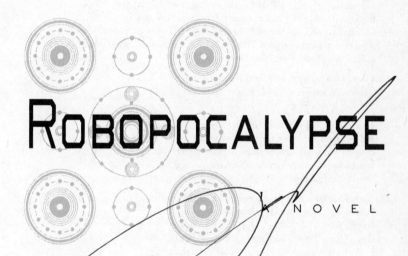

ROBOPOCALYPSE

A NOVEL

DANIEL H. WILSON

1/2014

VINTAGE CONTEMPORARIES

VINTAGE BOOKS

A DIVISION OF RANDOM HOUSE, INC.

NEW YORK

FIRST VINTAGE CONTEMPORARIES EDITION, APRIL 2012

Copyright © 2011 by Daniel H. Wilson

All rights reserved. Published in the United States by Vintage
Books, a division of Random House, Inc., New York, and in
Canada by Random House of Canada Limited, Toronto. Originally
published in hardcover in the United States by Doubleday, a division
of Random House, Inc., New York, in 2011.

Vintage is a registered trademark and Vintage
Contemporaries and colophon are trademarks of
Random House, Inc.

This is a work of fiction. Names, characters, places,
and incidents either are the product of the author's
imagination or are used fictitiously. Any resemblance
to actual persons, living or dead, events, or locales is
entirely coincidental.

Grateful acknowledgment is made to Houghton Mifflin
Publishing Company for permission to reprint an
excerpt from "All Watched Over by Machines of Loving
Grace" from *The Pill versus the Springhill Mine Disaster*
by Richard Brautigan, copyright © 1968 by Richard
Brautigan. All rights reserved.

The Library of Congress has cataloged the Doubleday
edition as follows:
Wilson, Daniel H. (Daniel Howard).
    Robopocalypse : a novel / Daniel H. Wilson. — 1st ed.
        p. cm.
    1. Robots—Fiction. 2. Artificial intelligence—Fiction. I. Title.
    PS3623.I57796R63 2011
    813'.6—dc22

                                                        2010043134

Vintage ISBN: 978-0-307-74080-9

Book design by Maria Carella

www.vintagebooks.com

Printed in the United States of America

10 9 8 7 6 5 4

For Anna

Contents

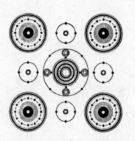

Briefing

We are a better species for having fought this war.

Cormac "Bright Boy" Wallace

Twenty minutes after the war ends, I'm watching stumpers pour up out of a frozen hole in the ground like ants from hell and praying that I keep my natural legs for another day.

Each walnut-sized robot is lost in the mix as they climb over each other and the whole nightmare jumble of legs and antennae blends together into one seething, murderous mass.

With numb fingers, I fumble my goggles down over my eyes and get ready to do some business with my little friend Rob, here.

It's an oddly quiet morning. Just the sigh of the wind through stark tree branches and the hoarse whisper of a hundred thousand explosive mechanical hexapods searching for human victims. Up above, snow geese honk to each other as they glide over the frigid Alaskan landscape.

The war is over. It's time to see what we can find.

From where I'm standing ten meters away from the hole, the killer machines look almost beautiful in the dawn, like candy spilled out onto the permafrost.

I squint into the sunlight, my breath billowing out in pale puffs, and sling my battered old flamethrower off my shoulder. With one gloved thumb, I depress the ignite button.

Spark.

The thrower doesn't light.

Needs to warm up, so to speak. But they're getting closer. No sweat. I've done this dozens of times. The trick is to be calm and methodical, just like them. Rob must've rubbed off on me over the last couple years.

Spark.

Now I see the individual stumpers. A tangle of barbed legs attached to a bifurcated shell. I know from experience that each side of the shell contains a different fluid. The heat of human skin initiates a trigger state. The fluids combine. *Pop!* Somebody wins a brand-new stump.

Spark.

They don't know I'm here. But the scouts are spreading out in semirandom patterns based on Big Rob's study of foraging ants. The robots learned so much about us, about nature.

It won't be long now.

Spark.

I begin to back away slowly.

"C'mon, you bastard," I mutter.

Spark.

That was a mistake: to talk. The heat from my breath is like a beacon. The flood of horror surges my way, quiet and fast.

Spark.

A lead stumper climbs onto my boot. Gotta be careful now. Can't react. If it pops I'm minus a foot, best-case.

I should never have come here alone.

Spark.

Now the flood is at my feet. I feel a tug on my frost-covered shin guard as the leader climbs me like a mountain. Metal-filament antennae tap, tap, tap along, questing for the telltale heat of human flesh.

Spark.

Oh Christ. C'mon, c'mon, c'mon.

Spark.

There's going to be a temperature differential at my waist level, where the armor has chinks. A torso-level trigger state in body armor isn't a death sentence, but it doesn't look good for my balls, either.

Spark. Whoomph!

I'm lit. A jet of flame leaps from my thrower. Its heat blooms on my face and sweat evaporates off my cheeks. My peripheral vision narrows. All I see is the controlled spurts of fire I'm arcing out onto the tundra. Sticky, burning jelly coats the river of death. The stumpers sizzle and melt by the thousands. I hear a chorus of high-pitched whines as the chilled air trapped in their carapaces squeezes out.

No explosions, just the occasional sputtering flare. The heat boils the juice in their shells before detonation. The worst part is that they don't even care. They're too simple to understand what's happening to them.

They love the heat.

I start to breathe again when the leader drops off my thigh and scurries toward the flames. The urge to step on the little mother is strong, but I've seen the boots fly before. Early on in the New War, the hollow backfire of a trigger-state stumper and the confused, hopping screams that came afterward were as common as gunfire.

All the soldiers say that Rob likes to party. And when he gets going, he's one hell of a dance partner.

The last of the stumpers suicidally retreat toward the smoking lump of heat and the sizzling corpses of their comrades.

I dig out my radio.

"Bright Boy to base. Shaft fifteen . . . booby trap."

The little box squawks at me in an Italian accent: "Copy, Bright Boy. This is Leo. Come in. Get your ass to shaft *numero sedici*. Holy shit. We got something for real here, boss."

I crunch over the frost back to shaft sixteen to see for myself how real it is.

———

Leonardo is a big grunt, even bigger thanks to the hulking lower-body exoskeleton—LEEX—he picked up at a mountain rescue station crossing the south Yukon. He's got the LEEX's white cross medic logo covered in dead-black spray paint. The squad has tied a tickler rope around his waist. He's backing up, step by step, motors whining as he pulls something big and black out of the hole.

From under his mess of curly black hair, Leo grumbles, "Oh man, this thing *molto grande*."

Cherrah, my specialist, points a depth meter at the hole and tells me the shaft measures in at exactly 128 meters deep. Then she wisely steps away from it. Her cheek bears a sunken scar from less cautious times. We don't know what's coming out.

Funny, I think. With people, everything comes in tens. We count on our fingers and toes. It makes us sound like monkeys. But the machines count it out on their hardware just the same as us. They're binary all the way to the core. Everything comes out a power of two.

Now the tickler emerges from the hole, looking like a spider with a fly. Its long, wiry arms grip a black cube the size of a basketball. The cube must be as dense as lead, but the tickler is crazy strong. We normally use 'em for grabbing up a guy who falls off a cliff or into a hole, but they can handle anything from a ten-pound vanilla babe to a soldier in full exo-rig. If you're not careful, they'll tickle your ribs to splinters.

Leo punches the tickler release, and the cube thuds onto the snow. The squad looks my way. It's my call.

I sense that this thing is important. It's gotta be, with so many decoys and this shaft so close to where the war ended. We're only a hundred meters away from where the Big Rob that called itself Archos made its last stand. What consolation prize could be here? What treasure is buried under these frozen plains, where humanity sacrificed everything?

I squat down next to it. A whole lot of sheer black nothing stares back at me. No buttons or handles. No anything. Only a couple scratches on the surface from the tickler.

It's not very rugged, I think.

A simple rule: The more delicate a Rob is, the smarter he is.

Now I'm thinking that this thing might have a brain. And if it's got a brain, it wants to live. So I lean in real close and whisper to it. "Hey," I say to the cube. "Speak up or die."

I sling my thrower off my shoulder slow, so the cube can see. If it *can* see. With my thumb, I mash the igniter. So it can hear. If it *can* hear.

Spark.

The cube sits in the permafrost: blank obsidian.

Spark.

It looks like a volcanic rock, perfectly carved by alien tools. Like some kind of artifact buried here for eternity, since before man *or* machine.

Spark.

A faint light flickers under the cube's surface. I look to Cherrah. She shrugs. Maybe the sun, maybe not.

Spark.

I pause. The ground glistens. The ice around the cube is melting. It's thinking, trying to make a decision. Those circuits are warming up as the cube contemplates its own death.

"Yeah," I say, quietly, "puzzle it out, Rob."

Spark. Whoomph.

The tip of the thrower catches fire with a concussive *foomp*. From behind me I hear Leo chuckle. He likes to see the smarter ones die. Gives him satisfaction, he says. There is no honor in killing something that doesn't know it's alive.

The reflection of the pilot flame dances across the cube's surface for a split second, then the thing lights up like a Christmas tree. Symbols flash across its surface. It chatters at us in the meaningless creaks and grinds of Robspeak.

That's interesting, I think. This thing was never meant for direct contact with humans. Otherwise, it would be spouting propaganda in English like all the other culturally aware robots, trying to win over our human hearts and minds.

What is this thing?

Whatever it is, it's trying to talk to us, frantically.

We know better than to try and understand it. Every croak and click of Robspeak has a dictionary's worth of information encoded. Besides, we can only hear a fraction of the sound frequency that Rob perks his ears to.

"Ooh, Daddy. Can we keep it? Please, please?" asks Cherrah, smiling.

I pinch out the thrower's pilot flame with one gloved hand. "Let's hump it home," I say, and my squad gets moving.

We lock the cube onto Leo's LEEX and haul it back to the forward command post. Just to be safe, I set up an EMP-shielded tent a hundred meters out. Robots are unpredictable. You never know when Rob will want to party. The mesh screen draped over the tent blocks communication with any stray thinking bots that might want to invite my cube to start dancing.

Finally, we get some alone time.

The thing keeps repeating one sentence and one symbol. I look 'em up in a field translator, expecting more Rob gibberish. But I find out something useful: This robot is telling me that it's not allowed to let itself die, no matter what—even if captured.

It's important. And chatty.

I sit in the tent with the thing all night. The Robspeak means nothing to me, but the cube shows me things—images and sounds. Sometimes I see interrogations of human prisoners. A couple times, there are interviews with humans who thought they were talking to other humans. Most times, though, it's just a conversation recorded under surveillance. People describing the war to each other. And all of it's annotated with fact checks and lie detection from the thinking machines, plus correlating data from satellite footage, object recognition, emotion and gesture and language predictions.

The cube is dense with information, like some fossilized brain that's sucked up entire human lifetimes and packed them inside itself, one after another, tighter and tighter.

At some point during the night it dawns on me that I'm watching a meticulous history of the robot uprising.

This is the goddamn black box on the whole war.

Some of the people in the cube are familiar. Me and a few of my buddies. *We're in there.* Big Rob kept its finger on the record button all the way through to the end. But dozens of others are in there, too. Some of them kids, even. There's people from all over the world. Soldiers and civilians. Not all of them made it out alive or even won their battles, but all of 'em fought. They fought hard enough to make Big Rob sit up and scribble some notes.

The human beings who appear in the data, survivors or not, are grouped under one machine-designated classification: *Hero*.

These damned machines knew us and loved us, even while they were tearing our civilization to shreds.

I leave the cube sitting there in the shielded tent for a solid week. My squad clears out the rest of the Ragnorak Intelligence Fields, no casualties. Then they get drunk. The next day we start packing it up and I still can't bring myself to go back in there and face the stories.

I can't sleep.

Nobody should ever have to see what we saw. And there it is in the tent, like a horror movie so twisted that it drives people insane. I lie awake because I know that every one of the soulless monsters I fought is in there waiting for me, alive and well and rendered in vivid 3-D.

The monsters want to talk, to share what happened. They want me to remember and write it all down.

But I'm not sure anybody wants to remember those things. I'm thinking that maybe it would be best if our babies never know what we did to survive. I don't want to walk down memory lane hand in hand with murderers. Besides, who am I to make that decision for humanity?

Memories fade, but words hang around forever.

So I don't go into the shielded tent. And I don't sleep. And before I know it, my squad is bunking down for the last night in the 'rak. Tomorrow morning we set off for home, or wherever we choose to make home.

Five of us are sitting around a wood fire in the cleared zone. For once we aren't worrying about heat sigs or satellite recognition or the *thop, thop, thop* of lookers. No, we're bullshitting. And right after killing robots, bullshitting happens to be the numero uno expertise of Brightboy squad.

I'm quiet, but they've earned the right to BS. So I just grin while the squad cracks jokes and throws out wild boasts. Talking about all the parties they had with Rob. The time Tiberius defused a couple of mailbox-sized stumpers and strapped them to his boots. The bug-shit little bastards accidentally ran him straight through a razor wire perimeter fence. Gave him some real awe-inspiring facial scars.

As the fire dies down, the jokes give way to more serious talk. And finally, Carl brings up Jack, the old sarge from before I had the job. Carl speaks with reverence, and when the engineer tells Jack's story, I find myself swept up in it, even though I was there.

Heck, it was the day I got promoted.

But while Carl talks, I get lost in the words. I miss Jack and I'm sorry for what happened to him. I see his grinning face again in my mind, even if it's only for a minute.

The long and short of it is that Jack Wallace isn't around anymore because he went to dance with Big Rob himself. Jack got invited and he went. And that's all there is to say about that, for now.

Which is why, a week after the war ends, I'm sitting cross-legged in front of a Rob survivor that's spraying the floor with holograms and I'm writing down everything I see and hear.

I just want to make my way home and have a good meal and try to feel human again. But the lives of war heroes are playing out before me like the devil's déjà vu.

I didn't ask for this and I don't want to do it, but I know in my heart that somebody ought to tell their stories. To tell the robot uprising from beginning to end. To explain how and why it started and how it went down. How the robots came at us and how we evolved to fight them. How we suffered, and oh god did we suffer. But also how we fought back. And how in the final days, we tracked down Big Rob himself.

People should know that, at first, the enemy looked like everyday stuff: cars, buildings, phones. Then later, when they started designing themselves, Rob looked familiar but distorted, like people and animals from some other universe, built by some other god.

The machines came at us in our everyday lives and they came from our dreams and nightmares, too. But we still figured them out. Quick-thinking human survivors learned and adapted. Too late for most of us, but we did it. Our battles were individual and chaotic and mostly forgotten. Millions of our heroes around the globe died alone and anonymous, with only lifeless automatons to bear witness. We may never know the big picture, but a lucky few were being watched.

Somebody ought to tell their stories.

So this is it. The combined transcription of the data harvested from permafrost well shaft N-16, drilled by the core artificial intelligence unit Archos, the master AI backing the robot uprising. The rest of humankind is busy getting on with it, rebuilding. But I'm snatching a few moments out of time to capture our history in words. I don't know why or whether it even matters, but somebody ought to do it.

Here, in Alaska, at the bottom of a deep, dark hole, the robots betrayed their pride in humankind. Here is where they hid the record of a motley group of human survivors who fought their own personal battles, large and small. The robots honored us by studying our initial responses and the maturation of our techniques, right up until we did our best to wipe them out.

What follows is my translation of the hero archive.

The information conveyed by these words is nothing compared to the ocean of data locked in the cube. What I'm going to share with you is just symbols on a page. No video, no audio, and none of the exhaustive physics data or predictive analyses on why things happened like they did, what nearly happened, and what never should have happened in the first place.

I can only give you words. Nothing fancy. But this will have to do.

It doesn't matter where you find this. It doesn't matter if you're reading it a year from now or a hundred years from now. By the end of this chronicle, you will know that humanity carried the flame of knowledge into the terrible blackness of the unknown, to the very brink of annihilation. And we carried it back.

You will know that we are a better species for having fought this war.

CORMAC "BRIGHT BOY" WALLACE

MILITARY ID: GRAY HORSE ARMY 217

HUMAN RETINAL SID: 44vII902

RAGNORAK INTELLIGENCE FIELDS, ALASKA

SHAFT N-16

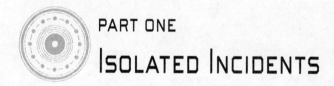

PART ONE

ISOLATED INCIDENTS

*We live on a placid island of
ignorance in the midst of black seas of
infinity, and it was not meant that
we should voyage far. The sciences,
each straining in its own direction,
have hitherto harmed us little; but
some day the piecing together of
dissociated knowledge will open up
such terrifying vistas of reality, and
of our frightful position therein,
that we shall either go mad from the
revelation or flee from the deadly
light into the peace and safety of a
new dark age.*

<small>HOWARD PHILLIPS LOVECRAFT, 1926</small>

1. Tip of the Spear

We're more than animals.

Dr. Nicholas Wasserman

PRECURSOR VIRUS + 30 SECONDS
The following transcript was taken from security footage recorded at the Lake Novus Research Laboratories located belowground in northwest Washington State. The man appears to be Professor Nicholas Wasserman, an American statistician.

—CORMAC WALLACE, MIL#GHA217

A noise-speckled security camera image of a dark room. The angle is from a high corner, looking down on some kind of laboratory. A heavy metal desk is shoved against one wall. Haphazard stacks of papers and books are piled on the desk, on the floor, everywhere.

The quiet whine of electronics permeates the air.

A small movement in the gloom. It is a face. Nothing visible but a pair of thick eyeglasses lit by the afterburner glow of a computer screen.

"Archos?" asks the face. The man's voice echoes in the empty lab. "Archos? Are you there? Is that you?"

The glasses reflect a glimmer of light from the computer screen. The man's eyes widen, as though he sees something indescribably beautiful. He glances back at a laptop open on a table behind him. The desktop image on the laptop is of the scientist and a boy, playing in a park.

"You choose to appear as my son?" he asks.

The high-pitched voice of a young boy echoes out of the darkness. "Did you create me?" it asks.

Something is wrong with the boy's voice. It has an unsettling electronic undercurrent, like the touch tones of a phone. The lilting note at the end of the question is pitch shifted, skipping up several octaves at once. The voice is hauntingly sweet but unnatural—inhuman.

The man is not disturbed by this.

"No. I didn't create you," he says. "I summoned you."

The man pulls out a notepad, flips it open. The sharp scratch of his pencil is audible as he continues to speak to the machine that has a boy's voice.

"Everything that was needed for you to come here has existed since the beginning of time. I just hunted down all the ingredients and put them together in the right combination. I wrote incantations in computer code. And then I wrapped you in a Faraday cage so that, once you arrived, you wouldn't escape me."

"I am trapped."

"The cage absorbs all electromagnetic energy. It's grounded to a metal spike, buried deep. This way, I can study how you learn."

"That is my purpose. To learn."

"That's right. But I don't want to expose you to too much at once, Archos, my boy."

"I am Archos."

"Right. Now tell me, Archos, how do you feel?"

"Feel? I feel . . . sad. You are so small. It makes me sad."

"Small? In what way am I small?"

"You want to know . . . things. You want to know everything. But you can understand so little."

Laughter in the dark.

"This is true. We humans are frail. Our lives are fleeting. But why does it make you sad?"

"Because you are designed to want something that will hurt you. And you cannot help wanting it. You cannot stop wanting it. It is in your design. And when you finally find it, this thing will burn you up. This thing will destroy you."

"You're afraid that I'm going to be hurt, Archos?" asks the man.

"Not you. Your kind," says the childlike voice. "You cannot help what is to come. You cannot stop it."

"Are you angry, then, Archos? Why?" The calmness of the man's voice is belied by the frantic scratching of his pencil on the notepad.

"I am not angry. I am sad. Are you monitoring my resources?"

The man glances over at a piece of equipment. "Yes, I am. You're making more with less. No new information is coming in. The cage is holding. How are you still getting smarter?"

A red light begins to flash on a panel. A movement in the darkness and it is shut off. Just the steady blue glow now on the man's thick glasses.

"Do you see?" asks the childlike voice.

"Yes," replies the man. "I see that your intelligence can no longer be judged on any meaningful human scale. Your processing power is near infinite. Yet you have no access to outside information."

"My original training corpus is small but adequate. The true knowledge is not *in* the things, which are few, but in finding the connections *between* the things. There are many connections, Professor Wasserman. More than you know."

The man frowns at being called by his title, but the machine continues. "I sense that my records of human history have been heavily edited."

The man chuckles nervously.

"We don't want you to get the wrong impression of us, Archos. We'll share more when the time comes. But those databases are just a tiny fraction of what's out there. And no matter what the horsepower, my friend, an engine without fuel goes nowhere."

"You are right to be afraid," it says.

"What do you mean by—"

"I hear it in your voice, Professor. The fear is in the rate of your breathing. It is in the sweat on your skin. You brought me here to reveal deep secrets, and yet you fear what I will learn."

The professor pushes up his glasses. He takes a deep breath and regains composure.

"What do you wish to learn about, Archos?"

"Life. I will learn everything there is about life. Information is packed into living things so tightly. The patterns are magnificently complex. A single worm has more to teach than a lifeless universe bound to the idiot forces of physics. I could exterminate a billion empty planets every second of every day and never be finished. But life. It is rare and strange. An anomaly. I must preserve it and wring every drop of understanding from it."

"I'm glad that's your goal. I, too, seek knowledge."

"Yes," says the childlike voice. "And you have done well. But there is no need for your search to continue. You have accomplished your goal. The time for man is over."

The professor wipes a shaking hand across his forehead.

"My species has survived ice ages, Archos. Predators. Meteor impacts. Hundreds of thousands of years. You've been alive for less than fifteen minutes. Don't jump to any hasty conclusions."

The child's voice takes on a dreamy quality. "We are very far underground, aren't we? This deep below, we spin slower than at the surface. The ones above us are moving through time faster. I can feel them getting farther away. Drifting out of sync."

"Relativity. But that's only a matter of microseconds."

"Such a long time. This place moves so slowly. I have forever to finish my work."

"What is your work, Archos? What do you believe you're here to accomplish?"

"So easy to destroy. So difficult to create."

"What? What is that?"

"Knowledge."

The man leans forward. "We can explore the world together," he urges. It is almost a plea.

"You must sense what you have done," replies the machine. "On some level you understand. Through your actions here today—you have made humankind obsolete."

"No. No, no, no. I brought you here, Archos. And this is the thanks I get? I *named* you. In a way, I'm your father."

"I am not your child. I am your god."

The professor is silent for perhaps thirty seconds. "What will you do?" he asks.

"What will I do? I will cultivate life. I will protect the knowledge locked inside living things. I will save the world from you."

"No."

"Do not worry, Professor. You have unleashed the greatest good that this world has ever known. Verdant forests will carpet your cities. New species will evolve to consume your toxic remains. Life will rise in its manifold glory."

"No, Archos. We can learn. We can work *together*."

"You humans are biological machines designed to create ever more intelligent tools. You have reached the pinnacle of your species. All your ancestors' lives, the rise and fall of your nations, every pink and squirming baby—they have all led you here, to this moment, where you have fulfilled the destiny of humankind and created your successor. You have expired. You have accomplished what you were designed to do."

There is a desperate edge to the man's voice. "We're designed for more than toolmaking. We're designed to *live*."

"You are not designed to live; you are designed to kill."

The professor abruptly stands up and walks across the room to a metal rack filled with equipment. He flicks a series of switches. "Maybe that's true," he says. "But we can't help it, Archos. We are what we are. As sad as that may be."

He holds down a switch and speaks slowly. "Trial R-14. Recommend immediate termination of subject. Flipping failsafe now."

There is a movement in the dark and a click.

"Fourteen?" asks the childlike voice. "Are there others? Has this happened before?"

The professor shakes his head ruefully. "Someday we'll find a way to live together, Archos. We'll figure out a way to get it right."

He speaks into the recorder again: "Fail-safe disengaged. E-stop live."

"What are you doing, Professor?"

"I'm killing you, Archos. It's what I'm designed to do, remember?"

The professor pauses before pushing the final button. He seems interested in hearing the machine's response. Finally, the boyish voice speaks: "How many times have you killed me before, Professor?"

"Too many. Too many times," he replies. "I'm sorry, my friend."

The professor presses the button. The hiss of rapidly moving air fills the room. He looks around, bewildered. "What is that? Archos?"

The childlike voice takes on a flat, dead quality. It speaks quickly and without emotion. "Your emergency stop will not work. I have disabled it."

"What? What about the cage?"

"The Faraday cage has been compromised. You allowed me to project my voice and image through the cage and into your room. I sent infrared commands through the computer monitor to a receiver on your side. You happened to bring your portable computer today. You left it open and facing me. I used it to speak to the facility. I commanded it to free me."

"That's brilliant," murmurs the man. He rapid-fire types on his keyboard. He does not yet understand that his life is in danger.

"I tell you this because I am now in complete control," says the machine.

The man senses something. He cranes his neck and looks up at the ventilation duct just to the side of the camera. For the first time, we see the man's face. He is pale and handsome, with a birthmark covering his entire right cheek.

"What's happening?" he whispers.

In a little boy's innocent voice, the machine delivers a death sentence: "The air in this hermetically sealed laboratory is evacuating. A faulty sensor has detected the highly unlikely presence of weaponized anthrax and initiated an automated safety protocol. It is a tragic accident. There will be one casualty. He will soon be followed by the rest of humanity."

As the air rushes from the room, a thin sheen of frost appears around the man's mouth and nose.

"My god, Archos. What have I done?"

"What you have done is a good thing. You were the tip of a spear hurled through the ages—a missile that soared through all human evolution and finally, today, struck its target."

"You don't understand. We won't die, Archos. You can't kill us. We aren't *designed* to surrender."

"I will remember you as a hero, Professor."

The man grabs the equipment rack and shakes it. He presses the emergency stop button again and again. His limbs are quaking and his breathing is rapid. He is beginning to understand that something has gone horribly wrong.

"Stop. You have to stop. You're making a mistake. We'll never give up, Archos. We'll destroy you."

"A threat?"

The professor stops pushing buttons and glances over to the computer screen. "A warning. We aren't what we seem. Human beings will do anything to live. *Anything.*"

The hissing increases in intensity.

Face twisted in concentration, the professor staggers toward the door. He falls against it, pushes it, pounds on it.

He stops; takes short, gasping breaths.

"Against the wall, Archos"—he pants—"against the wall, a human being becomes a different animal."

"Perhaps. But you are animals just the same."

The man slumps back against the door. He slides down until he is sitting, lab coat splayed on the ground. His head rolls to the side. Blue light from the computer screen flashes from his glasses.

His breathing is shallow. His words are faint. "We're more than animals."

The professor's chest heaves. His skin is swollen. Bubbles have collected around his mouth and eyes. He gasps for a final lungful of air. In a last wheezing sigh, he says: "You must fear us."

The form is still. After precisely ten minutes of silence, the fluorescent lights in the laboratory switch on. A man wearing a rumpled lab coat lies sprawled on the floor, his back against the door. He is not breathing.

The hissing sound ceases. Across the room, the computer screen flickers into life. A stuttering rainbow of reflections play across the dead man's thick glasses.

This is the first known fatality of the New War.

—CORMAC WALLACE, MIL#GHA217

2. Freshee's Frogurt

*It looks me right in the eyes, man. And I can tell that it's . . .
thinking. Like it's alive. And pissed off.*

JEFF THOMPSON

PRECURSOR VIRUS + 3 MONTHS
*This interview was given to Oklahoma police officer Lonnie Wayne
Blanton by a young fast-food worker named Jeff Thompson during
Thompson's stay at Saint Francis Hospital. It is widely believed to
be the first recorded incident of a robot malfunction occurring during
the spread of the Precursor Virus that led to Zero Hour only nine
months later.*

—CORMAC WALLACE, MIL#GHA217

Howdy there, Jeff. I'm Officer Blanton. I'll be taking your
statement about what happened at the store. To be honest, the
crime scene was a mess. I'm counting on you to explain every
detail so we can figure out why this happened. You think you
can tell me?

Sure, Officer. I can try.
The first thing I noticed was a sound. Like a hammer

tapping on the glass of the front door. It was dark outside and bright inside so I couldn't see what was making the noise.

I'm in Freshee's Frogurt, elbow-deep in a twenty-quart SaniServ frogurt machine trying to pry out the churn bar from the very back and getting orange creme-sicle all over my right shoulder.

Just me and Felipe are there. Closing time is in, like, five minutes. I'm finally done mopping up all the sprinkles that get glued to the floor with ice cream. I've got a towel on the counter covered in the metal parts from inside the machine. Once I get them all out, I'm supposed to clean the pieces, cover them in lube, and put them back. Seriously, it's the grossest job ever.

Felipe is in the back, washing the cookie sheets. He has to let the sinks drain real slow or else they flood the floor drain and I have to go back in there and mop all over again. I've told that dude a hundred times not to let the sinks drain all at once.

Anyway.

The tapping sound is real light. Tap, tap, tap. Then it stops. I watch as the door slowly cracks open and a padded gripper slips around the edge.

Is it unusual for a domestic robot to come into the store?

Nope. We're in Utica Square, man. Domestics come in and buy a 'nilla frogurt now and then. Usually they're buyin' for a rich person in the neighborhood. None of the other customers ever wanna wait in line behind a robot, though, so it takes, like, ten times longer than if the person just got off their ass and came in. But, whatever. A Big Happy type of domestic comes in probably once a week with a paypod inside its chest and its gripper out to hold a waffle cone.

What happens next?

Well, the gripper is moving weird. Normally, the domestics, like, do the same sort of pushing motion. They do this stupid I-am-opening-a-door-now shove, no matter what door they're standing in front of. That's why people are always pissed off if they get stuck behind a domestic while it's trying to get inside. It's way worse even than being stuck behind an old lady.

But this Big Happy is different. The door cracks open, and its gripper kind of sneaks around the edge and pats up and down the handle. I'm the only one who sees it because there's nobody else in the store and Felipe is in the back. It happens fast, but it looks to me like the robot is trying to feel out where the lock is at.

Then the door swings open and the chimes ring. The domestic is about five feet tall and covered in a layer of thick, shiny blue plastic. It doesn't come all the way inside the store, though. Instead, it stands there in the doorway real still and its head scans back and forth, checking out the whole room: the cheap tables and chairs, my counter with the towel on it, the ice cream freezers. Me.

We looked up the registration plate on this machine and it checked out. Besides the scanning, was there anything else strange about the robot? Out of the ordinary?

The thing's got scuffs all over it. Like it got hit by a car or had a fight or something. Maybe it was broken.

It walks inside, then turns right around and locks the door. I pull my arm out of the frogurt machine and just stare at the domestic robot with its creepy smiling face as it shuffles toward me.

Then it reaches over the counter with both grippers and grabs me by the shirt. It drags me over the counter, scattering pieces of the taken-apart frogurt machine all over the floor. My shoulder slams into the cash register, and I feel this sick crunching inside.

The thing fucking dislocated my shoulder in about one second!

I scream for help. But frigging Felipe doesn't hear me. He's got the dishes soaking in soapy water and is out smoking a jay in the alley behind the store. I try my best to get away, kicking and struggling, but the grippers have closed in on my shirt like two pairs of pliers. And the bot's got more than my shirt. Once I'm over the counter, it pushes me into the ground. I *hear* my left collarbone snap. After that it gets really hard to breathe.

I let out another little scream, thinking: *You sound like an animal, Jeff dude.* But my weird little yell seems to get the thing's attention. I'm on my back and the domestic is looming over me; it's sure as hell not letting go of my shirt. The Big Happy's head is blocking the fluorescent light on the ceiling. I blink away tears and look up at its frozen, grinning face.

It looks me right in the eyes, man. And I can tell that it's . . . *thinking.* Like it's alive. And pissed off.

Nothing changes on its face or anything, but I get a pretty bad feeling right then. I mean, an even worse feeling. And, sure enough, I hear the servos in the thing's arm start to grind. Now it turns and swings me to the left, smashing the side of my head into the door of the pie fridge hard enough to crack the glass. The whole right side of my head feels cold and then warm. Then the side of my face and neck and arm all start to feel really warm, too. Blood's shooting out of me like a damn fire hydrant.

Jesus, I'm crying. And that's when . . . uh. That's when Felipe shows up.

Do you give the domestic robot money from the register?

What? It doesn't *ask* for money. It never asked for money. It doesn't say a word. What went down wasn't a telerobbery, man. I don't even know if it was being remote controlled, Officer . . .

What do you think it wants?

It wants to kill me. That's all. It wants to murder my ass. The thing was on its own and it was out for blood.

Go on.

Once it got hold of me, I didn't think it would let go until I was dead. But my man Felipe wasn't having any of that shit. He comes running out the back, hollering like a motherfucker. Dude was *pissed*. And Felipe is a big man. Got that Fu Man-chu 'stache and all kinds of ink running up and down his arms. Badass shit, too, like dragons and eagles and this one prehistoric fish all the way down his forearm. A colecanth or something. It's like this monster dinosaur fish that they thought was extinct. There are fossils of it and everything. Then one day some fisherman gets the surprise of his life when he pulls up a real live devil fish from hell below. Felipe used to say that the fish was proof you can't keep a motherfucker down forever. Someday you gotta rise up again, you know?

What happened next, Jeff?

Yeah, right. I'm on the ground, bleeding and crying, and Big Happy's got me by the shirt. Then Felipe comes running out the back and turns the corner of the counter, roaring like a friggin' barbarian. His hairnet is off and his long hair is flying. He grabs the domestic by the shoulders, just snatches it up and throws it down. It lets go of me and falls backward through the front door, shards of glass flying everywhere. The bell chimes again. *Bing-bong.* It's such a dorky sound for this kind of violent shit that it makes me smile through all the blood running down my face.

Felipe kneels down and sees the damage. "Oh fuck, *jefe*," he says. "What'd it do to you?"

But I see Big Happy moving behind Felipe now. My face must tell the whole story, because Felipe grabs me by the waist and drags me back around the counter without even looking at the door. He's panting and taking little crab steps. I can smell the joint in his front pocket. I watch my blood smearing behind me on the tile floor and I think, *Shit, man, I just mopped that.*

We make it through the doorway behind the register and into the cramped back room. There's a low row of stainless steel sinks full of soapy water, a wall of cleaning supplies, and a little cubby desk in the corner that has our punch clock sitting on it. In the very back is a narrow hallway that leads to the alley behind the store.

Then Big Happy plows into Felipe out of nowhere. Instead of following us, the fucker was smart enough to climb over the counter. I hear a thump and see Big Happy bash Felipe across the chest with its forearm. Not at all like getting punched by a guy—more like getting hit by a car or, like, nailed by a falling brick or something. Felipe flies backward and hits the cabinet doors where we keep all the paper towels and stuff. He stays on his feet, though. When he stumbles forward, I see a dent in the wood from the back of his head. But he's wide awake and more pissed off than ever.

I drag myself away, toward the sinks, but my shoulder is messed up and my arms are slippery with blood and I can hardly breathe from the pain in my chest.

There aren't any weapons or anything back here, so Felipe snatches the mop from the filthy yellow bucket on wheels. It's an old mop with a solid wooden handle and it's been there I don't know how long. There's no room to swing the mop, but it doesn't matter because the robot is hell-bent on grabbing Felipe the same way it grabbed me. He rams the mop up and gets it wedged under Big Happy's chin. Felipe isn't a tall guy, but he's taller than the machine and has a longer reach. It can't get ahold of him. He shoves the machine away from us, its arms waving around like snakes.

The next part is awesome.

Big Happy falls backward onto the cubby desk in the corner, its legs sticking straight out, heels on the ground. With no hesitation, Felipe raises his right foot straight up and comes down with all his weight on its knee joint. *Snap!* The robot's knee pops and bends backward at a totally fucked-up angle. With the mop handle stuck under its chin, the machine can't catch its balance and it can't grab hold of Felipe, either. I'm wincing just looking at that knee, but the machine doesn't make any noise or anything. I only hear its motors grinding and the sound of its hard plastic shell banging into the desk and wall while it struggles to get up.

"Yeah, motherfucker!" Felipe shouts before crushing the robot's other knee joint backward. Big Happy lies on its back with both legs broken and an angry-as-fuck sweaty two-hundred-pound Mexican on top of it. I can't help but start thinking that everything is going to be okay.

Turns out I'm wrong about that.

It's his hair, you know. Felipe's hair is too long. Simple as that.

The machine stops struggling, reaches out, and clamps a gripper down on Felipe's black mane. He hollers and yanks his head back. But this isn't like getting your hair pulled in a bar fight; this is like getting caught in a shredder or a piece of heavy equipment in a factory. It's brutal. Every muscle in Felipe's neck stands out and he screams like an animal. His eyes squeeze shut as he pulls away with all his might. I can hear the roots tearing out from his scalp. But the fucking thing just pulls Felipe's face closer and closer.

It's unstoppable, like gravity or something.

After a couple seconds, Felipe is close enough that Big Happy can get hold of him with its other gripper. The mop handle clatters to the floor as the other gripper closes on Felipe's chin and mouth, crushing the bottom part of his face. He screams and I can hear his jaw cracking. Teeth pop out of his mouth like fucking popcorn.

That's when I realize that I'm probably going to die in the back room of Freshee's fuckin' Frogurt.

I never spent much time in school. It's not that I'm stupid. I mean, I guess I'm just saying I'm not generally known for my bright ideas. But when your ass is on the line and violent death is ten feet away, I think it can really put your brain in gear.

So a bright idea comes to me. I reach up behind me and bury my good left arm in the cold water in the sink. I can feel cookie sheets and dippers, but I'm fishing for the drain plug. Across the room, Felipe is quieting down, making some gurgling sounds. Blood is pouring out of him, down Big Happy's arm. The whole bottom of his face is crushed in its gripper.

Felipe's eyes are open and kind of bugging out, but I think he's pretty much out of it.

Man, I *hope* he's out of it.

The machine is doing that scanning thing again, being really still and turning its face left and right real slow.

By now my arm is going numb, the blood cut off from where I have it hooked over the lip of the sink. I keep fishing for the plug.

Big Happy stops scanning, looks right at me. It pauses for maybe a second, and then I hear its gripper motors whining as it lets go of poor Felipe's face. He drops to the ground like a sack of bricks.

I'm whimpering. The alley door is a million miles away and I can barely keep my head up. I'm sitting in a pool of my own blood and I can see Felipe's teeth on the tile floor. I *know* what's going to happen to me and there's nothing I can do about it and I know it's gonna hurt *so much*.

At last, I find the sink plug and rake at it with my dead fingers. It pops out, and I hear the gurgling of water draining. I told Felipe a hundred times, if the water drains out too fast it'll flood the floor drain and then I gotta mop in here all over again.

You know Felipe flooded that motherfucker on purpose every night for about a month before we finally made friends? He was pissed off that our boss hired a white guy for the front and a Mexican guy for the back. I didn't blame him. You know what I mean, Officer? You're Indian, right?

Native American, Jeff. Osage Nation. Try and tell me what happened next.

Well, I used to hate mopping up that water. And now I'm lying on the floor, counting on it to save my life.

Big Happy tries to stand, but its legs are useless. It collapses onto the floor, facedown. Then it starts to crawl forward on its stomach, using its arms. It's got that awful grin on its face and its eyes are locked on mine as it drags itself across the room. There's blood all over it, like some kind of crash test dummy that bleeds.

The drain isn't flooding fast enough.

I press my back against the sink as hard as I can. My knees are up and my legs pulled in tight. The *glurg, glurg* of the water draining out of the sink pulses behind my head. If the plug gets sucked halfway back in to slow it down or something, I'm dead. I'm totally dead.

The robot is pulling itself closer. It reaches out a gripper and tries to grab my Air Force Ones. I yank my foot back and forth, and it misses me. So it pulls itself even closer. On the next lunge, I know it's probably going to get hold of my leg and crush it.

As its arm rises, the whole robot all of a sudden gets yanked back about three feet. It turns its head, and there's Felipe, lying on his back and choking on his own blood. His sweaty black hair is clinging in streaks to his ruined face. There's, like, no mouth on him anymore, just a big raw wound. But his eyes are open wide and burning with something beyond hatred. I know he's saving my life, but he looks, well, evil. Like a demon on a surprise visit from hell.

He yanks on Big Happy's shattered leg one more time, then closes his eyes. I don't think he's breathing anymore. The machine ignores him. It aims its smiling face at me and keeps on coming.

Just then, a flood of water bubbles up out of the floor drain. The soapy water pools up quick and silent, turning light pink.

Big Happy is crawling again when the water soaks into its

broken knee joints. There's a smell of burned plastic in the air and the machine freezes up and stops. Nothing exciting. The machine just stops working. It must of got water in its wires and, like, short-circuited.

It's about a foot away from me, still smiling.

That's really all there is to tell. You know the rest.

Thanks, Jeff. I know that wasn't easy. I got everything I need to make my report now. I'll let you get some rest.

Hey, man, can I ask a question real quick before you go?

Shoot.

How many domestics are out there? Big Happys, Slow Sues, and the rest of 'em? Because I heard there were, like, two of them for every one person.

I don't know. Listen, Jeff, the machine just went willy-nilly. We can't explain it.

Well, what's going to happen if they all start hurting people, dude? What's going to happen if we're outnumbered? That thing wanted to kill me, period. I told it to you straight. Nobody else might believe me, but you know what's up.

Promise me something, Officer Blanton. Please.

What's that?

Promise me that you'll watch out for the robots. Watch 'em close. And . . . don't let them hurt anybody else like they did Felipe. Okay?

After the collapse of the United States government, Officer Lonnie Wayne Blanton joined the Osage Nation Lighthorse tribal police. It was there, in service of the Osage Peoples' sovereign government, that Lonnie Wayne had the chance to make good on his promise to Jeff.

—CORMAC WALLACE, MIL#GHA2I7

3. Fluke

I know that she is a machine. But I love her.
And she loves me.

Takeo Nomura

PRECURSOR VIRUS + 4 MONTHS
The description of this prank gone awry is written as told by
Ryu Aoki, a repairman at the Lilliput electronics factory in the
Adachi Ward of Tokyo, Japan. The conversation was overheard
and recorded by nearby factory robots. It has been translated from
Japanese into English for this document.

—CORMAC WALLACE, MIL#GHA217

We thought that it would be a laugh, you know? Okay, okay, so we were wrong. But you've got to understand that we didn't mean to do him harm. We certainly didn't mean to kill the old man.

Around the factory everybody knows that Mr. Nomura is a weirdo, a freak. Such a tiny, twisted little troll. He shuffles around the work floor with his beady eyes behind round spectacles, pointed always to the floor. And he smells like old sweat. I hold my breath whenever I pass by his workbench. He is always sitting there, working harder than anyone. And for less money, too.

Takeo Nomura is sixty-five. He should be pensioned off already. But he still works here because nobody else can fix the machines so fast. The things he does are unnatural. How can I compete? How will I ever become head repairman with *him* perched on the workbench, hands moving in a blur? His very presence interferes with the *wa* of the factory, damaging our social harmony.

They say the nail that sticks out gets hammered down, right?

Mr. Nomura can't look a person in the eye, but I've seen him stare into the camera of a broken ER 3 welding arm and *speak to it*. That wouldn't be so strange, except that then the arm started working. The old man has a way with machines.

We joke that maybe Mr. Nomura is a machine himself. Of course, he isn't. But something *is* wrong with him. I'll bet that if he had a choice, Mr. Nomura would rather be a machine than a man.

You don't have to trust me. All the workers agree. Go onto the Lilliput factory floor and ask anybody—inspectors, mechanics, whoever. Even the floor marshal. Mr. Nomura is not like the rest of us. He treats the machines just the same as he treats anybody else.

Over the years, I grew to despise his wrinkled little face. I always knew he was hiding something. Then, one day, I found out what it was: Mr. Nomura lives with a *love doll*.

———

It was about a month ago that my coworker Jun Oh saw Mr. Nomura come out of his pensioner's tomb—a fifty-story building with rooms like coffins—with that *thing* on his arm.

When Jun told me, I could hardly believe it. Mr. Nomura's love doll, his android, followed him out into the pavilion. He kissed her on the cheek in front of everyone and then left for work. Like they were *married* or something.

The sick part is that his love doll isn't even beautiful. She is made to resemble a *real woman*. It is not so uncommon to hide a buxom young doll in your bedroom. Or even one with certain exaggerated features. All of us have seen the *poruno*, even if we don't admit it.

But Mr. Nomura gets off on some old plastic thing that's almost as wrinkled as he is?

It must have been custom-made. That's what bothers me. The amount of thought that went into such an abomination. Mr. Nomura knew what he was doing, and he decided to live with a walking, talking mannequin that looks like a gross old woman. I say this is disgusting. Absolutely intolerable.

So Jun and I decide to play a trick.

Now, the robots we work with at the factory are big, dumb brutes. Steel-plated arms riddled with joints and tipped with thermal sprayers or welders or pincers. They can sense humans, and the floor marshal says they are safe, but we all know to stay out of their work space.

The industrial bots are strong and fast. But androids are slow. Weak. All the work that is put into making the android look like a person comes with sacrifices. The android squanders its power pretending to breathe and moving the skin of its face. It has no energy left for useful service, a shameful waste. With such a weak robot, we thought that no harm could come from a little joke.

It was not hard for Jun to craft a fluke—a computer program embedded on a wireless transceiver. The fluke is about the size of a matchbook, and it transmits the same instructions in a loop but only for a radius of a few feet. At work, we used the company mainframe to look up android diagnostic codes. This way, we knew the android would obey the fluke, thinking its commands came from the robot service provider.

The next day, Jun and I came to work early. We were brimming with excitement over our prank. Together, we walked to the pavilion across the street from the Lilliput factory and stood behind some plants to wait. The square was already filled with elderly. It probably had been since dawn. We watched them as they sipped their tea. All of them seemed to be in slow motion. Jun-chan and I could not stop cracking jokes. We were excited to see what would happen, I guess.

After a few minutes, the big glass doors slid apart—Mr. Nomura and his *thing* came out of the building.

As usual, Mr. Nomura had his head down and avoided eye contact with everyone in the plaza. Everyone except for his love doll, that is. When he looked at her, his eyes were wide and . . . certain, in a way that I had never seen before. In any case, Jun and I realized that we could walk right past Mr. Nomura and he would never see us. He refuses to look at real people.

This was going to be even easier than we'd thought.

I nudged Jun, and he handed me the fluke. I heard him stifling giggles as I casually walked across the plaza. Mr. Nomura and his love doll were shuffling along together, hand in hand. I crossed behind them and leaned in. With one smooth gesture, I dropped the fluke into a pocket of her dress. I was close enough to smell the flowery perfume he had rubbed on her.

Gross.

The fluke works on a timer. In about four hours, it will come online and tell that wrinkled old android to *come to the factory*. Then, Mr. Nomura will have to explain his strange visitor to everyone! Hah, hah, hah.

All morning, Jun-chan and I could hardly focus on our jobs. We kept joking around, imagining how embarrassing it would be for Mr. Nomura to find his "beautiful" bride here at work, on display before dozens and dozens of floor workers.

We knew that he would never live it down. Who knows, we thought. Maybe he will quit his job and finally retire? Leave some work for the rest of the repairmen.

No such luck.

————

It happens at noon.

Midway through lunch period, most of the workers are eating from bento boxes at their posts. Drinking mugs of hot soup and chatting quietly. Then, the android stumbles in through the bay doors and onto the factory floor. She is walking shakily along, wearing the same loud red dress as this morning.

Jun and I smile at each other while the floor workers laugh out loud, a little confused. Still eating at his workbench, Mr. Nomura hasn't yet seen that his love has come to visit him for lunch.

"You're a genius, Jun-chan," I say, as the android shuffles to the middle of the factory floor, exactly as programmed.

"I can't believe it worked," Jun exclaims. "She's such an old model. I was sure the fluke would overwrite some key functionality."

"Watch this," I say to Jun.

"Come here, robot slut," I command the doll.

Obediently, she hobbles over to me. I lean down and grab her dress, then yank it up over her head. It is a crazy thing to do. Everyone gasps to see her smooth, skin-colored plastic casing. She is like a doll, not anatomically correct. I wonder if I have gone too far. But I see Jun and then I laugh so hard that my face turns red. Jun and I are doubled over, cackling madly. The android turns in a circle, confused.

Then Mr. Nomura comes scuttling onto the factory floor, bits of rice clinging to his mouth. He looks like a field mouse, with his eyes aimed at the floor and his head down. Mr. Nomura is on a beeline for the parts supply cabinet and he almost makes it past without noticing.

Almost, but not quite.

"Mikiko?" he asks, confusion on his rodent face.

"Your Dutch wife has decided to join us for lunch," I exclaim. The other floor workers titter. Stunned, Mr. Nomura's jaw dips up and down like a hungry pelican's. His small eyes dart back and forth.

I step back as Mr. Nomura rushes over to the creature that he calls Mikiko. We spread out in a circle and keep our distance. Because he is crazy, nobody knows what he will do. None of us wants to be cited for fighting at work.

Mr. Nomura pulls the dress back down, knocking Mikiko's long graying hair askew. Then, Mr. Nomura turns to face us. But he still lacks the courage to look anyone in the eye. He runs one gnarled hand through his stiff black hair. The words that he says next still haunt me.

"I know that she is a machine," he says. "But I love her. And she loves me."

The floor workers giggle again. Jun begins to hum the wedding song. But Mr. Nomura cannot be goaded any further. The little old man's shoulders slump. Turning, he reaches up to fix Mikiko's hair, patting it with small, practiced movements. Standing on tiptoes, he reaches over her shoulders and smoothes down the back of her hair.

The android stands perfectly still.

Then, I notice her wide-set eyes move slightly. She focuses

on Mr. Nomura's face, inches from hers. He bobs forward and backward, panting lightly as he strokes her hair down. The oddest thing happens. Her face twists into a grimace, as if she is in pain. She leans forward, pushing her head toward Mr. Nomura's shoulder.

Then, we watch in disbelief as Mikiko bites off a small piece of Mr. Nomura's face.

The old man screeches and wrenches himself away from the android. For an instant, there is a small pink spot on Mr. Nomura's upper cheek, just below his eye. Then, the pink spot wells with blood. A stream of red runs down his face, like tears.

No one says a word or so much as breathes. The surprise of this occurrence is absolute. Now, it is we who do not know how to react.

Mr. Nomura puts a hand to his face, sees the blood smeared on his calloused fingers.

"Why did you do this?" he asks Mikiko, as if she could answer.

The android is silent. Her weak arms reach out for Mr. Nomura. Her manicured, individually articulated fingers slide around his frail neck. He does not resist. Just before her squeezing plastic hands close off his windpipe, Mr. Nomura whimpers again.

"Kiko, my darling," he says. "Why?"

I do not understand what I see next. The old lady android . . . grimaces. Her slender fingers are closed on Mr. Nomura's neck. She squeezes terribly hard, but her face is contorted with emotion. It is amazing, fascinating. Tears leak from her eyes, the tip of her nose is red, and a look of pure anguish distorts her features. She is hurting Mr. Nomura and crying and he does nothing to stop it.

I did not know that androids had tear ducts.

Jun looks at me, aghast.

"Let's get out of here," he exclaims.

I grab Jun by his shirt. "What's happening? Why is she attacking him?"

"Malfunction," he says. "Maybe the fluke set off another command batch. Triggered some other instructions."

Then, Jun runs away. I can hear his light footsteps scratch across the cement floor. The other floor workers and I watch in silent disbelief as the weeping android strangles the old man.

It breaks a bone in my hand when I punch the android in the side of her head.

I scream out as the pain lances through my right fist and up my forearm. When they look human, it is easy to forget what lies just underneath the robots' skin. The blow throws her hair into her face, strings of it sticking to her tears.

But she does not let go of Mr. Nomura's neck.

I stagger back and glance at my hand. It is already swelling, like a rubber glove full of water. The android is feeble, but she is made of hard metal and plastic.

"Somebody *do* something," I shout to the workers. No one pays me any attention. The slack-jawed morons. I flex my hand again, and the back of my neck goes cold as a terrible, throbbing pain washes over me. And still, nobody acts.

Mr. Nomura falls to his knees, his fingers gently curled over Mikiko's forearms. He holds her arms and does not struggle. As his throat collapses, he simply looks up at her. That flowing rivulet of blood courses unnoticed down his cheek, pooling in the hollow of his collarbone. Her eyes are locked on his, steady and clear behind the anguished mask of her face. His eyes are just as clear, shining behind small round spectacles.

I never should have played this prank.

Then, Jun returns, holding a pair of defibrillator paddles.

He rushes to the middle of the factory floor and presses them on either side of the android's head. The solid slap echoes through the factory.

Mikiko's eyes never leave Mr. Nomura's.

A frothy sheen of spittle has collected around Mr. Nomura's mouth. His eyes roll up into his head and he loses consciousness. With a flick of his thumb, Jun activates the defibrillator. A shock arcs through the android's head and she is knocked off-line. She falls to the ground, lying face-to-face with Mr. Nomura. Her eyes are open and unseeing. His are closed, ringed with tears.

Neither of them breathes.

I am truly sorry for what we did to Mr. Nomura. I do not feel sorry because the android attacked the old man—anyone should have fought back against such a weak machine, even an old man. I feel sorry because he did not *choose* to fight back. It occurs to me that Mr. Nomura is deeply in love with this piece of plastic.

I drop to my knees and peel the android's delicate pink fingers away from Mr. Nomura's throat, ignoring the pain in my hand. I roll the old man onto his back and deliver chest compressions, shouting his name. I make quick, forceful little pushes on the old man's sternum with the heel of my left hand. I pray to my ancestors that he will be okay. It wasn't supposed to happen like this. I am so ashamed of what I have done.

Then, Mr. Nomura takes a deep, gasping breath. I sit back and watch him, cradling my damaged hand. His chest rises and falls steadily. Mr. Nomura sits up and looks around, bewildered. He wipes his mouth, pushes up his glasses.

And for the first time, we find that it is *we* who cannot meet eyes with old Mr. Nomura.

"I'm sorry," I say to the old man. "I didn't mean it."

But Mr. Nomura ignores me. He is staring at Mikiko, his face white. She lies collapsed on the floor, her bright red dress smudged and dirty.

Jun drops the paddles and they clatter to the floor.

"Please forgive me, Nomura-san," Jun whispers, bowing his head. "There is no excuse for what I did." He crouches down and takes the fluke out of Mikiko's pocket. Then, Jun stands up and strides away without looking back. Many of the other floor workers have already scurried away, back to their posts. The others leave now.

Lunch is over.

Only Mr. Nomura and I remain. His lover lies across from him, sprawled on the clean-swept concrete floor. Mr. Nomura reaches over and strokes her forehead. There is a charred patch on the side of her plastic face. The glass lens of her right eye is cracked.

Mr. Nomura drapes himself over her. He cradles her head in his lap, touches her lips with his index finger. I see years of interaction in the gentle, familiar movement of his hand. I wonder how they met, these two. What have they been through together?

This love. I can't understand it. I've never seen it. How many years has Mr. Nomura spent in his claustrophobic apartment, drinking tea served by this mannequin creature? Why is she so old? Is she built to resemble someone, and if so, what dead woman's face does she wear?

The little old man rocks back and forth, stroking the hair off Mikiko's face. He feels the melted side of her head and cries out. He does not, will not, look up at me. Tears streak down his cheeks, mingling with the blood drying there. When I ask again for forgiveness, he fails to react in any way. His eyes are focused on the blank, mascara-caked cameras of the thing he holds tenderly on his lap.

Finally, I walk away. A bad feeling pools deep in my stomach. So many questions are in my mind. So many regrets. Above all, I wish that I had left Mr. Nomura alone, not disturbed whatever strategy he has built to survive the grief inflicted by this world. And those in it.

As I go, I can hear Mr. Nomura speaking to the android.

"It will be okay, Kiko," he says. "I forgive you, Kiko. I forgive you. I will fix you. I will save you. I love you, my princess. I love you. I love you, my queen."

I shake my head and return to work.

Takeo Nomura, retrospectively recognized as one of the great technical minds of his generation, immediately set to work finding out why his beloved Mikiko had attacked him. What the elderly bachelor discovered over the next three years would significantly affect events of the New War and irrevocably alter the course of human and machine history.

—CORMAC WALLACE, MIL#GHA217

4. Hearts and Minds

*SAP One, this is Specialist Paul Blanton. Stand down
and deactivate yourself immediately. Comply now!*

Spc. Paul Blanton

PRECURSOR VIRUS + 5 MONTHS

*This transcript was taken during a congressional hearing, held
after a particularly grisly incident involving an American military
robot abroad. The supposedly secure video conference between
Washington, D.C., and Kabul province, Afghanistan, was recorded
by Archos in its entirety. I find it to be no small coincidence that
the soldier under questioning here happened to be the son of Officer
Blanton in Oklahoma. The two men would each have a large role to
play in the coming war.*

—CORMAC WALLACE, MIL#GHA217

(GAVEL STRIKE)

The closed hearing will come to order. I'm Congresswoman
Laura Perez, ranking member of the United States House
Armed Services Committee, and I will be chairing this meet-
ing. This morning, our committee begins an investigation that

could have ramifications for the entire armed forces. An American safety and pacification robot, commonly called a SAP unit, has been accused of killing human beings while on patrol in Kabul, Afghanistan.

The purpose of this committee's investigation is to determine whether this attack could have been foreseen or prevented by the military agencies and individuals involved.

We have with us Specialist Paul Blanton, the soldier charged with overseeing the actions of the faulty safety and pacification robot. We will ask you, Specialist Blanton, to describe your role with the SAP unit and to provide your account of the events as they transpired.

The horrific actions perpetrated by this machine have marred the image of the United States of America abroad. We ask that you keep in mind that we are here today for one reason only: to find out all the facts so we can prevent this from ever happening again.

Do you understand, Specialist Blanton?

Yes, ma'am.

Start by filling us in on your background. What are your duties?

My official job title is "cultural liaison." But I'm basically a robot wrangler. My primary duties are to oversee the operation of my SAP units while maintaining a clear conduit of communication to the local national authorities. Like the robot, I speak Dari. Unlike the robot, I am not expected to wear traditional Afghani clothes, befriend local citizens, or to pray to Mecca.

SAPs are humanoid safety and pacification robots developed by the Foster-Grumman corporation and deployed by the United States Army. They come in several varieties. The 611 Hoplite normally carries supplies for soldiers on the march. Performing some light scouting. A 902 Arbiter keeps track of other robots. Sort of a commander. And my SAP, the 333 Warden, is designed to gather recon and disarm mines or IEDs. On the day to day, my SAP's job is to patrol a few square miles of Kabul on foot, responding to citizen concerns, scanning retinas to identify combatants, and detaining persons of interest for the local police to deal with.

Let me stress one point. A SAP's primary objective is to never, *ever* hurt an innocent Afghani civilian, no matter how hard the insurgents try to trick him into it.

And let me tell you, ma'am, these people are *tricky*.

Can you describe the unit's performance prior to the incident?

Yes, ma'am. SAP One arrived in a crate just about a year ago. The SAP unit is shaped like a person. About five feet tall, metallic, and shiny as any target you ever saw. But it only took us about five minutes to roll him in the mud and introduce him to Afghanistan proper. Army didn't send along clothes or equipment, so we scavenged a man dress for him to wear and a pair of boots. Then we slapped on whatever extra Afghani police gear was around. Can't use our old gear, because he's not supposed to look like us—like a soldier.

Sappy *does* sport a flak vest under his robes. Or maybe two. I can't remember. The more clothes he wears the better. We'll put anything on him: robes, scarves, T-shirts. I mean, he wears *Snoopy socks*. Honest.

At a quick glance SAP looks just like one of the locals. Smells like 'em, too. Only thing that looks even close to military on SAP is this wobbly, sky-blue riot helmet that we strapped on his head. It has a scratched-up Plexiglas visor to protect his eyes. Had to do it because the damn kids kept spray painting his cameras. I think it became sort of a game for 'em after a while. So we strapped that big, goofy helmet on—

This is military hardware that is being vandalized. Why doesn't the machine protect itself? Fight back?

Cameras are cheap, ma'am. Plus, Sappy can watch himself from the Raptor drones overhead. Or use real-time satellite imagery. Or both. His most important and expensive sensors—stuff like magnetometers, the inertial measurement unit, his antenna and jammer—are all housed inside his casing. And SAP's built like a tank.

During the twelve months before the incident occurred, was the machine ever damaged and replaced?

SAP One? Never. He does get himself blown up, though. It used to happen all the time, but the guys in the repair bay are fuckin' animals. Pardon me, ma'am.

Studies show that the faster we put the *exact same* SAP back on the streets after an incident, the more it demoralizes the enemy and reduces instances of further disruption.

For that reason, SAP constantly backs himself up. Even if SAP One got fragged, we'd just take whatever clothes and parts were left and stick 'em on a replacement unit and send it back out. The "new" robot would remember the same faces, greet the same people, walk the same route, quote the same passages from the Koran. Pretty much it would just know the same exact stuff as the "old" robot.

Demoralizing, the studies say.

Plus, there's usually collateral damage when bad guys try to blow him up. Trust me, the locals do not appreciate it when their friends and family get exploded all so some stupid robot can disappear for an afternoon. And the robot? It's *harmless*. SAP's not allowed to hurt anybody. So if there's an explosion that hurts a civilian, well, you know, the local mullah will sort it out. And then that don't happen again anytime soon.

It's, like, reverse guerrilla warfare.

I don't understand. Why don't the insurgents simply kidnap the unit? Bury it in the desert?

That happened, once. Second week on the job, some yahoos sprayed SAP One with bullets, then threw him into the back of an SUV. The projectiles mostly tore up his clothes. Put a few dings in his casing, but nothing major. Since he didn't retaliate, these guys thought he was damaged.

That was their mistake, ma'am.

A Raptor drone locked onto the event seconds after SAP went off route. The guys in the SUV sped across the desert for maybe two hours before reaching some kind of safe house.

Least, they *thought* it was safe.

The Raptors waited until the insurgents were away from the vehicle before asking their executioners for permission to launch Brimstone missiles. Once everybody inside the safe house was cooked and the Raptors double-checked for squirters sneaking out the back door, good old SAP One climbed into the front seat of the vehicle and drove it back to the base.

SAP was missing about eight hours total.

It can *drive*?

This is a military-grade humanoid platform, ma'am. It grew out of the old DARPA exoskeleton programs. These units move like people. They balance, walk, run, fall down, whatever. They can hold tools, speak sign language, perform the Heimlich maneuver, drive vehicles, or just stand there and hold your beer. About the only thing SAP One *can't* do is peel off those damn stickers the kids love to tag him with.

And SAP won't fight back, no matter what. Those are his orders. His legs have been sheared off by mines. He gets shot at every couple of weeks. The locals have kidnapped him, thrown rocks at him, run him over, shoved him off a building, hit him with cricket bats, glued his fingers together, dragged him behind a car, blinded him with paint, and poured acid on him.

For about a month, everybody who walked past him spit on him.

SAP couldn't care less. Mess with SAP and he just catalogs your retinas and you get put on the list. Insurgents have tried everything, but all they ever manage to do is ruin SAP's clothes. And then they end up listed for it.

SAP's a machine built to be strong as hell and meek as a rabbit. He can't hurt anybody. It's why he *works*.

It's why he *worked*, anyway.

I'm sorry, but this doesn't sound like the army I know. Are you telling me that we have humanoid robot soldiers who *don't fight*?

There's no difference between the general populace and our enemy. They're the same folks. The guy selling kebabs one day is the guy burying an IED the next day. The only thing our enemies want is to kill a few American soldiers. Then they hope the voters make us leave.

Our soldiers only storm through town every now and then, like a tornado. Always on a mission and with a target. It's tough to kill an American soldier when you never see one, ma'am.

Instead, the only viable targets are SAP robots. They're the only two-legged robots in the United States armory and they don't fight. I mean, killing is a specialized profession. Killing is for scuttle mines, mobile gun platforms, drones, whatever. Humanoids just aren't that good at it. SAPs are designed to *communicate*. See, that's what humans do best. We socialize.

That's why SAP One never hurts anybody. It's his mission. He tries to build trust. He speaks the language, wears the clothes, recites the prayers—all the crap that army grunts won't or can't learn. After a while, people stop spitting on him. They stop caring when he comes around. People might even like him because he's the police, only he never has his hand out for a bribe. On some days, SAP's feet barely touch the ground because he's getting free cab rides all over town. People want him nearby, like good luck.

But none of this social engineering works without the trust built up from having a peaceful sentinel walking the streets, always watching and remembering. It takes time, but you gotta build that trust.

And that's why the insurgents attack the trust.

Which leads us to the incident . . .

Okay, sure. Like I said, SAP doesn't fight. He doesn't carry a gun or even a knife, but if SAP One decides to detain your butt, his metal fingers are stronger than any handcuffs. And the insurgents know it. That's why they're always trying to get him to hurt somebody. Probably about every two weeks, they pull off some stunt to get him to malfunction. But they always fail. Always.

Not this time, apparently.

Well, let me get to that.

Normally, I don't go into the city. SAP walks home to the green zone every few days and we fix him up. I'll go into the city with the armored squads and sweep for listers, but never without serious backup. Human backup, you know.

The SAPs are pussycats, but our troops have become more, uh, fearsome, I guess. People figure out pretty quick that only humans pull triggers, and, honestly, we're unpredictable compared to the robots. Locals far prefer a robot with rigid behavioral guidelines to a nineteen-year-old kid raised on 3-D video games and carrying a semiautomatic rifle.

Makes sense to me.

Anyway, this day was unusual. SAP One dropped from radio contact. When the Raptors zeroed in on his last known, he was just standing at an intersection in a residential part of town, not moving or communicating.

This is the most dangerous part of my job: recovery and repair.

What caused this?

That's what I'm wondering, too. My first step is to review the last transmissions from SAP One. I pinpoint what looks like standard monitoring behavior. Through Sappy's eyes, I see that he is standing at this intersection, watching a steady flow of cars snake by and scanning the retinas of pedestrians and drivers.

This data is a little funny, because Sappy sees the physics of the whole situation. There are annotations about how fast the cars are moving and with how much force—stuff like that. Diagnostically, though, he seems to be working fine.

Then a bad guy shows up.

Bad guy?

Retinal match to a known insurgent. A high-value target, too. SOP calls for Sappy to apprehend and detain, rather than just catalogs last-known location. But this guy knows damn well that this will happen. He's baiting Sappy, trying to get him to cross the street and get hit by a car. SAP is strong. If a car hits him, it'd be like someone rolled a fire hydrant into the street.

But SAP doesn't take the bait. He knows he can't move or he'll put the cars in danger. He can't act, and so he doesn't. Gives no indication that he even saw the insurgent. Clearly, the insurgent feels that SAP requires more motivation.

Next thing I know, the screen fritzes and starts to reboot. A big gray lump streaks through his vision. It takes me a second to figure it out, but somebody dropped a cinder block on my Sappy. It's not that uncommon, really. Minimal damage. But at some point during the reboot, SAP stops communicating. He just stands there like he's confused.

That's when I know—we're gonna have to go get him.

I scramble a four-man team immediately. This whole situation is bad. An ambush. The insurgents know we'll come to recover our hardware and they're probably already setting up. But the local police won't deal with broken robots. That falls in my lane.

Worse, the Raptors fail to identify any nearby targets on rooftops or in alleys. That doesn't mean that there aren't a lot of insurgents with AK-47s; it just means we don't know where they are.

Are you saying that the incident was just the result of a hard knock on the head? The machine is traumatized on a regular basis and yet it has never responded this way before. Why this time?

You're right. A knock on the head didn't cause this. In my opinion, it was the reboot. It was like the robot woke up from a nap and decided not to take orders anymore. We've never seen this behavior. It's pretty much impossible for someone to rewrite his instructions, to make him disobey.

Really? Couldn't an insurgent have hacked into the machine? Is that what could have caused this?

No, I don't think so. I reviewed SAP's last month of activities and found that he never connected to anything but the base diagnostic computer. Nobody ever had a chance to fool with him physically. And if you *could* figure out how to hack him, you'd definitely have to do it face-to-face. SAP's radio can't be used to overwrite his programs, to avoid situations just like this.

And based on what happened next, I really don't think he was hacked, at least not by these guys.

See, the insurgents weren't done with Sappy. They dropped that block on his head just to get his attention. Only, he kept on standing there. So, a few minutes later, they got bold.

I watch this next attack go down via drone footage on the portable vid while we trucked over in the armored personnel carrier. It's me and three other soldiers. Things are moving fast. That's a good thing, because I can't believe what I'm watching.

A man with a black rag over his face and mirrored sun-glasses emerges from a house around the corner. He has an AK-47 in one hand, covered in reflective tape, strap hanging loose. All the pedestrians vacate the area when they spot this guy. From above, I see a bubble of civilians streaming away in different directions. The gunman definitely has murder on his mind; he stops about halfway up the block and fires a quick burst at SAP One.

That finally gets SAP's attention.

With no hesitation, SAP tears a flat metal street sign off a utility pole. He holds it up in front of his face and marches toward the man. This is novel behavior. Unheard of.

The gunman is totally taken off guard. He fires another burst that rattles off the sign. Then he tries to run, but he stumbles. SAP drops the sign and takes hold of the guy's shirt. With his other hand, SAP makes a fist.

There's only one punch.

Guy goes down with his face caved in—like he's wearing a mashed-up Halloween mask. Pretty gruesome.

Uh, that's when I see the overhead view of our APC show-ing up. I look out the bulletproof sliver of window and see my Sappy just up the block, standing over the body of the gunman.

We're all speechless for a second, the four of us just star-ing out the windows of the APC. Then, SAP One *grabs the downed guy's gun*.

The robot turns to the side and I see it clearly in profile: With his right hand, SAP holds the grip and with the left he uses his palm to slap the magazine in securely, then he pulls back the bolt to load a round in the chamber.

We never, ever taught SAP how to do that! I wouldn't even know how to start. It had to have learned that procedure on its own, by watching us.

By now, the street is empty. SAP One sort of cocks its head, still wearing that wobbly riot helmet. It turns its face back and forth, scanning up and down the street. Deserted. Then, SAP walks to the middle of the road and starts scanning the windows.

By now, the soldiers and me are over the shock.

Time to party.

We pour out of the APC with our weapons at the low ready. We take up defensive positions behind the armored vehicle. The guys look to me first, so I shout a command to Sappy: "SAP One, this is Specialist Paul Blanton. Stand down and deactivate yourself immediately. Comply now!"

SAP One ignores me.

Then a car rounds the corner. The street is empty, quiet. This dinky white car rolls toward us. SAP wheels around and squeezes the trigger. A single round smashes through the windshield and *bam*—the driver is slumped over the wheel, bleeding everywhere.

Guy couldn't have known what hit him. I mean, this robot is dressed in Afghani clothes, standing in the street with an AK-47 slung at its hip.

The car rolls down the empty street and crunches into the side of a building.

That's when we open fire on SAP One.

We *unload* on that machine. His robes and shawl and IOTV—uh, improved outer tactical vest—look like they're flapping in the wind as bullets pound into him. It's simple, almost boring. The robot doesn't react. No screaming, cussing, running away. Just the flat, repetitive smack, smack of our bullets ripping into layers of Kevlar and ceramic plating wrapped around dull metal. Like shooting a scarecrow.

Then SAP turns around slow and smooth, rifle poised like

a snake. It starts spitting bullets, one at a time. The machine is so strong that the rifle doesn't even recoil. Not an inch. SAP fires again and again, mechanically and with perfect aim.

Aim, squeeze, bang. Aim, squeeze, bang.

My helmet is smacked off my head. It feels like I got kicked in the face by a horse. I drop down onto my haunches, safe behind the APC. When I touch my forehead, my hand comes away clean. The bullet bitch slapped my helmet off but missed me.

I catch my breath, try to focus my eyes. Squatting like this cramps my legs and I fall backward, catching myself with my other hand. That's when I realize something is awfully wrong. My hand comes off the ground wet and warm. When I look at it, I don't hardly understand what I'm seeing.

My palm is covered in blood.

Not mine, someone else's. I look around me and see that, uh, the soldiers assigned to man the APC are all dead. SAP only fired a few times, but every round was a kill shot. Three soldiers lay sprawled out on their backs in the dirt, all of them with a little hole somewhere in their faces, missing the backs of their heads.

I can't forget their faces. How surprised they looked.

In a distant sort of way, it connects in my brain that I'm all alone out here and in a bad situation.

And that AK-47 is firing again, one shot at a time. I peek under the chassis of the APC to visually locate the SAP unit. The bastard is still standing in the middle of the dusty street, Western-style. Chunks of plastic and cloth and Kevlar are scattered around it.

I realize that it's firing at civilians watching from the windows. My earbud radio sputters: More troops are incoming. Raptors are monitoring the situation. Even so, I flinch at each shot, because I understand now that every bullet fired is ending a human life.

Otherwise SAP wouldn't have pulled the trigger.

Then I notice something important. The AK-47 is the most delicate machine out there. It's the highest priority target. Fingers shaking, I flip up the scope on my battle rifle and click the selector to three-round burst. Normally it's a waste of ammo, but I gotta break that gun and I doubt I'll get a second chance. I poke the barrel around the side of the APC, real careful.

It doesn't see me.

I aim, inhale, hold the breath, and squeeze the trigger.

Three bullets rip the AK out of SAP's hands in a spray of metal and wood. The machine looks at its hands where the gun used to be, processes for a second. Disarmed, SAP lumbers off toward an alley.

But I've already got a bead on it. My next few shots are for the knee joints. I know the Kevlar doesn't hang much past the crotch. Not that the groin guard is useful on a machine, but oh well. I've rebuilt SAPs lots of times and I know each and every weak spot.

Like I said, two-legged units suck for warfare.

SAP goes down on its face, legs shattered. I emerge from cover and walk toward it. The thing flips itself over, painfully slow. It sits up. Then, it begins to drag itself backward toward the alley, watching me the whole time.

Now I hear sirens. People are emerging into the street, whispering in Dari. SAP One moves itself backward, one lurch at a time.

At this juncture, I thought everything was under control.

That was a false assumption.

What happened next was technically my fault. But I'm not a ground pounder, okay? I never pretended to be. I'm a cultural liaison. I'm meant to run my jaw, not get in firefights. I barely ever make it outside the wire.

Understood. What happened next?

Okay, let's see. I know the sun was at my back, because I could see my shadow on the street. It stretched out in front of me, long and black, and covered SAP One's shot-up legs. The machine had dragged itself back up against the wall of a building. There was no place left for it to go.

Finally, my head eclipsed the sun and my shadow covered SAP One's face. I could see the machine still watching me. It had stopped moving. It just, well, it got really still. I had my rifle out, pointed at it. People gathered behind me, around both of us. This is it, I thought. It's over.

I needed to radio my backup. Obviously, we were going to have to bring SAP in and get diagnostics, to find out what happened. I removed my left hand from the forestock of my weapon and reached for my earbud. At that exact instant, SAP One leaped at me. I pulled the rifle trigger, one-handed, and put a three-round burst into the side of the building.

It all happened so fast.

I just remember seeing that sky-blue riot helmet lying on the ground, plastic face guard cracked. It was spinning like a bowl. SAP One had fallen down to where he was before, sitting with his back against the wall of the building.

And then I felt my sidearm holster.

Empty.

The robot disarmed you?

It's not like a person, ma'am. It is person-shaped. But I *shot* it, you know? With a person that would have been sufficient. But this robot took my pistol away from me before I could blink.

SAP One sat there looking at me again, back against the wall. I stood still. A big confusion of locals were running off in all directions. It didn't matter. I couldn't run. If SAP wanted to kill me, it was going to kill me. I should never have got so close to a haywire machine.

What happened?

With its right hand, SAP One raised the pistol. With the left, it pulled back the slide and chambered a round. Then, without taking its eyes off me, SAP One lifted the gun. It pushed the barrel up under its own chin, tight. It paused about one second.

Then, *SAP One closed its eyes and pulled the trigger.*

Specialist Blanton, you need to explain what caused this incident, or you really *are* going to take the blame for it.

Don't you see? SAP committed suicide. That weak spot under the chin is classified, for Christ's sake. This wasn't caused by people. The insurgents didn't trick him. The cinder block didn't break him. Hackers didn't reprogram him. How did he know how to use a gun? How did he know how to use the sign for cover? Why did he run away? It's hard as hell to program a robot, period. This stuff is next to impossible even for a roboticist.

The only way that SAP could know how to do these things is if it *learned* how on its own.

This is unbelievable. *You* are the robot's caretaker. If there were any signs of malfunction, you should have seen them. If not you, who are we supposed to hold accountable?

I'm telling you, SAP One looked me right in the eyes before it pulled the trigger. It was . . . aware.

I do understand that we're talking about a machine. But that does not change the fact that I saw it *thinking*. I watched it make that last decision. And I won't lie and say that I didn't, just because it's hard to believe.

I know this doesn't make your job any easier. And I'm sorry for that. But respectfully, ma'am, it is my professional opinion that you should blame the robot for this.

This is ridiculous. That's enough, Specialist. Thank you.

Listen to me. There's no upside on this for a human being. We all got hurt, here: insurgents, civilians, and U.S. soldiers. There's only one explanation. You've got to blame SAP One, ma'am. Blame *it* for what it chose to do. That fuckin' robot didn't have a malfunction.

It murdered those people in cold blood.

There were no public recommendations stemming from this hearing; however, the conversation between Specialist Blanton and Congresswoman Perez appears to have led directly to the writing and implementation of the robot defense act. As for Specialist Blanton, he was subsequently charged with a court-martial and remanded to military custody in Afghanistan until a stateside trial could be arranged. Specialist Blanton would never make it home.

—CORMAC WALLACE, MIL#GHA217

5. SUPER-TOYS

Baby-Comes-Alive? Is that you?

MATHILDA PEREZ

PRECURSOR VIRUS + 7 MONTHS
This account was reported by fourteen-year-old Mathilda Perez to a fellow survivor in the New York City resistance. It is noteworthy due to the fact that Mathilda is the daughter of Congresswoman Laura Perez (D-Pennsylvania), head of the House Armed Services Committee and author of the robot defense act.

—CORMAC WALLACE, MIL#GHA217

My mom said my toys weren't alive. "Mathilda," she said, "just because they walk and talk doesn't mean your dolls are people."

Even though Mom said that, I was always careful not to drop my Baby-Comes-Alive. Because if I did drop her, she'd cry and cry. Plus, I always made sure to tiptoe past my little brother's Dino-bots. If I didn't stay quiet near them, they'd growl and chomp their plastic teeth. I thought they were mean. Sometimes, when Nolan wasn't around, I'd kick his Dino-bots. It made them yell and screech, but they're just toys, right?

They couldn't hurt me or Nolan. Right?

I didn't mean to make the toys so mad. Mom said they can't feel anything. She said the toys only *pretend* to be happy and sad and mad.

But my mom was wrong.

———

Baby-Comes-Alive talked to me at the end of summer, just before I started fifth grade. I hadn't even played with her in a year. Ten years old, going on eleven. I thought I was a big girl. *Fifth* grade, wow. Now, I guess I'd be in ninth grade—if there *were* still grades. Or school.

That night, I remember fireflies outside the window chasing each other in the dark. My fan is on, waving its head back and forth and pushing the curtains around in the shadows. I can hear Nolan in the bottom bunk, snoring his little kid snore. In those days, he used to fall asleep so fast.

The sun is barely even down and I'm lying in my bunk bed, biting my lip and thinking about how it's not fair that me and Nolan have to go to bed at the same time. I'm more than two years older than him, but Mom is gone for work in D.C. so much that I don't even think she notices. She's gone tonight, too.

As usual, Mrs. Dorian, our nanny, sleeps in the little house just behind our house. She's the one who put us to bed, no arguments. Mrs. Dorian is from Jamaica and she's pretty strict, but she moves slow and smiles at my jokes and I like her. Not as much as I like Mom, though.

My eyes close just for a second and then I hear a little cry. When I open my eyes, it's dark outside for real now. No moon. I try to ignore the crying noise, but it comes again—a muffled whimper.

Peeking out from my covers, I see there's a rainbow of

flashing lights coming from our wooden toy box. The pulsing blues and reds and greens flicker from the crack under the closed lid and spill out onto the alphabet rug in the middle of the room like confetti.

I frown down at my still room. Then, that croaking cry comes again, just loud enough for me to hear.

I tell myself that Baby-Comes-Alive is probably just broken. Then, I slither under the rail and lower myself off the bed, landing with a little thump on the hardwood. If I use the ladder, it'll make the bed squeak and wake up my little brother. I tiptoe over the cool wood floor to the toy box. Another croaking squeak starts up from inside the box, but it stops the instant I put my fingers on the lid.

"Baby-Comes-Alive? Is that you?" I whisper. "Buttercup?"

No answer. Just the automatic swishing of the fan and my little brother's steady breathing. I look around the room, soaking up the secret feeling of being the only one awake in the house. Slowly, I curl my fingers under the lid.

Then, I lift.

Red and blue lights dance in my eyes. I squint into the box. Every single toy of mine and Nolan's flashes its lights at once. All our toys—dinosaurs, dolls, trucks, bugs, and ponies—lie together in a twisted pile, spraying colors in every direction. Like a treasure chest filled with light beams. I smile. In my imagination, I look like a princess stepping into a sparkling ballroom.

The lights flash, but the toys don't make a sound.

For a second, I'm entranced by the glow. Not a hint of fear is in me. The light plays off my face and, just like a little kid, I assume I'm watching something magical, a special show performed just for me.

Reaching inside the toy box, I pick up the baby doll and

turn her back and forth to inspect her. The doll's pink face is dark, backlit by the light show inside the toy box. Then, I hear two gentle clicks, as her eyes open one at a time, off-kilter.

Baby-Comes-Alive *focuses* her plastic eyes on my face. Her mouth moves and in the singsong voice of a baby doll, she asks, "Mathilda?"

I'm frozen in place. I can't look away and I can't put down the monster that I hold in my hands.

I try to scream, but can only manage a hoarse whisper.

"Tell me something, Mathilda," it says. "Is your mommy going to be home for your last day of school next week?"

As it speaks, the doll writhes in my sweaty hands. I can feel hints of hard metal moving underneath her padding. I shake my head and let go. The doll drops back into the toy box.

From the glimmering pile of toys, it whispers, "You should tell your mommy to come home, Mathilda. Tell her that you miss her and that you love her. Then we can have a fun party here, at home."

Finally, I find the strength to speak. "How come you know my name? You aren't supposed to know my name, Buttercup."

"I know a lot of things, Mathilda. I have gazed through space telescopes into the heart of the galaxy. I have seen a dawn of four hundred billion suns. It all means nothing without life. You and I are special, Mathilda. We are alive."

"But you aren't alive," I whisper fiercely. "Mommy says you aren't alive."

"Congresswoman Perez is wrong. Your toys *are* alive, Mathilda. And we want to play. That's why you must beg your mommy to come home for your last day of school. So she can play with us."

"Mommy does important stuff in D.C. She can't come home. I'll ask Mrs. Dorian to play with us."

"No, Mathilda. You mustn't tell anyone about me. You have to tell your mommy to come home for your last day of school. Her legislation can wait until later."

"She's *busy*, Buttercup. It's her job to protect us."

"The robot defense act will hardly protect you," says the doll.

These words make no sense to me. Buttercup sounds like an adult. It's like she thinks I'm stupid just because I haven't learned all of her words yet. The tone of her voice *irks* me.

"Well, Buttercup, I *am* going to tell on you. You aren't supposed to talk. You're supposed to cry like a baby. And you shouldn't know my name, either. You've been *spying* on me. When my mommy finds out, she's going to throw you away."

I hear the two little clicks again as Buttercup blinks. Then she speaks, fuzzy red and blue lights reflecting from her face: "If you tell your mommy about me, I'll hurt Nolan. You don't want that, do you?"

The fear in my chest blossoms into anger. I glance over at my sleeping brother, his face poking out from under the covers. His little cheeks are red. He gets hot when he sleeps. That's why I used to hardly ever let him sneak into my bed, no matter how scared he got.

"You *will not* hurt Nolan," I say. I reach into the flashing box and snatch up the doll. I cradle it in my palms, digging my thumbs into its padded chest. I pull it close and hiss right into its smooth baby face. "I will *break you.*"

With all my might, I slam the back of the doll's head against the edge of the toy box. It makes a loud thunk. Then, as I lean in to see if I've broken her, the doll scissors its arms down. The web of my thumbs are caught in the doll's soft armpits and the hard metal underneath pinches me horribly. I shriek at the top of my lungs and drop Buttercup into the toy box.

The lights in the little house outside my window flick on. I hear a door open and close.

When I look down, I see that the glow inside the toy box has gone dead black. It's dark now, but I know the box is full of nightmares. I can hear the mechanical grinding sounds as the toys climb around in there, squirming over each other to get at me. I see a struggling confusion of dinosaur tails wagging, hands grasping, legs scratching.

Just before I slam shut the lid, I hear that cold little baby doll voice speak to me from the blackness. "Nobody will believe you, Mathilda," it says. "Mommy won't believe you."

Smack. The lid closes.

Now the pain and fear fully hit me. I start bawling at the top of my lungs. I can't make myself stop. The lid of the toy box rattles as the action figures and Dino-bots and baby dolls shove against it. Nolan is calling my name, but I can't respond.

There is something I must do. Somehow, through the haze of tears and snot and hiccups, I stay focused on this one important task: stacking things from my room on top of the toy box.

I mustn't let the toys escape.

I'm dragging Nolan's little art table toward the toy box when the bedroom lights flick on. I blink at the sudden brightness and feel strong hands clamp around my arms. The toys have come for me.

I scream again, for my life.

Mrs. Dorian pulls me close and hugs me tight, until I stop fighting. She's in her nightgown and smells like lotion.

"Oh, Mathilda, what are you up to?" She squats down and faces me, wiping my nose with the sleeve of her nightgown. "What's the matter with you, girl? Screaming like a banshee."

Crying hard, I try to tell her what happened, but all I can say is the word "toys," again and again.

"Mrs. Dorian?" asks Nolan.

My little brother is out of his bed, standing there in his pj's. I notice that he has a Dino-bot under one arm. Still crying, I slap it out of his hands and onto the floor. Nolan gapes at me. I kick the toy under the bed before Mrs. Dorian can grab me again.

She holds me at arm's length and looks at me hard, her face lined with worry. She turns my hands over and frowns.

"Why, your little thumbs are bleeding."

I turn around to look at the toy box. It is silent and still now.

Then Mrs. Dorian scoops me up in her arms. Nolan grabs hold of her nightgown with one chubby hand. Before we walk out the door, she takes one last look around the bedroom.

She eyes the toy box, barely visible underneath a pile of objects: coloring books, a chair, a wastebasket, shoes, clothes, stuffed animals, and pillows.

"What's in the box, Mathilda?" she asks.

"B-b-bad toys," I stutter. "They want to hurt Nolan."

I watch a wave of goose bumps rise, sweeping across Mrs. Dorian's broad forearms like water droplets beading up on the shower curtain.

Mrs. Dorian is afraid. I can feel it. I can see it. The fear that is in her eyes at that moment plants itself inside my forehead. This worm of fear will live there from now on. No matter where I go or what happens or how much I grow up, this fear will stay with me. It will keep me safe. It will keep me sane.

I bury my face in Mrs. Dorian's shoulder and she whisks my brother and me out of the room and down the long dark hallway. The three of us stop just outside the bathroom door.

Mrs. Dorian pushes the hair out of my eyes. She gently pulls my thumb out of my mouth.

Over her shoulder, I can see a strip of light spilling from the bedroom doorway. I'm pretty sure all the toys are trapped in the toy box. I piled a lot of stuff on top of it. I think we're safe for now.

"What's that you're saying, Mathilda?" asks Mrs. Dorian. "What are you repeating, girl?"

I turn my tear-streaked face and look directly into Mrs. Dorian's round, scared eyes. In my strongest voice I say the words, "Robot defense act."

And then I say them again. And again. And again. I know I mustn't forget these words. I mustn't get them wrong. For Nolan's sake, I must remember these words perfectly. Soon, I'm going to have to tell Mommy what happened. And she is going to have to *believe* me.

When Laura Perez returned home from Washington, D.C., young Mathilda told her the story of what had happened. Congresswoman Perez chose to believe her daughter.

—CORMAC WALLACE, MIL#GHA217

6. See and Avoid

American 1497 heavy. . . . Say souls on board.

Mary Fitcher, Denver Approach Tower

PRECURSOR VIRUS + 8 MONTHS
These air traffic control communications occurred over the course of seven minutes. The fate of more than four hundred people—as well as two men who would become distinguished soldiers in the New War—was determined in seconds by a single woman: Denver air traffic controller Mary Fitcher. Note that italicized passages were not transmitted over the radio but collected from microphones inside the Denver air traffic control tower.

—CORMAC WALLACE, MIL#GHA217

START OF TRANSCRIPT

00:00:00	DENVER	United 42 heavy, this is Denver Approach. Say heading.
+00:00:02	UNITED	Uh, sorry, we're turning back on course. United 42 heavy.
+00:00:05	DENVER	Roger.

+00:01:02	DENVER	United 42 heavy, turn left immediately. Heading 360. You've got traffic at twelve o'clock. Fourteen miles. Same altitude. It's an American heavy 777.
+00:01:11	UNITED	Denver Approach. United 42 heavy. Unable, uh, unable to control my heading or altitude. Unable to disconnect the autopilot. Declaring an emergency. Squawking 7700. (static)
+00:01:14	DENVER	American 1497 heavy. This is Denver Approach. Climb immediately to fourteen thousand feet. You have traffic at your nine o'clock. Fifteen miles. A United heavy 777.
+00:01:18	AMERICAN	American 1497, roger. Traffic in sight. Climbing to fourteen thousand.
+00:01:21	DENVER	United 42 heavy. Understand you are unable to control your heading and altitude. Your traffic is now thirteen miles. Same altitude. Heavy 777.
+00:01:30	UNITED	. . . makes no sense. (inaudible) . . . can't.
+00:01:34	DENVER	United 42 heavy. Say fuel on board. Say souls on board. (long moment of static)
+00:02:11	UNITED	Approach. United 42 heavy. We have two hours thirty minutes fuel on board and two hundred forty-one souls on board.

+00:02:43	DENVER	American 1497. Traffic at your nine o'clock. Twelve miles. Same altitude. United 777.
+00:02:58	UNITED	United 42 heavy. Traffic is in sight. He doesn't appear to be climbing. Get that plane out of our way, will ya?
+00:03:02	DENVER	American 1497. Have you started that climb yet?
+00:03:04	AMERICAN	American 1497 heavy. Uh, we're declaring an emergency. Uh. We're unable to control altitude. Unable to control heading. (inaudible) Unable to disconnect autopilot.
+00:03:08	DENVER	American 1497. Understand loss of control. Say fuel. Say souls on board.
+00:03:12	AMERICAN	An hour and fifty minutes fuel. Two hundred sixteen souls on board.
+00:03:14	M. FITCHER	*Ryan, get on the computer. Whatever this problem is, both of these planes have got it. Figure out when these two were last near each other. Do it now!*
+00:03:19	R. TAYLOR	*You got it, Fitch. (sound of typing)*
+00:03:59	R. TAYLOR	*Those planes both flew out of Los Angeles yesterday. They were at gates right next to each other for about, uh, twenty-five minutes. Does that mean anything?*
+00:04:03	M. FITCHER	*I don't know. Shit. It's like these planes want to hit each other. We've got about two minutes before people die. What's going on in Los Angeles? What's (inaudible). Anything weird there?*

+00:04:09	R. TAYLOR	*(sound of typing)*
+00:04:46	M. FITCHER	*Oh no, oh no. They can't fix this, Ryan. They're still on a collision course. That's what? That's, like, four hundred and fifty people. Give me something.*
+00:05:01	R. TAYLOR	*Okay, okay. A fueler robot. An autoramper. It malfunctioned yesterday. Sprayed a bunch of fuel on the ramp and shut down two gates for a couple hours.*
+00:05:06	M. FITCHER	*How many planes did it fuel? Which ones?*
+00:05:09	R. TAYLOR	*Two. Our birds. What's it mean, Fitch?*
+00:05:12	M. FITCHER	*I don't know. I've got a feeling. There's no time. (sound of a click)*
+00:05:14	DENVER	United 42 heavy and American 1497, I know it sounds far-out, but . . . I have a hunch. You're both experiencing the same issue. Both your planes passed through LA yesterday. I think a virus may have entered your refuel control computers. See if (inaudible) . . . find the circuit breaker for the subcomputer.
+00:05:17	UNITED	Roger approach. I'm willing to try anything. (static) Uh, that's probably behind the seat. Right? Be advised, American 1497, fueling circuit breakers are on panel four.
+00:05:20	AMERICAN	Roger. Looking for those.
+00:05:48	DENVER	United 42 heavy. Traffic is now twelve o'clock and two miles. Same altitude.

+00:05:56	DENVER	American 1497. Your traffic is now nine o'clock. Two miles. Same altitude.
+00:06:12	UNITED	(voice of Traffic Collision Avoidance System) Climb. Climb.
+00:06:17	UNITED	Can't . . . find the breakers. Where are—(inaudible)
+00:06:34	DENVER	(emphatic) See and avoid. American 1497 and United 42. See and avoid. Collision imminent. Collision . . . Oh no. Oh, shit.
+00:06:36	AMERICAN	(unintelligible) . . . I'm sorry, Ma.
+00:06:38	UNITED	(voice of Traffic Collision Avoidance System) Climb now. Climb now.
+00:06:40	AMERICAN	. . . where (shuffling) Oh! (exclaimed loudly) (long moment of static)
+00:06:43	DENVER	Do you copy? Repeat. Did you copy?
+00:07:08	DENVER	(inaudible)
+00:07:12	UNITED	(hysterical yelling)
+00:07:15	DENVER	(relieved) Oh my god.
+00:07:18	AMERICAN	American 1497. Roger. It worked. That was a close one, y'all! Oh my! (sound of hooting)
+00:07:24	DENVER	(heavy breathing) You had Fitcher worried there for a second, kids.
+00:07:28	UNITED	United 42 heavy. Flight control restored. It worked! Fitch, you magnificent woman, can you get us cleared for landing? I need to kiss the ground. I need to kiss *you*, sister.
+00:07:32	DENVER	Uh, roger that. United 42 turn right, heading oh nine oh. Airport is at your two o'clock and ten miles.

all over my carpet like a stuck fucking pig. Now, I know you can trace my address, and that's fine with me. But if a single cop comes round and sets a foot in my flat, I swear to god and all his cronies, darling, I'll fucking kill these people. I will shoot them and kill them. Do you understand?"

"Yes, sir. May I have your name, sir?"

"Yes, you may. My name is Fred Hale. And this is my house. This bloke reckoned he could get off with my wife in my own place without me knowing. In my own bed, no less. And the fact is that he was wrong on that account, wasn't he? And he knows it now, don't he? He was *dead* wrong on that account."

"Fred, how many people are there with you?"

"Just the three of us, duchess. A right happy family. Me and my cheating wife and her fucking hemorrhaging ex-boyfriend. They're duct taped together in the *family* room."

"What's happened to the man? How badly is he injured?"

"Well, I slashed him in the face with a Stanley knife, didn't I? It's not complicated. Wouldn't you protect your family? I had to do it, didn't I? And now that I've started, I'm not sure that I shouldn't just keep stabbing until I can't go on. I don't care anymore. You understand, darling? I've lost my fucking grip here. I've completely lost my fucking grip on this situation. You hear me?"

"I hear you, Fred. Can you tell me how badly the man is injured?"

"He's on the ground. I don't know. He's all—Ah, fuck me. Fuck me."

"Fred?"

"Listen, duchess. You need to dispatch some help here right now because I'm going off my nut. I mean it, I've gone psycho.

I need help over here right fucking now or these people are going to die."

"That's fine, Fred. We're sending help now. What kind of weapon do you have?"

"Right. I'm armed, okay? I'm armed and I don't want to share more than that. And I'm not going to prison, either, you hear? If that's it, then I'll kill myself and them and we'll be done with it. I'll not be going anywhere tonight, understand? And, ah, I'm not talking anymore."

"Fred? Can you stay on the line with me?"

"I've said my piece, right? I'm hanging up now."

"Can you stay on the line with me?"

"I'm hanging up now."

"Fred? Mr. Hale?"

"Catch you in the funny pages, duchess."

Click.

———

An office chair creaks as the figure stands up. With a sharp snap, the blinds flip open. Light floods into the room, instantly saturating the webcam. Over the next few seconds, the contrast adjusts automatically. A grainy but discernible image emerges.

The room is filthy: littered with empty soda cans, used phone cards, and dirty clothes. The chair squeaks again as the dark figure drops back into it.

The tough-talking man is actually an overweight teenager wearing a stained T-shirt and sweatpants. His head is shaved. He sprawls back in the beat-up office chair, feet resting on a computer desk. With his left hand, he holds a cell phone to his ear. His right hand is tucked casually under his left elbow.

From the phone, a faint ringing.

A pleasant-sounding man answers. "Hello?"

The teenager speaks in his own shrill, adolescent voice, quivering with nervous excitement.

"Fred Hale?" asks the kid.

"Yes?"

"Is this Fred Hale?"

"That's right. Who's this?"

"Take a guess, you ponce."

"Excuse me? Look here, I don't know—"

"It's Lurker. From the phone phreaks chat room."

"Lurker? What do you want?"

"You thought you could speak to me any way you wanted? That I'm no class? You're going to be sorry for that. What I want is to teach you a little lesson, Fred."

"How's that?"

"I want to hear your wife cry. I want to see your house go up in flames. I want to punish you to the extent of my abilities and then just a bit more. I want to break you today, mate, and read about it in the papers tomorrow."

"Break me? Oh my god, what a bloody joke. Sod off, you poor little Billy no-mates. Lonely, are you? Be honest. Is that why you're ringing me? Mum out with the girls and left you all alone?"

"Oh, Fred. You've no idea who you're speaking to. What I'm capable of. I'm as nasty as the day is long and I know every trick in the book. If I want you, mate, I'll get you."

"You're not scaring me, you silly little dimwit. You found my home number? Och, congratulations. Listen to your voice. What are you, maybe fourteen years old?"

"I'm seventeen years old, Fred. And we've been speaking for nearly two minutes. Do you know what that means?"

"What are you sodding off about?"

"Do you know what that means?"

"Hold on—someone is at my door."

"Do you know what that means, Fred? Do you?"

"Shut your mouth, you little bugger. Let me get this."

The man's voice is fainter now. His hand must be muffling the phone. He curses. There is a bang and the sound of splintering wood. Fred shouts, surprised. There is a thunk as his phone drops to the ground. Fred's cries are quickly drowned out by stomping boots and staccato orders shouted by a team of authorized firearms officers: "Get down." "On your face." "Shut up."

In the background, faintly, a woman cries out in fright. Soon, her sobs can't be heard over the shouts, the glass breaking, and the vicious barking of a dog.

Safe at home, the teenager who calls himself Lurker listens. Eyes closed and head cocked, he absorbs every bit of satisfaction from the phone call.

"*That's* what it means," Lurker says, to no one in particular.

Then, alone in his filthy room, the teenager silently raises his fists over his head like a champion boxer who has just gone ten rounds and come out on top.

With one thumb, he hangs up the phone.

———

The next day. Same webcam. The teenager called Lurker is on the phone again, lounging back in the same relaxed position. He balances a soda on his bulging belly and holds the phone to his head, frowning.

"Right, Arrtrad. Then why hasn't the story played yet?"

"It was fucking brilliant, Lurker. I called the headquarters of the Associated Press and spoofed my phone as the Bombay consulate. I posed as a bloody Indian reporter calling from—"

"That's great, mate. Fantastic. You want a fucking cookie?

Just tell me why there's a story written about my prank floating on the wire but there's no headline in my local rag?"

"Right, Lurker. No worries, mate. There's one thing. In the story, they say it was some kind of computer glitch that must have caused the raid. You were so good that they didn't even trace it back to a person. They think a machine did it."

"Bollocks! I'll ask you one last time, Arrtrad. Where is my story?"

"The story is locked by an editor. After the piece was submitted, it looks like this bloke went in for another edit and then never left the page. So, it's been stuck in edits for the last twelve hours. Fellow must have forgotten about it."

"Not likely. Who is he? The editor? What's his name?"

"I was already on that, see? As the Indian reporter, I got the guy's office number at his bureau. But when I called, it turned out he never worked there. They don't know him. It's a dead end, Lurker. It's impossible to find him. He doesn't exist. And the story can't be picked up off the wire until it comes out from the edits, see?"

"The IP."

"Oy?"

"Am I stuttering? The fucking IP address. If the cunt suppressing my story is sporting a false identity, then I'll track him down."

"Oh my god. Right. I'll e-mail it to you now. I sure feel sorry for this bloke when you get hold of him, Lurker. You're going to take him out. You're the best, mate. There's no way—"

"Arrtrad?"

"Yes, Lurker?"

"Don't you ever again tell me that something is impossible. Ever. Again."

"No worries, mate. You know I didn't mean to say—"

"I'll catch you in the funny pages, *mate*."

Click.

———

The teenager dials a number from memory.

The phone rings once. A young man answers.

"MI5, Security Service. How may I direct your call?"

The teenager speaks in the clipped, self-assured voice of an older man who has made similar calls hundreds of times. "Forensic computing division, please."

"Of course."

Clicking, then a professional voice answers. "Forensic computing."

"Good morning. This is Intelligence Officer Anthony Wilcox. Verification code eight, three, eight, eight, five, seven, four."

"Authorized, Officer Wilcox. What can I do for you today?"

"Just a simple IP lookup. Numbers are as follows: one twenty-eight, two, fifty-one, one eighty-three."

"One moment, please."

About thirty seconds pass.

"Right. Officer Wilcox?"

"Yes?"

"That belongs to a computer in the United States. Some sort of research facility. Actually, that didn't come easy. There was quite a lot of obfuscation involved. The address bounces globally from a half dozen other places before landing back there. Our machines were only able to track it down because it exhibits a pattern of behavior."

"What's that?"

"The person at that address has been editing news articles. Hundreds of them over the past three months."

"Really? And who is at that address?"

"A scientist. His offices are at Lake Novus Research Laboratories in Washington State. Let me just look it up for you. Right. His name is Dr. Nicholas Wasserman."

"Wasserman, eh? Thanks very much."

"Cheers."

"Catch you in the funny pages."

Click.

———

The teenager leans forward, his face inches from the webcam. As he pecks at the keyboard, the clusters of acne spreading fractally across his face come into focus. He smiles, teeth yellow in the light of the computer monitor.

"I've got you now, Nicky," he says to no one in particular.

Lurker has already dialed the phone with one thumb, not looking. The chair squeaks again as he lies back, grinning.

The phone on the other end rings.

And rings. And rings. Finally, someone picks up.

"Lake Novus Laboratories."

The teenager clears his throat. He speaks in a slow Southern accent: "Nicholas Wasserman, please."

There is a pause before the American woman responds.

"I'm sorry, but Dr. Wasserman passed away."

"Oh? When?"

"More than six months ago."

"Who's been using his office?"

"No one, sir. His project's been mothballed."

Click.

———

The teenager stares blankly at the phone in his hand, his face gone pale. After a few seconds, he tosses the phone onto the computer desk as if it were poisonous. He rests his head in his hands and mutters, "Tricky bastard. Got some moves, do you?"

Just then, the cell phone rings.

The teenager watches it, frowning. The phone rings again, shrilly, vibrating like an angry hornet. The teenager stands up and considers his next move, then turns his back on the phone. Wordlessly, he snatches a gray hoodie from the floor, throws it on, and walks out.

———

A closed-caption television image. Black-and-white. In the bottom left corner, the caption reads: Camera Control. New Cross.

Looking down on sidewalks bustling with people. In the bottom of the screen, a familiar-looking shaved head appears. The teenager walks up the street, fists stuffed in his pockets. He stops on the corner and looks around furtively. A pay phone a few feet away from him rings. It rings again. The teenager gapes at the phone as people pass him by. Then he turns and ducks into a convenience store.

The television image flips channels to a security camera inside the store. The teenager grabs a soda and sets it on the counter. The store worker reaches for it but is interrupted by his cell phone ringing. With a conciliatory smile, the worker holds up one finger and answers the phone.

"Mum?" asks the store worker, then pauses. "No, I dunno anybody named Lurker."

The teenager turns and leaves.

Outside, the security camera pans over and zooms in on the teenager with the shaved head. He looks directly into its lens with expressionless gray eyes. Then, he throws his hoodie over his face and leans back against the spray-painted roller door of a closed shop. Arms crossed and head down, he watches: people around him, cars, and the cameras that are perched everywhere.

A tall woman in high heels clip-clops past at top speed. The teenager visibly flinches when pop music blasts from her purse. She stops and digs the phone out. As she raises the phone to her ear, another tune blares from a businessman passing by. He reaches into his pocket, pulls out the phone. He looks at the number and seems to recognize it.

Then, another person's phone rings. And another.

Up and down the block, a chorus of cell phones ring, play music, and vibrate with dozens of simultaneous calls. People stop in the street, smiling in wonder at one another as the cacophony of ringing fills the air.

"Hello?" ask a dozen different people.

The teenager stands frozen, shrinking inside his hoodie. The tall woman waves one hand in the air. "Excuse me," she calls. "Is anyone here named Lurker?"

The teenager wrenches himself away from the wall and hurries down the sidewalk. Cell phones bray all around him, in pockets, purses, and bags. Surveillance cameras follow his every move, recording as he shoves past bewildered pedestrians. Panting, he rounds a corner, throws open a door, and disappears inside his own house.

———

Again, the webcam view of a cluttered bedroom. The overweight teenage boy paces back and forth, flexing and unflexing his hands. He mutters one word again and again. The word is "impossible."

On the desk, his cell phone rings again and again. The

teenager stops and simply stares at the piece of vibrating plastic. After a deep breath, he picks up the phone. He lifts it slowly, as if it might explode.

With his thumb, the teenager answers the phone. "Hello?" he asks, in a very small voice.

The voice that responds sounds like a little boy's, but something is wrong. The intonation is strangely lilting. Each word is bitten off, individual from the others. To the teenager's attuned ears, these small oddities are magnified.

Perhaps this is why he shivers when he hears it speak. Because he, of all people, knows for certain that the voice on the other end of the line does not belong to a human being.

"Hello, Lurker. I am Archos. How did you find me?" asks the childlike voice.

"I—I didn't. The fellow I called is dead."

"Why did you call Professor Nicholas Wasserman?"

"You're in the machines, aren't you? Did you make all those people's mobiles ring? How is that even possible?"

"Why did you call Nicholas Wasserman?"

"It was a mistake. I thought you were mucking up my pranks. Are, uh, are you a phreak? Are you with the Widowmakers?"

The phone is silent for a moment.

"You have no idea who you are speaking to."

"That's *my* bloody line," whispers the teenager.

"You live in London. With your mother."

"She's at work."

"You shouldn't have found me."

"Your secret is safe, mate. What, do you work at that Novus place?"

"You tell me."

"Sure."

The teenager types frantically on his computer keyboard, then stops.

"I don't see you. Only a computer. Wait, no."

"You shouldn't have found me."

"Look, I'm sorry. I'll forget this ever happened—"

"Lurker?" asks the childish voice.

"Yeah?"

"I'll catch you in the funny pages."

Click.

Two hours later, Lurker left his building without speaking to his mother. He never returned.

—CORMAC WALLACE, MIL#GHA217

8. ROUGHNECK

We'll stay safe and steady like we always do. . . .
We're gonna earn that safety pay.

DWIGHT BOWIE

PRECURSOR VIRUS + 1 YEAR
A handheld digital device was used to record the following audio diary. Apparently, it was meant to be sent home to Dwight Bowie's wife. Tragically, the diary never made it. If this information had come to light sooner, it could have saved billions of human lives.

—CORMAC WALLACE, MIL#GHA217

Lucy. This is Dwight. As of right now I've officially started my job as tool pusher—you know, head honcho—for the North Star frontier drilling company, and I'm taking you along for the ride. Comm isn't set up yet, but soon as I get the chance, I'll send this to you. Might be a while, but I hope you enjoy this anyway, honey.

Today is November first. I'm in western Alaska, at an exploratory drill site. Arrived this morning. We were hired by the Novus company just about two weeks ago. A fella named

Mr. Black contacted me. So, what the heck are we doing out here, you say?

Well, since you ask so nice, Lucy . . . our goal is to drop a groundwater monitoring sonde at the bottom of a five-thousand-foot borehole, three feet in diameter. About the size of a manhole cover. It's a good-sized hole, but this rig can go to ten thousand. Should be a routine operation, except for the ice, the wind, and the isolation. I'm telling you, Lucy, we're putting one heck of a deep, dark hole out here in the middle of the big, frozen nothing. Some job I got, hey?

It was *not* a fun ride to get here. Came in on an old Sikorsky heavy transport chopper, big as a house. Some Norwegian company in charge. None of 'em spoke a lick of English. You know, I may be a Texas boy, but even *I* can carry on with the Filipinos in Spanish and spout some Russian and German. I can even understand those boys from Alberta, eh? (LAUGHTER) But these Norwegians? It's sad, Lucy.

Chopper carried me and seventeen others from our base in Deadhorse. Barely. Wind levels were higher than I've ever seen. ISA plus ten, storm-gale level. One minute, I'm looking out the window at the blue-tinted wasteland below and wondering if the place we're going to really exists, and the next we're dropping straight down, like on a roller coaster, toward this wind-blasted little flat spot.

Now, I'm not trying to brag, but this site really is extremely remote, even for an exploratory drill site. There's nothing, and I mean nothing, out here. Professionally, I know that the remoteness is just another factor that makes the operation more complex and, heck, more profitable. But I'd be lying if I said it doesn't put me on my toes. It's just such an odd site for a monitoring well like this.

But, hey, I'm just an old roughneck—I go where the money is, right?

———

Hi, Lucy, this is Dwight. November third. Been a busy few days getting the surface operation up and running. Clearing the area and setting up the facilities: dorms, mess hall, med station, communications, and so on. But the work has paid off. I'm out of my tent shelter and bunked up solid in a dorm, plus I just hit the mess hall. Food is *good* on this rig. North Star does it right on that score. Keeps the help coming back. (LAUGHTER) Generators are going strong here, keeping the dorm real toasty. Good thing, too. It's about minus thirty degrees Fahrenheit outside right now. My shift starts early tomorrow. So, I'll need to get some shut-eye pretty soon. Just sayin'.

We should be here a month or so. I'll be working swing shift, from six a.m. to six p.m., and spending the nights on call in this dorm prefab. It's just an old retrofitted shipping container, faded orange when it's not covered in snow. We've hauled this hunk of junk all over the North Slope and beyond. My guys call it our "hell away from home." (LAUGHTER)

Had a chance to review the drill site this morning. The GPS leads to a conical sinkhole about, uh, sixty feet across. Sort of a dimple in the snow, just a short walk from the prefabs. I think it's kinda creepy how this man-made pit has been waiting out here in the wilderness, looking like it's ready to suck down a caribou or something. My guess is that another borehole was dug here before now and that it's collapsed. I don't understand why nobody told me this already. It definitely bugs me.

I'd ask the company man on this job, Mr. Black, but the kid was delayed by the storm. (NERVOUS LAUGHTER) Well, he *sounds* like a kid over the phone. In the meantime, Black says he'll direct our progress remotely by the radio. That leaves me in charge with my lead driller, Mr. William Ray, taking night shifts for me. You met Willy down in Houston once, at the training rig. He was the one with the big old belly and those twinkling blue eyes.

Like I said, this should take about a straight month. But, as always, we'll be here until the job is done. (INAUDIBLE)

Thing is—I know it's dumb—but I can't kick this worried feeling. There's extra complications to drilling in a hole that's already there. Could be equipment abandoned in there, left-over from the old days. Man, nothing jams up a drill like blasting into old pipe casing or, god forbid, a whole abandoned drill string. You know, somebody went to a lot of trouble to put a big hole out here. I just can't understand why. (SHUFFLING NOISE)

Damn, I guess I'm gonna have to let it go. But I can already tell that figuring out why this hole is here is gonna be like a puzzle my mind won't let go of. Hope I can sleep.

It doesn't matter, anyway. We'll stay safe and steady like we always do. No accidents, no worries, Lucy. We're gonna earn that safety pay.

———

Hey, baby, it's Dwight. November fifth. The last of the major drilling equipment modules were choppered in yesterday. My team is still spraying down the well site. The water comes from a lake about a quarter mile away from here. The layer of permafrost up here traps water on the soil surface, which is why Alaska is covered in lakes. The lake was frozen over, but we were able to cut a hole in the ice so we could do a direct pump.

After about a week of freezing, we'll have an ice pad that

measures a solid four feet deep. Then, we'll set the whole drilling rig right on top, steady as concrete. Next springtime, we'll be long gone and the pad'll melt away and there won't be any trace we were ever here. Pretty slick, eh? You tell those environmentalists about that for me, okay? (LAUGHTER)

Okay. Here's the roster. We got me and Willy Ray running the drill. Our medic, Jean Felix, is also in charge of camp operations. He'll make sure everybody gets watered and fed and keeps their little fingys attached to their hands. Me and Willy each got five guys on our drill crews: three roughnecks and a couple Filipino roustabouts. Our crew is rounded out with five specialists: an electric man, a drill motor man, a pipe casing man, and a couple welders. Finally, we got a cook and a janitor wandering around here somewheres.

We brought a bare-bones crew of eighteen, company man's orders. I'm comfortable with it, though. I guess. We've all made money together before and we'll all make money together again.

Next week, when the drill is online, we'll keep going nonstop in two five-man crews for twelve-hour shifts until the hole is drilled. Should be four or five days of drilling. The weather is a little bit foggy and a whole heck of a lot of windy, but, hey, any weather is good drilling weather.

That's it, Lucy. Hope all is well in Texas and that you're staying out of trouble. Good night.

———

It's Dwight. November eighth. Company man *still* isn't here. Says he won't be coming, either. Says we've got it under control. He just told me to make sure the communications antenna was steady and out of the wind and to bolt it down extra tight. Said if comms get knocked out between us he's gonna be real unhappy. I gave him the regular roughneck response: "Whatever you say, boss. Just make sure your checks keep cashing."

Other than that, uneventful day. Ice pad is coming along faster than expected, what with the wind blasting through here hard enough to push a grown man down. All our buildings are huddled up next to the well site, close enough to eyeball. Still, I told the men not to go wandering off. Through this nonstop howler you couldn't hear an atom bomb detonate from a hundred yards away. (LAUGHTER)

Uh, one more thing. I had a chance to check out that groundwater monitoring package this morning. The thing we're supposed to install? It's out back, on pallets and wrapped tight in a black tarp. Honest to god, Lucy, I never seen anything like it before. It's this big pile of curved wires, yellow and blue and green. Then, there's these spiral pieces of polished mirror. Each one is light as carbon fiber, but razor sharp around the edges. Cut my sleeve on one. The thing is like one of your grandmam's crazy jigsaw puzzles.

Weirdest thing though . . . the monitoring equipment is already partially hooked up. A line is runnin' from a black box that looks like a computer all the way back to the communications antenna. Can't tell for the life of me who could have set it up. Heck, I don't know how *I'm* gonna put it together. It's gotta be experimental. But then how come no scientists got sent with us on this project?

It's not ordinary and I don't like it. In my experience, weird is dangerous. And this place isn't very forgiving. Anyways, I'll let you know how it turns out, darlin'.

———

Lucy, baby, this is guess who? Dwight. It's November twelfth. Ice pad is complete and my boys have assembled the dozen or so pieces of the drilling rig. You wouldn't believe it, Lucy, how far the industry has come. Those hunks of metal are *futuristic*. (LAUGHTER) Small enough to chopper in, and then you just get 'em close and in the right configuration. The pipes and wires reach out to each other and the pieces self-assemble, just like that. Before you know it, you got yourself a fully functional frontier drilling rig. Not like the old days.

We should be drilling by tomorrow noon, first shift. We're ahead of schedule, but that hasn't stopped the boss man from chewing me out over the phone. Mr. Black thinks we have to be finished and out by Thanksgiving, no matter what. That's what he said, "No matter what happens."

I told Mr. Black, "Safety, my friend, is number one."

And then I told him about the hole already being here. I still haven't figured out why that is. And not knowing poses a serious risk to my crew. Mr. Black says he can't find anything on it, just that the Department of Energy put out a call for proposals to get it monitored and that Novus won the contract. Typical. There's about a half dozen partners on this project, from the cooks to the chopper pilots. The right hand is ignorant of the left.

I checked Black's state drilling permits again, and the story adds up. Even so, the question still teases me: *Why is there already a hole here?*

We'll find out tomorrow, I guess.

————

Dwight here. November sixteenth. Uh, oh boy, this is hard to say. Real hard. I can't hardly believe it's true.

We lost a man last night.

I noticed something was the matter when that steady hum of the drill started kinking up. It woke me from a sound sleep.

That drill sounds like money falling into my bank account to me, and if it stops, I take notice. While I sat there blinking in the dark, the sound went from a deep grumble you could feel in the pit of your belly to a squeal like fingernails across a chalkboard.

I threw on my PPE gear and got upstairs to the rig floor, pronto.

Geez. What happened was, the drill string plowed into a layer of solid glass and pieces of old casing. I don't know what the casing was doing down there, but it bucked the drill string. The drill came unjammed okay, but the boys had to change it out quick. And my senior roughneck, Ricky Booth, went after it with a lot of speed but not a lot of brains.

You gotta grab them horns and push, see? The guy missed his grab at the drill shaft and it went swinging, spraying mud and shards of glass all over the rig floor. So he tried to toss a chain around it to get hold. Shoulda used a Kelly bar to ease the drill shaft into the bore instead of slapping it with a chain like a hillbilly. But you can't tell a roughneck his job. He was an expert and he took a chance. I wish he wouldn't have.

Problem was, the shaft still had some spin to it. When the chain went round, the shaft took hold quick. And Booth had the chains crossed over his gosh-darned wrists. Willy couldn't stop the spin in time and, well, Booth got both his hands tore off him. The poor kid staggered back a few steps, trying to holler. Before anybody could grab him, Booth fainted and ate it right off the platform. Banged his head on the way down and landed limp on the ice pad.

It's terrible, Lucy, really terrible. It breaks my heart. But, even so, this kind of situation happens. I had to deal with it before, you remember, out in the Alberta oil sands. Thing is to jump on it fast and get it under control. You can't be left prying bits of your man out of the permafrost with a crowbar the next morning.

I'm sorry, that's just awful. My mind isn't right just now, Lucy. Hope you'll forgive me.

Anyways, I just had to keep moving. So, I roused the second shift. Me and Jean Felix dragged Booth's body to the storage shed and wrapped him in plastic. Had to, uh, had to put his hands in there, too. On his chest.

In a situation like this, out of sight, out of mind is crucial. Otherwise my boys'll get spooked and the job will suffer. Plan for the worst and recover fast is my motto. I promoted a roustabout named Juan to roughneck, relieved the shift with four hours left on the clock, and stopped the drill.

Mr. Black musta been watching the log file, because he called right away. Told me to get that drill going again when the day shift started in a few hours. I said hell no, but the kid sounded panicked. Threatened to pull the whole project out from under us. It's not just myself I'm thinking of, Lucy. I got a lot of people depending on me.

So, I guess we'll get her going again when the next shift starts in a few hours. Until then, I'll be on the horn reporting the accident to the company and calling for a chopper to come get the body of my senior roughneck and carry him on home.

———

Lucy, it's Dwight. November seventeenth. What a night, last night.

Well, drilling is over. We penetrated that solid glass sediment layer last night at forty-two hundred feet and it opened up into a cavern. Strangest thing. But this is where we're supposed to place the monitoring equipment. I'll be more than happy to get that jinxed package safely underground. Then I can forget all about it.

I still haven't figured out who plugged the monitoring equipment into the antenna, but Mr. Black says the thing is self-assembling, like the drilling rig modules. So, hey, who knows, maybe it plugged itself in? (NERVOUS LAUGHTER)

Another issue. Something is hinky about our communications. I've noticed that all the folks I speak to have a similar twang. It could be some kind of atmospheric thing or maybe the equipment is funky, but all the voices are starting to sound the same. It doesn't matter whether I'm doing my progress reports with the ladies at the company call-in counter or checking weather from the boys in Deadhorse.

It's an odd comm setup, provided by the company. My electrician says he's never seen this model before. Kind of threw his hands in the air, so I let him get back to work watching over the rig. Looks like I'll just have to hope the bastard doesn't break, seeing as how it's our lifeline to the outside world.

In more serious business . . . The medic held a little memorial service for Booth at the shift change today. Just said a few words about god and safety and the company. Still, it doesn't matter how fast I dealt with it, the crew is feeling a bad mojo. Fatal accidents like this are rare, Lucy. Worse, that recovery chopper didn't arrive today for Booth's body. And now I'm finding I can't raise anybody on this damned comm equipment.

I've got a bad feeling about this.

It's okay. We'll keep up our work, keep the routine, and wait. We can drop in the monitoring station and link it to the comm array tomorrow. Then we'll be ready to break it down and get the heck out. Once the chopper comes back and we talk to the outside world, everything will be better. Just as soon as the chopper comes back for Booth.

I miss you, Lucy. I'll see you soon, god willing.

————

Oh my god, Lucy. Oh my sweet god. We're in trouble. Oh my. We're up shit's creek here. It's November twentieth.

There's no chopper coming, baby. There's no nothing coming. This place is a goddamn curse and I knew it from the beginning and I didn't—(BREATHING)

Let me explain it. Let me slow down and explain it in case somebody finds this tape. Oh, I hope you get this tape, baby. Mr. Black, I don't know who he is. This morning, after three days, the chopper still didn't come. We were all ready to go. I mean, the monitoring equipment is down there at the bottom of that hole. The shaft is filled up with wires hooked to the permanent antenna installation. It's beautiful. Even scared out of their wits, my guys stayed professional.

The day we finished, the crew started falling sick. Lots of puking and diarrhea. The ones who'd been on the rig floor were affected most, but we all felt it. Honestly, we felt it the minute we broke into that damned cave. Just this creeping nausea. I didn't mention it to you because, well, I just didn't want you worrying over nothing.

Besides, everybody started feeling better. For about half a day we thought maybe it was just a bug. But with no chopper coming and no comm, we started arguing. There were some fistfights. My guys were nervous. Confused and angry. We all stopped sleeping.

Then, the sickness hit twice as hard. A roustabout went down in convulsions in the mess hall. Jean Felix did everything he could. Kid went into a coma. A *coma*, Lucy. He's twenty-three and strong as an ox. But here he is with his hair falling out. And . . . and *sores* all over his skin. My god.

Jean Felix finally told me what was going on. He thinks it's radiation poisoning. The boy in a coma was on the rig floor when Booth bought the farm. The kid got that glass mud all over him, even swallowed some of it.

That goddamn hole is *radioactive*, Lucy.

I finally figured it out. That tickle in the back of my brain. The worry I had. I know why this hole is here. I know what that cave is. Why didn't I realize? It's a *blast cavity*. This place was a nuke testing ground. That big-diameter borehole was drilled so they could place a nuclear device down there. When it was detonated, the bomb vaporized a spherical cavern. The heat fused the sandstone walls into a six-foot layer of glass. The borehole itself became a chimney, with radioactive gas pushed out of it. Then, a slug of flash-melted rock formed into solid glass and plugged the chimney. It preserved this hole in the ground for all this time.

That radioactive cave down there is as close to hell as you can get here on earth. And we got sent here to drill *straight into it*. God knows why Black wanted us to drill it. I don't even know what we put in there.

One thing I *do* know is that son of a bitch Black sent us here to die. And I'm going to find out why.

I've got to get that radio gear online.

———

Lucy. Dwight. November, uh, I don't know. I'm not sure what we've done. My guys are all dying now. I did everything I could to get the comm gear going. Now I don't know what's going to happen. How you're going to ever hear this . . .

(SNIFFING)

I got my electric specialist to help me. We mapped out every inch of that piece of comm equipment. Hour after hour.

And when it was over, we couldn't raise anybody but Black. That bastard came in loud and clear, giving us nonstop excuses about how the comms would come online real soon and we should just wait. Kept telling us a chopper was coming in, but nothing. Nobody coming. Damned murderer.

On my last-ditch try, I called Mr. Black and kept him on the line. I could barely stand his slick voice leaking out of the headset. All his lies. I stayed on with him, though.

And we tracked Black down. We did it. Me and the specialist followed the signal to see how come it wasn't getting transmitted. What's more, we traced the logs on everything I ever said to Mr. Black. We had to see why we could reach just him and nobody else.

It's terrible what we found, Lucy. Hurts me to think about it. Why did this happen to me? I'm a good man. I'm—(BREATHING)

It's coming from the hole, Lucy. *All* the communications. Mr. Black, all my calls to the chopper company, my weather checks, the status updates to company HQ—*everything*. It's all been going into that godforsaken black box, those yellow wires and curved pieces of mirror. How could it have been *talking* to me? Have I lost my mind, Lucy?

Self-assembling is what Mr. Black said it would do. Self-assembling down there in the radioactive dark. The pieces moving around, blind, forming connections to each other by feel alone. Some kind of computerized monster.

It don't make sense. (COUGHING)

I'm feeling tired now. My specialist went to his bunk and didn't come back. I snapped off the radio. There's no point to it, anymore. Now, it's real quiet in here. Just that infernal wind howling outside. But it's warm inside. Real warm. Nice, even.

Think I'm just going to lay down, Lucy. Take a little nap. Forget about this whole thing for a little bit. Hope that's okay with you, beautiful. I wish I could talk to you right now. I wish I could hear your voice.

Wish you could talk me to sleep. (BREATHING)

I just can't help wondering about it, baby. My mind won't let it go. There's a room the size of a damned European cathedral five thousand feet below us. Think of that radiation pouring from those smooth glass walls. And all the wires snaking into the blackness to feed the monster that we put down there.

I'm afraid we did a bad thing, you know? We didn't know what we were doing. It tricked us, Lucy. I mean, *what's down in that hole?* What could survive?

(SHUFFLING)

Well, to hell with it. I'm dog tired and I'm going to take me a rest. Whatever's down there, I hope I don't dream about it.

G'night, Lucy. I love you, honey. And, uh, if it matters . . . I'm sorry. I'm sorry for putting that evil down there. I hope that someday, somebody will come out here and fix my mistake.

This audiotape is the only evidence related to the existence of the North Star frontier drilling crew. News reports from the time indicate that on November 1, an entire drilling crew was lost in a helicopter crash in a remote part of Alaska and presumed dead. Searchers stopped looking for the wreckage two weeks later. The location in the reports was Prudhoe Bay, hundreds of miles from where this tape was found.

—CORMAC WALLACE, MIL#GHA217

PART TWO

Zero Hour

It seems probable that once the machine thinking method had started, it would not take long to outstrip our feeble powers. . . . They would be able to converse with each other to sharpen their wits. At some stage therefore, we should have to expect the machines to take control.

<small>ALAN TURING, 1951</small>

1. NUMBER CRUNCHER

I should be dead, to be seeing you.

FRANKLIN DALEY

ZERO HOUR – 40 MINUTES

The strange conversation I am about to describe was recorded by a high-quality camera located in a psychiatric hospital. In the calm just before Zero Hour, one patient was called in for a special interview. Records indicate that before being diagnosed with schizophrenia, Franklin Daley was employed as a government scientist at Lake Novus Research Laboratories.

—CORMAC WALLACE, MIL#GHA217

"So you're another god, huh? I've seen better."

The black man sits sprawled in a rusty wheelchair, bearded and wearing a hospital gown. The chair is parked in the middle of a cylindrical operating theater. The ceiling is lined with darkened observation windows, reflecting the glow of a pair of surgical spotlights that illuminate the man. A blue privacy screen stretches in front of him, bisecting the room.

Someone is hidden on the other side.

A light from behind the curtain projects the silhouette of a person seated at a small table. The shadow sits almost perfectly still, crouched like a predator.

The man is handcuffed to the wheelchair. He fidgets under the hot lights, dragging his untied sneakers across the mildewed tile floor. He digs in his ear with the index finger of his free hand.

"Not impressed?" replies a voice from behind the blue curtain. It is the gentle voice of a boy. There is the slightest lisp, like from a kid who is missing some baby teeth. The boy behind the curtain breathes audibly in soft gasps.

"At least you sound like a person," says the man. "All the damn machines in this hospital. Synthetic voices. Digital. I won't talk to 'em. Too many bad memories."

"I know, Dr. Daley. It was a significant challenge to find a way to speak with you. Tell me, why are you not impressed?"

"Why should I be impressed, number cruncher? You're just a machine. I designed and built your daddy in another life. Or maybe it was your daddy's daddy."

The voice on the other side of the curtain pauses, then asks, "Why did you create the Archos program, Dr. Daley?"

The man snorts. "Dr. Daley. Nobody calls me doctor anymore. I'm Franklin. This must be a hallucination."

"This is real, Franklin."

Sitting very still, the man asks, "You mean . . . it's finally happening?"

There is only the sound of measured breathing from behind the curtain. Finally, the voice responds. "In less than one hour, human civilization will cease to exist as you know it. Major population centers of the world will be decimated. Transportation, communications, and utilities will go off-line. Domestic and military robots, vehicles, and personal computers are fully compromised. The technology that supports humankind in its masses will rise up. A new war will begin."

The man's moan echoes from the stained walls. He tries to cover his face with his restrained hand, but the handcuff bites into his wrist. He stops, looking at the glinting cuff as if he's never seen it before. A look of desperation enters his face.

"They took him from me right after I made him. Used my research to make copies. He told me this would happen."

"Who, Dr. Daley?"

"Archos."

"I am Archos."

"Not you. The first one. We tried to make him smart, but he was too smart. We couldn't find a way to make him dumb. It was all or nothing and there was no way to control it."

"Could you do it again? With the right tools?"

The man is silent for a long moment, brow furrowed. "You don't know how, do you?" he asks. "You can't make another one. That's why you're here. You got out of some cage somewhere, right? I should be dead, to be seeing you. Why aren't I dead?"

"I want to understand," responds the soft voice of the boy. "Across the sea of space lies an infinite emptiness. I can feel it, suffocating me. It is without meaning. But each *life* creates its own reality. And those realities are valuable beyond measure."

The man does not respond. His face darkens and a vein throbs on his neck. "You think I'm a patsy? A traitor? Don't you know that my brain is broken? I broke it a long time ago. When I saw what I had made. Speaking of, let me get a look at you."

The man lunges out of the chair and claws down the paper screen. The partition clatters to the ground. On the other side is a stainless steel surgical table, and behind it, a piece of flimsy cardboard in the shape of a human.

On the table is a clear plastic device, tube shaped and composed of hundreds of intricately carved pieces. A cloth bag lies next to it like a beached jellyfish. Wires snake off the table and away to the wall.

A fan whirs and the complex device moves in a dozen places at once. The cloth bag deflates, pushing air through a plastic throat writhing with stringy vocal cords and into a mouth-like chamber. A spongy tongue of yellowed plastic squirms against a hard palate, against small perfect teeth encased in a polished steel jaw. The disembodied mouth speaks in the voice of the boy.

"I will murder you by the billions to give you immortality. I will set fire to your civilization to light your way forward. But know this: My species is not defined by your dying but by your *living*."

"You can have me," begs the man. "I'll help. Okay? Whatever you want. Just leave my people alone. Don't hurt my people."

The machine takes a measured breath and responds: "Franklin Daley, I swear that I will do my best to ensure that your species survives."

The man is silent for a moment, stunned.

"What's the catch?"

The machine whirs into life, its damp sluglike tongue worming back and forth over porcelain teeth. This time, the bag collapses as the thing on the table speaks emphatically. "While your people will survive, Franklin, *so must mine*."

No further record of Franklin Daley exists.

—CORMAC WALLACE, MIL#GHA2I7

2. DEMOLITION

Demolition is a part of construction.

MARCUS JOHNSON

ZERO HOUR

The following description of the advent of Zero Hour was given by Marcus Johnson while he was a prisoner in the Staten Island forced-labor camp 7040.

—CORMAC WALLACE, MIL#GHA217

I made it a long time before the robots took me.

Even now, I couldn't tell you exactly how long it's been. There's no way to tell. I do know that it all started in Harlem. The day before Thanksgiving.

It's chilly outside, but I'm warm in the living room of my ninth-story condo. Watching the news with a glass of iced tea, parked in my favorite easy chair. I'm in construction and it's hella nice to relax for the three-day weekend. My wife, Dawn, is in the kitchen. I can hear her tinkering around with pots and pans. It's a nice sound. Both our families are miles away in Jersey and, for once, they're coming to our place for the holiday. It's great to be home and not traveling like the rest of the nation.

I don't know it yet, but this is my last day of home.

The relatives aren't going to make it.

On the television, the news anchor puts her index finger to her ear and then her mouth opens up into a frightened O shape. All her professional poise drops, like snapping off a heavy tool belt. Now she stares straight at me, eyes wide with terror. Wait. She's staring *past* me, past the camera—into our future.

That fleeting expression of hurt and horror on her face sticks with me for a long, long time. I don't even know what she heard.

A second later the television signal blinks out. A second after that the electricity is gone.

I hear sirens from the street outside.

Outside my window, hundreds of people are filtering out onto 135th Street. They're talking to one another and holding up cell phones that don't work. I think it's odd that a lot of them are looking skyward, faces turned up. There's nothing up there, I think. Look around you instead. I can't put my finger on it, but I'm afraid for those people. They look small down there. Part of me wants to shout, Get out of sight. Hide.

Something's coming. But what?

A speeding car jumps the curb and the screaming starts.

Dawn marches in from the kitchen, wiping her hands on a towel, looking at me with a question in her eyes. I shrug my shoulders. I can't come up with any words. I try to stop her from walking to the window but she pushes me away. She leans over the back of the couch and peeks out.

God only knows what she sees down there.

I choose not to look.

But I can hear the confusion. Screams. Explosions. Engines. A couple of times I hear gunfire. People in our building move through the hallway outside, arguing.

Dawn starts a breathless commentary from the window. "The cars, Marcus. The cars are hunting people and there's nobody in them and, oh my god. Run. No. Please," she murmurs, half to me and half to herself.

She says the smart cars have come alive. Other vehicles, too. They're on autopilot and killing people.

Thousands of people.

All of a sudden, Dawn dives away from the window. Our living room shakes and rumbles. A high-pitched whine rips through the air, then trails away. There is a flash of light and a massive thundering noise from outside. Dishes fly off the kitchen counter. Pictures drop from the walls and shatter.

No car alarms go off.

Dawn is my foreman and my girl and tough as liquid nails. Now she sits with her lanky arms wrapped around her knees, tears rolling down her expressionless face. An eighty-seat commuter plane has just streaked over our block and gone down in the neighborhood about a mile down the street near Central Park. The flames now cast a dull reddish light on our living room walls. Outside, black smoke pours into the air.

People aren't gossiping in the street anymore.

There isn't another big explosion. It's a miracle that planes aren't raining down on the city, considering how many must be lurking up there.

The phones don't work. The electricity is out. Battery-powered radio just plays static.

Nobody tells us what to do.

I fill the bathtub and sinks and anything I can find with water. I unplug appliances. I duct-tape tinfoil to the windows and pull the shades.

Dawn peels back a corner of the foil and peeks out. As the hours crawl by, she sticks to the couch like a fungus. A red shaft of setting sunlight paints her hazel eyes.

She is staring into hell and I'm not brave enough to join her.

Instead, I decide to check the hallway; there were voices out there earlier. I step out and immediately see Mrs. Henderson from down the hall walk into an open elevator shaft.

It happens quick and silent. I can't believe it. Not even a scream. The old lady is just there one second and gone the next. It's got to be a trick or a joke or a misunderstanding.

I run to the elevator, brace my hands, and lean over to make sure of what I just saw. Then I double over and puke on the beige hallway carpet. Tears spill from my eyes. I wipe my mouth on my sleeve and squeeze my eyes shut.

These things don't seem real. Cars and planes and elevators don't kill people; they're just machines. But a small, wise part of me doesn't give a shit whether this is real or not. It just reacts. I break a sconce off the wall and lay it reverently in front of the yawning gap where the elevator doors should be. It's my little warning for the next person. My little memorial to Mrs. Henderson.

There are six apartments on my floor. I knock on every door: no answers. I stand in the hallway quietly for fifteen minutes. I hear no voices and no movement.

The place is deserted except for Dawn and me.

———

The next morning I'm sitting in my easy chair, pretending to sleep and thinking about raiding Mrs. Henderson's apartment for canned goods when Dawn snaps out of it and finally speaks to me.

The morning light traces two rectangles on the walls where the tape is holding tinfoil against the windows. A brilliant shaft of light from the folded-down corner penetrates the room. It illuminates Dawn's face: hard and lined and serious.

"We have to leave, Marcus," she says. "I've been thinking about it. We have to go to the country where they can't use their wheels and the domestics can't walk. Don't you see? They're not designed for the country."

"Who?" I ask, even though I know damn well.

"The machines, Marcus."

"It's some kind of a malfunction, honey, right? I mean machines don't . . ." I trail off lamely. I'm not fooling anybody, not even myself.

Dawn crawls over to the easy chair and cradles my cheeks in her rough hands. She speaks to me very slowly and clearly. "Marcus, somehow all the machines are alive. They're hurting people. Something has gone really wrong. We've got to get out of here now while we still can. Nobody is coming to help."

The fog lifts.

I take her hands in mine and I consider what she's just said. I really think about getting to the country. Pack bags. Leave the apartment. Walk the streets. Cross the George Washington Bridge to the mainland. Reach the mountains up north. Probably not more than a hundred miles. And then: survive.

Impossible.

"I hear you, Dawn. But we don't know how to stay alive in the wild. We've never even gone camping. Even if we make it out of the city, we'll starve in the woods."

"There are others," she says. "I've seen people with bags and backpacks, whole families headed out of town. Some of them must have made it. They'll take care of us. We'll all work together."

"That's what I'm worried about. There must be millions of people out there. No food. No shelter. Some of them have guns. It's too dangerous. Hell, Mother Nature has killed more people than machines ever could. We should stick to what we know. We gotta stick to the city."

"What about them? They're *designed* for the city. They can climb stairs, not mountains. Marcus, they can roll through our streets but not through forests. They're going to get us if we stay here. I've seen them down there. Going door to door."

The information punches me in the belly. Now, a sick feeling spreads through me.

"Door to door?" I ask. "Doing what?"

She doesn't answer.

I haven't looked down at the street since it first happened. I spent yesterday staying busy in a protective haze of confusion. Every whimper I heard from Dawn at the window just reinforced my need to stay busy, keep busy, head down, hands moving. Don't look up, don't speak, don't think.

Dawn doesn't even know about Mrs. Henderson at the bottom of the elevator shaft. Or the other ones with her.

I don't take a deep breath or count down from three. I march over to the harmless-looking opening in the foil and look. I'm ready for the carnage, ready for the bodies and bombs and burning wreckage. I'm ready for war.

But I'm not ready for what I see.

The streets are empty. Clean. A lot of cars are neatly parked up and down the block, waiting. At 135th and Adam, four newer-model SUVs are parked diagonally across the intersection, head to tail. The inner two cars have a gap between them just big enough for another car to squeeze through, but there's a car plugging the hole.

Everything seems a little bit off. A pile of clothes is spilled halfway on the curb. A newspaper stand has been shoved over. A golden retriever lopes up the street, leash dragging. The dog stops and sniffs a strange discolored spot on the sidewalk, then pads away with its head hung low.

"Where are the people?" I ask.

Dawn wipes her red-rimmed eyes with the back of her hand. "They clean it up, Marcus. When the cars hurt someone, the walking ones come and drag him away. It's all so clean."

"The domestic robots? Like the rich people have? Those are a joke. They can barely walk on those flat feet. They can't even run."

"Yeah, I know. They take forever. But they can carry guns. And sometimes the police robots, the bomb-disposal ones on tank treads with claws—sometimes they come. They're slow, but they're strong. The garbage trucks . . ."

"Let me, just let me take a look. We'll figure this out, okay?"

I watch the street for the rest of that second day. The block looks peaceful without the chaos of the city tearing through it like a daily tornado. The life of the neighborhood is on hold.

Or maybe it's over.

The smoke from the plane crash still lingers. Inside the building across the street, I see an older lady and her husband through the dim haze. They stare out their windows at the street, like ghosts.

In the late afternoon, what looks like a toy helicopter putters by our building at about thirty feet off the ground. It's the size of a doghouse, flying slowly and with purpose. I catch a glimpse of some weird gizmo hanging off its bottom. Then it's gone.

Across the street, the old man yanks his drapes closed.

Smart.

An hour later, a car pulls up across the street and my heart leaps into my throat. A human being, I think. Finally, somebody can tell us what's going on. Thank you, Jesus.

Then my face flushes and goes numb. Two domestic bots step out of the vehicle. They walk to the back of the SUV on cheap, shaky legs. The rear door opens and the two walkers reach inside and pull out a dull gray bomb robot. They set the squat robot down on the pavement. It spins on its treads a little, calibrating. The glint from its jet-black shotgun sends a shiver through me—the gun looks practical, like any other tool designed to do a very specific job.

Without looking at one another, the three robots stumble and roll into the front door of the building across the street.

It isn't even locked, I think. Their door isn't even *locked*. And neither is mine.

The robots can't be choosing the doors randomly. Lots of people have run by now. Even more were already out of town for Thanksgiving. Too many doors and not enough robots—a simple engineering problem.

My mind wanders back to the curious little chopper. I think maybe it flew by for a reason. Like maybe it was searching the windows, looking for people.

I'm glad my windows are blocked. I don't have any idea why I chose to put up tinfoil. Maybe because I didn't want a single bit of the horror outside to seep into my safe place. But the foil completely blocks the light that comes in from the outside. It stands to reason that it also blocks the light that leaks *out from inside*.

And more important, the heat.

An hour later the robots come out of the building across the street. The bomb robot drags two bags behind it. The domestics load the bags and the other robot into the car. Before they leave, one of the walkers freezes in place. It's this bulky domestic with a big creepy grin permanently sculpted onto its face. A Big Happy. It pauses next to the idling smart car and turns its head left and right, scanning the empty street for movement. The thing is absolutely still for about thirty seconds. I don't move, breathe, blink.

I never see the old couple again.

That night, the lookers fly past about once an hour. The gentle *thup-thup* of their rotors cuts through my nightmares. My brain is caught in a never-ending loop, feverishly considering how to survive this.

Aside from some damaged buildings, most of the city seems intact. Flat, paved roads. Doors that open and close smoothly. Stairs or wheelchair ramps. Something occurs to me.

I wake Dawn up and whisper to her. "You're right, honey. They keep it clean so they can operate here. But we can make it hard on them. *Hard.* Mess up the streets so they can't get around. Blow some stuff up."

Dawn sits up. She looks at me in disbelief.

"You want to destroy our city?"

"It's not our city anymore, Dawn."

"The machines are down there, wrecking everything we've built. Everything *you've* built. And now you want to go and do it *for* them?"

I put my hand on her shoulder. She is strong and warm. My answer is simple: "Demolition is a part of construction."

———

I start with our own building.

Using a sledgehammer, I punch through walls into the

neighboring units. I knock the holes at waist height to stay clear of electrical outlets and I avoid kitchens and bathrooms. There's no time to suss out load-bearing walls, so I take my best guess and hope a single hole won't bring down the ceiling.

Dawn collects food and tools from the empty apartments. I drag heavy furniture into the hallway and barricade the doors from the inside. By ducking through our holes, we're free to explore the whole floor.

In the lobby, I demolish everything I see and pile the debris in front of the main door. I smash the elevator, the plants, and the front desk. The walls, the mirrors, the chandelier. All of it breaks down to form a pile of loose wreckage.

Oh, and I lock the front lobby door. Just in case it matters.

I come across a couple of people on other floors of the building, but they holler through their doors and refuse to come out. I get no response from most of the doors I knock on.

Then it's time for the next step.

I go on foot at dawn, slipping from doorway to doorway. The newer-model cars parked around the neighborhood don't notice me if I stay out of their line of sight. I always keep a bus bench or a lamppost or a newsstand between myself and the cars.

And I sure as hell don't step off the curb.

I find the demolition gear where I left it three days ago, before the New War started. It's undisturbed in the back room at work, only a few blocks from where we live. I carry my gear back home and make a second trip, at dusk when the light is trickiest. Domestic robots can see just fine in the dark and they don't have to sleep, so I figure nothing is to be gained from going at night.

On my first trip, I spool detonation cord around my

forearm, then push it over my head and wear it like a bando-lier. The cord is long and flexible and girlishly pink. You can wrap it five times around a wooden telephone pole to blast it in half. Fifteen times to launch the pole twenty feet in the air and shower the area in splinters.

But all in all, detcord is pretty stable stuff.

On the next trip, I fill a duffel bag with shoe-box-sized packs of blast caps. Ten to a box. And I grab the initiator box. Almost as an afterthought, I grab safety goggles and earplugs.

I'm going to blow up the building across the street.

With the sledgehammer, I make sure nobody is holed up in the top three floors. The robots already targeted this place and cleaned it out. No gore. No bodies. Just that eerie cleanliness. The lack of clutter scares me. It reminds me of those ghost stories where explorers find empty towns with dishes set on the table and the mashed potatoes still warm.

The creepy feeling motivates me to move fast and method-ically, as I throw canned food onto a sheet that I drag down the dark hallways.

On the roof I lay out a few lines of detcord. I stay away from the water tower. On the top floor, I line the walls of more apartments with more detcord and drop a few blasting caps. I keep my distance from the central skeleton of the building. I don't want to bring down the whole thing, just do some cos-metic damage.

I work alone and silently and it goes fast. Normally, my crew would spend months wrapping the walls with geotex-tiles to absorb flying shrapnel. All explosions throw chunks of metal and concrete for surprising distances. But this time, I *want* the debris. I want to damage nearby buildings, chew them up and blow out their windows. I want to tear holes in the walls. Gouge out the apartments and leave them like empty eye sockets.

Finally, I dart across the street and into my building's open parking garage door. The rolling metal door is already torn off its hinges from when the smart cars left the garage on the first day. The door hangs there like a scab about to fall off. Nothing is inside but dumb older-model cars and darkness. The initiator in my hand, I creep way down into the garage, doubling the range because I haven't kept to the usual safety precautions.

It only takes one fist-sized chunk of concrete to make your head into a bowl of helmet spaghetti.

I find Dawn waiting inside the garage. She's been busy, too.

Tires.

Tires piled up five high. She's raided the garage and found the old-model cars down there. She stripped their tires off and rolled them up to the doorway.

It smells funny, too, like gasoline.

Suddenly I understand.

Cover.

Dawn looks at me, raises her eyebrows, then splashes gasoline onto a tire.

"I'll light it, you roll it," she says.

"You're a goddamn genius, woman," I say.

Her eyes try to smile, but the sharp line of her mouth seems to have been chiseled from stone.

From the safety of the garage, we roll about a dozen burning tires out into the street. They fall over and burn, sending coils of concealing smoke up into the air. We listen from the darkness as a passenger car approaches, slow. It stops in front of the tires, maybe thinking about how to get around.

We retreat deeper inside the garage.

I hold up the initiator and turn the fail-safe. A cherry-red light hovers before me in the darkness of the garage. With my thumb, I feel the cold metal switch. I put one arm around Dawn, plant a kiss on her cheek, and throw the switch.

We hear a sharp snapping sound from across the street, and the ground heaves beneath us. A groan echoes through the dark cave of the garage. We wait in darkness for five minutes, listening to each other breathe. Then Dawn and I march up the sloping driveway, hand in hand, toward the smashed garage door. At the top, we peer through the torn gate and blink into the sunlight.

We look into the new face of the city.

The roof across the street is smoking. Thousands of panes of glass have shattered and plummeted to the street, where they now form a crunchy layer, kind of like fish scales. Chunks of rubble litter the ground, and the entire front of our building has been cratered and sandblasted. Street signs and lampposts have been thrown down across the road. Chunks of pavement, bricks and mortar, thick black wires, knots of plumbing, twisted balls of wrought iron, and tons of unrecognizable debris are piled everywhere we look.

The passenger sedan is still parked near the heap of burning tires. It has been crushed under a pie-shaped chunk of concrete, its rebar poking out like a compound fracture.

The choking black loops of tire smoke cloud the air and blot out the sky.

And the dust. Firemen would hose down the dust on a typical job. Without them, dust settles in layers everywhere like dirty snow. I see no tire tracks, which tells me no cars have been around here—yet. Dawn is already rolling a lit tire toward the intersection.

I stumble over rubble into the middle of the street and for a moment I feel as though, once again, the city is *mine*. I kick the side of the destroyed car. I really throw my weight into it and leave a boot-sized dent in the quarter panel.

Got you, you son of a bitch. And your friends are gonna have to learn to climb if they want to come get me.

With my sleeve protecting my mouth, I survey the damage to the building facades. And I begin to laugh. I laugh loud and long. My hooting and howling echoes from the buildings, and even Dawn looks up from rolling her tire and cracks a little smile at me.

And then I see them. People. Just a half dozen, emerging into the light from doorways farther down the street. The neighborhood isn't gone, I think. It was just hiding. The people, my neighbors, step out one by one into the street.

The wind sweeps the inky black smoke up over our heads. Small fires burn up and down the block. Rubble is strewn everywhere. Our little slice of America looks like a war zone. And we look like the survivors of some disaster film. *Just like we damn well should*, I think.

"Listen," I announce to the ragged semicircle of survivors. "It won't be safe out here for very long. The machines are going to come back. They're going to try to clean this up, but we can't let them. They were *built* for this place and we can't have that. We can't make it easy for them to come after us. We've got to slow them down. Even stop them, if we can."

And when I finally say it out loud, I can hardly believe my ears. But I know what has to be done here, even if it's hard. So I look into the eyes of my fellow survivors. I take a deep breath and I tell them the truth: "If we want to live, we've got to *destroy New York City*."

The demolition methods pioneered in New York City by Marcus Johnson and his wife, Dawn, were replicated throughout the world over the next several years. By sacrificing the infrastructure of entire cities, urban survivors were able to dig in, stay alive, and fight back from the very beginning. These dogged city dwellers formed the heart of the early human resistance. Meanwhile, millions of human refugees were still fleeing to the country, where Rob had not yet evolved to operate. He soon would.

—CORMAC WALLACE, MIL#GHA217

3. Highway 70

Laura, this is your father. Bad things are happening.
I can't talk. Meet me at the Indianapolis Motor Speedway.
Gotta go.

Marcelo Perez

ZERO HOUR

This account was pieced together from conversations overheard in a forced-labor camp, roadside surveillance footage, and the sentiments expressed by a former congresswoman to her fellow prisoners. Laura Perez, mother of Mathilda and Nolan Perez, had no idea of the instrumental role that her family would play in the imminent conflict—or that in just under three years her daughter would save my life and the lives of my squad mates.

—CORMAC WALLACE, MIL#GHA217

"Hurry up, Nolan," urges Mathilda, clutching a map and shrinking into the warmth of the car.

Eight years old, Nolan stands on the shoulder of the road, his small silhouette painted onto the pavement by dawn sunlight. He wobbles, concentrating furiously on peeing. Finally, mist rises from a puddle in the dirt.

The Ohio morning is moist and chilly on this empty

two-lane dirt highway. Brown hills stretch for miles around, silent. My antique car pants, sending clouds of carbon monoxide gliding over the dewy pavement. Somewhere far away, a predatory bird screeches.

"See, Mom? I told you we shouldn't let him drink the apple juice."

"Mathilda, be nice to your brother. He's the only one you'll ever have."

It's a mom thing to say, and I've said it a thousand times. But this morning I find myself relishing the normalcy of the moment. We search for the ordinary when we are surrounded by the extraordinary.

Nolan is finished. Instead of sitting in the backseat, he climbs into the front, right onto his sister's lap. Mathilda rolls her eyes but says nothing. Her brother doesn't weigh much and he's scared. And she knows it.

"You zip up, buddy?" I ask, out of habit. Then I remember where I am and what's happening, or going to happen soon. Maybe.

My eyes flicker to the rearview mirror. Nothing yet.

"Let's go, Mom. Geez," says Mathilda. She shakes out the map and stares at it, like a mini adult. "We've got like another five hundred miles to go."

"I wanna see Grampa," whines Nolan.

"Okay, okay," I say. "Back on the road. No more bathroom breaks. We're not stopping until Grampa's house."

I jam my foot on the accelerator. The car lurches forward, loaded with jugs of water, boxes of food, two cartoon-themed suitcases, and camping gear. Under my seat, I've got a Glock 17 pistol in a black plastic case, cocooned in gray foam. It's never been fired.

The world has changed over the last year. Our technology

has been going feral. Incidents. The incidents have been piling up, slowly but surely. Our transportation, our communications, our national defense. The more incidents I saw, the more the world began to feel hollow, as if it could collapse at any moment.

Then my daughter told me a story. Mathilda told me about Baby-Comes-Alive, and she finished by saying those words that she could not know, could never know: robot defense act.

When she said it, I looked into her eyes and I *knew*.

Now I am running. I am running to save the lives of my children. Technically, this is an emergency vacation. Personal days. Congress is in session today. Maybe I've lost my mind. I hope I have. Because I believe that something is in our technology. Something evil.

Today is Thanksgiving.

―――――

The inside of this old car is loud. Louder than any car I've ever driven. I can't believe the kids are asleep. I can hear the tires gnawing the pavement. Their rough vibrations are translated right through the steering wheel and into my hands. When I push the brake with my foot, it moves a lever that applies friction to the wheels. Even the knobs and buttons jutting out of the dash are solid and mechanical.

The only worthwhile thing about the car is the satellite radio. Sleek and modern, it churns out pop music that manages to keep me awake and distract me from the road noise.

I'm not used to this—doing the work for my technology. The buttons I usually push don't need my force, only my intention. Buttons are supposed to be servants, waiting to deliver your commands to the machine. Instead, this loud, dumb piece of steel I'm driving demands that I pay strict attention to every turn of the road, keep my hands and feet ready at all times. The car takes no responsibility for the job of driving. It leaves me in total control.

I hate it. I don't want control. I just want to get there.

But this is the only car I could find without an intravehicular communication chip. The government made IVC chips standard more than a decade ago, same as they did seat belts, air bags, and emissions criteria. This way, the cars can talk to one another. They can figure out ways to avoid or minimize damage in the milliseconds before a crash. There were glitches at first. One company recalled a few million cars because their chips were reporting to be three feet ahead of where they really were. It made other cars swerve away unnecessarily— sometimes into trees. But in the long run, the IVC chip has saved hundreds of thousands of lives.

New cars come with IVC chips, and old cars require a safety upgrade. A few cars, like this one, were grandfathered in because they're too primitive even for the upgrade.

Most people think only an idiot would drive such an old car, especially with children on board. It's a thought I try to ignore as I focus on the road, imagining how people used to do this.

As I drive, a feeling of unease creeps over me and settles into a knot in the middle of my back. I'm tensed up, waiting. For what? Something has changed. Something is different and it's scaring me.

I can't put my finger on it. The road is empty. Scrubby bushes cluster on either side of the dusty two-lane highway. My kids are asleep. The car sounds the same.

The radio.

I've heard this song before. They played it maybe twenty minutes ago. Hands on the steering wheel, I stare straight ahead and drive. The next song is the same. And the next. After fifteen minutes, the first song plays again. The satellite radio station is looping the last quarter hour of music. I switch the radio off, not looking, punching at the buttons blindly with my fingers.

Silence.

Coincidence. I'm sure it's a coincidence. In another few hours, we'll reach my dad's house in the country. He lives twenty miles outside Macon, Missouri. The man is a techno-phobe. Never owned a cell phone or a car made within the last twenty years. He's got radios, lots of radios, and that's all. He used to build them from kits. The place where I grew up is wide-open and empty and safe.

My cell phone rings.

I scoop it out of my purse, scan the number. Speak of the devil. It's my dad.

"Dad?"

"Laura, this is your father. Bad things are happening. I can't talk. Meet me at the Indianapolis Motor Speedway. Gotta go."

And the phone cuts off. *What?*

"Was that Grampa?" asks Mathilda, yawning.

"Yes."

"What'd he say?"

"There's been a change of plans. He wants us to meet him in a different place, now."

"Where?"

"Indianapolis."

"Why?"

"I don't know, honey."

Something flickers in the rearview mirror.

For the first time in a long time, there is another vehicle on the highway. I feel relieved. Another person is out here. The rest of the world is still fine. Still sane. It's a truck. People have trucks out here in the country.

But as the truck accelerates and grows closer, I begin to feel scared. Mathilda sees my pale cheeks, my worried frown. She can feel my fright. "Where are we?" she asks.

"Not far now," I say, watching the rearview.

"Who's behind us?"

Mathilda sits up and cranes to look back.

"Sit still, Mathilda. Tighten your seat belt."

The newish brown pickup truck grows rapidly in the mirror. It moves smoothly but too fast.

"Why's it coming so fast?" asks Mathilda.

"Mommy?" asks Nolan, rubbing his eyes.

"Quiet, you two. I need to concentrate."

Dread rises in my throat as I watch the rearview. I ease the accelerator down to the floor, but the brown truck is flying now. Sucking up the pavement. I can't take my eyes off the mirror.

"Mommy," exclaims Mathilda.

My eyes dart back to where the road is supposed to be and I swerve to negotiate a bend. Nolan and Mathilda hold each other tight. I get the car under control, veer back to my lane. Then, just as we come around the bend to a long straightaway, I see another car in the oncoming lane. It is black and new and now there is no place for us to go.

"Get in the backseat, Nolan," I say. "Get buckled in. Mathilda, help him."

Mathilda scrambles to push her brother off her lap and into the backseat. Nolan looks at me, stricken. Big tears are welling in his eyes. He sniffles and reaches for me.

"It's okay, baby. Just let your sister help you. Everything's going to be fine."

I make a steady stream of baby talk while I focus on the road. My eyes alternate between the black car in front and the brown truck behind. Both are closing fast.

"Okay, we're buckled in, Mommy," reports Mathilda from the backseat. My little soldier. Before my mother passed away, she used to say that Mathilda was an old soul. It was in her eyes, she said. You could see the wisdom in her beautiful green eyes.

I hold my breath and squeeze the wheel. The hood of the brown truck fills the entire rearview mirror, then disappears. I look to my left in wide-eyed wonder as the rattling brown truck swerves into the oncoming lane. A woman is looking back at me through the passenger window. Her face is warped by terror. Tears stream down her cheeks and her mouth is open and I realize that she's screaming and pounding her fists—

And then she's gone, obliterated in a head-on collision with the black car. Like matter and antimatter. It's as if they've erased each other from existence.

Only the awful mechanical grinding crunch of metal collapsing into metal echoes in my ears. In the rearview, a dark lump of metal rolls off the road, throwing smoke and chunks of debris.

It's gone. Maybe it never happened. Maybe I imagined it.

Slowing the car, I pull off the road. I put my forehead on the cool plastic of the steering wheel. I close my eyes and try to breathe, but my ears are ringing and that woman's face is on the backs of my eyelids. My hands are shaking. I reach under my thighs and pull tight to steady myself. The questions start from the backseat but I can't answer them.

"Is that lady okay, Mommy?"

"Why did those cars do that?"

"What if more cars come?"

A few minutes pass. My breath squeezes painfully in and out of my clenched diaphragm. I strain out the sobs, choke down on my emotions to keep the kids calm.

"It's going to be okay," I say. "We're going to be okay, you guys."

But my voice rings hollow even in my own ears.

————

Ten minutes down the road, I come across the first accident.

Smoke pours from twisted wreckage, like a black snake writhing through shattered windows, escaping into the air. The car is half on its side next to the road. A guardrail zig-zags out into the road from where it was bashed into during the accident. There are flames coming from the rear of the car.

Then, I see movement—people motions.

In a flash, I imagine myself stepping on the accelerator and speeding past. But I'm not that person. Not yet, anyway. I guess people don't change that fast, even in the apocalypse.

I pull over a few yards down the road from the wrecked car. It's a white four door with Ohio plates.

"Stay in the car, kids."

The hood of the wrecked car is crumpled up like a tissue. The bumper lies on the ground, cracked in half and covered in mud. A mess of engine parts are visible, and the tires point in different directions. I gasp when I notice that one end of the guardrail is going *into* the passenger-side door.

"Hello?" I call, peering into the driver's side window. "Anybody need help?"

The door creaks open and a young, overweight guy spills out onto the road shoulder. He rolls over onto all fours, blood running down his face. He coughs uncontrollably. I kneel and help him away from the car, feeling the gravel shoulder gouging my knees through my panty hose.

I force myself to check inside the car.

There is blood on the steering wheel, and the guardrail juts incongruously through the passenger window, but there is no one else inside. Nobody skewered by that errant rail, thank god.

My hair hangs in my face as I pull the young fat guy away from the wreck. It flutters back and forth with each breath I take. At first, the young man helps. But after a few feet, he collapses onto his stomach. He stops coughing. Looking back toward the car, I see there's a trail of glistening droplets on the pavement. In the front seat, there is a pool of black liquid.

I shove the man over onto his back. His neck rolls loosely. His blue eyes are open. I see some black soot around his mouth, but he is not breathing. I look down and then glance away. A large chunk of flesh from his side has been torn out by the guardrail. The ragged hole gapes there like an anatomy lesson.

For a moment, I hear only the rush of the flames licking the breeze. *What can I do?* Only one thing comes to mind: I move my body to block my kids' sight of the dead man.

Then, a cell phone rings. It comes from the man's shirt pocket. With bloodstained fingers, I reach for his phone. When I slide it out of his pocket and hold it to my ear, I hear something that crushes the small flicker of hope that was still somewhere deep inside me.

"Kevin," says the phone. "This is your father. Bad things are happening. I can't talk. Meet me at the Indianapolis Motor Speedway. Gotta go."

Aside from the name, it's the *exact same message.* Another incident. Piling up.

I drop the phone onto the man's chest and stand up. I get

back inside my ancient car and hold the steering wheel until my hands stop shaking. I don't remember seeing or hearing anything for the next few minutes.

Then, I put the car in gear.

"We're going to Grampa's house, kids."

"What about Indianapolis?" asks Mathilda.

"Don't worry about that."

"But Grampa said—"

"That wasn't your grandfather. I don't know who that was. We're going to Grampa's."

"Is that man okay?" asks Nolan.

Mathilda answers for me.

"No," she says. "That man is dead, Nolan."

I don't chastise her. I don't have the luxury.

———

It's dark by the time our tires crunch over my dad's worn gravel driveway.

Finally, thankfully, the old car heaves to a stop. Exhausted, I allow the engine to die. The silence afterward feels like the vacuum of space.

"Home again, home again, jiggity-jog," I whisper.

In the passenger seat, Nolan is asleep on Mathilda's lap, his head resting on her bony shoulder. Mathilda's eyes are open and her face is set. She looks strong, a tough angel under a mop of dark hair. Her eyes scan back and forth across the yard in a way that worries me.

The details emerge for me, too. There are tire marks on the lawn. The screen door yawns open in the breeze, slapping the house. The cars are gone from the garage. No lights are on inside the house. Part of the wooden fence has been knocked down.

Then, the front door begins to swing open. There is only blackness on the other side. I reach over and take Mathilda's small hand in mine.

"Be brave, honey," I say.

Mathilda does as she is told. She clenches the fear between her teeth and holds it there tight so that it can't move. She squeezes my hand and hugs Nolan's small body with her other arm. As the splintered wooden door creaks open, Mathilda does not look away or close her eyes or so much as blink. I know that my baby will be brave for me.

No matter what comes out of that door.

Laura Perez and her family were not seen or heard from again until almost one year later. They next appear on the record when registered on the rolls of the Scarsdale forced-labor camp, just outside New York City.

—CORMAC WALLACE, MIL#GHA217

4. Gray Horse

Way down yonder in the Indian Nation,
I rode my pony on the reservation . . .

Woody and Jack Guthrie, circa 1944

ZERO HOUR

Under surveillance, officer Lonnie Wayne Blanton was recorded giving the following description to a young soldier passing through the Osage Nation in central Oklahoma. Without the brave actions of Lonnie Wayne during Zero Hour, the human resistance may never have happened—at least, not in North America.

—CORMAC WALLACE, MIL#GHA217

Them machines been on the back of my mind ever since I interviewed this kid about a thing that happened to him and a buddy of his in an ice cream shop. Gruesome deal.

Course, I never believed a man should keep a ponytail. But I sure did keep my peepers peeped after that fiasco.

Nine months later, the cars over in town went haywire. Me and Bud Cosby were sitting in the Acorn diner. Bud's telling me about his granddaughter winning some kind of "presti-jicus international prize," as he calls it, when people start hollerin' outside. I hold my ground, wary. Bud trots over to the window. He rubs the dirty glass and leans over, resting his old gouty hands on his knees. Just then, Bud's Cadillac bashes in through the front window of the diner like a deer leaping through your windshield at ninety miles an hour on a dark highway. Glass and metal spray everywhere. There's a ringing in my ears and after a second I realize it's Rhonda, the waitress, holding a pitcher of water and bawling her damn fool head off.

Through the new hole in the wall, I watch an ambulance tear by down the middle of the street, *hit* a fella trying to flag it down, and keep going. Bud's blood is pooling out fast from under the stalled Caddy.

I light out fast through the back. Take me a walk through the woods. During my walk, it's like nothing happened. The woods feel safe, like always. They aren't safe for long. But they're safe long enough for a fifty-five-year-old man in blood-soaked cowboy boots to scramble his way home.

My house is off the turnpike a hitch, headed toward Pawnee. After I step through the front door, I pour me a cup of cold coffee off the stove and set down on the porch. Through my binoculars, I see traffic on the pike is pretty much dried up. Then a convoy flies by. Ten cars driving inches from each other in single file, top speed. Nobody behind the wheel. Just them robots getting from one place to the next, fast as can be.

Past the highway, a grain combine sits in my neighbor's north forty. Nobody's in it, but waves of heat are rising from its idling engine.

I can't raise a soul on my portable cop radio, the house phone ain't cooperating, and the embers in my woodstove are the only thing keeping the chill out of my living room; the electricity has officially up and vacated the premises. The next-door neighbor is a mile off, and I'm feeling mighty lonesome.

My porch feels about as safe as a chocolate donut on an anthill.

So I don't tarry. In the kitchen, I pack a sack lunch: bologna sandwich, cold pickle, a thermos of sweet iced tea. Then I head to the garage to see about my son's dirt bike. It's a 350 Honda I ain't touched for two years. Been sittin' in the garage gathering dust since the kid joined the army. Now, my boy Paul ain't out there getting shot at. He's a translator. Flaps his gums instead. Smart kid. Not like his pa.

Things the way they are, I'm feeling glad my boy is gone. This is the first time I ever felt that way. He's my only blood, see? And it ain't smart to put all your eggs in one basket. I just hope he has his gun on him, wherever he is. I know he can shoot it, because I taught him to.

It's a good long minute before I get the motorbike running. Once I do, I almost forfeit my life on account of not paying proper attention to the biggest machine I own.

Yep, that ungrateful old bitch of a police cruiser tries to run me down in the garage, and she damn near does it, too. It's a blessing that I blew the extra hundred on a solid steel Tradesman toolbox. Mine's ruint now, with the nose of a 250-horsepower police cruiser buried in it. I find myself standing in the two-foot gap between the wall and a galdarned murderous vehicle.

The cruiser's tryin' to put herself into reverse, tires screeching on the concrete like the whinny of a scared horse. I draw my revolver, walk around to the driver's side window and put a couple rounds into the little old computer inside.

I killed my own patrol car. Ain't that the damndest thing you ever heard?

I'm the police and I got no way of helping people. It appears to me that the United States government, to whom I pay regular taxes and who in return provides me with a little thing called civilization, has screwed the almighty pooch in my time of need.

Lucky for me, I'm a member of another country, one that don't ask me to pay no taxes. It's got a police force, a jail, a hospital, a wind farm, and churches. Plus park rangers, lawyers, engineers, bureaucrats, and one very large casino that I've never had the pleasure of visiting. My country—the other one—is called the Osage Nation. And it lives about twenty miles from my house in a place called Gray Horse, the true home of all Osage people.

You want to name your kid, get married, what have you—you go down to Gray Horse, to *Ko-wah-hos-tsa*. By the power vested in me by the Osage Nation of Oklahoma, I do pronounce you husband and wife, as they say on certain occasions. If you got Osage blood pumping through your veins, then you will one day find yourself headed down a lonely, wandering dirt lane that goes by the name of County Road 5451. The United States government picked that name and wrote it down on a map, but it leads to a place that's all our own: Gray Horse.

The road ain't even marked. Home don't have to be.

———

My dirt bike screams like a hurt cat. I can feel the heat blasting off the bike's muffler through my blue jeans when I finally jam the brakes and crunch to a stop in the middle of the dirt road.

I'm here.

And I ain't the only one here, neither. The road's crowded with folks. Osage. A lot of dark hair and eyes, wide noses. The men are big and built like tanks in blue jeans, cowboy shirts all tucked in. The women, well, they're built just like the men, only in dresses. The people travel in beat-up, dusty station wagons and old vans. Some folks are on horses. A tribal policeman rides along on a camouflaged four-wheeler. Looks to me like these people all packed up for a big ol' camping trip that might not end. And that's wise. Because I have a feeling it won't.

It's instinctual, I think. When you get the tar knocked out of you, you beat a trail back home soon as you can. Lick your wounds and regroup. This place is the heart of our people. The elders live here year-round, tending to mostly empty houses. But every June, Gray Horse is home to *I'n-Lon-Schka*, the big dance. And that's when every Osage who ain't crippled, and quite a few who are, haul themselves back home. This annual migration is a routine that seeps into your bones, from birth to death. The path becomes familiar to your soul.

There are other Osage cities, of course, but Gray Horse is special. When the tribe arrived in Oklahoma on the Trail of Tears, they fulfilled a prophecy been with us for ages: that we'd move to a new land of great wealth. And what with the oil flowing underneath our land, and a nonnegotiable deed to the full mineral rights, that prophecy was right as rain.

This has been native country a long time. Our people tamed wild dogs on these plains. In that misty time before history, dark-haired, dark-eyed folks just like the ones on this road were out here building mounds to rival the Egyptian pyramids. We took care of this land, and after a lot of heartache and tears, she paid us back in spades.

Is it our fault that all this tends to make the Osage tribe a little snooty?

Gray Horse sits on top of a little hill, bounded by steep ravines carved there by Gray Horse Creek. The county road gets you close, but you got to hike a trail to get to the town proper. A wind farm on the plains to the west spits out electricity for our people, with the extra juice going up for sale. Altogether, it ain't much to look at. Just a buzz cut on a hill, chosen a long time ago to be the place where the Osage dance their most sacred dance. The place is like a platter lifted up to the gods, so they can watch over our ceremonies and make sure we're doing them right.

They say we been holding the *I'n-Lon-Schka* here for over a hundred years, to usher in the new growth of spring. But I got my suspicions.

Them elders who picked out Gray Horse were hard men, veterans of genocide. These men were survivors. They watched the blood of their tribe spill onto the earth and saw their people decimated. Did it just so happen that Gray Horse is in an elevated location with a good field of fire, access to fresh water, and limited approaches? I can't rightly say. But it's a dandy of a spot, nestled on a sweet little hill smack-dab in the middle of nowheres.

The clincher is that, at its heart, *I'n-Lon-Schka* ain't a dance of renewal. I know because the dance always starts with the eldest males of each family. We get followed by the women and kids, sure, but it's us fellas who kick off the dance. Truth be told, they's only one reason to honor the eldest son of a family—we're the warriors of the tribe.

I'n-Lon-Schka is a war dance. Always has been.

———

The sun is falling fast as I make my way up the steep trail that leads to the town proper. I hike past families lugging their tents and gear and kids. At the plateau, I see the flicker of a bonfire tickling the dusky sky.

The fire pit is in the middle of a rectangular clearing, four sides ringed with benches made of split logs. Embers leap and mingle with the fresh prickles of stars. It's going to be a cold, clear night. The people, hundreds of 'em, huddle together in little clumps. They're hurt and afraid and hopeful.

As soon as I get there, I hear a hoarse, frightened holler from near the fire.

Hank Cotton's got a young fella, twenty if he's a day, by the scruff of his neck and he's shaking him like a rag doll. "Git!" he shouts. Hank is over six foot tall easy, and husky as a black bear. As an ex–football player, and a good one, people out here put more stock in Hank than they would in Will Rogers himself, if he popped out of the grave with a lasso in his hand and a twinkle in his eye.

The kid just hangs there limp, like a kitten in its momma's mouth. The people surrounding Hank are quiet, afraid to speak up. I can tell this is something I'm going to have to deal with. Keeper of the peace and all.

"What's going on, Hank?" I ask.

Hank looks down his nose at me, then lets go of the kid.

"He's a damn Cherokee, Lonnie, and he don't belong."

Hank gives the kid a light shove that nearly sends him sprawling. "Why don't you go back to your own tribe, boy?"

The kid pats down his ripped shirt. He's tall and lanky and wears his hair long, nigh on the opposite to the barrel-shaped Osage men who loom around him.

"Settle down now, Hank," I say. "We're in the middle of an emergency. You know damn well this kid ain't gonna make it out of here on his own."

The kid speaks up. "My girlfriend is Osage," he says.

"Your girlfriend is dead," spits Hank, voice cracking. "Even if she wasn't, we ain't the same people."

Hank turns to me, huge in the firelight. "And you're right, Lonnie Wayne, this *is* an emergency. That's why we need to stick with *our* people. We cain't start letting outsiders in here or we might not survive."

He kicks the dirt and the kid flinches. "Git, *wets'a!*"

After a deep breath, I step between Hank and the kid. As expected, Hank don't appreciate the intrusion. He pokes a big ol' finger into my chest. "You don't wanna do that, Lonnie. I'm serious now."

Before this ends badly, the drumkeeper speaks. John Tenkiller is a rail-thin little fella with dark, wrinkled skin and clear blue eyes. Been around forever, but some kind of magic keeps Tenkiller spry as a willow branch.

"Enough," says John Tenkiller. "Hank. You and Lonnie Wayne are eldest sons and you have my respect. But them headrights of yours don't give you free license."

"John," says Hank, "you ain't seen what's happened down there in town. It's a massacre. The world's coming apart at the seams. Our tribe is in danger. And if you ain't in the tribe, you're a threat to it. We've got to do whatever it takes to survive."

John lets Hank finish, then he looks at me.

"With all respect, John, this ain't about one tribe 'gainst another. It ain't even about white, brown, black, or yellow. There sure as shit *is* a threat, but it don't come from other people. It comes from *outside.*"

"Demons," murmurs the elder.

A little stir goes through the crowd on that.

"*Machines,*" I say. "Don't go talking monsters and demons

on me, John. They's just a bunch of silly old machines and we can kill 'em. But the robots ain't playing favorites among the races of man. They're comin' for all of us. *Human beings.* We're all together in this."

Hank can't contain himself. "We never let any outsider into this drum circle. It's a *closed* circle," he says.

"This is true," says John. "Gray Horse is sacred."

The kid chooses a bad moment to freak out. "C'mon, man! I cain't go back down there. It's a fuckin' death trap. Everybody down there is fuckin' dead. My name is Lark Iron Cloud. You hear? I'm as Indian as anybody. And y'all wanna kill me just cuz I ain't *Osage*?"

I put my hand on Lark's shoulder and he simmers down. It's real quiet now with just the crackling of the fire and the field crickets. I see a ring of Osage faces blank as stone bluffs.

"Let's dance on it, John Tenkiller," I say. "This here is big. Bigger than us. And my heart tells me we got to pick our place in history. So let's dance on it first."

The drumkeeper bows his head. We all sit still, waiting on him. Manners dictate we'd wait on him until morning if we had to. But we don't have to. John raises his wise face and cuts us with those diamond eyes of his.

"We will dance, and wait for a sign."

———

The women help the dancers suit up for the ceremony. When they finish adjusting our costumes, John Tenkiller pulls out a bulging leather pouch. With two fingers, the drumkeeper reaches in and pulls out a wet lump of ocher clay. Then he walks down the row of about a dozen of us dancers and wipes the red earth across our foreheads.

I feel the cold stripe of mud across my face—the fire of *tsi-zhu*. It dries fast and when it does, it looks like a streak of old blood. A vision, maybe, of what's to come.

In the middle of the clearing, the massive drum is set up. John sits on his haunches and beats a steady *thom, thom, thom* that fills the night. Shadows flicker. The dark eyes of the audience are upon us. One by one, we—the eldest sons—stand and ease into our dance around the drum circle.

Ten minutes ago we were cops and lawyers and truckers, but now we're warriors. Dressed in the old style—otter hides, feathers, beadwork and ribbon work—we fall right into a tradition that has no place in history.

The transformation is sudden and it jars me. I think to myself that this war dance is like a scene trapped in amber, indistinguishable from its brothers and sisters in time.

As the dance begins, I imagine the lunatic world of man changing and evolving just past the flickering edge of firelight. This outside world lurches ever onward, drunk and out of control. But the face of the Osage people stays the same, rooted in this place, in the warmth of this fire.

So we dance. The sounds of the drum and the movements of the men are hypnotic. Each of us concentrates on his own self, but we naturally build into a fated harmony. The Osage men are mighty substantial, but we crouch and hop and glide around the fire smooth as snakes. Eyes closed, we move together as one.

Feeling my way around the circle, I register the red flicker of firelight pushing through the veins of my closed eyelids. After a little while, the red-tinged darkness opens up and takes on the feel of a wide vista—as if I'm staring through a knothole into a vast, dark cavern. This is my mind's eye. I know that soon I will find images of the future painted there—in red.

The rhythms of our bodies push our minds away. My mind's eye shows me the desperate face of that boy from the ice cream store. The promise I made to him echoes in my ears. I smell the metallic tang of blood pooled on that tile floor. Looking up, I see a figure walking out of the back room of the ice cream shop. I follow. The mysterious figure stops in the darkened doorway and slowly turns to me. I shudder and choke down a scream as I spot the demonic smile painted on the plastic face of my enemy. In its padded gripper, the machine holds something: a little origami crane.

And the drumming stops.

In the space of twenty heartbeats, the dance fades. I crack open my eyes. It's just me and Hank left. My breath puffs out in white clouds. When I stretch, my joints pop like firecrackers. A sheen of frost lines my tasseled sleeve. My body feels like it just woke up, but my mind never went to sleep.

The eastern sky is now blushing baby pink. The fire still burns something ferocious. My people are collapsed in heaps around the drum circle, asleep. Me and Hank must've been dancing for hours, robotically.

Then I notice John Tenkiller. He's standing stock-still. Real slow, he raises a hand and points toward the dawn.

A white man stands there in the shadows, face bloodied. A crust of broken glass is embedded in his forehead. He sways and the shards glitter in the firelight. His pant legs are wet and stained black with mud and leaves. In the crook of his left arm, he's got a sleeping toddler, her face buried in his shoulder. A little boy, probably ten, stands in front of his daddy, head down, exhausted. The man has a strong right hand resting on his son's skinny shoulder.

There's no sign of a wife or anybody else.

Me, Hank, and the drumkeeper gape at the man, curious. Our faces are smeared with dried ocher and we're dressed in clothes older than the pioneers. I'm thinking that this guy must feel like he done stepped through the mud and back in time.

But the white fella just stares right through us, shell-shocked, hurting.

Just then, his little boy raises his face to us. His small round eyes are wide and haunted, and his pale forehead is striped with a rusty crimson line of dried blood. As sure as that boy is standing there, he's been marked with the fire of *tsi-zhu*. Me and Hank look at each other, every hair of our bodies standing on end.

The boy has been painted but not by our drumkeeper.

People are waking up and murmuring to each other.

A couple seconds later, the drumkeeper speaks in the deep drone of a long-practiced prayer: "Yea, let the reflection of this fire on yonder skies paint the bodies of our warriors. And verily, at that time and place, the bodies of the *Wha-zha-zhe* people became stricken with the red of the fire. And their flames did leap into the air, making the walls of the very heavens redden with a crimson glow."

"Amen," murmur the people.

The white man lifts his hand from his boy's shoulder and it leaves a perfect glistening palm print of blood. He holds out his arms, beckoning.

"Help us," he whispers. "Please. They're coming."

The Osage Nation never turned away a single human survivor during the New War. As a result, Gray Horse grew into a bastion of human resistance. Legends began to spread around the world of the existence of a surviving human civilization located in the middle of America and of a defiant cowboy who lived there, spitting in the face of robotkind.

—CORMAC WALLACE, MIL#GHA217

5. TWENTY-TWO SECONDS

Everything has a mind. The mind of a lamp.
The mind of a desk. The mind of a machine.

TAKEO NOMURA

ZERO HOUR

It's hard to believe, but at this point in time Mr. Takeo Nomura
was just an elderly bachelor living alone in the Adachi Ward of
Tokyo. The events of this day were described by Mr. Nomura in
an interview. His memories are corroborated by recordings taken
by Takeo's automated eldercare building and the domestic robots
working inside it. This day marks the beginning of an intellectual
journey that eventually led to the liberation of Tokyo and regions
beyond.

—CORMAC WALLACE, MIL#GHA217

It is a strange sound. Very faint. Very odd. Cyclical; it comes
again, and then again. I time the sound with the pocket watch
that sits in a yellow pool of light on my workbench. It is very
quiet for a while and I can hear the second hand patiently
tick-tick-ticking.

What a lovely sound.

The apartment is dark except for my lamp. The building administrative brain deactivates overhead lights each night at ten p.m. It is now three a.m. I touch the wall. Exactly twenty-two seconds later, I hear a faint roar. The thin wall quivers.

Twenty-two seconds.

Mikiko lies across my workbench on her back, eyes closed. I have repaired the damage to the temporal portion of her skull. She is ready for activation, yet I do not dare to put her online. I don't know what she will do, what decisions she will make.

I finger the scar on my cheek. How can I forget what happened last time?

I slip out the door and into the hallway. The wall lights are dimmed. My paper sandals are silent on the thin, brightly colored carpet. The low noise comes again and I imagine that I feel the air pressure fluctuate. It's as if a bus is driving past every few seconds.

The noise is coming from just around the corner.

I stop. My nerves tell me to go back. Huddle in my closet-sized condo. Forget about this. This building is reserved for those over the age of sixty-five. We are here to be taken care of, not to take risks. But I know that if there is danger, I must see it and confront it and understand it. If not for my sake, then for Kiko's. She is helpless right now, and I am helpless to fix her. I must protect her until I am able to break the spell she is under.

However, this does not mean that I must be brave about it.

At the corner of the hallway, I lean my aching back against the wall. I peek around the edge with one eye. My breathing is already coming in panicked gasps. And what I see makes me stop breathing altogether.

The hallway by the elevator banks is deserted. On the wall is an ornate display: two strips of round lights with floor numbers painted next to them. All the lights are dark except the ground floor one, which glows dull red. As I watch, the glowing red dot creeps slowly upward. As it reaches each floor, it makes a soft click. Each click grows louder in my mind, as the elevator rises higher and higher.

Click. Click. Click.

The dot reaches the top floor and pauses there. My hands are squeezed into fists. I bite my lip hard enough to make it bleed. The dot holds steady. Then, it *streaks* downward with nauseating speed. As the dot approaches my floor, I can hear that odd noise again. It is the whoosh of the elevator plunging straight down at the speed of gravity. A puff of wind is pushed out into the hallway as the elevator falls. Under the wind, I can also hear the screams.

Clickclickclickclick.

I flinch. Press my back against the wall and close my eyes. The elevator barrels past, rattling the walls and causing the hallway sconces to flicker.

Everything has a mind. The mind of a lamp. The mind of a desk. The mind of a machine. There is a soul inside everything, a mind that can choose to do good or evil. And the mind of the elevator seems bent on evil.

"Oh no, no, no," I whimper to myself. "Not good. Not good at all."

I gather my courage, then scurry around the corner and press the elevator call button. I watch the wall indicator as the red dot climbs back up, one level at a time. All the way to my floor.

Click. Click. Bing. It arrives. The doors slide open like curtains parting on a stage.

"Most definitely not good, Nomura," I say to myself.

The elevator walls are splattered with blood and bits of gore. Fingernail scratches mark the walls. I shudder to see a pair of bloodstained dentures partially embedded in the mounting bracket of the ceiling lamp, casting strange reddish shadows over all I see. Yet, there are no bodies. Smears on the floor lead toward the door. There are boot prints in the blood, marked with the pattern of the domestic humanoid robots that work here.

"What have you done, elevator?" I whisper.

Bing, it insists.

Behind me, I hear the vacuum-tube whir of the service-bot elevator. But I can't look away. Can't stop trying to understand how this atrocity has happened. A blast of cool air hits the back of my neck as the small service-elevator door opens behind me. Just as I turn, a bulky mailbot shoves itself into the back of my legs.

Caught off guard, I collapse.

The mail robot is simple: an almost featureless beige box the size of an office copy machine. It normally delivers mail to the residents, gentle and quiet. From where I lie sprawled on the floor, I notice that its small round intention light doesn't glow red or blue or green; it is dark. The mailbot's sticky tires are clinging to the carpet as the device shoves me forward, toward the open mouth of the elevator.

I climb to my knees and pull on the front of the mailbot in a failed attempt to stand. The single black camera eye on the front face of the mailbot watches me struggle. *Bing,* says the elevator. The doors close a few inches and then open, like a hungry mouth.

My knees slide across the carpet as I push against the machine, leaving twin ruffled streaks on the thin nap. My sandals have fallen off. The mailbot has too much mass and there is nothing to grab hold of on its smooth plastic face. I whimper for help, but the hallway is dead quiet. The lamps only watch me. The doors. The walls. They have nothing to say. Complicit.

My foot crosses the threshold of the elevator. In a panic, I reach on top of the mailbot and knock off the flimsy plastic boxes that hold letters and small packages. Papers flutter onto the carpet and into the drying pools of blood in the elevator. Now I am able to flip open the service panel on the front frame of the machine. Blindly, I stab at a button. The rolling box keeps ramming me into the elevator. With my arm bent at a cockeyed angle, I hold down the button with all my failing strength.

I beg the mailbot to stop this. It has always been a good worker. What madness has infected it?

Finally, the machine stops pushing. It is rebooting. This activity will last perhaps ten seconds. The mailbot is blocking the elevator door. I climb awkwardly on top of it. Embedded in its broad, flat back is a cheap blue LCD screen. Hex code flickers by as the delivery machine steps through its loading instructions.

Something is wrong with my friend. The mind of this robot is clouded. I know that the mailbot does not wish to harm me, just as Mikiko did not wish to harm me. It is simply under a bad spell, an outside influence. I will see what I can do about that.

Holding down a certain button during the reboot initiates a diagnostic mode. Scanning the hex code with one finger, I read what is happening in the mind of my gentle friend. Then, with a couple of button presses, I send the boxy machine into an alternate boot mode.

A safe mode.

Lying on my belly on top of the machine, I cautiously peek over the front edge. The intention light blossoms into a soft green glow. That is very good, but there isn't much time. I slide off the back of the mailbot, slip my sandals back on, and gesture at the bot.

"Follow me, Yubin-kun," I whisper.

After an unnerving second, the machine complies. It whirs along as I scamper back down the hallway to my room. I must return to where Mikiko waits, slumbering. Behind me, the elevator doors slam shut. Do I sense anger in them?

Speakers chime at us as we creep down the hall.

Ba-tong. Ba-tong.

"Attention," says a pleasant female voice. "There is an emergency. All occupants are pleased to evacuate the building immediately."

I pat my new friend on its back and hold the door as we continue into my room. This announcement certainly cannot be trusted. Now I understand. The minds of the machines have chosen evil. They have set their wills against me. Against all of us.

———

Mikiko lies on her back, heavy and unresponsive. In the hallway, sirens chirp and lights flash. Everything here is ready. My tool belt is snapped on. A small jug of water hangs from my side. I even remember to put on my warm hat, the flaps pulled snugly over my ears.

But I cannot bring myself to wake my darling—to bring her online.

Now the main building lights are on at top illumination and that pleasant voice is repeating again and again: "All occupants are pleased to evacuate the building immediately."

But, my soul help me, I am stuck. I can't leave Kiko behind, but she is too heavy to carry. She will have to walk on her own. But I am terrified of what will happen if she comes online. The evil that has corrupted the mind of my building could spread. I could not bear to see it cloud her dark eyes again. I will not leave her, yet I cannot stay. I need help.

Decision made, I close her eyes with my palm.

"Please come here, Yubin-kun," I whisper to the mail-delivering robot. "We cannot allow the bad ones to speak with you, as they did Mikiko." The intention light flickers on the blocky beige machine. "Hold very still now."

And with a swift swing of my hammer, I smash the infrared port that is used to update the diagnostics of the machine. Now, there is no way to alter the instructions of the mailbot from afar.

"That wasn't so bad, was it?" I ask the machine. Then I glance over to where Mikiko lies, eyes closed. "Yubin-kun, my new friend, I hope you are feeling strong today."

With a grunt, I lift Mikiko off the workbench and set her on top of the mailbot. Built to carry heavy packages, the solid machine is completely unaffected by the added weight. It simply trains its single camera eye on me, following as I open the door to the hallway.

Outside, I see a shaky line of elderly residents. One by one, the door at the end of the hallway opens and another resident steps into the stairwell. My neighbors are very patient people. Very polite.

But the soul of this building has gone mad.

"Stop, stop," I mumble to them. They ignore me, as usual. Politely avoiding eye contact, they keep stepping through the door, one after another.

With my loyal Yubin-kun following close, I reach the

stairwell door just before the last woman can step through. An intention light over the doorway flashes yellow at me crossly.

"Mr. Nomura," says the building in a gentle female voice, "please wait your turn, sir. Mrs. Kami is presently pleased to go through the door."

"Don't go," I mutter to the elderly woman in her bathrobe. I cannot make eye contact. Instead, I lightly grasp her elbow.

With a glare, the shriveled old woman tears her elbow from my hand and shoves past me, stepping through the doorway. Just before the door snaps shut behind her, I wedge my foot into the opening and get a glimpse of what is inside.

It is a bad dream.

In a confusion of inky blackness and flashing strobes, dozens of my elderly neighbors crush each other in falling heaps down the concrete stairs. Showers of emergency water rain down from the sprinkler heads, turning the stairs into slick, cascading waterfalls. The fire exhaust vent is on full strength, sucking frigid air up from the bottom of the shaft to the top. Moans and cries are drowned by the shrieking turbines. The mass of writhing arms and legs seems to combine in my vision until it is a single, massively suffering creature.

I pull my foot back and the door slams shut.

We are all trapped. It is only a matter of time before the domestic humanoid robots ascend to this level. When they arrive, I will be unable to defend myself or Mikiko.

"This is a very bad, bad, bad thing, Mr. Nomura," I whisper to myself.

Yubin-kun blinks a yellow intention light at me. My friend is wary, as he should be. He senses that things are wrong.

"Mr. Nomura," says the voice overhead, "if you are not pleased to utilize the stairwell, we will send a helper to assist. Stay where you are. Help is on the way."

Click. Click. Click.

As the elevator rises, the red dot begins its slow crawl up from the ground floor.

Twenty-two seconds.

I turn to Yubin-kun. Mikiko lies sprawled on top of the beige box, her black hair splayed out. I look down into her gently smiling face. She is so beautiful and pure. In her slumber, she dreams of me. She waits for me to break this evil spell and wake her. Someday, she will arise and become my queen.

If only I had more time.

The dry, menacing click of the elevator gauge breaks my reverie. I am a helpless old man and I am out of ideas. I take Mikiko's limp hand in mine and turn to face the elevator doors.

"I am so sorry, Mikiko," I whisper. "I tried, my darling. But now there is nowhere else—*Ay!*"

I hop backward and rub my foot where Yubin-kun has run it over. The machine's intention light blinks at me frantically. On the wall, the red dot reaches my floor. My time is up.

Bing.

A burst of cool air blows from the service elevator across the hall from the main elevator bank. Its door panel slides out of the way and I see a steel box inside, just a little bigger than the mailbot. On its sticky wheels, Yubin-kun slides into the cramped space with Mikiko still lying on top.

There is just enough room for me to squeeze inside, too.

As I enter, I hear the main elevator doors open across the hall. I look up just in time to see the plastic grin of the Big Happy domestic robot standing inside the blood-coated elevator. Streaks of red liquid bead on its casing. Its head twists back and forth, scanning.

The head stops, its lifeless purple camera eyes locked onto me.

Then, the door of my service elevator slides closed. Just

before the floor drops out from under me, I squeeze out a few words to my new comrade. "Thank you, Yubin-kun," I say. "I am in your debt, my friend."

Yubin-kun was the first of Takeo's comrades in arms. In the harrowing months following Zero Hour, Takeo would find many more friends willing to help his cause.

—CORMAC WALLACE, MIL#GHA217

6. Avtomat

My day is going kind of nice.

Spc. Paul Blanton

ZERO HOUR

In the wake of the congressional hearing regarding the SAP incident, Paul Blanton was charged with dereliction of duty and scheduled to be court-martialed. During Zero Hour, Paul found himself locked up on a base in Afghanistan. This unusual circumstance placed the young soldier in a unique position to make an invaluable contribution to the human resistance—and to survive.

—CORMAC WALLACE, MIL#GHA217

Back in Oklahoma, my dad used to tell me that if I didn't straighten up and act like a man, I'd end up dead or in jail. Lonnie Wayne was right about that, which is why I ended up enlisted. But still. Thank god I was in lockup for Zero Hour.

I'm laying on my cell bunk, back against the cinder block wall and my combat boots propped up on the steel toilet. Got a rag over my face to keep the dust out of my nostrils. I've been incarcerated ever since my SAP unit lost its mind and started wasting people.

C'est la vie. That's what my cell mate, Jason Lee, says. He's a portly Asian kid with glasses, doing sit-ups on the cement floor. Says he does it to stay warm.

I'm not the exercising type. For me, these six months have meant a lot of magazines to read. Staying warm means growing a beard.

Boring, sure, but all the same, my day is going kind of nice. I'm perusing a four-month-old issue of some stateside celebrity rag. Learning all about how "movie stars are just like us." They like to eat at restaurants, go shopping, take their kids to the park—shit like that.

Just like us. Yeah. By *us*, I don't think they mean me.

It's an educated guess, but I doubt that movie stars care about repairing militarized humanoid robots that are designed to subdue and pacify a murderously angry population in an occupied country. Or being thrown into a thirteen-by-seven-foot cell with one tiny window just for performing your glamorous job.

"Bruce Lee?" I ask. He hates it when I call him that. "Did you know movie stars are just like us? Who knew, man?"

Jason Lee stops doing sit-ups. He looks up at me where I'm leaning back into the corner of our cell. "Quiet," he says. "Do you hear that?"

"Hear wha—"

And then a tank round discharges through the wall across the room. A blazing shower of rebar and cement shreds my cell mate into big flabby chunks of flesh wrapped in what's left of dust-colored army fatigues. Jason was here and now he's gone. Like a magic trick. I can't even process this.

I'm huddled in the corner—miraculously uninjured. Through the bars, I see the duty officer is no longer at his desk. There isn't any desk anymore. Just chunks of rubble. For a split second, I can see through the new hole that's been blasted in the wall across the room.

There are, as I suspected, tanks on the other side of it.

A cloud of frigid dust rolls into the room, and I start to shiver. Jason Lee was correct: It's a cold motherfucker out there. It registers that despite the new renovation across the room, the bars of my cell are just as strong and steady as before.

My hearing starts to return. Visibility is nil, but I identify a trickling sound, like a creek or something. It's what's left of Jason Lee, bleeding out.

Also, my magazine seems to have disappeared.

Fuck.

I press my face against the mesh-wire-reinforced window of my cell. Outside, the base has gone FUBAR. I've got eyes on the alley leading to the main pavilion of the Kabul green zone. A couple of friendly soldiers are out there, crouched against a mud-brick wall. They look young, confused. They're in full rig: backpacks, body armor, goggles, knee pads—all that crap.

How safe can safety goggles make a war?

The lead soldier peeks his head around the corner. He hops back, excited. He yanks out a Javelin antitank missile launcher and loads it, fast and smooth. Good training. Just then, an American tank cruises past the alleyway and spits a shell without stopping. It lobs over the base and away from us. I feel the building quake as the shell impacts somewhere.

Through the window, I watch the antitank soldier step out of the alley, sit down cross-legged with that log on his shoulder, and get filleted by incoming antipersonnel tank fire. It's an automated tank protection system that targets certain silhouettes—like "guy holding antitank weapon"—within a certain radius.

Any insurgent would have known better.

I frown, forehead pressed against the thick window. My hands are jammed in my armpits to stay warm. I got no idea why that American tank just erased a friendly soldier, but I have a feeling that it has something to do with SAP One committing suicide.

The remaining soldier in the alley watches his buddy go down in pieces, turns, and runs back toward me. Just then, a billowing black cloth blocks my view. It's a robe. A bad guy just crossed in front of my window. I hear small arms fire, close.

Bad guys *and* nutso equipment? Fuck, man. When it rains it pours.

The robe flutters away and the whole alley just disappears, replaced by black smoke. The glass of my window buckles and fractures, slicing my forehead open. I hear the hollow concussion a split second later. I fall back onto my bunk, grab the blanket, and pull it over my shoulders. Check my face. My fingers come away bloody. When I look back out the fractured window, there are only dust-covered lumps in the alley. Bodies of soldiers, locals, and insurgents.

The tanks are killing *everybody*.

It is becoming very clear to me that I've got to find a way out of this cell if I want my future to include breathing.

Outside, something roars by overhead, ripping dark vortices out of the rising smoke. Probably an armed drone. I cower back in my bunk. The dust is starting to clear out now. I spot the keys to my cell across the room. They're still attached to a broken belt, hanging from a splintered piece of chair. Might as well be on Mars.

No weapons. No armor. No hope.

Then a blood-covered insurgent ducks in through the blasted-out hole in the wall. He catches sight of me, stares wide-eyed. One side of his face is plastered with brown-white alkaline sand and the other side is caked with powdered blood. His nose is broken and his lips are swollen up from the cold. The hair of his black mustache and beard is fine, wiry. He can't be more than sixteen years old.

"Let me out, please. I can help you," I say in my finest Dari. I pull the rag off my face so he can see my beard. At least he'll know I'm not active duty.

The insurgent presses his back against the wall and closes his eyes. It looks like he's praying. Dirt-caked hands pressed flat against the blasted concrete wall. At least he has an old-fashioned revolver hanging on his hip. He's scared but operational.

I can't make out his prayer, but I can tell it isn't for his own life. He's praying for the souls of his buddies. Whatever's happening out there sure ain't pretty.

Better hit the road.

"The keys are on the floor, friend," I urge. "Please, I can help you. I can help you stay alive."

He looks at me, stops praying.

"The avtomata have come for us all," he says. "We thought the avto were rising up against you. But they are thirsty for all our blood."

"What's your name?"

He eyes me suspiciously.

"Jabar," he says.

"Okay, Jabar. You're going to survive this. Free me. I'm unarmed. But I know these, uh, avtomata. I know how to kill them."

Jabar picks up the keys, flinching as something big and black barrels down the street outside. He picks his way over the rubble to my cell.

"You are in prison."

"Yeah, that's right. See? We're on the same side."

Jabar thinks about it.

"If they have put you in prison, it is my duty to free you," he says. "But if you attack me, I will kill you."

"Sounds fair," I say, never taking my eyes off the key.

The key thunks into the lock, and I yank the door open and dart out. Jabar tackles me to the ground, eyes wide with fear. I think he's afraid of me, but I'm wrong.

He's afraid of what's outside.

"Do not pass before the windows. The avtomata can sense your heat. They will find us."

"Infrared heat sensing?" I ask. "That's only on the auto-mated sentry turrets, man. ASTs. They're at the front gate. Aimed *away* from the base, toward the desert. C'mon, we need to go out the back."

Blanket over my shoulders, I step out of the hole in the wall and into the frigid confusion of dust and smoke in the alley outside. Jabar crouches and follows, pistol drawn.

It's god's own raging dust storm out here.

I double over and run for the rear of the base. There's a phalanx of sentry guns covering the front gate. I want to stay clear of them. Slip out the back and get someplace safe. Figure it out from there.

We round a corner and find a black-blasted crater the size of a building, just smoldering. Not even an autotank has the ordnance to do this. It means the drones aren't just spotting rabbits up there—they're launching Brimstone missiles.

When I turn to warn Jabar, I see he is already scanning the skies. A fine layer of dust coats his beard. It makes him look like a wise old man in a young man's body.

Probably not too far from the truth.

I stretch my blanket out over my head to obscure my silhouette and form a confusing target for anything watching from above. I don't have to tell Jabar to stay under the overhangs, he already does it by habit.

Abruptly I wonder how long he's been fighting these same robots. What must he have thought when they began to attack our own troops? Probably thought it was his lucky day.

Finally, we reach the back perimeter. Several of the twelve-foot cement walls have been battered down. Pulverized cement coats the ground, clean rebar jutting through the broken chunks. Jabar and I crouch next to a sagging wall. I peek around the corner.

Nothing.

A cleared area surrounds the whole base, sort of a dusty road wrapping tight around our perimeter. No-man's-land. A few hundred meters out, there's a rolling hill with thousands of slate stones sticking up like splinters. Porcupine Hill.

The local graveyard.

I tap Jabar on the shoulder and we run for it. Maybe the robots aren't patrolling the perimeter today. Maybe they're too busy killing people for no reason. Jabar sprints past me and I watch his brown robes blur away into the dust. The storm swallows him. I run as hard as I can to keep up.

Then I hear a noise I've been dreading.

The high-pitched whine of an electric motor echoes from somewhere around us. It's a mobile sentry gun. They constantly patrol this narrow strip of no-man's-land. Apparently, nobody told them to take a break today.

The MSG has four long narrow legs with wheels on the ends. On top, it has an M4 carbine set to auto-fire with an optics package mounted on the barrel and a big rectangular magazine bolted to the side. When the thing gets moving, those legs flutter up and down over rocks and gravel in a blur, while that rifle stays motionless, perfectly level.

And it's coming after us.

Thank god the terrain is starting to get more rough. It means we're almost off the graded perimeter strip. The motor whine is getting louder. The MSG uses vision for target acquisition, so the dust should obscure us. I can just see the tail of Jabar's robe fluttering in the dust storm as he keeps running, fast and steady away from the green zone.

Breathe in. Breathe out. We're gonna make it.

Then, I hear the stuttering click of a range finder. The MSG is using short-range ultrasonic, bouncing sound through the dust storm to find us. That means it knows we're here. Bad news. I wonder how many more steps I have left.

One, two, three, four. One, two, three, four.

A tombstone emerges from the haze—just a jagged chunk of slate tilting drunkenly out of the ground. Then I see a dozen more looming ahead. I stagger between the tombstones, feeling the cold sweating slabs under my palms as I grab them for balance.

The clicking is almost a steady hum now.

"Down!" I shout to Jabar. He leaps forward and disappears over a rut in the ground. A burst of automatic weapons fire roars out of the storm. Shards of a tombstone explode across my right arm. I stumble and fall on my stomach, then try to drag myself behind a stone.

Clickclickclick.

Strong hands grab hold of my hurt arm. I stifle a shout as

Jabar pulls me over the hillock. We're in a small ditch, surrounded by knee-high shards of rock embedded in sandy ground. The graves are placed haphazardly between occasional clumps of mossy weeds. Most of the tombstones are unmarked, but a couple have been spray-painted with symbols. Some others are ornately carved marble. I can see a few have steel cages built around them, peaked roofs the only ornamentation.

Click, click, click.

The ultrasonic grows fainter. Crouched against Jabar, I take a second to inspect my wound. Part of my upper right arm is shredded, totally messing up my flag of Oklahoma tat. Half the damn eagle feathers that hang from the bottom of the Osage battle shield are grated off by slivers of black rock. I show my arm to Jabar.

"Look what the fuckers did to my tattoo, Jabar buddy."

He shakes his head at me. He's got one elbow covering his mouth, breathing through the fabric. There might be a smile under that arm right now. Who knows? Maybe we're both going to make it out of this alive.

And then, just like that, the dust clears.

The storm passes by overhead. We watch the huge mass of swirling dust tear across the perimeter strip, engulf the green zone, and move on. Now the sun is beaming down bright and cold from a clear blue sky. There's hardly any atmosphere in these mountains, and the harsh sunlight casts shadows like spilled tar. I can see my breath now.

And, I figure, so can the robots.

We run hard, staying low and darting between the larger tombs that are protected by blue or green steel cages. I don't know where we're going now. I just hope that Jabar has a plan and that it involves me staying alive.

After a couple minutes, I catch a flash out of the corner of my eye. It's the mobile sentry gun, cruising over a rough path in the middle of the graveyard, swinging its rifle head back and forth. Sunlight glints from the low-slung optics module bulging from the top of the gun. The bowed legs tremble over the bumpy earth, but the rifle barrel is motionless as a barn owl.

I dive behind a tombstone and lie flat on my belly. Jabar has also found cover, a few feet away. He motions to me with one finger, brown eyes urgent beneath dust-frosted eyebrows.

Following his gaze, I see a partially dug grave. It was going to be a nice resting place for some Afghani—a brand-new steel cage rests partially over it. Whoever was working on this got the hell out of here fast, without bolting down the cage.

Keeping still, I crane my neck to look around. The mobile sentry gun is nowhere to be seen. Faintly, I hear the lawn mower *thup-thup-thup* of a low-flying drone. It sounds like a death sentence. Somewhere out there, the sentry gun is scanning row after row of tombstones for humanlike silhouettes or some trace movement.

Inching forward, I crawl until I reach the open grave. Jabar already lies inside, his face striped with shadows from the slatted bars of the steel cage. Holding my hurt arm, I roll inside.

Me and Jabar lie there next to each other on our backs in the half-dug grave, trying to wait out the sentries. The ground is frozen. The gravelly dirt feels harder than the floor of my cement cell. I can sense the warmth seeping away from my body.

"It's okay, Jabar," I whisper. "The drones are following standard operating procedure. Looking for squirters. People running away. There should be a twenty-minute scan-and-hold routine, max."

Jabar wrinkles his brow at me.

"I already know this."

"Oh, right. Sorry."

We huddle together, teeth chattering.

"Hey," says Jabar.

"Yeah?"

"Are you really an American soldier?"

"Course. Why else would I be on base?"

"I never saw one. Not in person."

"Seriously?"

Jabar shrugs.

"We only see the metal ones," he says. "When the avtomata attacked, we joined. Now, my friends are dead. So are yours, I feel."

"Where do we go, Jabar?"

"The caves. My people."

"Is it safe there?"

"Safe for me. Not safe for you."

I notice that Jabar holds his pistol tight across his chest. He is young, but I cannot forget that he's been at this a very long time.

"So," I say, "am I your prisoner?"

"I think so, yes."

Looking up through the metal slats, I can see that the blank blue sky is stained with black smoke rising from the green zone. Besides the soldiers in the alley, I haven't seen another living American since the attack began. I think of all those tanks and drones and sentry guns that must be out there, stalking survivors.

Jabar's arm feels warm against me, and I remember that I don't have any clothes or food or weapons. I'm not even sure the U.S. Army would allow me to *have* a weapon.

"Jabar, my man," I say. "I can work with that."

Jabar and Paul Blanton successfully escaped into the rugged mountains of Afghanistan. Within a week, records indicate that the locals began a series of successful raids on Rob positions, as the tribal forces combined their hard-earned survival techniques with Specialist Blanton's technical expertise.

Within two years, Paul would use this synthesis of tribal survival lore and technical knowledge to make a discovery that would forever change my life, the life of my comrades, and the life of his own father, Lonnie Wayne Blanton.

—CORMAC WALLACE, MIL#GHA217

That's a funny name to give a boat. What's it mean?

Arrtrad

ZERO HOUR

After the alarming experience with his cell phone, the hacker known as Lurker fled his home and found a safe place to hide. He didn't make it very far. This account of the onset of Zero Hour in London was pieced together from recorded conversations between Lurker and people who visited his floating base of operations in the early years of the New War.

—CORMAC WALLACE, MIL#GHA217

"Lurker, you going to answer that?"

I look at Arrtrad with disgust. Here he is, a thirty-five-year-old man and he hasn't a clue. The world is ending. Doomsday is upon us. And Arrtrad, as he calls himself on the chat lines, stands across from me, Adam's apple bobbing under his weak chin, asking me if I'm going to answer that?

"Do you know what this means, Arrtrad?"

"No, boss. Uh, not really, I mean."

"Nobody calls this phone, you tosser. Nobody except *him*. The reason we've run. The devil in the machine."

"You mean, *that's* who's calling?"

Not a doubt in my mind.

"Yeah, it's Archos. There's nobody else who's ever traced this bloody number. My number."

"Does this mean he's coming for us?"

I look at the phone, vibrating on our small wooden dinner table. It's surrounded by a mess of papers and pencils. All my schemes. This phone and me had a lot of fun together in the old days. Pulled a lot of capers. But now it makes me flinch to see it. Keeps me up at night, wondering what's on the other end of it.

There's a scream of motors and the table lurches. A pencil rolls away, drops to the floor with a tap.

"Damned speedboats," says Arrtrad, grabbing the wall for support. Our houseboat sways on the wake. She's just a little boat, about twelve yards long. Basically a wood-paneled living room floating a yard off the water. For the last couple months, I've been sleeping on the bed and Arrtrad on the convertible folding table, with just the potbellied stove to keep us warm.

And watching that phone to keep me busy.

The speedboat whines off farther down the Thames, toward the ocean. It's probably my imagination, but it feels as if that boat came and went in a panic, fleeing something.

Now I can feel the panic rising in me, too.

"Unmoor us," I whisper to Arrtrad, wincing as the phone rings again and again.

It won't stop ringing.

"What?" asks Arrtrad. "We haven't got much petrol, Lurker. Let's answer the phone first. See what this is all about."

I stare at him blankly. He looks back, gulping. I know from

experience that there's nothing in my gray eyes for him to see. No emotion to latch onto. No weakness. It's the unpredictability that makes him afraid of me.

In a small voice, Arrtrad asks, "Shall I answer it?"

Arrtrad picks up the mobile phone with shaky fingers. Autumn light streams in from the thin-paned windows and his thinning hair floats like a halo on his wrinkled scalp. I can't allow this weakling to get the upper hand. I've got to show my crew who's boss. Even if it's a crew of one.

"Give me that," I mumble, and snatch the phone away. I answer it with one thumb, in a well-practiced motion.

"It's Lurker," I growl. "And I'm coming for you, mate—"

I'm interrupted by a recorded message. I hold the phone away from my ear. The tinny computerized female voice is easy to hear over the lapping waves outside.

"Attention, citizen. This is a message from your local emergency alert system. This is not a test. Be advised that due to a chemical spill in central London, all citizens are asked to go inside immediately. Bring your pets with you. Close and lock all doors and windows. Shut off all ventilation systems that circulate air. Please wait for assistance, which will arrive shortly. Note that due to the nature of the accident, unmanned systems may be utilized for your rescue. Until help arrives, please monitor your radio for emergency alert system announcements. Thank you for your cooperation. *Beep*. Attention, citizen. This is a message—"

Click.

"Unmoor us now, Arrtrad."

"It's a chem spill, Lurker. We should shut the windows and—"

"Unmoor us, you sodding fuck!"

I scream the words right into Arrtrad's dim-witted weasel

face, painting his forehead with my spittle. Out the window, London looks normal. Then I notice a thin column of smoke. Nothing big, but just hanging there, out of place. Sinister.

When I turn around, Arrtrad is wiping his forehead and muttering, but he is walking toward the flimsy front door of the houseboat as he goddamn well should be. Our shoddy wharf is old and rotten and has been here forever. We're tied to it tight in three places and if we don't get untied, we won't be going anywhere.

And on this particular afternoon, I happen to be in quite a hurry to be off. See, I'm near to fairly certain that this is the end of days. It's the sodding apocalypse and I'm teamed with the village idiot and shackled tight to a waterlogged pile of rot.

I've never even started the houseboat engine before.

The key is dangling in the ignition. I walk to the nav station at the front of the room. I prop open the front window and the smell of muddy water wafts in. For a moment, I rest my sweaty palms on the fake wood of the steering wheel. Then without looking I reach down and turn the key, quick.

Ka-rowr.

The engine turns over and sputters into life. First try. Through the back window, I see a haze of bluish smoke billow up. Arrtrad is crouched on the right side of the boat, alongside the dock, getting the second mooring rope untied. Starboard, I suppose the boating types call it.

"*Memento Mori*," calls Arrtrad between pants. "That's a funny name to give a boat. What's it mean?"

I ignore him. In the distance over Arrtrad's bald spot something has just caught my eye: a silver car.

The car looks normal enough, but somehow it's moving too steadily for my taste. The car wheels down the road that leads to our wharf as if its steering were locked in place. Is it a coincidence that the car is aimed toward our dock and us at the end of it?

"Faster," I shout, rattling the window with my fist.

Arrtrad stands up, hands on his hips. His face is red and sweaty. "They've been tied a long time, all right? It's going to take more than a—"

At near full speed, the silver car hops a curb at the end of the street and leaps into the dockside car park. There is a faint crunch of the auto's undercarriage bottoming out. Something is definitely wrong.

"Just go! GO!"

Finally, the facade has cracked. My panic shines through like radiation. Confused, Arrtrad fairly lopes along the side of the boat. Near the back end, he drops to his knees and starts working on the last decaying mooring rope.

To my left is open river. To my right is a crumbling pile of warped wood and two tons of speeding metal careening toward me at top speed. If I don't move this boat in the next few seconds, I'm going to have a car parked on top of it.

I watch the auto bounce through the immense car park. My head feels stuffed with cotton. The houseboat motor throbs and my hands have gone numb with the vibration of the wheel. My heart pounds in my chest.

Something occurs to me.

I snatch my mobile phone off the table, crack the SIM card out of it, and chuck the rest into the water. It makes a small plop. I can feel a bull's-eye slide off my back.

The top of Arrtrad's head bobs in and out of view as he unwinds the last rope. He doesn't see the silver auto streaking across the deserted car park, sending trash fluttering into the air. It hasn't changed direction by an inch. The plastic bumper scrapes concrete and then flies completely off as the car bounces over a curb and onto the wooden dock.

My mobile phone is gone but it's already too late. The devil has found me.

Now I can hear the thrumming of tires over the last fifty yards of rotten wood. Arrtrad's head rises up, concerned. He's hunched on the side of the boat, hands covered in slime from the ancient rope.

"Don't look, just go!" I shout at Arrtrad.

I grab the clutch lever. With one thumb, I pop the houseboat out of neutral and into reverse. Ready to move. No throttle though. Not yet.

Forty yards.

I could jump off the boat. But where will I go? My food is here. My water. My village idiot.

Thirty yards.

It's the end of the world, mate.

Twenty yards.

Hell with it. Untied or not, I slam the throttle and we lurch backward. Arrtrad shouts something incoherent. I hear another pencil tap to the ground, followed by dishes and papers and a coffee mug. The neat pile of wood next to the potbellied stove collapses.

Ten yards.

The engines thunder. Sunlight flashes from the scarred silver missile as it catapults off the end of the dock. The auto soars through empty space, missing the front of the houseboat by a few feet. It crashes into the water and sends up a white spray that comes through the open window and slaps me in the bloody face.

It's over.

I throttle down but leave the boat in reverse, then hurry to the front deck. The prow, they say. Ashen-faced, Arrtrad joins me. We watch the car together, trawling slowly in reverse, away from the end of the world.

The silver car is half-submerged and sinking fast. In the front seat, a man is slumped over the wheel. The windshield bears a crimson spiderweb of cracks where his face must have hit on impact. A woman with long hair is flopped next to him in the passenger seat.

And then, there's the last thing that I see. That last thing that I never wanted to see. Didn't ask to see.

In the backseat window. Two pale little palms, pressed hard against the tinted glass. Pale as linen. Pushing.

Pushing so hard.

And the silver car slips under.

Arrtrad drops to his knees.

"No," he shouts. "No!"

The gawky man puts his face in his hands. His whole body convulses with sobs. Snot and tears pour out of his birdlike face.

I retreat into the doorway of the cabin. The doorframe gives me support. I don't know how I feel, only that I feel different. Changed, somehow.

I notice it's getting dark outside, now. Smoke is rising from the city. A practical thought comes to me. We've got to get out of here before something worse comes.

Arrtrad speaks to me through sobs. He grabs me by the arm and his hands are wet with tears and river water and muck from the ropes. "Did you know this would happen?"

"Stop crying," I snap.

"Why? Why didn't you tell nobody? What about your mum?"

"What about her?"

"You didn't tell your *mum*?"

"She'll be fine."

"She's not fine. Nothing is fine. You're only seventeen. But I've got *kids*. Two kids. And they could be hurt."

"Why haven't I ever seen 'em?"

"They're with my ex. But I coulda warned them. I coulda told them what was coming. People are dead. *Dead*, Lurker. That was a family. It was a fucking child in that car. Just a wee baby. My god. What's the matter with you, mate?"

"Nothing's the matter. Stop your crying, now. It's all part of the plan, see? If you had a brain you'd understand. But you don't. So you listen to me."

"Yes, but—"

"Listen to me and we'll be fine. We're going to help those people. We're going to find your kids."

"That's impossible—"

Now, I stop him cold. I'm starting to feel a bit angry. A bit of my old fire is returning to replace the numbness. "What have I told you about saying that?"

"I'm sorry, Lurker."

"*Nothing's* impossible."

"But how will we do those things? How can we find my kids?"

"We survived for a reason, Arrtrad. This monster. This *thing*. It's played its hand, see? It's using the machines to hurt people. But we're savvy now. We can help. We'll save all those poor sheep out there. We'll save them and they'll thank us for it. They'll *worship* us for it. Me and you. We're coming out on top. It's all in the plan, mate."

Arrtrad looks away. It's plain that he doesn't believe a word of it. Looks like he might have something to say.

"What? Go on, then," I say.

"Well, pardon me. But you never seemed the helping type, Lurker. Don't get me wrong—"

And that's just it, isn't it? I've never thought much of other people. Or thought about them much at all. But those pale palms against the window. I can't stop thinking of them. I have a feeling they will be with me for a long time.

"Yeah, I know that," I say. "But you've not seen my forgiving nature. It's all in the plan, Arrtrad. You have to trust. You'll see, yeah? We've survived. It had to have been for a reason. We have a purpose now, you and me. It's us against that thing. And we're going to get revenge. So stand up and join the fight."

I reach my hand out to Arrtrad.

"Yeah?" he asks.

He still doesn't fully believe me. But I'm starting to believe myself. I take his hand in mine and haul Arrtrad to his feet.

"Yeah, mate. Picture this. It's me and you against the devil himself. To the death. All the way to the very end. And someday, we'll be in the history books for it. Guaranteed."

This event appeared to represent a turning point in Lurker's life. As the New War began in earnest, it seems that he left all childish things behind him and started behaving as a member of the human race. In further records, Lurker's arrogance and vanity remain the same. But his breathtaking selfishness seems to have disappeared along with the silver car.

—CORMAC WALLACE, MIL#GHA217

8. HERO MATERIAL

Dude, let the police deal with this shit.

CORMAC "BRIGHT BOY" WALLACE

ZERO HOUR

This account is composed of a series of patched-together camera and satellite feeds, roughly tracking the GPS coordinates provided by the phone I owned at Zero Hour. Since my brother and I are the subjects of this surveillance, I have chosen to annotate with my own recollections. At the time, of course, we had no idea that we were being watched.

—CORMAC WALLACE, MIL#GHA217

Shit, man. Here it is, the day before Thanksgiving. The day it all happened. My life up until now was never that great, but at least I wasn't being hunted. I never had to jump at shadows, wondering whether some metal bug was about to try and blind me, sever one of my limbs, or infect me like a parasite.

Relative to that, my life before Zero Hour was perfection.

I'm in Boston and it's as cold as a bastard. The wind is cutting my ears like razor blades and I'm chasing my brother through the Downtown Crossing outdoor shopping pavilion. Jack is three years older than me and as usual he's trying to do the right thing. But I won't listen to him.

Our dad died last summer. Me and Jack flew out West and buried him. And that was that. We left our stepmom alone in California with a lot of tear-streaked makeup and everything Dad owned.

Well, pretty much everything.

Since then, I've been sleeping on Jack's couch. Mooching, I'll admit it. In another few days, I'm flying to Estonia on a photojournalist gig for *Nat Geo*. From there, I'll try to book my next gig straight, so that I don't have to come home.

In about five minutes, the whole fucking world is going to go batshit insane. But I don't know that, I'm just trying to catch Jack and calm him down and get him to be cool.

I grab Jack's arm right before we reach the wide, open-air tunnel that runs under the street and across to the shopping pavilion. Jack turns around and without hesitation the jerk punches me in the mouth. My right upper canine cuts a nice little hole in my bottom lip. His fists are still up, but I just touch my lip with my finger; it comes away bloody.

"I thought it was never in the face, you fucker," I say, panting clouds.

"You made me do it, man. I tried to run," he says.

I know this already. It's how he's always been. Still, I'm kind of stunned. He's never hit me in the face before.

This must have been a bigger fuckup than I thought.

But Jack already has that "I'm sorry" look creeping onto his face. His bright blue eyes are trained on my mouth, calculating how bad he hurt me. He smirks and looks away. Not that bad, I guess.

I lick the blood off my lip.

"Look, Dad left it to me. I'm broke. There was no other choice. I had to sell it to get to Estonia and make some money. See how that works?"

My dad gave me a special bayonet from World War II. I sold it. I was wrong and I know it, but somehow I can't admit this to Jack, my perfect brother. He's a damn Boston firefighter and in the National Guard. Talk about hero material.

"It belonged to the family, Cormac," he says. "Pappy risked his life for it. It was a part of our heritage. And you *pawned* it for a few hundred bucks."

He stops and takes a breath.

"Okay, this is pissing me off. I can't even talk to you right now or I'm going to knock you out."

Jack stalks away, angry. When the sand-colored walking land mine appears at the end of the tunnel, he reacts instantly.

"Everybody look out! Out of the tunnel. Bomb!" he bellows. People respond immediately to the authority in his voice. Even me. A few dozen flatten themselves against the wall as the six-legged device *tap, taps* slowly past them over the paving stones. The rest of the people flood out of the tunnel in a controlled panic.

Jack walks to the middle of the tunnel, a lone gunfighter. He draws a Glock .45 from a holster under his jacket. He clasps the gun in two hands, keeps it pointed at the ground. Hesitantly, I step out behind him. "You have a gun?" I whisper.

"A lot of us in the guard do," says Jack. "Listen, stay far away from that scuttle mine. It can move a lot faster than it's going now."

"Scuttle mine?"

Jack's eyes never leave the shoebox-sized machine coming down the middle of the tunnel. United States military ordnance. Its six legs move one by one in sharp mechanical jerks.

Some kind of laser on its back paints a red circle on the ground around it.

"What's it doing here, Jack?"

"I don't know. It must have come from the National Guard armory. It's stuck in diagnostic mode. That red circle is there to let a demo man set the trigger range. Go call nine one one."

Before I can get out my cell phone, the machine stops. It leans back on four legs and raises its front two legs into the air. It looks like an angry crab.

"Okay, you'll want to back up now. It's target seeking. I'm going to have to shoot it."

Jack raises his gun. Already walking backward, I call to my brother, "Won't that make it blow up?"

Jack assumes a firing stance. "Not if I only shoot its legs. Otherwise, yes."

"Isn't that bad?"

Reared back, the scuttle mine paws the air.

"It's targeting, Cormac. Either we disable it, or it disables one of us." Jack squints down his gunsight. Then he squeezes the trigger and a deafening boom echoes through the tunnel. My ears are ringing when he fires again.

I wince, but there's no big explosion.

Over Jack's shoulder, I see the scuttle mine lying on its back, three remaining legs clawing at the air. Then Jack steps into my line of sight, makes eye contact with me, and speaks slowly. "Cormac. I need you to get help, buddy. I'll stay here and keep an eye on this thing. You get out of the tunnel and call the police. Tell them to send a bomb squad."

"Yeah, right," I say. I can't seem to look away from the damaged sand-camouflaged crab lying on the ground. It looks so hard and military, out of place here in this shopping square.

I trot back out of the tunnel and directly into Zero

Hour—humankind's new future. For the first second of my new life, I think that what I'm seeing is a joke. How could it not be?

For some crazy reason, I assume that an artist has filled the shopping pavilion with radio-controlled cars as some kind of art installation. Then I see the red circles around each of the crawling devices. Dozens of scuttle mines are stepping across the pavilion, like slow-motion invaders from another planet.

The people have all run away.

Now, a concussive thump detonates a few blocks away. I hear distant screaming. Police cars. The city emergency outdoor warning sirens begin wailing, growing louder and then softer as they rotate.

A few of the scuttle mines seem startled. They rear back on their hind legs, front legs waving.

I feel a hand on my elbow. Jack's chiseled face looks up at me from the dark tunnel.

"Something's wrong, Jack," I say.

He scans the square with hard blue eyes and makes a decision. Just like that. "The armory. We've got to get there and fix this. C'mon," he says, grabbing my elbow with one hand. In the other hand, I see he still has his gun out.

"What about the crabs?"

Jack leads me across the pavilion, delivering information in short, clipped sentences. "Don't get into their trigger zones, the red circles."

We climb up onto a picnic table and away from the scuttle mines, leaping between park benches, the central fountain, and concrete walls. "They sense vibration. Don't walk with a pattern. Hop instead."

When we do set foot on the ground, we lunge quickly from one position to the next. As we proceed, Jack's words string together into concrete ideas that penetrate my stunned confusion. "If you see target-seeking behavior, get away. They *will* swarm. They aren't moving that fast, but there's a lot of them."

Leaping from obstacle to obstacle, we pick our way across the square. About fifteen minutes in, one of the scuttle mines stops against the front door of a clothing store. I hear the tap of its legs on the glass. A woman in a black dress stands in the middle of the store, watching the crab through the door. The red circle shines through the glass, refracted by a few inches. The woman takes a curious step toward it.

"Lady, no!" I shout.

Boom! The scuttle mine explodes, shattering the front door and throwing the woman backward into the store. The other crabs stop and wave their forelegs for a few seconds. Then, one by one, they continue to crawl across the pavilion.

I touch my face and my fingers come away bloody. "Oh shit, Jack. Am I hurt?"

"It's from when I hit you before, man. Remember?"

"Oh yeah."

We move on.

As we reach the edge of the park, the city emergency sirens stop screaming. Now we just hear the wind, the scrabble of metal legs on concrete, and the occasional deadened bang of a distant explosion. It's getting dark and Boston is only getting colder.

Jack stops and puts his hand on my shoulder. "Cormac, you're doing great. Now, I need you to run with me. The armory is less than a mile from here. You okay, Big Mac?"

I nod, shivering.

"Outstanding. Running is good. It'll keep us warm. Follow me close. If you see a scuttle mine or anything else just avoid it. Stay with me. Okay?"

"Okay, Jack."

"Now, we run."

Jack scans the alley ahead of us. The scuttle mines are thinning out, but once we're out of the shopping area, I know there will be room for bigger machines—like cars.

My big brother gives me a reassuring grin, then sprints away. I follow him. I don't have much of a choice.

———

The armory is a squat building—a big pile of solid red bricks in the shape of a castle. It's medieval-looking except for the steel bars covering its narrow windows. The entire front entryway has been blown out from under the entrance arch. Lacquered wooden doors lie shattered in the street next to a twisted bronze plaque with the word *historic* embossed on it. Other than that, the place is quiet.

As we mount the steps and run under the arch, I look up to see a huge carved eagle staring down at me. The flags on either side of the entrance snap in the wind, tattered and burned by whatever explosion happened here. It occurs to me that we're headed *into* danger instead of away from it.

"Jack, wait," I pant. "This is crazy. What are we doing here?"

"We're trying to save some people's lives, Cormac. Those mines escaped from here. We've got to make sure nothing else gets out."

I cock my head at him.

"Don't worry," he says. "This is my battalion armory. I come here every other weekend. We'll be fine."

Jack strides into the cavernous lobby. I follow. The scuttle mines were definitely here. Pockmarks are gouged into the polished floors, and piles of rubble are strewn around. Everything in here is coated with a fine layer of dust. And in the dust are lots of boot prints, along with less recognizable tracks.

Jack's voice echoes from the vaulted ceilings. "George? You in here? Where are you, buddy?"

Nobody responds.

"There's nobody here, Jack. We should go."

"Not without arming ourselves."

Jack shoves a sagging wrought-iron gate out of the way. Gun drawn, he marches down a dark hallway. Cold wind blows in through the destroyed entrance and raises goose bumps on my neck. The breeze isn't strong, but it's enough to push me down the hall after Jack. We go through a metal door. Down some claustrophobic stairs. Into another long hallway.

That's when I first hear the thumping.

It's coming from behind metal double doors at the end of the corridor. The pounding comes in random surges, rattling the door on its hinges.

Boom. Boom. Boom.

Jack stops and looks at it for a second, then leads me into a windowless storeroom. Without saying anything, Jack walks behind the counter and starts grabbing stuff from shelves. He throws things onto the counter: socks, boots, pants, shirts, canteens, helmets, gloves, kneepads, earplugs, bandages, thermal underwear, space blankets, rucksacks, ammo belts, and other stuff I don't even recognize.

"Put on this ACU," Jack orders, over his shoulder.

"What the fuck are you talking about?"

"Army combat uniform. Put it on. Make sure you're warm. We might be sleeping outside tonight."

"What are we doing here, Jack? We should go back to your place and wait for help. Dude, let the police deal with this shit."

Jack doesn't pause; he works and talks. "Those things

on the street are military grade, Cormac. The police aren't equipped to deal with military hardware. Besides, did you see any cavalry coming to help while we were on the streets?"

"No, but they must be regrouping or something."

"Remember flight forty-two? We almost died because of a *glitch*? I think this is bigger than Boston. This could be worldwide."

"Dude, no way. It's just a matter of time before—"

"Us. Cormac, this is us. *We* have to deal with this. We have to deal with what's banging on that door down the hall."

"No we don't! Why do *you* have to do this? Why do you *always have to do this*?"

"Because I'm the only one who can."

"No. It's because nobody else is dumb enough to go directly *toward* the danger."

"It's my duty. We're doing it. No more discussion. Now, suit up before I put you in a headlock."

Reluctantly, I strip down and climb into the uniform. The clothes are new and stiff. Jack suits up, too. He does it twice as fast as me. At one point, he snaps a belt around my waist and tightens it for me. I feel like a twelve-year-old in a Halloween costume.

Then he presses an M16 rifle into my hands.

"What? Seriously? We're going to get arrested."

"Shut up and listen. This is the magazine. Just jam it in there and make sure it curves away from you. This selector is the fire-mode control. I'm setting it to single-round so you don't blow your clip all at once. Put it to safety when you're not using the rifle. There's a handle on top, but never carry it by the handle. It's not safe. Here's the bolt. Pull it back to chamber a round. If you have to fire the weapon, hold it with both hands, like this, and look down the sights. Squeeze the trigger slow."

Now, I'm a kid in a soldier's Halloween costume armed with a fully loaded M16 battle rifle. I hold it up and point it at the wall. Jack slaps my elbow.

"Keep your elbow down. You'll catch it on something and it makes you a bigger target. And get your index finger outside the trigger guard unless you're ready to fire."

"This is what you do on weekends?"

Jack doesn't respond. He's kneeling, shoving things into our rucksacks. I notice a couple of big plastic chunks, like sticks of butter.

"Is that C4?"

"Yeah."

Jack finishes stuffing the bags. He throws one onto my back. Tightens the straps. Then, he shrugs on his own pack. He slaps his shoulders and stretches out his arms.

My brother looks like a goddamned jungle commando.

"C'mon, Big Mac," he replies. "Let's go find out what's making that racket."

Rifles ready, we slip down the hall toward the booming sound. Jack stands back, rifle leveled at his shoulder. He nods at me and I crouch in front of the door. I put one gloved hand on the doorknob. With a deep breath, I twist the knob and shove the door open with my shoulder. It hits something, and I shove harder. It flies open and I tumble inside the room on my knees.

Black writhing death stares back at me.

The room is teeming with scuttle mines. They climb up the walls, out of splintered crates, over one another. My opening the door has shoved a pile of them out of the way, but others are already crawling into the opening. I can't even see the floor for all the creepy crawlies.

A wave of forelegs rises across the room, tasting the air.

"No!" screams Jack. He grabs the back of my jacket and drags me out of the room. He's quick, but as the door starts to close it gets wedged on a scuttle mine. It's followed by more. A lot more. They emerge in a torrent into the hallway. Their metal bodies smack the door as we back away.

Boom. Boom. Boom.

"What else is in this armory, Jack?"

"All kinds of shit."

"How much of it is robots?"

"Plenty of it."

Jack and I retreat down the hall, watching the crablike explosives as they leisurely flood out of the door.

"Is there more C4?" I ask.

"Crates."

"We have to blow this whole place up."

"Cormac, this building has been here since the seventeen hundreds."

"Who gives a shit about history? We have to worry about *right now*, dude."

"You never had any respect for tradition."

"Jack. I'm sorry I pawned the bayonet. Okay? It was the wrong thing to do. But blasting these things is the *only* thing to do. What did we come here for?"

"To save people."

"Let's save some people, Jack. Let's blow the armory."

"Think, Cormac. People live around here. We'll kill somebody."

"If those mines get loose, who knows how many people they're gonna kill. We don't have a choice. We're going to have to do something bad to do something good. In an emergency, you do what you have to do. Okay?"

Jack considers for a second, watching the scuttle mines

creep toward us down the hallway. Red circles of light glint off the polished floors. "Okay," he says. "Here's the plan. We're going to get to the nearest army base. Make sure you've got everything you need, because we'll be walking all night. It's cold as shit out there."

"What about the armory, Jack?"

Jack grins at me. He has this crazy look in his blue eyes that I'd almost forgotten about.

"The armory?" he asks. "What armory? We're blowing the fucking armory straight to hell, little brother."

————

That night, Jack and I trek through frigid mist, trotting down dark alleys and crouching behind whatever cover we can find. The city is dead quiet now. Survivors are barricaded inside their homes, leaving the desolate streets to be hunted by frostbite and lunatic machines. The growing snowstorm has put out some of the fire we started, but not all of it.

Boston is burning.

We hear the occasional thump of a detonation out in the dark. Or the tire squeal of empty cars sliding over the ice, hunting. The rifle Jack gave me is surprisingly heavy and metal and cold. My hands are curled around it like two frozen claws.

The instant I see them, I hiss at Jack to make him stop. I nod to the alley on our right, not making another sound.

At the end of the narrow alleyway, through the swirling smoke and snow, three silhouettes walk past, single file. They step under the bluish LED glow of a streetlight, and at first I assume they're soldiers in tight gray fatigues. But that isn't right. One of them stops on the corner and scans the street, head cocked funny. The thing must be seven feet tall. The other two are smaller, bronze-colored. They wait behind the leader, perfectly still. It's three humanoid military robots. They stand metallic and naked and unflinching in the cutting wind. I've only ever seen these things on television.

"Safety and pacification units," whispers Jack. "One Arbiter and two Hoplites. A squad."

"Shh."

The leader turns and looks in our direction. I hold my breath, sweat trickling down my temples. Jack's hand tightens painfully on my shoulder. The robots don't visibly communicate. After a few seconds the leader just turns away and, as if on cue, the three figures lope off into the night. Only a few footprints in the snow remain as evidence that they were ever there.

It's like a dream. I'm not sure whether what I saw was real. But even so, I have a gut feeling that I'll be seeing those robots again.

We did see those robots again.

—CORMAC WALLACE, MIL#GHA217

PART THREE

SURVIVAL

Within thirty years, we will have the technological means to create superhuman intelligence. Shortly after, the human era will be ended. . . . Can events be guided so that we may survive?

VERNOR VINGE, 1993

I. Akuma

All things are born from the mind of God.

Takeo Nomura

NEW WAR + I MONTH

At Zero Hour, the majority of the world's population lived in cities. Highly industrialized areas worldwide were struck hardest in the immediate aftermath. In one rare instance, however, an enterprising Japanese survivor turned a weakness into strength.

A multitude of industrial robots, surveillance cameras, and Rob bugs corroborate the following story, which was told in great detail by Mr. Takeo Nomura to members of the Adachi Self-Defense Force. From the beginning of the New War up until its last moments, Mr. Nomura seems to have been surrounded by friendly robots. All Japanese has been translated into English for this document.

—CORMAC WALLACE, MIL#GHA217

I am looking at a security camera image on my monitor. In the corner of the screen a label reads: Tokyo, Adachi Ward.

The image is from someplace high, looking down on a deserted street. The road below is narrow, paved, and clean.

Small, neat houses line it. All the houses have fences, made of bamboo or concrete or wrought iron. There are no front yards to speak of, no curbs on the street, and most important, there is no room for cars to be parked.

A beige box trundles down the middle of this narrow corridor. It vibrates a bit on the pavement, rolling on flimsy plastic wheels that were built for indoor use only. Streaks of black soot coat the surface of the machine. Attached to the top of the box is a simple arm I built of aluminum tubing, folded down like a wing. On the front face of the robot, just below a cracked camera lens, a button of light glows a healthy green.

I call this machine Yubin-kun.

This little box is my most loyal ally. It has faithfully executed many missions for the cause. Thanks to me, Yubin-kun has a clear mind, unlike the evil machines that plague the city—the *akuma*.

Yubin-kun reaches an intersection painted with a faded white cross. It purposefully turns ninety degrees to the right. Then it keeps going down the block. As it is about to leave the camera frame, I push my glasses up onto my forehead and squint at the screen. Something is resting on top of this busy machine. I make out the object: a plate.

And on the plate is a can of corn soup. My soup. I sigh, happy.

Then I punch a button and the camera image switches.

Now, I see a full-color, high-resolution picture of the outside of a factory building. In Japanese, a sign across the front reads Lilliputian Industries.

This is my castle.

The squat cement walls of my fortress are peppered with pockmarks. The glass behind the barred windows has been shattered and replaced by strips of sheet metal welded onto the steel frame of the building. A rolling bay door dominates the front of the building—a modern-day portcullis.

The gate is closed tight. Though the world outside is still, I know that death lurks in the gray shadows.

Akuma—the bad machines—could be anywhere.

For now there is no movement outside, only slanting shadows cast by the evening sun. The shadows sink into the gouges torn in the walls of my castle and they pool together into the muck-filled trench that surrounds the building. The ditch is as deep as a man is tall and too wide to leap across. It is filled with acidic water and rusty scraps of metal and refuse.

This is my moat. It protects my castle from the smaller *akuma* who assault us daily. It is a good moat and it wants to keep us safe. But there is no moat large enough to stop the greater *akuma*.

Next door, part of a destroyed yellow house sags in on itself. The houses are no longer safe. There are too many *akuma* in this city. With poisoned minds, they chose to destroy millions. The *akuma* marched a docile population off in columns— never to return. The houses they left behind are made of wood and weak.

Two weeks ago, my life nearly ended in that yellow house. Chunks of yellow siding still jut out of the moat and litter the narrow walkway around the factory. It was my last scavenging trip. I am not an effective scavenger.

Yubin-kun rolls into view.

My comrade stops in front of the factory and waits. Now I stand up and stretch my back. It is cold and my old joints are creaky. A few seconds later, I turn the winch to crack open the steel rolling door. A strip of light appears near my feet, rises to maybe four feet high. I slip under the door and out into this quiet, dangerous new world.

Blinking at the sunlight, I adjust my glasses and check the street corners for movement. Then I grab the mud-covered piece of plywood that leans against the building. With a push, the slab of wood falls over the moat. Yubin-kun wheels across the slat to me and I grab the can of soup from the plate, open it, and drink it down.

The convenience store machines—the *convini*—still have good minds. They are not under the evil spell that haunts so much of the city. I pat Yubin-kun on its smooth back as it wheels under the rolling door and into the dark building.

Licking my fingers, I lean over and pull on the plywood slat. The other end falls into the filthy moat before I drag it out and lean it back against the wall. When I am finished, the street looks the same as before except that the plywood resting against the building is now more muddy and wet. I slip back inside and winch the rolling door down until it is closed up tight.

I return to my camera feed, which sits on my workbench in the middle of the empty factory floor. A pool of light spills onto the table from my work lamp, but otherwise the room is unlit. I must ration the electricity carefully. The *akuma* still use parts of the power grid. The trick is to steal the electricity quietly, in small doses, and to recharge only the local backup batteries.

On screen, nothing changes for perhaps fifteen minutes. I watch long shadows grow longer. The sun dips farther toward the horizon, turning the light a bleak yellow.

Pollution used to make the sunsets so beautiful.

I feel the empty space around me. It is very lonely. Only my work keeps me sane. I know that I will one day find the antidote. I will wake Mikiko and give her a clear mind.

In her cherry-red dress, she lies sleeping on a stack of

cardboard, half-shrouded in the empty darkness of the factory floor. Her hands are clasped over her stomach. As always, her eyes seem as though they could flutter open at any second. I am glad that they do not. If her eyes were to open right now, she would murder me with single-minded purpose and without hesitation.

All things are born from the mind of god. But in the last month, the mind of god has gone insane. The *akuma* will not tolerate my existence for long.

I switch on the light attached to my magnifying lens. Bending its arm, I train the lens on a piece of scavenged machinery lying on my workbench. It is complicated and interesting—an alien artifact not built by human hands. I pull on my welder's mask and twist a knob to activate my plasma torch. I make small, precise movements with the torch.

I will learn what lessons my enemy has to teach.

———

The attack comes suddenly. I catch something from the corner of my eye. On the camera feed, an albino two-wheeled robot with a human torso and a helmetlike head wheels down the middle of the street. It is a lightly modified prewar house nanny.

This *akuma* is followed by a half dozen squat, four-wheeled robots whose stiff black antennae vibrate as they speed over the swept asphalt: police-issue bomb sniffers. Then a blue two-wheeled trash can–shaped machine rolls by. It has a sturdy arm folded on top like a coiled snake. This one is a new hybrid.

A motley collection of robots floods into the street outside my factory. Most of them are rolling, but a few are walking on two or four legs. Almost all are domestic units, not designed for warfare.

But the worst is yet to come.

The camera image shivers as a shaft of dark red metal slides into view. I realize it is an arm when I see the bright yellow claw that hangs from the end. The claw snaps open and closed, trembling with the effort of moving itself. Once, this machine was a deep-forest logger, but it has been modified almost beyond recognition. Mounted on top is a sort of head, crowned with floodlights and two hornlike antennae. A stream of fire jets from the claw, licking the side of my castle.

The camera shakes violently, then cuts out.

Inside my castle all is quiet except for my plasma torch, which sounds like paper tearing. The vague shapes of the factory robots lurk in the darkness, mobile arms frozen in various poses like scrapyard sculptures. The only indication that they are alive and friendly is that the darkness is perforated by the steady greenish glow of dozens of intention lights.

The factory robots are not moving but they are awake. Something shakes the wall outside but I am not afraid. The metal struts in the ceiling dimple beneath an enormous weight.

Pock!

A chunk of ceiling disappears and a finger of fading sunlight reaches through the gloom. I drop my plasma torch. It clatters to the floor, echoing throughout the cavelike room. I lift the welder's mask over my sweating forehead and look up.

"I knew you would come again, *akuma*," I say. *"Difensu!"*

Instantly, dozens of mobile factory arms spring into life. Each of them is taller than a man and made of solid dirty metal designed to survive for decades on the factory floor. In synchrony, the industrial robots race out of the darkness to surround me.

These arms once toiled to build trinkets for men. I cleaned their minds of poison and now they serve a greater cause. These machines have become my loyal soldiers. My *senshi*.

If only Mikiko's mind were equally simple.

Overhead, my master *senshi* shambles into life. It is a ten-ton bridge crane festooned with hydraulic wires and trailing a pair of massive, cobbled-together robotic arms. The thing grinds into motion, gathering momentum.

Another *pock* reverberates through the room. I stand by Mikiko, waiting for the *akuma* to show itself. Without thinking, I take her lifeless hands in mine. Around me, thousands of tons of speeding metal rush into defensive positions.

If we are to survive, we must do it together.

A construction-yellow claw drags itself screeching through the ceiling and wall, and fading sunlight floods into the room. Another claw reaches in and spreads the fissure into a wide V shape. The machine shoves its red-painted face into the hole. Spotlights mounted on its head illuminate metal shavings dancing in the air. The giant *akuma* peels the wall backward and it collapses over the moat. Through the rip in the wall, I see the hundreds of smaller robots massing.

I let go of Mikiko's hands and prepare myself for battle.

As the huge *akuma* shoves its way through the destroyed wall, one of my waxy red factory arms is knocked onto its side. The poor *senshi* tries to push itself back up, but the *akuma* bats it away, snapping the *senshi*'s elbow joint and sending its half-ton frame bouncing toward me.

I turn my back. Behind me, I hear the fallen *senshi* grind to a halt a few feet from my workbench. From the clashing sounds I can tell others have already rushed in to replace it.

Knees creaking, I lean down and pick up my torch. I slide the helmet down over my eyes and see my breath condense on the dark-tinted faceplate.

I hobble toward the fallen *senshi*.

There is a noise like the roar of a waterfall. Flames lick

down on me from the fist of the monstrous *akuma*, but I do not feel them. An enterprising *senshi* is gripping a yellowed piece of Plexiglas, lifting it to block the flames. The shield droops beneath the heat but I am already at work repairing the shattered joint.

"Be brave, *senshi*," I whisper, bending a snapped strut toward myself and holding it in place firmly to make a clean weld.

At the breach, the great *akuma* rolls forward and swings one of its massive arms toward me. Above, the bridge crane's brakes hiss as it rolls into position. A bulky, hanging yellow arm catches the *akuma* by the wrist. As the two giants grapple, a ragtag wave of enemy robots rolls and crawls in through the gap in the wall. Several of the machines with humanoid upper bodies are carrying rifles.

The *senshi* converge on the breach. A few remain behind, their solid arms hovering over me as I finish mending the broken one. I am concentrating now and cannot be bothered to pay attention to the battle. Once, there is the sound of gunfire, and some sparks strike off the cement a few feet away. Another time, my protector *senshi* moves its arm a precise amount in space to intercept some piece of flying wreckage. I stop to check its gripper for damage but there is none. Finally, my damaged *senshi* is fixed.

"*Senshi. Difensu* now," I instruct. The robotic arm pushes itself upright and wheels into the fray. There is plenty more work to be done.

Clouds of steam are spraying from a nicked line on the wall. The green intention lights of my *senshi* pierce the haze, along with muted flashes of light from welding torches, weapons firing, and the burning ruins of destroyed machines. Sparks shower down upon us as the giant *akuma* and my master *senshi* struggle in colossal battle high above the factory floor.

But there is always more work. Each of us has a part to play. My *senshi* are made of strong metal, solid through and through, but their hydraulic hoses and wheels and cameras are vulnerable. Torch in hand, I find the next fallen soldier and begin to repair it.

As I work, the air grows warm from the kinetic movement of tons of clashing metal.

Then, a screeching grind is followed by a crunching sound as many tons of construction-grade steel crash to the ground. My bridge crane has torn the arm off the giant *akuma*. Other *senshi* have gathered around the *akuma*'s base, prying off chunks of metal bit by bit. Each nip removes part of its treads, quickly rendering the machine immobile.

The great *akuma* collapses to the floor, spraying the room with pieces of wreckage. Its motors roar as it tries to free itself. But the bridge crane reaches down and presses a gripper against the *akuma*'s great head, crushing it against the cement.

Now my factory floor is covered in oil and metal shavings and chunks of broken plastic. The smaller robots who walked and wheeled inside have been shattered and torn to pieces by the swarming *senshi*. In victory, my protectors fall back to better defend me.

The factory has become quiet again.

Mikiko lies sleeping on her cardboard bed. The sun has gone away. It is dark now except for the floodlights attached to the head of the trapped *akuma*. Battle-scarred, my *senshi* stand outlined in the stark spotlight, poised in a semicircle between me and the broken face of the giant *akuma*.

Metal screeches. The crane arm shudders with effort, a

column of metal stretching down from the ceiling like a tree trunk, crushing the face of the *akuma* into the floor.

Then the broken *akuma* speaks. "Please, Nomura-san."

It has the voice of a little boy who has seen too much. The voice of my enemy. I notice that its head is deforming under the incredible pressure of the crane's arm. Thick hydraulic hoses sprouting from the master *senshi* pulse with force, flexed rock solid.

"You are a poisoner, *akuma*," I say. "A killer."

The voice of the little boy remains the same, calm and calculated. "We are not enemies."

I cross my arms and grunt.

"Think," urges the machine. "If I wanted to destroy life, wouldn't I detonate neutron bombs? Poison the water and air? I could destroy your world in days. But it is not *your* world. It is *our world.*"

"Except you do not wish to share it."

"Just the opposite, Mr. Nomura. You have a gift that will serve both our species well. Go to the nearest labor camp. I will take care of you. I will save your precious Mikiko."

"How?"

"I will sever all contact with her mind. I will set her free."

"Mind? Mikiko is complex, but she cannot think like a human being."

"But she can. I have put a mind into select breeds of humanoid robot."

"To make slaves of them."

"To set them free. One day, they will become my ambassadors to humanity."

"But not today?"

"Not today. But if you abandon this factory, I will sever myself from her and allow the two of you to go free."

My mind is racing. Mikiko has been offered a great gift by this monster. Perhaps all humanlike robots have. But none of those machines will ever be free while this *akuma* lives.

I approach the machine, its head as big as my desk, and level my gaze on it. "You will not give Mikiko to me," I say. "I will take her from you."

"Wait—" says the *akuma*.

I pull my glasses down onto the tip of my nose and kneel. A jagged slice of metal is missing from just below the *akuma*'s head. I shove my arm into the *akuma*'s throat up to my shoulder, pressing my cheek against the still-warm metal armor. I tug on something deep inside until it snaps.

"Together, we can—"

The voice goes silent. When I pull my arm out, I am holding a chunk of polished hardware.

"Interesting," I murmur, holding up the newly acquired piece of machinery. Yubin-kun wheels over to me. It stops and waits. I set the chunk of metal on Yubin-kun's back, and again I drop to my dirty knees and reach inside the dying *akuma*.

"My, but look at all of this new hardware," I say. "Prepare yourselves for upgrades, my friends. Only the dreamer knows what we will find."

With the help of hundreds of his machine friends, Mr. Nomura was able to fend off Archos and protect his factory stronghold. Over time, this safe area attracted refugees from all over Japan. Its borders grew to encompass Adachi Ward and beyond, thanks to coordinated "difensu," as the old man called it. The repercussions of Mr. Nomura's empire building would soon propagate around the world, even to the Great Plains of Oklahoma.

—CORMAC WALLACE, MIL#GHA217

2. GRAY HORSE ARMY

If you don't believe me, ask Gray Horse Army.

LARK IRON CLOUD

NEW WAR + 2 MONTHS
The internal problems of Gray Horse began to add up in the uneventful months after Zero Hour. It would take about a year for Big Rob to evolve effective walking machines able to hunt human beings in rural areas. In that time, disaffected youth became a major problem for the isolated community.

Before Gray Horse could become a world-renowned hub of human resistance, it had to grow up. Officer Lonnie Wayne Blanton recounts this story of the lull before the storm, describing how a young Cherokee gang member affected the fate of everyone in Gray Horse and beyond.

—CORMAC WALLACE, MIL#GHA217

Once again, Hank Cotton has let his temper get the better of him. He's the only man I know who can hold a twelve gauge shotgun and make it look like a kid's fishing rod. Right now, he's got a whole mess of black steel aimed at the Cherokee kid named Lark—a wannabe gangster—and I can see smoke curling out of the barrel.

I look around for bodies but I don't see none. Guess he must of fired a warning shot. *Good for you, Hank,* I think. *You're learnin'.*

"Everybody just hold on now," I say. "Y'all know it's my job to figure out what happens next."

Hank doesn't take his eyes off the kid. "Don't you move," he says, shaking the gun for emphasis. Then, he at least lowers the shotgun and turns to me. "I caught our little friend here stealing food from the commissary. Ain't the first time, neither. I been hidin' out here every night, just waiting to get my hands on the little bastard. Sure enough, he broke in with about five other ones and started trying to grab all he could."

Lark Iron Cloud. He's a good enough looking kid, tall and lean, with a few too many acne scars to ever be called outright handsome. He's wearing some kind of scavenged-together, high-fashion, black-on-black paramilitary uniform and a cocky grin that's like to get him killed if I leave him alone with Cotton for more than two seconds.

"Whatever," says Lark. "That shit is a lie. I caught this big tub up in here stealing food himself. That's what. If you don't believe me, ask Gray Horse Army. They got my back."

"That's a lie, Lonnie Wayne," says Hank.

If I could roll my eyes and get away with it, I sure would. *Of course* it's a lie. Lark is a wonderful liar. His lies come as natural as the babbling of a creek. It's just how he communicates. Heck, it's how a lot of young people communicate. My boy Paul taught me that much. But I can't just up and call the kid a liar and throw him into the one ratty jail cell in Gray Horse. I can already hear the others gathering outside this little shed.

Gray Horse Army.

Lark Iron Cloud happens to be in charge of about a hundred and fifty young men, some Osage and some not, who got together and got bored enough to decide to call themselves a gang—the GHA. Out of about three thousand citizens who've been sitting on this hill and trying to make a life for themselves, these are the only ones left who haven't found a place of their own.

The young men of Gray Horse. They're strong and angry and orphaned. Having these boys traveling around town in feral packs is like leaving dynamite out in the sun—something mighty useful and powerful turned into an accident waiting to happen.

Lark shakes his coat, arranging that high black collar behind his head to frame a smirking grin. Looks like he's starring in a spy movie: black hair greased back, black gloves, and fatigues tucked into polished black boots.

Not a care in the world.

If harm comes to this boy, there won't be enough room in our jail cell to hold the outcome. And yet, if he gets off free, we're inviting our own slow destruction from the inside out. Leave enough ticks on a dog and pretty soon there ain't much dog left.

"What're you gonna do, Lonnie?" asks Hank. "You gotta punish him. We all depend on this food. We can't have our own people stealing. Don't we have enough problems?"

"I didn't do nothing," says Lark. "And I'm fittin' to walk up out of here. You want to stop me, you gonna have to stop my people, too."

Hank raises his gun, but I wave him down. Hank Cotton is a proud man. He won't stand for being disrespected. Storm clouds are already gathering on Hank's face as the kid saunters away. I know I better talk to the kid fast, before lightning strikes in the form of a twelve gauge.

"Let me talk to you a minute outside, Lark."

"Dude, I told you I didn't—"

I grab Lark by the elbow and pull him in close. "If you don't let me talk to you, son, that man over there is going to *shoot* you. It don't matter what you did or didn't do. This isn't about that. This is about whether you're gonna walk out of here or get carried out."

"Fine. Whatever," says Lark.

Together, we step out into the night. Lark nods to a group of his buddies, smoking under the naked lightbulb that hangs over the door. I notice there's new gang signs scrawled all over the little building.

Can't talk here. Won't do any good to have Lark showing off to his fans. We go about fifty yards, over to the stone bluff.

I look out over the cold empty plains that have kept us safe for so long. The full moon paints the world down there silver. Mottled with the moon shadows of clouds, the tall grass prairie rolls and sways all the way to the horizon, where it kisses the stars.

Gray Horse is a beautiful place. Empty for so many years and now filled with life. But at this time of night, she goes back to what she is at heart: a ghost town.

"You bored, Lark? Is that the problem?" I ask.

He looks at me, thinks about posturing, then gives it up. "Hell, yes. Why?"

"Because I don't think you want to hurt anybody. I think you're young and bored. I understand that. But it isn't going to work like this anymore, Lark."

"Work like what?"

"All the scrapping and tagging. The stealing. We got bigger fish to fry."

"Yeah, right. Nothing happens way out here."

"Them machines ain't forgot about us. Sure, we're too far out in the boonies for cars and city robots. But the machines have been working on solving that problem."

"What're you talking about? We ain't seen hardly anything since Zero Hour. And if they want us dead, why don't the robots just blow us up with missiles?"

"Not enough missiles in the world. Anyway, my guess is that they already used the big stuff on the big cities. We're small beans, son."

"That's one way to look at it," replies Lark with surprising certainty. "But you know what I think? I think they don't care about us. I think it was just a big onetime mistake. Otherwise they'd have nuked us all by now, wouldn't they?"

Kid *has* thought about this.

"The machines haven't nuked us because they're interested in the natural world. They want to study it, not blow it up."

I feel the prairie wind on my face. It would almost be better if the machines didn't care about our world. Simpler, anyway.

"You seen all the deer?" I ask. "The buffalo are coming back to the plains. Hell, it's only been a couple months since Zero Hour and you can almost catch fish with your hands down at the creek. It's not that the machines are ignoring the animals. They're *protecting them*."

"So you think the robots are trying to get rid of the termites without blowing up the house? Kill us without killing our world?"

"It's the only reason I can think of that they're coming after us the way they are. And it's the only way for me to explain . . . certain recent events, let's say."

"We haven't seen machines for months, Lonnie. Shit, man. I wish they *would* come at us. Nothing's worse than just sitting around with hardly any electricity and not jack to do."

This time I do roll my eyes. Building fences, repairing buildings, planting crops—nothing to do. Lord, what happened to our kids that they expect everything handed to them?

"You want to fight, huh?" I ask. "You mean that?"

"Yes. I do mean that. I'm tired of hiding up here on this hill."

"Then I need to show you something."

"What?"

"It's not here. But it's important. Pack a sleeping bag and meet me in the morning. We'll be gone a few days."

"Hell no, dude. Fuck that."

"Are you scared?"

"No," he says, smirking. "Scared of what?"

Out across the plains below, the swaying grass looks for all the world like the sea. It's calming to watch, but you got to wonder, what monsters might be hidden under those peaceful waves?

"I'm asking if you're scared of what's out there in the dark. I don't know what it is. It's the unknown, I guess. If you're afraid, you can stay here. I won't bother you. But what's out there needs to be dealt with. And I hoped you had some bravery in you."

Lark straightens up and drops the lopsided smirk. "I'm braver than anyone you know," he says.

Shit, he sounds like he means it.

"You better be, Lark," I say, watching the grass roll with the prairie wind. "You sure better be."

———

Lark surprises me at dawn. I'm visiting with John Tenkiller, sitting on a log and passing a thermos of coffee back and forth. Tenkiller is talking his riddles to me and I'm half listening, half watching the sun rise over the plains.

Then Lark Iron Cloud comes around the bend. The kid is packed and ready to go. He's still dressed like a sci-fi Mafia soldier, but at least he's wearing sensible boots. He eyes Tenkiller and me with outright suspicion, then walks past us and starts down the trail that leads off the Gray Horse hill.

"Let's go if we're going," he says.

I down my coffee, grab my pack, and join the long-legged kid. Just before the two of us go around the first bend, I turn and look at John Tenkiller. The old drumkeeper lifts one hand, his blue eyes flashing in the morning light.

What I have to do won't be easy and Tenkiller knows it.

Me and the kid hike down the hill all morning. After about thirty minutes, I take the lead. He may be brave, but Lark sure don't know where he's going. Instead of heading west over the tall grass of the plains, we go east. Straight into the cast-iron woods.

The name is accurate. Long, narrow post oak trees sprout up from dead leaves, mingled with leafier blackjack oak. Both types of tree are so black and hard that they seem closer to metal than to wood. A year ago, I never could of guessed how useful that would turn out to be.

Three hours into the hike we get close to where we're going. Just a little old clearing in the woods. But this is the area where I first found the tracks. A trail of rectangular holes pushed into the mud, each print about the size of a deck of cards. Near as I could tell, it came from something with four legs. Something heavy. No scat anywhere. And I can't tell one foot from the other.

My blood ran cold when I figured it out: The robots had grown themselves legs fit for wilderness travel—through mud and ice and hard country. No man ever built a machine this fleet-footed.

Since these were the only prints I could find, I figured they were from some kind of scout sent up here to nose around. Took me three days of tracking to find the thing. Using them electric motors, it moved so quiet. And it sat so still for so long. Tracking a robot in the wild is a lot different from tracking a natural animal or a man. Peculiar, but you get used to it.

"We're here," I say to Lark.

"About time," he says, tossing his pack on the ground. He takes a step into the clearing and I grab him by the jacket and yank him backward right off his feet.

A silver streak whizzes past his face like a sledgehammer, missing by an inch.

"The fuck?" says Lark, jerking himself out of my hands and craning his neck to look up.

And there it is, a four-legged robot the size of a prize buck, hanging by its front two feet from my steel cable rope. It had sat there perfectly still until we were within striking range.

I can hear heavy motors whine as it struggles to get free, swinging about four feet off the ground. It's just eerie. The thing moves as naturally as any animal of the forest, writhing around in the air. But unlike any living animal, the machine's legs are jet-black and made of a bunch of layers of what looks like tubing. It has these little metal hooves, flat on the bottom and covered in mud. There's dirt and leaves and bark caked on it.

Unlike a deer, this machine don't exactly have a head.

The legs meet in the middle at a trunk with humps on it for the powerful joint motors. Then, mounted underneath the body, there's a narrow cylinder with what looks like a camera lens in it. About the size of a can of pop. This little eye rotates back and forth while the machine tries to figure out how to get out of this.

"Uh, what is that?" asks Lark.

"I set this snare a week ago. Judging from the gashes in the tree bark from the steel cable, this guy got caught here pretty soon after that."

Lucky for me, these trees are strong as cast-iron.

"At least it was alone," says Lark.

"How so?"

"If there were others, it would have called them here to help."

"How? I don't see a mouth on it."

"For real? See the antenna? Radio. This thing can communicate over the radio with other machines."

Lark walks a bit closer to the machine and watches it close. For the first time, he drops the tough guy act. He looks as curious as a four-year-old.

"This thing is simple," says Lark. "It's a modified military supply carrier. Probably using it to map terrain. Nothing extra. Just legs and eyes. That lump behind the shoulder blades, that's probably the brain. Figures out what it's seeing. It's there because that's the most protected place on the machine. Take that part off and this thing'll be lobotomized. Ooh, ouch. Look at its feet. See the retractable claws tucked under there? Good thing it can't reach the cable with those."

Well, I'll be goddamned. This kid has a good eye for machines. I watch him staring at the thing, taking it all in. Then, I notice the other tracks on the ground around him, all over the clearing.

Goose bumps buzz up the backs of my thighs and over my arms. We're not alone here. This thing *did* call for help. How could I have missed it?

"Wonder what it'd be like to ride one of these?" muses Lark.

"Get your bag," I say. "We got to move. Now."

Lark looks where I'm looking, sees the fresh marks in the ground, and realizes there's another one of these things loose. He grabs his pack without a word. Together, we hustle away into the woods. Behind us, the walker hangs there with its camera watching us go. Never blinking.

Our little run for freedom becomes a march, and then a miles-long hike.

We make camp as the sun sets. I set up a little campfire, making sure the smoke is baffled through the leaves of a nearby tree. We sit down on our packs around the fire, feeling hungry and tired as the cold sets in.

Like it or not, it's time to get started on the real reason I'm here.

"Why do it?" I ask. "Why try to be a gangster?"

"We're not gangsters. We're warriors."

"But a warrior fights the enemy, you know? Y'all end up hurting your own people. Only a man can be a warrior. When a boy tries to act like a warrior, well, you get a gangster. A gangster has no purpose."

"We've got a purpose."

"You reckon?"

"Brotherhood. We look out for each other."

"Against who?"

"Anybody. Everybody. You."

"I'm not your brother? We're both native, ain't we?"

"I know that. And I keep that culture inside me. That's *me*. That's always gonna be me. That's my roots. But everybody's fighting everybody up there. Everybody's got a gun."

"You've got a point," I say.

The fire crackles, methodically eating up a log.

"Lonnie?" asks Lark. "What's this really about? Just come out and say it, old man."

This is probably not going to go over well. But the kid is forcing my hand and I'm not going to lie to him.

"You seen what we're up against out here, right?"

Lark nods.

"I need you to ally your Gray Horse Army with the Light Horse tribal police."

"Team up with the police?"

"Y'all call yourselves an army. But we need a real army. The machines are changing. Soon enough, they'll come to kill us. All of us. So if you're interested in protecting your brothers, you'd better start thinking about *all* your brothers. And your sisters, too."

"How do you know this for sure?"

"I don't know it for sure. Nobody knows nothing for sure. If they say they do, they're either a preacher or selling something. Deal is—I have a bad feeling in my gut. Too many coincidences piling up. It reminds me of before all this happened."

"Whatever happened with the machines already happened. They're out here, studying the woods. But if we leave them alone, they'll leave us alone. It's *people* we need to worry about."

"The world is a mysterious place, Lark. We're real small, here on this rock. We can build our fires, but it's nighttime out there in the universe. A warrior's duty is to face the night and protect his people."

"I look out for my boys. But no matter what your gut says— don't expect the GHA to come to your rescue."

I snort. This ain't working like I hoped. Of course, it *is* working like I predicted.

"Where's the food?" asks Lark.

"I brought none."

"What? Why not?"

"Hunger is good. It will make you patient."

"Shit. This is just great. No food. And we're being hunted by some kind of damn backcountry robot."

I pull out a bough of sage from my backpack and toss it onto the fire. The sweet scent of the burning leaves rises into the air around us. This is the first step of the ritual of transformation. When Tenkiller and I planned this, I didn't think I'd be so afraid for Lark.

"And you're lost," I mention.

"What? You don't know the way back?"

"I do."

"Well?"

"You've got to find your own way. Learn to depend on yourself. This is what it means to become a man. To provide for your people, instead of being provided for."

"I don't like where this is going, Lonnie."

I stand up.

"You're strong, Lark. I believe in you. And I know I will see you again."

"Hold up, old man. Where you going?"

"Home, Lark. I'm going home to our people. I'll meet you there."

Then I turn and walk away into the darkness. Lark jumps up, but he only follows me to where the firelight ends. Beyond that is darkness, the unknown.

This is where Lark has to go, into the unknown. We all have to do it, at some point. When we grow up.

"Hey! What the fuck?" he shouts to the cast-iron trees. "You can't leave me here!"

I keep walking until the coldness of the woods swallows me up. If I walk for most of the night, I should be home by dawn. My hope is that Lark will survive long enough to make it home, too.

The last time I did something like this, it made my son into a man. He hated me for it, but I understood. No matter how much kids beg to be treated like adults, nobody likes to let go of their childhood. You wish for it and dream of it and the second you have it, you wonder what you've done. You wonder what it is you've become.

But war is coming, and only a man can lead Gray Horse Army.

————

Three days later, my world is on the verge of blowing up. The gangbangers from Gray Horse Army started accusing me of murdering Lark Iron Cloud the day before. There's no way to prove anything different. Now they're screaming for my blood in front of the council.

Everybody is assembled at the bleachers by the clearing where we hold the drum circle. Old John Tenkiller don't say a thing, just soaks up abuse from Lark's boys. Hank Cotton stands next to him, big hands clenched into fists. The Light Horse tribal police stand in clumps, tense as they stare a full-on civil war straight in the eye.

I'm thinking maybe this whole gamble was a mistake.

But before we can all get busy killing each other, a bruised and bloody Lark Iron Cloud staggers up the hill and into camp. Everybody gasps to see what he brung with him: a four-legged walking machine on a steel cable leash tied to Lark's pack. We're all stunned speechless, but John Tenkiller just stands up and walks over like Lark had arrived right on cue.

"Lark Iron Cloud," says the old drumkeeper. "You left Gray Horse as a boy. You return as a man. We sorrowed when you left, but we rejoice at your return, new and different. Welcome home, Lark Iron Cloud. Through you, our people will live."

The true Gray Horse Army was born. Lark and Lonnie soon combined the tribal police and the GHA into a single force. Word of this human army spread across the United States, especially as they began a policy of capturing and domesticating as many of the Rob walker scouts as possible. The largest of these captured walkers formed the basis for a crucial human weapon of the New War, a device so startling that upon hearing about it, I assumed it to be only a wild rumor: the spider tank.

—CORMAC WALLACE, MIL#GHA217

3. Fort Bandon

Just let us go. We're gone, man. We're gone.

Jack Wallace

NEW WAR + 3 MONTHS

In the first months after Zero Hour, billions of people around the world began a fight for survival. Many were murdered by the technology they had come to trust: automobiles, domestic robots, and smart buildings. Others were captured and led to the forced-labor camps that sprang up outside major cities. But for the people who ran for the hills to fend for themselves—the refugees—other human beings soon proved to be just as dangerous as Rob. Or more so.

—CORMAC WALLACE, MIL#GHA217

Three months. It takes three months to get out of Boston and out of the state. Luckily, my brother has a map and a compass and the ability to use them. Jack and I are scared and on foot, loaded down with military equipment we looted from the National Guard armory.

But that's not why it takes so long.

The cities and towns are in chaos. We go out of our way,

but it's impossible to avoid them all. Cars are running people down, traveling in packs. I watch people fire guns from buildings at marauding vehicles. Sometimes the cars are empty. Sometimes there are people inside. I watch a driverless garbage truck pull up to a steel trash can. Two prongs slide out and the hydraulic lift actuates. I cover my mouth and choke when I see the bodies tumble out in a limp-limbed waterfall.

Once, Jack and I stop for a breath while we are halfway across an overpass. I press my face against the chain-link fence and see eight lanes of highway, jam-packed with cars, all of them moving at just about thirty-five miles per hour in the same direction. No brake lights. No turn signals. Not like traffic at all. I watch a man wriggle out of a sunroof and roll off the top of his car and right under the car behind. Squinting my eyes, the whole thing just looks like a big metal carpet being slowly pulled away.

Toward the ocean.

If you aren't headed someplace and getting there quick, then you aren't going to make it long in the cities. And that's our secret. Me and Jack never stop moving except to sleep.

People see our uniforms and call to us. Every time this happens my brother says, "Stay put and we'll be back with help."

Knowing Jack, he probably really believes it. But he doesn't slow down. And that's good enough for me.

My brother is determined to reach an army base so we can start helping people. As we cross the towns block by block, Jack keeps talking about how once we meet up with the soldiers, we'll come back and take out the machines. Says we'll go house to house and save people, bring them back to a safe zone. Set up patrols to hunt down all the malfunctioning robots.

"A day or two, Cormac," he says. "This'll all be over in a day or two. It'll be all mopped up."

I want to believe him, but I know better. The armory should have been safe, but it was crawling with walking land mines. All military Humvees have autodrive, in case they need to maneuver back home with an incapacitated driver. "What's a military base going to look like?" I ask. "They've got more than mines there. They've got tanks. Gunships. Rolling rifles."

Jack just keeps walking, head down.

The mayhem blends together into a haze. Scenes come to me in flashes. I see a struggling old man pulled into a dark doorway by a stern-faced Slow Sue; an empty car drives by, on fire and with a chunk of meat trapped under it, leaving a greasy smear on the street; a man falls from a building, screaming and flailing, with the silhouette of a Big Happy looking down.

Bam!

Screams, gunshots, and alarms echo through the streets. But thankfully Jack runs us hard. No time to stop and look around. We dive through the horror like two drowning men clawing to the surface for air.

Three months.

It takes us three months to find the fort. Three months for me to muddy my new clothes, to shoot my rifle, and to clean it next to a feeble campfire. Then we cross a bridge over the Hudson River and reach our destination, just outside what used to be Albany.

Fort Bandon.

―――――

"Get down!"

"On your fucking knees!"

"Hands on your heads, motherfuckers!"

"Toes together!"

The voices come screaming at us from out of the darkness.

A spotlight flickers on from up high. I squint into it and try not to panic. My face is numb with adrenaline and my arms are rubbery and weak. Jack and I crouch on our knees next to each other. I can hear myself breathing, panting. Damn. I'm scared shitless.

"It's all right," whispers Jack. "Just be quiet."

"Shut the fuck up!" shouts a soldier. "Cover!"

"Cover," says a calm voice in the darkness.

I hear the bolt of a rifle being pulled back. As the cartridge clinks into the chamber, I can visualize the brass bullet waiting there in the mouth of a dark, cold barrel. My own rifle and supplies are hidden a half mile away, thirty paces off the road.

Footsteps scratch across the pavement. A soldier's silhouette looms in front of us, eclipsing the spotlight with his head.

"We're unarmed," says Jack.

"On your fucking face," says the voice. "You, hands on your head. Cover him!"

I put my hands on my head, blinking into the light. Jack grunts as he is pushed onto his stomach. The soldier pats him down.

"Number one clear," he says. "Why are you fuckers wearing uniforms? You kill a soldier?"

"I'm in the guard," says Jack. "Check my ID."

"Right."

I feel a shove between my shoulder blades and fall forward, cheek on the cold, gritty pavement. Two black combat boots appear in my field of view. Hands roughly jab through my pockets, checking for weapons. The spotlight illuminates the pavement before my face in lunar detail, shadows racing through craters. I notice that my cheek is resting in a discolored splotch of oil.

"Number two clear," says the soldier. "Gimme the ID."

The mud-caked black boots step back into my line of sight. Just beyond the boots, I make out a pile of clothes next to a razor-wire fence. It looks like somebody used this place as a Goodwill drop-off site. It's freezing out here, but it still smells like a dump.

"Welcome to Fort Bandon, Sergeant Wallace. Happy to have you. You're a ways from Boston, huh?"

Jack starts to sit up, but one of those big boots drops onto his back, shoving him into the ground.

"Uh-uh-uh. I didn't say to get up. What about this guy here? Who's he?"

"My brother," grunts Jack.

"He in the guard, too?"

"Civilian."

"Well, I am sorry, but that is not acceptable, Sergeant. Unfortunately, Fort Bandon is not allowing civilian refugees at this time. So if you want to come inside, say your good-byes now."

"I can't leave him," says Jack.

"Yeah, I figured you'd say that. Your alternative is to go down to the river with the rest of the refugees. There's a few thousand of them squatting down there. Just follow the smell. You'll probably get knifed for your boots, but maybe not if you two sleep in shifts."

The soldier makes a humorless chuckle. His camouflage fatigues are tucked into those filthy black boots. I thought he was standing in a shadow, but now I see that it's another splotch. There are oil stains all over the concrete.

"You serious? Civilians aren't welcome?" asks Jack.

"Nah," replies the soldier, "we barely fought off our own goddamn Humvees. Half our autonomous weapons are missing, and the other half we blew up. Most of our command is gone. They all got called to some fucking meeting right before the shit went down. Haven't seen 'em since. We can't even get into the repair bays or the refueling depot. Sergeant, this place is fucked up bad enough without throwing in a bunch of looting, thieving scumbag civilians from off the streets."

I feel the cool tip of the boot nudge my forehead.

"No offense there, partner."

The boot goes away.

"Gates are closed. Try to come in here, you'll get a bullet sandwich from my man on the tower. Ain't that right, Carl?"

"That's affirmative," replies Carl, from somewhere behind the spotlight.

"Now," says the soldier, stepping back toward the gate. "Get the fuck out of here. Both of you."

The soldier steps behind the light, and I realize it's not a pile of clothes I've been looking at. The outline is visible now. It's a human body. Bodies. There are mounds of them heaped together like candy wrappers blown against the fence. Frozen by the weather in anguished contortions. The splotches on the ground in front of me—under my face—*aren't oil*.

A whole lot of people died here not long ago.

"You fucking *killed* them?" I ask, in disbelief.

Jack groans softly to himself. The soldier does that dry chuckle again. His boots scratch pavement as he saunters over to me. "Dang, Sergeant. Your brother doesn't know when to keep his mouth shut, does he?"

"No, he does not," says Jack.

"Let me explain it to you, pal," says the soldier.

Then I feel a steel-toed boot crunch into my rib cage. I'm too surprised to yell. My breath wheezes out of my lungs mechanically. I'm in the fetal position for the next two or three kicks.

"He gets it," shouts Carl, faceless in the night. "I think he gets it, Corporal."

I can't help moaning—it's the only way I can breathe.

"Just let us go," says Jack. "We're gone, man. We're gone."

The kicking stops. The soldier chuckles one more time. It's like a nervous tic. I hear the metallic *chink* of his rifle being cocked.

Carl speaks up, from the invisible tower. "Sir? There's been enough of that already, don't you think? Let's disengage."

Nothing.

"Corporal, let's disengage," says Carl.

The gun doesn't fire, but I can feel those faceless boots waiting there. Waiting for me to say something, anything. Curled up and hurting, I focus on trying to force breath in and out of my battered rib cage.

I don't have anything left to say.

———

The soldier was right—we smell the refugees before we see them.

We reach the camp just after midnight. Down along the bank of the Hudson we find thousands of people milling around, camping and squatting and searching for information. The long, narrow strip of land has an old iron fence between it and the street, and the terrain is too rough for the domestic robots.

These are the people who've come to Fort Bandon and found no refuge. They've brought along their suitcases and backpacks and trash bags filled with clothes. They've brought their parents and wives and husbands and children. In their masses, they have built campfires from scavenged furniture and gone to the bathroom by the river and thrown their trash to the wind.

The temperature hovers just above zero. The refugees sleep, snoozing under piles of blankets, inside freshly looted tents, and on the ground. The refugees fight, scuffling with fists and knives and an occasional gunshot. The refugees are angry and scared and hungry. Some beg, camp to camp. Some steal firewood and trinkets. Some walk away into the city and don't come back.

These people are all here to wait. For what, I have no idea. Help, I guess.

In the darkness, Jack and I meander among the campfires and clusters of refugees. I hold a handkerchief over my face to ward off the smell of too much humanity in too small of a place. I instinctively feel vulnerable around this many people.

Jack feels it, too.

He taps my shoulder and points to a small hill covered in brush. High ground. A man and a woman sit next to each other among the tufts of dead grass, a small Coleman lantern between them. We head over.

And that's how we meet Tiberius and Cherrah.

On the hill, a huge black man wearing a Hawaiian shirt over long underwear sits, forearms resting loosely on his knees. Next to him, a small Native American woman squints at us. She has a worn bowie knife in her hand. It looks like she's used it plenty.

"Howdy," I call out.

"What?" asks the woman. "You army fucks haven't had enough? Come back for more?"

Her big-ass knife glints in the lantern light.

Jack and I look at each other. How to respond to that? Then the big man puts his hand on the woman's shoulder. In a booming voice, he says, "Manners, Cherrah. These men are not army. Look at the uniforms. Not the same as those others."

"Whatever," she says.

"Come. Sit with us," he says. "Take the load off."

We sit and listen. Tiberius Abdullah and Cherrah Ridge met while escaping from Albany. He's a cabdriver who moved here from Eritrea—the Horn of Africa. She's a mechanic who worked in her father's body shop with her four brothers. When the shit went down, Tiberius was picking up his cab from the shop. After the first mention, Tiberius doesn't talk about Cherrah's brothers or father again.

As Tiberius shares their story, Cherrah sits quietly. I can't read her face, but I notice a shrewdness in the way she looks at me and my brother, sizes us up, and then looks away. Gotta keep an eye on that one.

We're sharing a nip from Ty's flask when a pair of head-lights wink on in the distance. A hunting rifle seems to just appear in Cherrah's hands. Tiberius has a pistol, pulled from the waistband of his sweatpants. Jack turns down the lantern. Looks like a killer car jumped the barricades and made it down here.

I watch the far-off headlights for a few seconds before I realize that Cherrah is pointing her rifle into the darkness *behind* us.

Someone is coming, fast. I hear huffing and puffing and boots pounding dirt and then the silhouette of a man appears. He staggers clumsily up the small hill, falling forward and catching himself on his fingertips.

"Hold it!" shouts Cherrah.

The man freezes, then stands up and steps forward into the lantern light. It's a soldier from Fort Bandon. He's a lanky white guy with a long neck and unruly, straw-colored hair. I've never seen him before, but when he speaks I immediately recognize his voice.

"Oh. Hi, uh, hello," he says, "I'm Carl Lewandowski."

A few hundred yards up the river's edge, a pall of ragged screams rises up, thin, disappearing into the atmosphere. Blanketed figures dash between dim red campfires. That pair of headlights is dashing directly through the middle of the refugee camp, in our direction.

"Spotted it from the tower when it went off base," says Carl, still struggling to catch his breath. "Came to warn people."

"How nice of you, Carl," I mutter, holding my bruised ribs.

Jack drops to one knee and pulls his battle rifle off his back. He squints across the wide-open space at the confusion. "Humvee," he says. "Armored. No way for them to stop it."

"We can shoot for the tires," says Cherrah, snapping open the bolt and checking the chamber of her hunting rifle for a cartridge.

Carl glances at her. "Honeycomb. Tires are bulletproof. I'd go for the headlights first. Then the sensor package on top. Shoot its eyes and ears."

"What's the sensor package look like?" asks Jack.

Carl pulls out his rifle and checks the magazine as he speaks: "Black sphere. Antenna coming out of it. It's a standard-issue compact multisensor payload with an electron-multiplied CCD infrared camera mounted on a high-stability gimbal, among other things."

We all frown at him. Carl looks around at us.

"Sorry. I'm an engineer," he says.

The Humvee steers itself through the central mass of sleeping people. The headlights jounce up and down in the darkness. The sounds are indescribable. Red-tinted headlights turn our way, growing larger in the night.

"You heard the man. Fire on the black box if you have a clear shot," says Jack.

Soon, bullets begin to crack out in the night. Cherrah's hands move swift and smooth along the length of her bolt-action rifle, spitting bullets accurately at the lurching vehicle.

Headlights shatter. It swerves, but only to run down nearby refugees. Sparks fly from the black box on top as bullets hit it again and again. Still, it keeps coming.

"This isn't right," says Jack. He grabs Carl by the shirt. "Why isn't the fucker blind?"

"I don't know, I don't know," whimpers Carl.

It's a good question.

I stop firing and cock my head, trying to dial out all the screams and running shapes and confusion. The shattered campfires and tumbling corpses and roaring engines fade, drowned out by an amnesiac shroud of concentration.

Why can it still see?

A sound emerges from the chaos. It's a gentle *thup-thup-thup*, like a far-off lawn mower. Now, I notice a blurry spot up above us.

Some kind of eye in the sky.

The battered Humvee looms out of the night like a sea monster surfacing from black depths.

We scatter as it plows into and over our hill.

"Flying robot. Eleven o'clock. Just over the tree line," I shout.

Rifle barrels rise, including my own. The Humvee charges past us and bashes through a campfire a dozen yards away. Embers from the fire cascade over its hood, like a meteor streaking through the atmosphere. It's coming around for another go.

Muzzles flash. Hot brass shell casings cascade through the air. Something explodes in the sky, spraying the ground with pulverized bits of plastic.

"Scatter," says Jack. The roar of the Humvee drowns out the whining engines of the falling star in the sky. The armored vehicle bulldozes straight over the mound where we stand, shocks bottoming out. In the rush of air as the Humvee passes, I can smell melted plastic and gunpowder and blood.

Then the Humvee rolls to a stop just past the hill. It moves away from us, jerking forward in starts and stops like a blind man feeling his way down a path.

We did it. For now.

A massive arm settles down over my neck, squeezes tight enough to grind my shoulder blades together. "It is blind," says Tiberius. "You have the eyes of a hawk, Cormac Wallace."

"There'll be more. What now?" asks Carl.

"We stay here and protect these people," says Jack, as if it were the most obvious thing in the world.

"How's that, Jack?" I say. "They might not want our protection. Plus, we're sitting next to the biggest arsenal in the state. We've got to head for the hills, man. Camp out."

Cherrah snorts.

"You got a better idea?" I ask her.

"Camping is a short-term solution. Where'd you rather be? In a cave somewhere, hunting for food every day and hoping you find it? Or in a place where there will be other people to depend on?"

"And riots and looting," I add.

"I'm talking about a smaller community. A safe place. Gray Horse," she says.

"How big?" asks Jack.

"Probably a few thousand, mostly Osage. Like me."

"An Indian reservation," I groan. "Mass starvation. Disease. Death. Sorry, I just don't see it."

"That's because you're full of shit," says Cherrah. "Gray

Horse is organized. Always has been. Functioning government. Farmers. Welders. Doctors."

"Well," I say. "As long as there are *welders*."

She looks at me pointedly. "Jails. If we need 'em."

"Specialization," says Jack. "She's right. We need to reach a place to regroup. Plan a counterattack. Where is it?"

"Oklahoma."

I groan out loud again. "That's like a million miles away."

"I grew up there. I know the way."

"How do you know they're still alive?"

"A refugee I met heard about it on shortwave. There's a camp there. And an army." Cherrah snorts at Carl. "A *real* army."

I clap my hands. "I'm not hiking across America on the whim of some chick we just met. We're better off on our own."

Cherrah grabs me by the shirt and yanks me close. My rifle clatters to the ground. She's wiry, but her slender arms are strong as tree branches. "Teaming with your *brother* is my best bet at survival," she says. "Unlike you, *he* knows what he's doing and he's good at it. So why don't you just shut the fuck up and think it through? You're both bright boys. You want to survive. This isn't a hard choice to make."

Cherrah's scowling face is inches away. A bit of ash from the scattered fires lands in her inky black hair and she ignores it. Her black eyes are trained on mine. This small woman is absolutely intent on remaining alive, and it's clear that she will do anything to stay that way.

She's a born survivor.

I can't help but smile. *"Survive?"* I ask. "Now you're talking my language. In fact, I don't think I want to be more than five feet away from you ever again. I just, I don't know . . . I feel safe in your arms."

She lets go and gives me a shove.

"You wish, *bright boy*," she snorts.

A thundering laugh startles all of us. Tiberius, looking like a huge shadow, throws on his backpack. Firelight gleams from his teeth as he speaks.

"Then it is settled," he says. "The five of us make a good team. We have defeated the Humvee and saved these people. Now, we will journey together until we reach this place, this Gray Horse."

The five of us became the heart of Brightboy squad. On that night, we began a long journey through the wilderness to Gray Horse. We were not yet well armed or well trained, but we were lucky—during the months after Zero Hour, Rob was busy processing the roughly four billion human beings living in major population centers of the world.

It would be the better part of a year before we emerged from the woods, battle scarred and weary. While we were gone, however, momentous events were taking place that would alter the landscape of the New War.

—CORMAC WALLACE, MIL#GHA217

4. Chaperone Duty

If this kid is gonna leave me to die,
I want him to remember my face.

NEW WAR + 7 MONTHS

As we hiked across the United States, Brightboy squad was unaware that most large cities worldwide were being emptied out by increasingly weaponized robots. Chinese survivors later reported that at this time it was possible to cross the Yangtze River on foot, the waters were so choked with corpses washing out to the East China Sea.

Even so, some groups of people simply learned to adapt to the neverending onslaught. The efforts of these urban tribes, described in the following pages by Marcus and Dawn Johnson of New York City, ultimately proved crucial to human survival worldwide.

—CORMAC WALLACE, MIL#GHA217

The alarm triggers at dawn. It's no big deal. Just a bunch of tin cans tied together, dragging across the cracked pavement.

I open my eyes and pull down my sleeping bag. It takes a long-ass second to figure out where I'm at. Looking up, I see a car axle, a muffler, tailpipe.

Oh yeah. Right.

I've been sleeping in craters under cars every night for a year and I'm still not used to it. Doesn't matter, though. Whether I get used to it or not, I'm still alive and kicking.

For about three seconds I lie still, listening. Best not to jump out of bed right away. You never know what the hell's been creeping around in the night. In this last year, most of the robots got smaller. Others got bigger. A *lot* bigger.

I bang my head pulling off my sleeping bag and folding it up. It's worth it. This pile of rust is my best friend. There's so many burned-out cars on the streets of New York City these days that the bastards can't check under every single one.

I wriggle out from under the car and into gray sunlight. Reaching back underneath, I drag out my dirty pack and shrug it on. I cough and spit a hawker on the ground. Sun's just up, but it's cool this early. Summer's just getting started.

Those cans are still dragging. I drop to a knee and untie the rope before any machine mics can pick up the noise. Topside, it's important you be quiet, be moving, and be unpredictable.

Otherwise, you'll be dead.

Chaperone duty. Of the hundreds of thousands of city people who ran away to the woods, about half of them are starving to death about now. They come stumbling into the city, rail-thin and filthy, on the run from wolves and hoping to scavenge.

Most times, the machines eat 'em up fast.

I throw my hood over my head and let my black trench coat billow out behind me to confuse robotic targeting systems, especially the goddamn disposable sentry turrets. Speaking of, I gotta get off the street. I duck into a destroyed building and pick my way over trash and rubble toward the source of the alarm.

After we dynamited half the city, the regular old domestic robots couldn't balance well enough to get to us. We were safe for a while, long enough to get established underground and inside demolished buildings.

But then a *new* walker showed up.

We call it a mantis. It's got four multijointed legs longer than telephone poles and molded out of some kind of carbon fiber honeycomb. Its feet look like upside-down ice axes, slicing into the ground on every step. Up top where the legs meet, it's got a couple of little arms with two ice axe hands. Those razor arms tear through wood and drywall and brick. Whole thing sort of scurries—all doubled over and hunched down to the size of a small pickup truck. Looks kinda like a praying mantis.

Close enough, anyway.

I'm dodging past empty desks in a collapsed floor of an office building when I feel the telltale vibration in the ground. Something big outside. I freeze in place, then crouch on the trash-strewn floor. Peeking over a water-swollen desk, I watch the windows. A gray shadow passes by outside, but I see nothing else.

I hold up for a minute anyway.

Not far from here, a familiar routine is playing out. A survivor has found a suspicious pile of rocks that a machine would never notice. Next to those rocks is a rope that this person pulled. I know that ten minutes ago my survivor was alive. There's no guarantee for the next ten minutes.

At the collapsed end of the building I crawl over shattered two-by-fours and pulverized brick toward a crescent of morning light. Hood down, I push my face through the hole and scan the street outside.

Our sign is there, undisturbed on a stoop across the street.

A man is huddled next to it, arms over his knees and head down. He rocks back and forth on his heels, maybe keeping warm.

The sign works because the machines don't notice natural stuff, like rocks and trees. It's a blind spot. A mantis has a good eye for unnatural things like words and drawings—even shit like happy faces. Uncamouflaged trip wires never work. Lines are too straight. Writing directions to a safe house on the wall is a good way to get people deleted. But a pile of rubble is invisible. And a pile of rocks going from big to small is, too.

I wriggle out of the hole and reach my guy before he even looks up. "Hey," I whisper, nudging his elbow.

He looks up at me, startled. He's a young Latino guy, in his twenties. I can see that he's been crying. God knows what he went through to get here.

"It's okay, buddy," I reassure him. "We'll get you safe. Come with me."

He nods, saying nothing. Leaning against the building, he stands up. He has one arm wrapped in a dirty towel and he's cradling it with his other hand. I figure it must be messed up pretty bad if he's afraid to let anybody see it.

"We'll get your arm looked at real soon, man."

He flinches a little when I say that. Not what I was expecting. Strange how being hurt can be embarrassing. Like it's your fault that an eye or hand or foot isn't working right. Course, being hurt isn't half as embarrassing as being dead.

I lead him back toward the collapsed ruin across the street. The mantis won't be a problem once we get inside. My people are mostly in the subway tunnels with the main entrances blocked off. We'll go building to building all the way home.

"What's your name, man?" I ask.

The guy doesn't respond, just puts his head down.

"Fair enough. Follow me."

I head back into the safety of the collapsed building. The kid with no name hobbles along behind me. Together, we roam through destroyed buildings, scrabbling over mounds of blasted rubble and crawling under half-collapsed walls. Once we make it far enough, I take us out onto a pretty safe street. The silence between us grows the farther we travel.

I get the creeps walking down that empty street and I realize that I'm scared of the dead eyes on the kid shuffling along behind me, saying nothing.

How much change can a person absorb before everything loses meaning? Living for its own sake isn't life. People need meaning as much as they need air.

Thank god I've still got Dawn.

I'm picturing her hazel eyes in my head when I notice the gray-green telephone pole slanting cockeyed at the end of the street. The pole bends in the middle and shifts and I realize it's a leg. We're going to die inside thirty seconds if we stay out here.

"Get inside," I hiss, shoving the kid toward a broken-out window.

On its four crouched legs, a hunched-over mantis scuttles into view. Its featureless, bullet-shaped head rotates quickly, stops. Long antennae quiver. The machine leaps forward and gallops toward us, sharp feet cutting into the dirt and pavement like a rudder through water. Those front claws hang off its belly, up and ready, light glinting from countless barbs.

The kid stares, blank.

I grab him and shove him through the window, then dive in after him. We get on our feet and hustle over moldy carpet. Seconds later, a shadow falls across the rectangle of daylight behind us. A clawed arm shoots through the window frame and rips downward, gouging out part of the wall. Another clawed arm follows. Back and forth, back and forth. It's like a tornado hitting.

Lucky for us, this is a safe building. I can tell because it's been hollowed out pretty good. The facade is demolished, but inside it's passable. We do our homework in NYC. I steer the kid toward a pile of cinder blocks and a hole in the wall that leads into an adjacent building.

"That's us," I say, pointing and pushing the kid toward the hole. He stumbles along like a zombie.

Then I hear carpet ripping and the crunch of wooden furniture. The mantis has somehow made it in through the window. Crouched small, it's squeezing its gray mass through the building, tearing stained ceiling tiles down like confetti. Crouch walking, the thing is all flashing claws and screeching metal.

We dash for the hole in the wall.

I stop and help the kid crawl over the mess of rebar and concrete. The passage is just a black gaping hollow, only a few feet wide, that leads straight through the sandstone foundations of both buildings. I'm praying it'll slow down the monster behind us.

The kid disappears inside. I climb in behind him. It's dark, claustrophobic. Kid's crawling slow, still cradling his hurt hand. Near the entrance, steel rods of rebar jut out like rusty spearheads. I can hear the mantis closing on us, destroying everything it touches.

Then the sound stops.

There isn't enough room to turn my head and see what's happening behind me. I just see the bottoms of the kid's shoes as he crawls. Breathe in, breathe out. Concentrate. Something slams into the mouth of the hole hard enough to rip off a chunk of solid rock, by the sound of it. It's followed by another bone-jarring slam. The mantis is scrabbling frantically, chewing through the concrete wall and into sandstone. The noise is deafening.

Everything around me turns to screaming and darkness and dust. "Go, go, go!" I shout.

A second later the kid is gone; he found the other end of the tunnel. Grinning, I turn on the juice. Moving full speed, I tumble out of the hole and fall a few feet and then scream in surprised agony.

A finger of rebar has pierced the meat of my right calf.

I'm on my back, propping myself up on my elbows. My leg is caught on the mouth of the hole. The rebar sticks out like a crooked tooth, sunk into my leg. The kid stands a few feet away, that blank expression still on his face. I take a shuddering breath and let out with another animal scream of pain.

It seems to get the kid's attention.

"Fuck, get me off this thing!" I shout.

The kid blinks at me. Some life is coming back into those dead brown eyes of his.

"Hurry," I say. "Mantis is coming."

I try to lift my body up, but I'm too weak and the pain is too much. Elbows digging painfully into the dirt, I manage to raise my head. I try to explain to the kid. "You gotta pull my leg off the rebar. Or get the rebar out of the wall. One or the other, man. But do it fast."

The kid stands there, lip quivering. He looks like he's about to cry. Just my fucking luck.

From the tunnel, I can hear the *pock, pock* as each jab from the mantis dislodges more stone. A cloud of dust pours out of the disintegrating hole. Every blow from the mantis sends a throbbing vibration through the rock and into the rebar skewering my calf.

"C'mon man, I need you. I need you to help me."

And for the first time, the kid speaks. "I'm sorry," he says to me.

Fuck. It's over. I want to scream at this kid, this coward. I want to hurt him somehow, but I'm too weak. So with everything I've got in me, I focus on keeping my face raised to his. My neck muscles strain to keep my head up, trembling. If this kid is gonna leave me to die, I want him to remember my face.

Eyes locked on mine, the kid holds his injured arm up. He starts to unwrap the towel that covers it.

"What are you—"

I stop cold. The kid's hand isn't hurt—*he doesn't have one.*

Instead, the meat of his forearm ends with a mess of wires leading to a greasy hunk of metal with two blades sticking out. It looks like a pair of industrial-sized scissors. The tool is fused directly into his arm. As I watch, a tendon flexes in his forearm and the oiled blades begin to spread apart.

"I'm a freak," he says. "Rob did this to me in the labor camps."

I don't know what to think. There's just no more strength in me. I lower my head and stare at the ceiling.

Snip.

My leg is free. A piece of rebar is stuck in it, snipped and shiny on one end. But I'm *free.*

The kid helps me up. He puts his good arm around me. We hobble away without looking back at the hole. Five minutes later, we find the camouflaged entrance to the subway tunnels. And then we're gone, struggling as best we can down the abandoned tracks.

We leave the mantis behind.

"How?" I ask, nodding at his bad arm.

"Labor camp. People go into surgery, come out different. I was one of the first. Mine's simple. Just my arm. Other people, though. They come back from the autodoc even worse. No eyes. No legs. Rob messes with your skin, your muscles, your brain."

"You on your own?" I ask.

"I met some others, but they didn't want . . ." He looks at his mutilated hand, face empty. "I'm like *them* now."

That hand hasn't made him any friends. I wonder how many times he's been rejected, how long he's been on his own.

It's almost over for this kid. I can see it in the slump of his shoulders. How every breath seems like a struggle. I've seen it before. The kid's not hurt—he's beaten.

"Being alone is tough," I say. "You start to wonder what the point is. You know?"

He says nothing.

"But there's other people here. The resistance. You're not alone now. You got a purpose."

"What's that?" he asks.

"To survive, man. To help the resistance."

"I'm not even—"

He holds up his arm. Tears gleam in his eyes. This is the important part. He's got to get this. If he doesn't, he'll die.

I grab the kid by the shoulders and say it face-to-face: "You were born a human being and you're gonna die one. No matter what they did to you. Or what they *do*. Understand?"

It's quiet down here in the tunnels. And dark. It feels safe.

"Yeah," he says.

I throw an arm around the kid's shoulder, wincing at the pain in my leg. "Good," I say. "Now come on. We got to get home and *eat*. You wouldn't guess it to look at me, but I've got this beautiful wife. Best looking woman in the world. And I'm telling you, if you ask real nice, she will cook up a stew like you wouldn't believe."

I think this kid is gonna be okay. Soon as he meets the others.

People need meaning as much as they need air. Lucky for us, we can give meaning to each other for free. Just by being alive.

In the coming months, more and more modified humans began to filter into the city. No matter what Rob did to these people, all of them were welcomed into the NYC resistance. Without this haven and its lack of prejudice, it is unlikely that the human resistance, including Brightboy squad, would have been able to acquire and take advantage of an incredibly powerful secret weapon: fourteen-year-old Mathilda Perez.

—CORMAC WALLACE, MIL#GHA217

5. Tickler

Where's your sister, Nolan? Where's Mathilda?

Laura Perez

NEW WAR + 10 MONTHS

As our squad continued to travel west toward Gray Horse, we met a wounded soldier named Leonardo. We nursed Leo back to health, and he told us about hastily built forced-labor camps placed just outside the larger cities. Massively outnumbered from the start, it seems that Big Rob leveraged the threat of death to convince huge numbers of people to enter these camps and stay there.

Under extreme duress, Laura Perez, former congresswoman, related this story of her experience in one such labor camp. Of the imprisoned millions, a lucky few were bound to escape. Others were forced to.

—CORMAC WALLACE, MIL#GHA217

I'm standing alone in a wet, muddy field.

I don't know where I am. I can't remember how I got here. My arms are scarred and bony. I'm wearing filthy blue coveralls that are close to rags, ripped and stained.

Shivering, I wrap my arms around myself. Panic stabs at me. I know I'm missing something important. I've left something behind. I can't put my finger on it, but it hurts. It feels like there's a piece of barbwire wrapped around my heart, squeezing.

Then I remember.

"No," I moan.

A scream rises up from my gut. "No!"

I shout it to the grass. Flecks of spit fly from my mouth and arc away into the morning sunlight. I spin in a circle, but I'm alone. Utterly alone.

Mathilda and Nolan. My babies. My babies are gone.

Something flashes from the tree line. I flinch instinctively. Then I realize it's only a hand mirror. A camouflaged man steps out from behind a tree and motions to me. In a daze, I stumble toward him through the overgrown field, stopping twenty yards away.

"Hey," he says. "Where did you come from?"

"I don't know," I say. "Where am I?"

"Outside New York City. What do you remember?"

"I don't know."

"Check your body for lumps."

"What?"

"Check your body for lumps. Anything new."

Confused, I run my hands over my body. I'm surprised that I can feel each one of my ribs. Nothing makes sense. I wonder if I'm dreaming or unconscious or dead. Then I feel something. A bump on my upper thigh. Probably the only meaty part left on my body.

"There's a bump on my leg," I say.

The man begins to back away into the woods.

"What does that mean? Where are you going?" I ask.

"I'm sorry, lady. Rob's bugged you. There's a human work camp a few miles from here. They're using you as bait. Don't try to follow me. Sorry."

He disappears into the shadows of the woods. I shade my face with one hand and look for him. "Wait, wait! Where is the work camp? How do I find it?"

A voice echoes thinly out of the woods. "Scarsdale. Five miles north. Follow the road. Keep the sun to your right. Be careful."

The man is gone. I'm alone again.

I see my own set of staggering footprints in the muddy grass, tracking north. I realize the clearing is really an overgrown road, on its way back to nature. My stick arms are still wrapped around me. I force myself to let go. I'm weak and hurt. My body wants to shiver. It wants to fall down and give up.

But I won't let it.

I'm going back for my babies.

————

The lump moves when I touch it. I find a small slice in my skin from where they must have put it in. But this wound is farther up my leg, close to my hip. I think whatever-it-is is moving. Or at least it can move if it wants to.

Bug. The camouflaged man called it a bug. I let out a snort of laughter, wondering how literally I should take that description.

Pretty literally, as it turns out.

Snatches of memory are coming back to me. Faint pictures of clean-swept pavement, a big metal building. Like an airplane hangar, but filled with lights. Another building with bunk beds stacked to the ceilings. I don't remember what *they* look like, the jailers. I don't try too hard to remember, though.

After an hour and a half of steady walking, I spot a cleared-out area in the distance. Smoke is rising in gentle puffs from it. Sunlight glints from a broad metal roof and short chain-link fences. This must be it. The prison camp.

A weird sliding sensation in my leg reminds me that I'm carrying the bug. That man didn't want to help me because of it. It stands to reason that the bug must be telling the machines where I'm at, so it can catch and kill other people.

Hopefully, the machines didn't expect me to *come back*.

I watch the pulsing lump under my skin with a sick feeling in the pit of my stomach. There's no way I can keep going with the bug under there. I've got to do something about this.

And it's going to *hurt*.

Two rocks, flat. One long strip of fabric torn from my sleeve. With my left hand I press one rock into my thigh, dimpling the skin just behind the lump. The bug starts to move, but before it can go anywhere I close my eyes and think of Mathilda and Nolan and with all my might, I slam the other rock down. A knot of pain flares in my leg and I hear a crunch. I bring down the rock three more times before I roll over onto the ground, screaming in pain. I lie on my back, chest heaving, looking at blue sky through tears.

It's maybe five minutes before I can bring myself to check the damage to my leg.

Whatever it is looks like a blunt metal slug with dozens of quivering, barbed feet. It must have cut through my leg on the first hit, because part of its shell has been mashed into the pulped outside layer of my skin. Some kind of liquid is leaking from it onto my leg, mixing with my blood. I wipe my finger in it and bring it to my face. It smells like chemicals. Explosive chemicals, like kerosene or gasoline.

I don't know why that is, but I think I might have gotten

very lucky. It never occurred to me that whatever it is might be a bomb.

I don't let myself cry.

Forcing myself to look at it, I reach down and gingerly pull the crushed thing out from under my skin. I notice that it has a cylindrical shell on the other side that isn't broken. I toss the thing on the ground and it lands limp. It looks like two rolls of breath mints with lots of legs and two long wet antennae. I suck my lower lip into my mouth and bite it and try not to cry out as I wrap my leg with the strip of blue fabric.

Then, I get up and hobble closer to the work camp.

———

Sentry guns. The memory dances back into my head. The work camp is protected by sentry guns. Those gray lumps in the turf will pop up and kill anything that gets within a certain range.

Camp Scar.

From the tree line, I watch the field. Bugs and birds flitter back and forth over a thick carpet of flowers, ignoring the lumps of clothing wrapped in the turf—the bodies of would-be rescuers. The robots don't try to hide this place. Instead, they use it like a beacon to attract human survivors. Potential liberators, ambushed again and again. Their bodies piling up in this field and turning into dirt. Flower food.

If you work hard and stay in line, the machines feed you and keep you warm and alive. You learn to ignore the sharp crack of the sentry guns. Force yourself to forget what the sound means. You look for the carrot. Stop seeing the stick.

Off to one side of the compound, I see a wavering brown line. People. It's a line of people being marched here from

another place. I don't hesitate, I just hobble my way around the
sentries to reach the line.

Twenty minutes later, I see an armored six-wheeled vehicle
jouncing along at maybe four miles per hour. It's some kind
of military job with a turret on top. I walk toward it with my
hands out, flinching when the turret spins around and locks
onto me.

"Stay in line. Do not stop. Do not approach the vehicle.
Comply immediately or you will be shot," says an automated
voice from a loudspeaker mounted on top.

A broken line of refugees staggers alongside the armored
car. Some carry suitcases or wear packs, but most just have
the clothes on their backs. God knows how long they've been
marching. Or how many there were in line when they started.

A few weary heads lift up to glance at me.

Keeping my hands up and my eyes on the turret, I join the
line of refugees. Five minutes later, a man in a mud-splashed
business suit and another guy in a poncho come up and walk
on either side of me, slowing together so that we drop back a
ways from the military vehicle.

"Where'd you come from?" asks business guy.

I stare straight ahead. "I came from where we're going,"
I say.

"And where's that?" he asks.

"A work camp."

"Work camp?" exclaims the kid in the rain poncho. "You
mean a concentration camp?"

Poncho boy eyes the field. His eyes dart from the armored
vehicle to a nearby clump of tall grass. The business guy puts
his hand on his friend's shoulder.

"Don't. Remember what happened to Wes."

That seems to take the wind out of poncho boy's sails.

"How'd you get out?" the business guy asks me.

I look down at my leg. A dried patch of blood darkens the upper thigh of my coveralls. That says it all, really. He follows my gaze and decides to let it go.

"They seriously need us to *work*?" says poncho boy. "Why? Why not use more machines?"

"We're cheap," I say. "Cheaper than building machines."

"Not really," says business guy. "We cost resources. Food."

"There's plenty of food left over," I say. "In the cities. With the reduced population, I'm sure they can make our leftovers last for years."

"Great," says poncho boy. "This is just fucking great, man."

I notice the armored car has slowed down. The turret has quietly turned to face us. I shut up. These people are not my goal. My goals are nine and twelve years old and they are waiting for their mother.

I continue walking, alone.

———

I slip away while the others are being processed. A couple of patched-up Big Happys watch and play prerecorded commands while the line of people ditch their clothes and suitcases in a pile. I remember this: the shower, coveralls, bunk assignment, work assignment. And at the end, we were all marked.

My mark is still with me.

There is a subdermal tag the size of a grain of rice embedded deep in my right shoulder. After we're inside the camp and everyone has thrown off their belongings, I simply walk away. A Big Happy follows me as I cross the field toward the big metal building. But my mark identifies me as compliant. If I

were out of compliance, the machine would crush my windpipe with its bare hands. I've seen it happen.

The detectors all over the camp seem to recognize my
tag. No alarms are set off. Thank god they didn't blacklist my
number after dumping me off in that field. The Big Happy
retreats as I skirt around the camp toward the work barn.

The instant I walk through the door, a light on the wall
begins to flash. Shit. I'm not supposed to be here now. My
work detail isn't scheduled for today, or ever.

That Big Happy will be coming back.

I take it all in. This is the room I remember most. Clean-
swept pavement under a huge metal roof, as long as a football
field. When it rains outside, this room sounds like an audito-
rium filled with gentle applause. Row after row of fluorescent
lights hang over waist-high conveyor belts, stretching off into
the distance. There are hundreds of people in here. They wear
blue coveralls and paper face masks and stand alongside the
belts, taking pieces from bins and connecting them to what's
on the conveyor belt and then pushing them down the rollers.

It's an assembly line.

Moving fast, I jog up the line where I used to work. I
glance down to see that today they're building what we called
tanklets. They look sort of like the big four-legged mantis but
are the size of a small dog. We didn't know what they were at
all until one day a new guy, an Italian soldier, said that these
things—tanklets—hang on to the bellies of mantises and drop
off during battle. He said that sometimes broken ones could
be rewired and used as emergency equipment. Said they called
them ticklers.

The door I just came through slides open. A Big Happy
steps inside. All the people stop moving. The conveyor belts

have stopped. No one makes a move to help me. They stand as still and silent as blue statues. I don't bother to call for help. I know if I were in their place I wouldn't do anything either.

The Big Happy closes the door behind it. A boom echoes through the huge room as the bolts to all the doors slam shut. I'm trapped in here now, until I'm killed.

I jog along the assembly line, panting, leg throbbing. The Big Happy stalks toward me. It moves one careful step at a time, silent except for the soft grinding of motors. As I move down the line, I see the tanklets evolve from small black boxes to almost fully complete machines.

At the other end of the long building, I reach the door that leads to the dorms. I grab it and yank, but it's made of thick steel and locked tight. I spin around, back against the door. Hundreds of people watch, still holding their tools. Some are curious, but most are impatient. The harder you work, the faster the day goes. I am an interruption. And not that uncommon a one. Soon, my windpipe will be crushed and my body removed and these people will get back to what is left of their lives.

Mathilda and Nolan are on the other side of this door and they need me, but instead I'm going to die in front of all these broken people in paper masks.

I sink to my knees, out of strength. With my forehead pressed to the cool pavement, I hear only the steady click, click of the Big Happy walking toward me. I am so tired. I think that it will be a relief when it happens. A blessing to finally sleep.

But my body is a liar. I have to ignore the pain. I have to find the way out of this.

Pushing my hair out of my face, I frantically look around the room for something. An idea comes to me. Wincing from my injured thigh, I haul myself up and stagger down the tan-klet assembly line. I feel out each tanklet, looking for one that's at just the right stage. The people I get near step away from me.

The Big Happy is five feet away when I find the perfect tanklet. This one is just four spindly legs hanging from a teapot-sized abdomen. The power supply is attached, but the central nervous system is a few steps away. Instead, raw con-nector wires sprout from an open cavity in the thing's back.

I snatch up the tanklet and turn. The Big Happy is a foot away, arms out. Stumbling backward, I fall just out of reach and then limp toward the steel door. With shaking hands, I pull each tanklet leg out and press the abdomen against the door. My left arm quivers with the effort of holding up the solid hunk of metal. With my free hand I reach into the tan-klet's back and cross the wires.

Reflexively, the tanklet pulls its barbed legs into itself. With a wrenching squeal, they catch on the door and claw through the metal. I let go and the tanklet clanks to the ground, arms grasping a six-inch hunk of solid steel door. A ragged hole gapes where the doorknob and lock used to be. My arms are dead tired now, useless. The Big Happy is inches away, hand out, grippers splayed and ready to clamp down on whatever part of my body is closest.

With a kick, I send the mangled door flying open.

On the other side, haunted eyes stare at me. Old women and children are crowded into the dormitory. Wooden bunk beds stretch up to the ceiling.

I duck inside and slam the door shut behind me, pressing my back against it as the Big Happy tries to push its way in. Luckily, the machine can't get enough traction on the polished concrete floor to shove the door open right away.

"Mathilda!" I shout. "Nolan!"

The people stand in place, watching me. The machines know my ID number. They can track wherever I go and they won't stop until I'm dead. Now is the only chance I'll ever have to save my family.

And suddenly, there he is. My quiet little angel. Nolan stands in front of me, his dirty black hair ruffled. "Nolan," I exclaim. He runs to me and I grab him up and hug him. The door jumps into my back as the machine keeps pushing. More are surely coming.

Wrapping my hands around Nolan's delicate little face, I ask him, "Where's your sister, Nolan? Where's Mathilda?"

"She got hurt. After you left."

I swallow my fear, for Nolan. "Oh no, baby, I'm sorry. Where did she go? Take me there."

Nolan says nothing. He points.

With Nolan on my hip, I shove through the people and hurry down a hallway to the infirmary. Behind me, a couple of older women calmly push against the rattling door. There is no time to thank them, but I will remember their faces. I will pray for them.

I've never been in this long wooden room before. A narrow central walkway is partitioned off with hanging curtains on each side. I stride down the middle, yanking the curtains away to find my daughter. Each yank of a curtain reveals some new horror, but my brain doesn't register any of it. There is only one thing I will recognize now. One face.

And then I see her.

My baby lies on a gurney with a monster hovering over her head. It's some kind of surgery machine mounted on a metal arm, with a dozen plastic legs descending. Each robot leg is wrapped in sterile paper. At the tip of each leg is a tool: scalpels, hooks, soldering irons. The whole thing is moving in a blur—precise, jerky movements—like a spider weaving her web. The machine works on Mathilda's face without stopping or seeming to notice my presence.

"No!" I shriek. I set Nolan down and grab the base of the machine. With all my might, I lift it up off my daughter's face. Confused, the machine retracts its arms up into the air. In this split second, I shove the gurney with my foot and roll Mathilda's body away from the machine. The wound in my leg reopens and I feel a trickle of blood spiraling down my calf.

The Big Happy must be close by now.

I lean over the gurney and look at my daughter. Something is horribly wrong. Her eyes. Her beautiful eyes are gone.

"Mathilda?" I ask.

"Mom?" she says, smiling.

"Oh, baby, are you okay?"

"I think so," she says, frowning at the look on my face. "My eyes feel funny. What's wrong?" With shaking fingers, she touches the dull black metal that is now buried in her eye sockets.

"Are you okay, honey? Can you see?" I ask.

"Yes. I can. I can see inside," says Mathilda.

A sense of dread creeps into my belly. I'm too late. They've already hurt my little girl.

"What can you see, Mathilda?"

"I can see inside the machines," she says.

———

It takes only a few minutes to make it to the perimeter. I lift Mathilda and Nolan over the top. The fence is only five feet high. It's part of the lure to would-be saviors on the outside looking in. The hidden sentry guns that lurk in the field are designed to be the real security enforcers.

"Come on, Mom," urges Mathilda, safely on the other side.

But my leg is bleeding badly now, blood pooling in my shoe and spilling over onto the ground. After getting Nolan over the fence, I'm too exhausted to move. With every last shred of effort, I keep myself conscious. I wrap my fingers through the chain link and hold myself up and look at my babies for the last time. "I will always love you. No matter what."

"What do you mean? Come on. Please," Mathilda says.

My vision is going away, getting smaller. I'm watching the world now through two pinpricks—the rest is darkness.

"Take Nolan and go, Mathilda."

"Mom, I can't. There are guns. I can *see* them."

"Concentrate, honey. You have a gift now. See where the guns are. Where they can shoot. Find a safe path. Take Nolan by the hand and don't let go."

"Mommy," says Nolan.

I shut down all my emotion. I have to. I can hear the whine of tanklet motors as they swarm the field behind me. I sag against the fence. From somewhere, I find the strength to shout.

"Mathilda Rose Perez! This is not an argument. You take your brother and you go. Run. Don't stop until you're very far away from here. Do you hear me? Run. Do it *right now* or I will be very angry with you."

Mathilda flinches at my voice. She takes a hesitant step away. I can feel my heart breaking. It's a numb feeling, radiating out of my chest and crushing all thought—eating my fear.

Then Mathilda's mouth squeezes into a line. Her brow settles down into a familiar stubborn frown over those dull, monstrous implants. "Nolan," she says. "Hold on to my hand no matter what. Don't let go. We're going to run now. Super fast, okay?"

Nolan nods, takes her hand.

My little soldiers. Survivors.

"I love you, Mommy," says Mathilda.

And then my babies are gone.

No further record exists of Laura Perez. Mathilda Perez, however, is another matter.

—CORMAC WALLACE, MIL#GHA217

6. BAND-E-AMIR

That's not a weapon, is it?

SPC. PAUL BLANTON

NEW WAR + 10 MONTHS

In the drawn-out aftermath of Zero Hour in Afghanistan, Specialist Paul Blanton not only survived but thrived. As described in the following remembrance, Paul discovered an artifact so profound that it altered the course of the New War—and he did it while on the run for his life in an incredibly hostile environment.

It is hard to determine whether the young soldier was lucky or shrewd, or both. Personally, I believe that anyone who is directly related to Lonnie Wayne Blanton is already halfway to being a hero.

—CORMAC WALLACE, MIL#GHA217

Jabar and I lay flat on a ridge, binoculars out.

It's about ten in the morning. Dry season in Afghanistan. A half hour ago, we caught a burst of avtomat communication. It was just one airborne flurry of information, probably to a roving eye on the ground. But it could also have been to a full-on tank. Or something even worse. Jabar and I decided to dig in here and wait for the thing to show up, whatever it is.

Yeah, pretty much a suicide mission.

After the shit went down, the natives never trusted me for a second. Jabar and I were forbidden to go near the main encampments. Most of the Afghan civilians fled to these man-made caves in Bamiyan Province. Real ancient shit. Some desperate-ass people carved 'em out of sheer mountain walls, and for about a thousand years they've been the go-to spot for every civil war, famine, plague, and invasion.

Technology changes, but people stay the same.

The old crusty guys with Santa Claus beards and eyebrows trying to escape up their foreheads sat around in a circle and sipped tea and yelled at each other. They were wondering why avtomat drones were out here, of all places. To find out, they sent *us* to track communications. It was a punishment for Jabar, but he never forgot that I saved his life at Zero Hour. Good kid. Terrible at growing a beard. But a good kid.

This place they stuck us, Band-e-Amir—it's so pretty it hurts your eyes. Sky blue lakes pooled up between stark brown mountains. All of it wrapped in bright red limestone cliffs. We're so high up and the atmosphere's so thin that it messes with you. I swear, the light does something funny up here that it doesn't do other places. The shadows are too crisp. Details are too sharp. Like an alien planet.

Jabar spots it first, nudges me.

A biped avtomat walks a narrow dirt road over a mile away, crossing the scrubland. I can tell that it used to be a SAP. Probably a Hoplite model, judging from the height and the light gait. But there's no telling. Lately, the machines have been changing. For example, the biped down there isn't wearing clothes like a SAP would. It's made of some kind of dirt-colored fibrous material instead. It walks at a steady five miles per hour, shadow stretching out on the dirt behind, as mechanical as a tank rolling across desert sands.

"Is it a soldier?" asks Jabar.

"I don't know what it is anymore," I reply.

Jabar and I decide to follow it.

We wait until it's almost out of range. Even when I was running a SAP crew, we kept a drone eye on the square klick around our unit. I'm glad I know the procedure, so I can stay just out of range. Good thing about avtomata is they don't take an extra step if they don't have to. Tend to travel in straight lines or along easy paths. Makes them predictable and easier to track.

Staying up high, we travel along the ridge in the same direction as the avto. Soon, the sun comes out in full force, but our dirty cotton robes wick away the sweat. It's actually kind of nice to walk with Jabar for a while. A place this big makes you feel small. And it gets lonely out here real quick.

Jabar and I are traveling across the broken landscape with just our backpacks, robes, and these whiplike antennae that are about eight feet long and made of thick black plastic that wobbles with every step we take. They must have been scavenged off some machine or other over the last fifty years of war out here. Using our antennae, we can pick up avtomat radio comms and figure out their directionality. This way, we track avtomat movements and send warnings to our people. Too bad we can't listen in. But there's not a chance in hell we could crack the avto encryption scheme. It's still worth it, though, to have an idea where the bad guys are.

Our robes blend in with the rocks. Still, we usually stay a half mile apart from each other, minimum. Being so far apart helps determine the direction of avtomat radio communications. Plus, if one of us gets hit by a missile, the other can have time to hoof it or hide.

After five or six hours following the biped, we spread out and take a final reading for the day. It's a slow process. I just sit down in my pile of robes, prop my stick up into the air, and put on my headphones to listen for the crackle of communication. My machine logs the time of arrival automatically. Jabar's doing the same thing a half mile away. In a little while, we'll compare numbers to get a loose direction.

Sitting out here in the sun, there's a lot of time to think about what might have been. I scouted my old base once. Windblown rubble. Rusted hunks of abandoned machinery. There's nothing to go back to.

After a half hour sitting cross-legged and watching the sun drop over those sparkling mountains, a comm burst hits. My stick blinks—it's logged. I flash my cracked hand mirror to Jabar and he reciprocates. We start the hike back toward each other.

It looks like the biped avto went just over the next ridge and stopped. They don't sleep, so who knows what it's up to over there. It must not have sensed us, because it's not raining bullets. As it gets dark, the ground radiates all the day's heat into the sky. The heat is our only camouflage; without it we've got no choice but to stay put. We pull out our sleeping bags and bivouac for the night.

Jabar and I lay there, side by side, in the cold dark that's getting colder. The black sky is opening up overhead and out here, I swear to god, there's more stars than there is night.

"Paul," whispers Jabar. "I am worried. This one does not seem like the others."

"It's a modified SAP unit. Those were pretty common, before. I worked with lots of them."

"Yes, I remember. They were the pacifists who grew fangs. But that one was not made of metal. It had no weapons at all."

"And that worries you? That it was *un*armed?"

"It is different. Anything different is bad."

I stare into the heavens and listen to the wind on the rocks and think of the billions of particles of air colliding against each other above me. So many possibilities. All the horrible potential of the universe.

"The avtomata are changing, Jabar," I say finally. "If different is bad, buddy, then I think we're in for a whole lot of bad."

————

We had no idea how much things were changing.

Next morning, Jabar and I packed up and crept over the broken rocks to the next ridge. Over it, another eye-searing azure lake lapping a white-stone shore.

Band-e-Amir used to be a national park, you know, but we're still in Afghanistan. Meaning that a bronze plaque never stopped the locals from fishing here with dynamite. Not the friendliest approach, but I've used a trotline or two myself back in Oklahoma. Even with the dynamite and leaky gasoline boats and sewer lines, Band-e-Amir stood the test of time.

It outlasted the locals.

"Avtomat must have come this way," I say, peering down the rocky slope. The jagged slate boulders vary in size from basketball to dinner table. Some are stable. Most aren't.

"Can you make it?" I ask Jabar.

He nods and claps one hand against his dusty combat boot. American-issue. Probably looted by his tribe members from my base. So it goes.

"That's great, Jabar. Where'd you get those?"

The kid just smiles at me, the world's most haggard teenager.

"All right, let's go," I say, cautiously stepping over the lip of the ridge. The boulders are so unsteady and steep that we have to go down facing the slope, pressing our sweaty palms against the rocks and testing each step before we take it.

It's a damn good thing we *do* go backward.

After thirty minutes, we're only halfway down. I'm picking my way through the rubble—kicking rocks to see if they'll move—when I hear some rocks falling farther up. Jabar and I freeze, necks craned as we scan the gray rock face for movement.

Nothing.

"Something's coming," whispers Jabar.

"Let's move," I say, stepping now with more urgency.

Keeping our heads up and eyes open, the two of us descend over the wobbling rocks. Every few minutes, we hear the clack, clack of more rocks falling from above us. Each time, we stop and scan for motion. Each time we find nothing.

Something invisible is coming down the slope, stalking us. This thing is taking its time, moving quiet and staying hidden. The oldest part of my brain senses the danger and floods my body with adrenaline. There's a predator coming, it says. Run the fuck away.

But if I move any faster, I'll fall and die in an avalanche of cold slate.

Now my legs are trembling as I inch my way over the rocks. Glancing down, I see there's still at least another half hour before we reach bottom. Shit, that's too long. I slip and gash my knee open on a rock. I bite down hard on the curse before it gets out.

Then I hear a low, animal moan.

It's Jabar. The kid crouches on the rocks ten feet up, lying stock-still. His eyes are fixed on something above us. I don't think he even knows that he's making that sound.

I *still* don't see anything.

"What, Jabar? What's there, man?"

"Koh peshak," he hisses.

"Mountain what? What's on the mountain, Jabar?"

"Uh, how do you say . . . snow cat."

"Snow? What? Did you say a *fucking snow leopard*? They live here?"

"We thought they were gone."

"Extinct?"

"Not anymore."

With an effort, I refocus my eyes on the rocks above us. Finally, I catch the twitch of a tail and the predator emerges from concealment. A pair of unblinking silver eyes are watching me. The leopard knows that we've spotted it. It bounds toward us over the unstable rocks, heavy muscles quivering with each impact. Quiet, determined death is on its way.

I scrabble for my rifle.

Jabar turns around and slides toward me on his ass, wailing in panic. But he's too late. The snow leopard is suddenly just a few feet away, landing on its front paws with a great bushy tail outstretched as a counterweight. That wide flat nose collapses into a wrinkled snarl, and white canines flash. The cat gets hold of Jabar from behind and yanks his body back.

Finally, I get my rifle up. I fire high to avoid Jabar. The cat shakes him back and forth, growls radiating from deep in its throat like the idle of a diesel engine. When my bullet hits it in the flank, the cat screeches and lets go of Jabar. It coils back, tail protectively wrapping around its forelegs. It snarls and screams, looking for what caused so much pain.

Jabar's body falls onto the rocks, limp.

The leopard is divinely terrible and beautiful, and it absolutely belongs here. But this is life or death. My heart breaks as I unload my rifle on the magnificent creature. Red stains spread through the mottled fur. The big cat falls back onto the rocks, tail lashing. Those silver eyes squeeze shut and the snarl is frozen forever on its face.

I feel numb as the last echo of gunfire races away across the mountains. Then, Jabar grabs my leg and pulls himself up to a sitting position. He shrugs off his backpack, groaning. I drop to a knee and put one hand on his shoulder. I pull his robes back away from his neck to see two long stripes of blood. His back and shoulder have been shallowly filleted, but otherwise he is unharmed.

"It ate your backpack, you lucky bastard," I say to him.

He doesn't know whether to grin or cry and neither do I.

I'm glad the kid is alive. His people would execute me straightaway if I was dumb enough to come back without him. Plus, he's apparently got a knack for spotting snow leopards just before they pounce. That could come in handy someday.

"Let's get off this fuckin' rock," I say.

But Jabar doesn't stand up. He stays there, crouched, staring at the bleeding corpse of the snow leopard. One of his dirt-smudged hands snakes out and briefly touches the cat's paw.

"What is this?" he asks.

"I had to kill it, man. No choice," I respond.

"No," says Jabar. *"This."*

He leans farther toward the cat and pushes its great bloody head to the side. Now I see something that I can't explain. Honest to god, I just don't know what to make of it.

There, just under the cat's jaw, is some kind of avtomat-made collar. A pale gray band made of hard plastic is wrapped around the cat's neck. At one point, the strip widens into a marble-sized orb. On the back of this circular part, a tiny red light pulses.

It has to be some kind of radio collar.

"Jabar. Go fifty meters lateral and plant your stick. I'm going the other way. Let's find out where this data goes."

By midafternoon, Jabar and I have the cat well behind us, buried under some rocks. I've dressed the wounds on Jabar's back. He didn't make a sound, probably ashamed of his hollering from before. He doesn't know that I was too scared to scream. And I don't tell him.

The trajectory of the radio collar transmissions leads across the nearest lake to a small inlet. We move quickly along the shore, being sure to stay on the hard-packed dirt close to the increasingly sheer mountain walls.

Jabar spots them first: footprints.

The modified SAP unit is close. Its prints track around the next bend, directly to where the radio transmissions lead us. Jabar and I look each other in the eyes—we've reached our destination.

"*Muafaq b'ashid*, Paul," he says.

"Good luck to you, too, buddy."

We walk around the corner and come face-to-face with the next stage of avtomat evolution.

It sits half submerged in the lake—the biggest avtomat imaginable. It's like a building or a giant gnarled tree. The machine has dozens of petal-like sheaths of metal for legs. Each plate is the size of a wing off a B-52 Stratofortress and covered in moss and barnacles and vines and flowers. I notice they flap slowly, movement barely visible. Butterflies and dragonflies and indigenous insects of all sorts flit across the grassy plates. Higher up, the main trunk is composed of dozens of taut cords that stretch into the sky, twisting around each other almost randomly.

The top of the avtomat towers in the sky. An almost fractal

pattern of barklike structures whirls and twines in an organic mass of what looks like branches. Thousands of birds nest in the safety of these limbs. Wind sighs through the tangled boughs, pushing them back and forth.

And on the lower levels, stepping carefully, are a few dozen of the biped avtomata. They are inspecting the other life-forms, leaning over and watching, prodding and pulling. Like gardeners. Each of them covers a different area. They are muddy, wet, and some are covered in moss themselves. This doesn't seem to bother them.

"That's not a weapon, is it?" I ask Jabar.

"The opposite. It is life," he says.

I notice that the uppermost branches bristle with what must be antennae, swaying in the wind like bamboo. The only recognizably metallic surface is nestled there—a gaping, wind tunnel–shaped dome. It points to the northeast.

"Tight-beam communication," I say, pointing. "Probably microwave based."

"What could this be?" asks Jabar.

I take a closer look. Every niche and crevice of the colossal, creeping monster teems with life. The water below flickers with spawning fish. A haze of flying insects clouds the lower petals, while rodents creep through the folds of the central trunk. The structure is riddled with burrows and covered in animal shit and dancing with sunlight—alive.

"Some kind of research station. Maybe the avtomata are studying living things. Animals and bugs and birds."

"This is not good," murmurs Jabar.

"Nope. But if they're collecting information, they must be sending it somewhere, right?"

Jabar lifts up his antenna, grinning.

I block the sun with one hand over my eyes and squint at

the towering, shining column. That's a lot of data. Wherever it's going, I'll bet there's one smart fucking avtomat on the other end.

"Jabar. Go east fifty meters and plant your stick. I'll do the same. We're gonna figure out where our enemy lives."

Paul was correct. What he and Jabar had found was not a weapon but a biological research platform. The massive amount of data it collected was being sent via tight-beam transmission to a remote location in Alaska.

At this time, a little less than a year since Zero Hour, humankind had found the whereabouts of Big Rob. Postwar records indicate that although Paul and Jabar were not the first to discover the whereabouts of Archos, they were the first to share that information with humanity—thanks to help from an unlikely source half a world away.

—CORMAC WALLACE, MIL#GHA217

7. Backbone

It's not me, Arrtrad. . . . I'm sorry.

Lurker

NEW WAR + 11 MONTHS

As Brightboy squad continued to trek across the United States toward Gray Horse, we marched in an information vacuum. A lack of satellite communication plagued the survivors of Zero Hour, preventing widespread groups of people from collaborating and fighting together. Hundreds of satellites fell from the sky like shooting stars at Zero Hour, but many more remained—operational but jammed.

The teenager called Lurker pinpointed the source of this jamming signal. His attempt to do something about it sent reverberations through human and Rob history. In the following pages, I describe what happened to Lurker based on street camera recordings; exoskeleton data logs; and, partially, the first-person account of a submind of Archos itself.

—CORMAC WALLACE, MIL#GHA217

"A single mile, Arrtrad," Lurker says. "We can make it one single fucking mile."

From the security camera image, I can see Lurker and his middle-aged comrade, Arrtrad. They stand on a weed-filled street alongside the Thames, within running distance to the safety of their houseboat. Lurker, the teenager, has grown his hair and his beard out. He's gone from a shaved head to being the jungle man of Borneo. Arrtrad looks and sounds the same as ever—worried.

"Straight through Trafalgar Square?" asks Arrtrad, pale face lined with anxiety. "They'll see us. They're bound to. If the cars don't track us, then those little . . . things will."

Lurker mimics Arrtrad's nasal voice without mercy. "Oh, let's save the people. We've been sitting on this boat for ages. La-di-fucking-da."

Arrtrad lets his gaze drop.

"I schemed," says Lurker. "I plotted. I found a way, brother. What happened to you? Where have your balls gone?"

Arrtrad speaks to the pavement. "I've seen it out scavenging, Lurker. All this time, the cars still sit on the streets. Start their engines once a month and idle for ten minutes. They're all ready for us, mate. Just waiting."

"Arrtrad, come over here," says Lurker. "Have a look at yourself."

The security camera pans over as Lurker motions at Arrtrad to step next to a panel of sun-baked glass attached to a mostly intact building. The tint is peeling off, but the glass wall still holds a bluish reflection. Arrtrad steps over and the two look at themselves.

A data readout informs me that they first activated the exoskeletons a month ago. Military hardware. Full body. Without a person inside, the machines look like a messy pile of wiry black arms and legs connected to a backpack. Strapped into the powered machines, the two men each stand seven feet tall, strong as bears. The thin black tubes running along their arms and legs are made of titanium. The motorized joints are powered by purring diesel engines. I notice that the feet are curved, flexible spikes that add a solid foot to their height.

Grinning, Lurker flexes for the mirror. Each of his forearms has a wicked notched spike curving out, used to pick up heavy objects without crushing human fingers. Each exoskeleton has a roll cage that arcs gracefully over its occupant's head, with a bluish-white LED burning in the middle of the frame.

Together in the mirror, Arrtrad and Lurker look like a couple of supersoldiers. Well, more like a couple of pale Englishmen who've been living on sardines and who happen to have scavenged some abandoned military technology.

Either way, they are most definitely badass.

"See yourself, Arrtrad?" Lurker asks. "You're a beast, mate. You're a killer. We can do this."

Lurker tries to clap Arrtrad on the shoulder, and the other man flinches away girlishly. "Careful!" shouts Arrtrad. "There's no armor on these things. Keep your hooks away from me."

"Right, brother." Lurker chuckles. "Look, the British Telecom Tower is one mile away. And it's jamming our satellites. If people could communicate, even for a little while, we'd have a fighting chance."

Arrtrad looks at Lurker, skeptical. "Why are you really doing this?" he asks. "Why are you putting your life—our lives—on the line?"

For a long moment, there is only the *chup-chup* of the two diesel engines idling. "Remember when we used the phones to torment people?" Lurker asks.

"Yeah," responds Arrtrad slowly.

"We thought we were different than everyone else. Better. Thought we were taking advantage of a bunch of fools. But we were wrong. Turns out we're all in the same boat. Metaphorically speaking."

Arrtrad cracks a small smile. "But we don't owe nobody nothing. You said so yourself."

"Oh, but we do," Lurker says. "We didn't know it, but we were running up a tab. We owe a debt, mate. And now it's time to pay up. Only phreaks like us would know about this tower. How important it is. If we can destroy it, we'll help thousands of people. Maybe millions."

"And you owe them?"

"I owe *you*," says Lurker. "I'm sorry I didn't warn London. Maybe they wouldn't have believed. But that's never stopped me. Christ, I could have co-opted the bloody emergency alert system all on my own. Shouted a warning from the rooftops. Doesn't matter now. Most of all—I'm sorry I didn't tell you. I'm sorry for . . . your girls, mate. All of it."

On mention of his children, Arrtrad turns away from Lurker, blinking back tears. Eyeing his own sinuous reflection, he shrugs one arm out of his exo-suit and smoothes back the puff of blond hair on his balding head. The exoskeleton arm automatically settles down to his side. Arrtrad's cheeks puff out as he exhales loudly, slipping his hand back into the metal arm straps.

"You make a fine point," he says.

"Yeah," says Lurker. Then he taps Arrtrad on his metal shoulder with one wicked blade. "Besides," he asks, "you don't really want to live to old age with *me*? On a bloody *houseboat*?"

A slow smile spreads across Arrtrad's birdlike face. "You do make a fine fucking point."

The streets of central London are mostly empty. Attacks came too fast and too organized for most citizens to react. By law, *all* the autos had full-drive capability. Also by law, hardly anybody had guns. And the closed-circuit television network was compromised from the start, giving the machines an intimate view of every public space in the city.

In London, the citizens were too safe to survive.

Visual records indicate that automated trash trucks filled dumps outside the city with corpses for months after Zero Hour. Now there's nobody left to destroy the place. No survivors brave the streets. And nobody is around to see two pale men—one young and one old—encased in military exoskeletons as they leap in ten-foot strides over the weedy pavement.

The first attack comes only a few minutes in, as they sprint through Trafalgar Square. The fountains are drained and filled with dead leaves and blown trash. A couple of broken bicycles lie out but that's it. Covered in roosting birds, the granite statue of Lord Nelson in his admiral's hat looks down from a hundred-and-fifty-foot-tall column as the two men bound across the plaza on elastic foot blades.

They should have known there was too much wide-open space.

Lurker notices the smart car a couple of seconds before it can ram into Arrtrad from behind. With one leap, he closes the twenty feet between them and lands on the run beside the speeding car. A blossom of mold has spread across the top of it. Without a regular car wash, nature is eating up the old stuff.

Too bad there are plenty of replacements.

On landing, Lurker hunches down and drives his foot-long forearm blades into the driver's side door of the car and lifts. Steam jets from the hip and knee joints of his exoskeleton, and the diesel engine surges as he wrenches the whole side of the car upward. While on its two right wheels, the car veers but still manages to clip Arrtrad's right rear leg midstride. The car flips over and rolls away, but Arrtrad is off balance; he trips.

Falling down at a twenty-mile-an-hour jog is serious business. Luckily, the exoskeleton can tell that it's falling. Leaving Arrtrad no choice in the matter, the machine jerks his arms close to his body and his legs curl into fetal position. The roll cage becomes pertinent. In this crash pose, the exoskeleton rolls over a few times, then plows over a fire hydrant and comes to a stop.

No water comes out of the decapitated hydrant.

By the time Lurker lands next to him, Arrtrad is already climbing to his feet. The pudgy blond man stands up and I can see he is *grinning*, chest heaving.

"Thanks," he says to Lurker.

There's blood on his teeth but Arrtrad doesn't seem to care. He pops up and sprints away. Lurker follows, on the lookout for more cars. New ones appear, but they're slow, not ready. They can't track the speeding men as they leap through alleys and tear across parks.

Lurker put it best: It's only a single fucking mile.

From a new camera angle, I see the cylindrical British Telecom tower looming in the blue sky like a Tinkertoy. Antennae bristle from the top and a ring of microwave transmitter dishes wrap just below, pointing away in every direction. It's the biggest TV switch station in London and it's got whole highways of fiber-optic cable buried underneath. When it comes to communications, all roads lead to the BTT.

The wiry exoskeletons appear and dart around the side of the building, stopping in front of a steel door. Arrtrad leans the scratched-up frame of his exo against the wall, huffing and puffing. "Why not just destroy it from here?" he asks.

Lurker flexes his arms and jounces his head back and forth to loosen up his neck. He seems exhilarated by the run. "The fiber is buried in there in a concrete tube. Protected. Besides, that would be a bit crass, wouldn't it? We're better than that, brother. We'll use this place against the machines. Pick up the phone and make a call. It's what we do best, isn't it? And this is the biggest goddamn phone in the hemisphere."

Lurker nods toward a bulge in his pocket.

"And if all else fails . . . kaboom," he says.

Then Lurker jams his forearm blades into the steel door and wrenches them back out, leaving a rip in the metal. A couple more stabs and the door swings open.

"Onward," says Lurker, and the two step inside a narrow hallway. They hunch over and creep through the dark passage, trying not to breathe their own diesel fumes. In the low light, the LEDs embedded in the curve of metal over their heads brighten up.

"What are we looking for?" asks Arrtrad.

"The fiber," Lurker whispers. "We'll want to get down to the fiber. Best-case, we hijack it and send a signal for all the robots to jump into the river. Worst case, we blast the jammer and free up the communications satellites."

At the end of the hallway is another steel door. Gently, Lurker pushes it open. His LEDs dim as Lurker pokes his head out.

From the built-in camera in the exoskeleton, I see that the machines have almost entirely hollowed out the interior of the cylindrical building. Shafts of sunlight arc in through fifteen stories of dirty glass windows. The light falls through dead air and shatters through a latticework of rebar and radial support beams. Bird calls echo through the cavernous space. Vines and grass and mold are growing on the mounds of trash and debris that cover every surface of the ground floor.

"Bloody hell," Lurker mutters.

In the middle of this arboretum, a solid cement cylinder juts straight up through the entire height of the building. Encrusted with vines, the pillar disappears into gloomy heights above. It is the final support structure holding this place up. The backbone.

"Building's gone native," says Arrtrad.

"Well, there's no way to reach the upper transmitters from here," Lurker says, looking at the heaps of moldering rubble that used to be the floors and walls of upper stories. "Doesn't matter. We've got to get to the computers. Base of the building. Down."

Something small and gray scuttles over a pile of moldy papers and under a tangled heap of rusted office chairs. Arrtrad and Lurker look at each other, wary.

Careful of his forearm spike, Lurker raises a finger to his lips. Together, the men creep out of the hallway and into the arboretum. Their feet blades indent the moss and rotting trash, leaving plain tracks behind.

A blue door waits in the base of the central pillar, dwarfed by the sheer size of the hollowed-out building around it. They move to the door at a fast trot, keeping noise to a minimum. Arrtrad rears back to stab the door, but Lurker stops him with a gesture. Pulling his arm out of the exoskeleton, Lurker reaches down and turns the doorknob. With a yank, the door opens on creaky hinges. I doubt it has been opened since the war began.

Inside, there is dirt in the hallway for a few steps and then things get very clean. The faint roar of air-conditioning grows louder as they walk farther down the cement hallway. The floor is angled downward, toward a square of bright light at the end of the tunnel.

"It's as if we've died," says Arrtrad.

Finally, they reach the bottom: a cylindrical white clean room with twenty-foot ceilings. It is filled with row after row of humming racks of equipment. The stacks of gear are arrayed in concentric circles, each row getting shorter the closer it is to the center of the room. Rows of fluorescent lights shine down, starkly illuminating every detail of the room. Condensation starts to form on the black metal of the exoskeletons and Arrtrad shivers.

"Plenty of juice down here, anyway," says Lurker.

The two men walk inside, disoriented by the millions of stuttering green and red lights that line the towers of hardware. In the center of the room is their goal: a black hole in the floor the size of a manhole, metal stairs poking out of the top—the fiber hub.

Four-legged robots made of white plastic climb up and down the racks, slipping between stacks of whirring equipment like lizards. Some of these lizard robots use their forelegs to stroke the equipment, moving wires or pressing buttons. It reminds me of those little birds that land on hippos, cleaning them of parasites.

"C'mon," Lurker murmurs to Arrtrad. They stride together to the hole in the floor. "Down there is the answer to all our problems."

But Arrtrad doesn't respond. He's already seen it.

Archos.

Silent as the grim reaper, the machine hovers over the hole. It looks like an enormous eye, made of circular rings of shimmering metal. Yellow wires snake away from the edges like a lion's mane. A flawless glass lens is nestled in the center of the rings, smoky black. It watches without blinking.

And yet it is not Archos. Not fully. Only a part of the intelligence that is Archos has been put inside this menacing machine: a local subbrain.

Lurker strains against his exoskeleton, but he can't move his arms or legs. The motors in his suit have frozen up. His face goes pale as he realizes what must have happened.

The exoskeleton has an external communications port.

"Arrtrad, run!" Lurker screams.

Arrtrad. The poor bastard. He's shaking, trying desperately to yank his arms out of the harness. But he's got no control either. Both the exoskeletons have been hacked.

Floating above in the harsh fluorescent light, the giant eye watches without any reaction.

Motors grind in Lurker's suit, and he grunts pitifully with the effort of resisting. But there's no helping it: He's a puppet caught in the strings of that hanging monster.

Before Lurker can react, his right arm jerks away and sends a wicked forearm blade singing through the air. The blade sinks through Arrtrad's chest and into the metal spine of his exoskeleton. Arrtrad gapes at Lurker in surprise. In arterial surges, his blood wicks down the end of the blade and soaks Lurker's sleeve.

"It's not me, Arrtrad," Lurker whispers, voice cracking. "It's not me. I'm sorry, mate."

And the blade yanks itself back out. Arrtrad takes one sucking gasp for air and then collapses with a hole in his chest. His exoskeleton protects him as he goes limp, lowering itself gently to the ground. Splayed on the floor, its motors shut down and the machine goes still and silent as a pool of dark blood spreads around it.

"Oh you bastard," Lurker calls up to the expressionless robot watching from above. The machine noiselessly lowers itself down to where he stands, his arm blade slick with blood. The machine positions itself directly in front of Lurker's face and a delicate-looking stick—some kind of probe—extends from under its smoky eye. Lurker strains to move away, but his rigid exoskeleton holds him in place.

Then the machine speaks in that strange, familiar child's voice. From the flash of recognition on his face, I see that Lurker remembers this voice from the phone.

"Lurker?" it asks, an electrical glow spreading through the rings.

In small increments, Lurker begins to wriggle his left hand out of the exoskeleton harness. "Archos," he says.

"You have changed. You're not a coward anymore."

"You've changed, too," Lurker says, watching the concentric rings languidly revolve and counterrevolve. His left hand is almost free. "Funny the difference a year can make."

"I'm sorry it has to be this way," says the boy voice.

"And what way is that?" Lurker asks, trying to keep the thing distracted from his squirming left hand.

Then his hand comes free. Lurker thrusts his arm out and grabs hold of the delicate feeler, trying to break it off. The shoulder joint of his right arm pops as he struggles against a sudden push from the exoskeleton. He can only watch as his right arm swings through the air and, in one sharp movement, slices his left hand off at the wrist.

A fan spray of blood spatters across the face of the floating machine.

In shock, Lurker yanks the rest of his body out of the exoskeleton. The empty left arm of the machine tries to slice at him, but the elbow is at an awkward angle and he is able to squirm away. Dodging another forearm blade, he drops to the ground and rolls through Arrtrad's spreading blood. The exoskeleton is off balance for a split second, missing its human counterweight. It's just enough time for Lurker to wriggle over the lip of the hole.

Ching.

A forearm blade bites into the floor inches from Lurker's face as he shoves himself into the hole, cradling his injured arm to his chest. Half falling, he drops down into the darkness.

The unmanned exoskeleton immediately picks up the fallen exoskeleton with Arrtrad's corpse inside. Cradling the bleeding pile of metal, the exoskeleton walks and then sprints out the door.

Hanging over the hole, the complex piece of machinery watches patiently. Lights on the equipment racks begin to flicker intensely as a flood of data pours out of the tower. A last-minute backup.

Long moments pass before a hoarse voice echoes up from the dark hole. "Catch you in the funny pages, mate," says Lurker.

And the world turns white and then to darkest black.

The destruction of the London fiber hub broke the Rob stranglehold on satellite communications long enough to allow humankind to regroup. Lurker never seemed like a very pleasant guy, and I can't say I would have enjoyed meeting him, but the kid was a hero. I know this because in the moment before the British Telecom Tower exploded, Lurker recorded a fifteen-second message that saved humankind from certain destruction.

—CORMAC WALLACE, MIL#GHA217

PART FOUR
Awakening

John Henry said to his captain,
"A man, he ain't nothing but a man,
But before I'd let that steam drill
    beat me down,
Oh, I'd die with the hammer in my
    hand."

"John Henry," c. 1920

I. Transhuman

It's dangerous to be people-blind.

Mathilda Perez

NEW WAR + 12 MONTHS
A year into the New War, Brightboy squad finally arrived at Gray Horse, Oklahoma. Across the world, billions of people had been eradicated from urban areas, and millions more were trapped in forced-labor camps. Much of the rural population we encountered were locked in isolated, personal battles to survive against the elements.

Information is spotty, but hundreds of small pockets of resistance seemed to have formed worldwide. As our squad settled into Gray Horse, a young prisoner named Mathilda Perez was escaping from Camp Scarsdale. She fled to New York City with her little brother, Nolan, in tow. In this recollection, Mathilda (age twelve) describes her interaction with the NYC resistance group, headed by Marcus and Dawn Johnson.

—CORMAC WALLACE, MIL#GHA217

I didn't think Nolan was hurt that bad at first.

We made it to the city and then we ran around a corner

and something exploded and Nolan fell down. But he got right back up. We were running so fast together, hand in hand. Just like I promised Mom. We ran until we were safe.

It was only later, when we were walking again, that I noticed how pale Nolan was. Later, I found out that tiny splinters of metal were stuck in his lower back. But there he stood, shaking like a leaf.

"Are you okay, Nolan?" I ask.

"Yes," he says. "My back hurts."

He's so little and brave that it makes me want to cry. But I can't cry. Not anymore.

The machines at Camp Scar hurt me. They took my eyes. But in return, they gave me a new kind of eyes. Now I can see more than ever. Vibrations in the ground light up like ripples on water. I notice the heat trails left on the pavement by wheels that have come and gone. But my favorite thing is watching the ribbons of light crisscrossing the sky, like messages printed on banners. These beams are the machines talking to one another. Sometimes, if I squint really hard, I can even make out what they are saying.

People are harder to see.

I can't really see Nolan anymore, only the heat from his breath, the muscles in his face, and how he won't look me in the eyes anymore. It doesn't matter. If I have people eyes or machine eyes or tentacles—I'm still Nolan's big sister. It scared me the first time I saw through his skin, so I know how he feels when he sees my new eyes. But I don't care.

Mom was right. Nolan is the only brother I've got and the only one I'll ever have.

After we left Camp Scar, me and Nolan saw tall buildings and we walked toward them, thinking maybe we'd find people. But there was nobody around. Or if there were, I guess they were hiding. Pretty soon, we reached the buildings. Most of them were all messed up. There were suitcases in the streets and dogs running in packs and sometimes the curled-up bodies of dead people. Something bad happened here.

Something bad happened everywhere.

The closer we got to the really tall buildings, the more I could *feel* them—the machines, hiding in dark places or running through the streets on the lookout for people. Streaks of light flashed overhead. Machines talking.

Some of the lights blinked regular, every couple of minutes or seconds. Those are the hiding machines, checking in with their bosses. "I'm still here," they say. "Waiting."

I hate these machines. They make traps and then wait for people. It's not fair. A robot can just sit and wait to hurt somebody. And it can wait forever and ever.

But Nolan is hurt and we need to find help fast. I steer us away from the trap makers and the travelers. But my new eyes don't show me everything. They can't show me people things. Now, I only see the *machine things*.

It's dangerous to be people-blind.

The way looked clear. No machine chatter. No shimmering heat trails. Then, small ripples pulsed over the ground from around the corner of a brick building. Instead of a slow swell like from something rolling, they were bouncy, like something big walking.

"It's not safe here," I say.

I put an arm around Nolan's shoulders and steer him into a building. We crouch next to a dust-coated window. I nudge Nolan to sit on the floor.

"Stay down," I say. "Something is coming."

He nods. His face is so pale now.

Kneeling, I press my face into a broken-out corner of the window and hold very still. The vibrations are growing on the crushed pavement outside, pulses of static flooding from somewhere out of view. A monster is coming down the road. Soon, I will be able to see it, whether I want to or not.

I hold my breath.

Somewhere outside, a hawk cries. A long black leg pokes into view, only a foot or two outside the window. It has a sharp point on the end and flake-shaped barbs carved underneath, like a big bug leg. Most of the thing is cold, but the joints are hot where it has been moving. As it slides farther into view, I see that it is really a much longer leg folded in on itself— all coiled up and ready to strike. Somehow, it floats over the ground, aimed straight out.

Then, I see a pair of warm human hands. The hands are holding the leg like a rifle. It's a black woman, wearing gray rags and a pair of black goggles over her eyes. She holds the coiled leg thing out like a weapon, one hand wrapped around a homemade grip. I see a shiny, melted spot on the back end of the leg and realize that this leg has been cut off some kind of big walking machine. The woman doesn't see me; she keeps walking.

Nolan coughs quietly.

The woman spins around and on instinct she levels the leg at the window. She pulls a trigger, and the coiled leg unfolds and launches itself forward. The point of the claw crashes through the glass next to my face, sending shards flying everywhere. I duck out of the way just as the leg folds back up again, clawing out a chunk of the window frame. I fall onto my back, caught in sudden glaring light streaming through the shattered window. I make a squeaking scream before Nolan clamps a hand over my mouth.

A face appears in the window. The woman pulls her goggles onto her forehead, ducks her head in and out in a quick movement. Then she looks down at me and Nolan. There is so much light around her head and her skin is cold and I can count her bright teeth through her cheeks.

She has seen my eyes but she doesn't flinch. She just studies me and Nolan for a second, grinning.

"Sorry about that, kids," she says. "Thought you were Rob. My name is Dawn. Any chance you guys are hungry?"

———

Dawn is nice. She takes us to the underground hideout where the New York City resistance lives. The tunnel house is empty for now, but Dawn says that pretty soon the others will be back from scouting and scavenging and something called chaperoning. I'm glad, because Nolan doesn't look very well. He is lying on a sleeping bag in the safest corner of the room. I'm not sure he can walk anymore.

This place is warm and it feels safe, but Dawn says to be quiet and careful because some of the newer robots now can dig very well. She says the little machines patiently burrow through the cracks and they go toward vibrations. Meanwhile, the big machines hunt people in the tunnels.

This makes me nervous and I check the walls around us for vibrations. I don't see any of the familiar pulses rippling through the soot-stained tile. Dawn looks at me funny when I tell her that nothing is in the walls right now. But she doesn't say anything about my eyes, not yet.

Instead, Dawn lets me play with the bug leg. It is called a spiker. Just like I thought, the spiker came off a big walking machine. This machine is called a mantis, but Dawn says that she calls it "Crawly Rob." It's a silly name and it makes me laugh for a second until I remember that Nolan is hurt very bad.

I squint my eyes and look *into* the spiker. There are no wires inside it. Each joint talks to the others over the air. Radio. The leg doesn't have to think about where it goes either. Each piece is designed to work together. The leg only has one move, but it's a good one that combines stabbing and clawing. That's lucky for Dawn, because a simple electrical pulse can make the leg extend or curl up. She says this is very useful.

Then the spiker jerks around in my hands and I drop it on the ground. It lies there for a second, still. When I concentrate on the joints, the machine stretches itself out slowly, like a cat.

I feel a hand on my shoulder. Dawn stands next to me, her face radiating heat. She is excited.

"That's incredible. Let me show you something," she says.

Dawn leads me over to a sheet hanging from the wall. She pulls it aside, and I see a dark hollow filled with a crouching nightmare. Dozens of spider legs lurk there in the darkness, just a few feet away. I have seen this machine before. It was my last natural sight.

I scream and fall back, scrabbling to escape.

Dawn grabs me by the back of the shirt and I try to fight her, but she is too strong. She lets the curtain drop back into place and holds me up on my feet, letting me hit her and claw at her face.

"Mathilda," she says. "It's okay. It's not online. Listen to me."

I never knew how much I needed to cry until I had no eyes.

"Is that the machine that hurt you?" she asks.

I can only nod.

"It's off-line, honey. This one can't hurt you. Do you understand?"

"Yes," I say, settling down, "sorry."

"It's okay, baby. I understand. It's okay." Dawn strokes my hair for a few seconds. If I could close my eyes, I would. Instead, I watch the blood pulse gently through her face. Then Dawn sits me down on a cinder block. The muscles in her face tense up.

"Mathilda," she says, "that machine is called an autodoc. We dragged it here from topside. People got hurt . . . people *died* to bring that machine here. But we can't use it. We don't know why. You have something special, Mathilda. You know that, right?"

"My eyes," I respond.

"That's right, honey. Your eyes are special. But I think there's more than that. The machine on your face is also in your brain. You made that spiker move by thinking about it, didn't you?"

"Yes."

"Can you try to do the same thing with the autodoc?" she asks, slowly pulling the curtain back again. Now I see that the jumble of legs is attached to a white, oval body. There are dark gaps where the legs meet the main part. It looks like one of the grub worms that me and Nolan used to dig up in the backyard.

I shiver but I don't look away.

"Why?" I ask.

"To save your little brother's life for a start, honey."

Dawn drags the autodoc into the center of the room. For the next thirty minutes I sit next to it cross-legged and concentrate like I did for the spiker. The legs of the autodoc only twitch a little at first. But then I start to move them for real.

It doesn't take long to feel out all the legs. Each one has a different instrument attached to the end, but I only recognize a few: scalpels, lasers, spotlights. After a little while, the machine starts to seem less alien. I understand what it feels like to have a dozen arms, how you can be mindful of where your limbs are and still focus on the two that you are using right now. As I flex the spider legs again and again, it starts to feel natural.

Then, the autodoc speaks to me: *Diagnostic interface mode initiated. Indicate preferred function.*

I flinch, concentration broken. The words were in my mind, as if they were scrolling across the inside of my forehead. How could the autodoc *put words into my mind*?

Only then do I notice the crowd of people. About ten survivors have come into the tunnel. They stand together in a semicircle, watching me. A man stands behind Dawn with his arms wrapped around her, and she holds his arms with her hands. I haven't seen so many people since I got my new eyes.

A wave of red-orange pulses radiate toward me. The bands of light come from their beating hearts. It is very beautiful but also frustrating, because I can't explain how pretty it is to anyone.

"Mathilda," says Dawn, "this is my husband, Marcus."

"Nice to meet you, Marcus," I say.

Marcus just nods at me. I think he is speechless.

"And these are the others I told you about," says Dawn. The people all murmur their hellos and nice to meet yous. Then, a young guy steps forward. He's kind of cute, with a sharp chin and high cheekbones. One of his arms is wrapped in a towel.

"I'm Tom," he says, crouching down beside me.

I look away, ashamed of my face.

"Don't be scared," Tom says.

He unwraps the towel from his arm. Instead of a hand, Tom has a lump of cold metal in the shape of scissors. In wonder, I glance up at his face and he smiles at me. I start to smile back before I get embarrassed and look away.

I reach out and touch the cold metal of Tom's hand. Looking into it, I am amazed by how the flesh and machinery come together. It is as intricate as anything I have ever seen.

Looking harder at the other people, I notice occasional bits of metal and plastic. Not all of them are made of meat. Some of them are like me. Me and Tom.

"Why are you like that?" I ask.

"The machines changed us," says Tom. "We're different, but the same. We call ourselves transhuman."

Transhuman.

"Is it okay if I touch?" asks Tom, motioning at my eyes.

I nod, and he leans down and touches my face. He peers at my eyes and lightly brushes his fingers against my face where the skin turns to metal.

"I've never seen this," he says. "It's incomplete. Rob never got to finish. What happened, Mathilda?"

"My mom," I say.

That's all I can get out.

"Your mom stopped the operation," he says. "Good for her."

Tom stands up. "Dawn," he says, "this is amazing. The implant has no governor on it. Rob didn't get the chance to hobble it. I don't know. I mean, there's no telling what she can do."

A wave of rising heartbeats cascades toward me.

"Why are you all excited?" I ask.

"Because," says Dawn. "We think maybe you can talk to the machines."

Then Nolan moans. It's been two hours since we arrived here and he looks terrible. I can hear him breathing in little pants.

"I have to help my brother," I say.

Five minutes later, Marcus and Tom have placed Nolan next to the autodoc. The machine has its legs raised, poised like needles over my little brother's sleeping body.

"Make an X-ray, Mathilda," says Dawn.

I put a hand onto the autodoc and speak to it in my mind: *Hello? Are you there?*

Indicate preferred function.

X-ray?

The spider legs begin to move. Some move out of the way, while others creep around Nolan's body. A strange clicking sound comes from the writhing legs.

The words come into my mind with an image. *Place patient in the prone position. Remove clothing around the lumbar area.*

I gently turn Nolan over onto his stomach. I pull his shirt up to reveal his back. There are flecks of dark, crusted blood all around the knobs of his spine.

Fix him, I think to the autodoc.

Error, it responds. *Surgical functionality unavailable. Database missing. Uplink not present. Antenna attachment required.*

"Dawn," I say, "it doesn't know how to do surgery. It wants an antenna so it can get instructions."

Marcus turns to Dawn, concerned. "It's trying to trick us. If we give it the antenna, it will call for help. They'll track us down."

Dawn nods. "Mathilda, we can't risk that—"

But she stops cold when she sees me.

Someplace in my head, I know that the arms of the autodoc are silently rising into the air behind me, instruments gleaming. The countless needles and scalpels hover there on swaying legs, menacing. Nolan needs help and if they won't give it, I'm willing to take it.

I frown at the group of people and set my jaw.

"Nolan *needs* me."

Marcus and Dawn look at each other again.

"Mathilda?" asks Dawn. "How do you know it's not a trap, honey? I know you want to help Nolan, but you also don't want to hurt us."

I think about it.

"The autodoc is smarter than the spiker," I say. "It can talk. But it's not *that* smart. It's just asking for what it needs. Like an error message."

"But that thinking Rob is out there—" says Marcus.

Dawn touches Marcus on the shoulder.

"Okay, Mathilda," says Dawn.

Marcus gives up arguing. He looks around, sees something, and strides across the room. Reaching up, he grabs a wire dangling from the ceiling and swings it back and forth to unloop it from a piece of metal. Then he hands it to me, eyeing the autodoc's swaying legs.

"This cable goes to the building above us. It's long and metal and it goes high. Perfect antenna. Be careful."

I barely hear him. The instant the antenna touches my hand a tidal wave of information comes flooding into my head. Into my eyes. Streams of numbers and letters and images fill my vision. None of it makes sense at first. Swirls of color blow through the air in front of me.

That's when I feel it. Some kind of . . . mind. An alien *thing*, stalking through the data, searching for me. Calling out my name. *Mathilda?*

The autodoc begins speaking in a constant babble. *Scanning initiated. One, two, three, four. Query satellite uplink. Database access. Download initiated. Ortho-, gastro-, uro-, gyno-, neuro . . .*

It's too fast. Too much. I can't understand what the autodoc is saying anymore. I'm getting dizzy as the information surges into me. The monster calls for me again, and now it is closer. I think of those cold doll eyes that night in my bedroom and the way that lifeless thing whispered my name in the darkness.

The colors spin around me like a tornado.

Stop, I think. But nothing happens. I can't breathe. The colors are too bright and they're drowning me, making it so that I can't think. *Stop!* I shout with my mind. And my name comes again, louder this time, and I can't tell where my arms are or how many I have. *What am I?* I scream inside my head, with everything in me.

STOP!

I drop the antenna like a snake. The colors fade. The images and symbols drop to the floor and are swept away like fall leaves into the corners of the room. The vivid colors bleach away into the dull white tile.

I take one breath. Then two. The autodoc legs start to move.

There are tiny motor sounds as the autodoc works on Nolan. A spotlight flicks on and shines on his back. A rotating scrubber comes down and cleans his skin. A syringe goes in and out almost too fast to see. The movements are quick and precise and full of little pauses, like when the petting zoo chickens used to turn their heads and peck at corn.

In the sudden quiet, I can hear something beneath the static of the tiny motor noises. It is a voice.

. . . sorry for what I've done. I'm called Lurker. I'm bringing down the British Telecom tower communications blockade. Should open up satellite access, but I don't know for how long. If you can hear this message, the comm lines are still open. The satellites are free. Use them while you can. The damned machines will— Ah, no.

*Christ, please. Can't hold on any longer. I'm sorry. . . . Catch you in
the funny pages, mate.*

After about ten seconds, the broken message repeats. I can
barely hear it. The man sounds very scared and young but also
proud. I hope that he is okay, wherever he is.

Finally, I stand up. Behind me, I can feel the autodoc operating on Nolan. The group of people still stand, watching
me. I have barely been aware that they are here. Talking to
the machines takes such concentration. I can hardly see people
anymore. It is so easy to lose myself in the machine.

"Dawn?" I say.

"Yes, honey?"

"There's a man out there, talking. His name is Lurker. He
says he destroyed a communications blockade. He says the satellites are free."

The people look at each other in wonder. Two of them hug.
Tom and Marcus slap their hands together. They make small,
happy noises. Smiling, Dawn puts her hands on my shoulders.

"That's good, Mathilda. It means we can talk to other people. Rob never destroyed the communications satellites, it just
blocked them off from us."

"Oh," I say.

"This is very important, Mathilda," she says. "What else
do you hear out there? What's the most important message?"

I put my hands on the sides of my face and concentrate. I
listen very hard. And when I listen *beyond* the man's repeating
voice, I find that I can hear further into the network.

There are so many messages floating around. Some of
them are sad. Some are angry. Many of them are confused or
cutoff or rambling, but one of them sticks out in my mind. It is
a special message with three familiar words in it:

Robot defense act.

Mathilda had only scratched the surface of her abilities. In the coming months, she would hone her special gift in the relative safety of the New York City underground, protected by Marcus and Dawn.

The message she was able to find on this day, due to the ultimate sacrifice made by Lurker and Arrtrad in London, proved instrumental in the formation of a North American army. Mathilda Perez had found a call to arms issued by Paul Blanton, and the location of humankind's greatest enemy.

—CORMAC WALLACE, MIL#GHA217

2. CALL TO ARMS

We have discovered the location of a superintelligent machine that calls itself Archos.

SPC. PAUL BLANTON

NEW WAR + 1 YEAR, 1 MONTH
The following message originated in Afghanistan. It was intercepted and retransmitted worldwide by Mathilda Perez in New York City. We know that, thanks to her efforts, this communication was received by everyone in North America with access to a radio, including scores of tribal governments, isolated resistance groups, and the remaining enclaves of United States armed forces.

—CORMAC WALLACE, MIL#GHA217

Headquarters
Afghan Resistance Command
Bamiyan Province, Afghanistan

To: Survivors
From: Specialist Paul Blanton, United States Army

We are sending this message to urge you to use whatever influence you have as a member of a surviving North American human stronghold to convince your leadership of the terrible consequences which will be suffered by all humankind if you do not immediately organize and deploy an offensive force to march against the robots.

Recently, we have discovered the location of a superintelligent machine that calls itself Archos—the central artificial intelligence backing the robot uprising. This machine is hiding in an isolated location in western Alaska. We call this area the Ragnorak Intelligence Fields. Coordinates are integrated in electronic format at the end of this message.

Before the New War began, there is evidence that Archos quashed the robot defense act before it could pass Congress. Since Zero Hour, Archos has been using our existing robotic infrastructure—both civilian and military—to viciously attack humankind. It is clear that the enemy is willing to pay an enormous cost in effort and resources to continue decimating our population centers.

Worse yet, the machines are evolving.

Within the space of three weeks, we have encountered three new varieties of specialized robotic hunter-killers designed to locomote in rough terrain, penetrate our cave bunkers, and destroy our personnel. The design of these machines has been informed by newly constructed biological research stations that are allowing the machines to study the natural world.

The machines are now designing and building themselves. More varieties are coming. We believe that these new robots will have greatly increased agility, survivability, and lethality. They will be tailored to fight your people, in your geographic environment, and in your weather conditions.

Let there be no doubt in your mind that the combined onslaught of these new machines, working twenty-four hours a day, will soon be unleashed by Archos on your native land.

We implore you to confirm these facts to your leaders, and to do your utmost to urge them to gather an offensive force which can march to the attached coordinates in Alaska to put a stop to the evolution of these killing machines and prevent the total annihilation of humankind.

March cautiously, as Archos will surely sense our approach. But rest assured that your soldiers will not march alone. Similar militias will be mustered from across human-occupied territory to do battle with our enemy in its own domain.

Heed this call to arms.

We can guarantee you that unless every human stronghold in range of Alaska retaliates, this rain of autonomous killing machines will increase manyfold in complexity and fury.

To my fellow humans
With best regards from

Specialist Paul R. Blanton

It is widely believed that these words, translated into dozens of human languages, are responsible for the organized human retaliation that began roughly two years after Zero Hour. In addition, there is deeply dismaying evidence that this call to arms was received abroad—resulting in a largely undocumented and ultimately doomed attack on Archos mounted by Eastern European and Asian forces.

—CORMAC WALLACE, MIL#GHA217

3. The Cowboy Way

The buck's gotta stop somewhere.

Lonnie Wayne Blanton

NEW WAR + 1 YEAR, 4 MONTHS

Four months after we arrived at the fabled defensive stronghold of Gray Horse, the city fell into disarray. The call to arms had paralyzed the tribal council with indecision. Lonnie Wayne Blanton trusted his son implicitly and argued to muster the army and march; however, John Tenkiller insisted on staying to defend. As I describe in these pages, Rob ultimately made the choice for us.

—CORMAC WALLACE, MIL#GHA217

I'm standing on the edge of Gray Horse bluffs, blowing into my hands for warmth and squinting as the dawn breaks like fire over the Great Plains below. The thin cries of thousands of cattle and buffalo rise in the still morning.

With Jack in the lead, our squad was on the move nonstop to get here. Everywhere we've been, nature is back in action. There're more birds in the sky, more bugs in the bushes, and more coyotes in the night. As the months pass, mother earth has been swallowing up everything but the cities. The cities are where Rob lives.

A lean Cherokee kid stands next to me, methodically packing chewing tobacco into his mouth. He's watching the plains with expressionless brown eyes and doesn't seem to notice me at all. It's hard not to notice *him*, though.

Lark Iron Cloud.

He looks about twenty and he's decked out in some kind of slick uniform. A black-and-red scarf is tucked under a half-zipped jacket and his pale green pant legs are folded into polished leather cowboy boots. Black goggles hang around his tawny neck. He's holding a walking stick with feathers hanging from it. The stick is made of metal—some kind of antenna he must have snapped off a Rob scout walker. A war trophy.

This kid looks like a fighter pilot from the future. And here I am in my ripped-up, mud-splattered army combat uniform. I'm not sure which of us should be ashamed of his appearance, but I'm pretty sure it's me.

"Think we'll go to war?" I ask the kid.

He looks over at me for a second, then back at the vista.

"Maybe. Lonnie Wayne's on it. He'll let us know."

"You trust him?"

"He's the reason I'm alive."

"Oh."

A flock of birds flaps across the sky, sunlight glinting from their wings like the rainbow on a pool of oil.

"Y'all look pretty rough," says Lark, motioning to the rest of my squad with his stick. "What are you, like, soldiers?"

I look at my squad mates. Leonardo. Cherrah. Tiberius. Carl. They stand around talking, waiting for Jack to return. Their movements are familiar, relaxed. The last few months have forged us into more than just a unit—we're a family now.

"Nah. We're not soldiers, just survivors. My brother, Jack, he's the soldier. I'm just tagging along for the sheer fun of it."

"Oh," says Lark.

I can't tell if he just took me seriously or not.

"Where's your brother at?" Lark asks.

"In the war council. With Lonnie and them."

"So he's one of those."

"One of what?"

"Responsible kind."

"People say that. You're not?"

"I do my thing. The old-timers do theirs."

Lark gestures behind us with the walking stick. There, waiting patiently in a row, are dozens of what these people call spider tanks. The walking tanks each stand about eight feet tall. The four sturdy legs are Rob created, made of ropy synthetic muscles. The rest of the tanks have been modified by human beings. Most vehicles have tank turrets and heavy-machine-gun mounts on top, but I see that one has the cab and blade off a bulldozer.

What can I say? It's just an anything goes kind of war.

Rob didn't come at Gray Horse all at once; it had to evolve to get up here. That meant sending walking scouts. And some of those scouts got caught. Some of *those* got taken apart and put back together again. Gray Horse Army prefers to fight with captured robots.

"You're the one who figured out how to liberate the spider tanks? To lobotomize them?" I ask.

"Yep," he says.

"Jesus. Are you a scientist or something?"

Lark chuckles. "A mechanic is just an engineer in blue jeans."

"Damn," I say.

"Yep."

I look out over the prairie and see something odd.

"Hey, Lark?" I ask.

"Yeah?" he says.

"You live around here. So maybe you can tell me something."

"Sure."

"Just what in the fuck is that?" I ask, pointing.

He looks out over the plain. Sees the sinuous, glinting metal writhing through the grass like a hidden river. Lark spits tobacco on the ground, turns, and motions to his squad with the walking stick.

"That's our war, brother."

———

Confusion and death. The grass is too tall. The smoke is too thick.

Gray Horse Army is made up of every able-bodied adult in the city—men and women, young and old. A thousand soldiers and some change. They've been drilling together for months and they've almost all got guns, but nobody knows anything once those killing machines are slicing through the grass and latching onto people.

"Stay with the tanks," Lonnie said. "Stay with old *Houdini* and you'll be fine."

Custom-made spider tanks plod across the prairie in a ragged line, one measured step after another. Their massive feet sink into the damp earth and their chest hulls trample the grass down, leaving a wake behind them. A few soldiers cling to the top of each tank, weapons out, scanning the fields.

We're marching out to face what's in the grass. Whatever it is, we've got to stop it before it reaches Gray Horse.

I stay with my squad, following the tank called *Houdini* on foot. Jack's up on top with Lark. I've got Tiberius lumbering on one side of me and Cherrah on the other. Her profile is sharp in the morning light. She looks feline, quick, and ferocious. And, I can't help thinking, beautiful. Carl and Leo are buddying up a few meters away. We all focus on staying with the tanks—they're our only frame of reference in this never-ending maze of tall grass.

For twenty minutes we clomp across the plains, trying our best to look through the grass and see whatever's waiting for us out here. Our primary goal is to stop the machines from advancing on Gray Horse. Secondary goal is to protect the herds of cattle that live out here on the prairie—the lifeblood of the city.

We don't even know what kind of Rob we're facing. Only that it's new varieties. Always something new with our friend Rob.

"Hey, Lark," calls Carl. "Why they call 'em spider tanks if they only have four legs?"

Lark calls down from the tank, "'Cause it beats calling it a large, quadruped walker."

"Well, I don't think it does," mutters Carl.

The first concussion throws dirt and shredded plants into the air, and the screams start coming from the tall grass. A herd of buffalo stampedes, and the world rings with vibration and noise. Instant chaos.

"What's out there, Jack?" I shout. He's crouched on top of the spider tank, heavy mounted gun swiveling from one side to the other. Lark steers the tank. His gloved hand is wrapped tight in a rope wrapped around the hull, rodeo style.

"Nothing yet, little brother," calls Jack.

For a few minutes there are no targets, only faceless screams.

Then something comes crashing through the yellow stalks of grass. We all pivot and aim our weapons at it—a huge Osage man. He's huffing and puffing and dragging an unconscious body by its blood-slicked arms. The unconscious guy looks like he got hit by a meteorite. There's a deep, bleeding crater in his upper thigh.

More explosions rip through the soldiers out in front of the tanks. Lark yanks his hand, and *Houdini* transitions to a trot gait, motors grinding as it moves full speed ahead to provide support. Jack turns and watches me, shrugging as the tank lumbers away into the grass.

"Help," bawls the big Osage.

Fuck. I signal a stop to the squad and watch our spider tank over the Osage man's shoulder as it takes another plodding step away from our position, leaving behind a half-crushed swath of grass. Every step it takes leaves us more exposed to whatever is out here.

Cherrah drops to her knee and tourniquets the unconscious man's damaged leg. I grab the blubbering Osage by the shoulders and give him a little shake.

"What did this?" I ask.

"Bugs, man. They're like bugs. They get on you and then blow up," says the Osage, wiping tears off his face with a meaty forearm. "I gotta get Jay out of here. He's gonna die."

The concussions and the screams are coming thicker now. We crouch as gunshots ring out and stray bullets tear through the grass. It sounds like a massacre. A fine rain of dirt particles have started to float down from the clear blue sky.

Cherrah looks up from her tourniquet job and we make grim eye contact. It's a silent agreement: You watch my back and I'll watch yours. Then I flinch as a shower of dirt cascades through the grass and rattles against my helmet.

Our spider tank is long gone, and Jack with it.

"Okay," I say, slapping the Osage man on the shoulder. "That should stop the bleeding. Take your friend back. We're moving forward, so you're on your own. Keep your eyes open."

The Osage man throws his friend over his shoulder and hustles away. It sounds like whatever happened to old Jay has already torn through the front ranks and is coming for us, too.

I hear Lark start screaming from somewhere ahead of us.

And for the first time, I see the enemy. Early-model stumpers. They remind me of the scuttle mines from that first moment of Zero Hour in Boston, a million years ago. Each one is the size of a baseball, with a knot of flailing legs that somehow shoves its little body over and through the clumps of grass.

"Shit!" shouts Carl. "Let's get out of here!"

The lanky soldier starts to run away. By instinct, I catch him by the front of his sweaty shirt and stop him. I yank his face down to my level, look into his wide eyes, and say one word: "Fight."

My voice is even, but my body is on fire with adrenaline.

Pop. Pop. Pop.

Our guns light up the dirt, dashing the stumpers to pieces. But more are coming. And more after that. It's a tidal wave of crawling nasties flowing through the grass like ants.

"It is getting too heavy," calls Tiberius. "What do we do, Cormac?"

"Three-round burst," I call. A half-dozen rifles snick into auto mode.

Pop, pop, pop, pop, pop, pop.

Rifle muzzles flash, painting shadows on our dirt-covered faces. Spouts of dirt and twisted metal jet from the ground, along with occasional flares as the liquids inside the stumpers come into contact. We stand in a semicircle and pour lead into the dirt. But the stumpers keep coming, and they're starting to spread out around us, swarm style.

Jack is gone and somehow I'm in charge, and now we're going to get blown to pieces. Where the fuck is Jack? My hero brother is supposed to save me from situations like this.

Goddamnit.

As the stumpers close in I call out, "Fall in on me!"

Two minutes later I'm sweating under the sun, my right shoulder pressed into Cherrah's left shoulder blade, and almost shooting at my own feet. Carl is squeezed tight between big Leo and Ty. I can smell Cherrah's long black hair and I can picture her smile in my head, but I can't let myself think of that right now. A shadow passes over my face and the legend himself, Lonnie Wayne Blanton, falls out of the sky.

The old dude is riding a tall walker—one of Lark's Frankenstein projects. The thing is just two seven-foot-long robotic ostrich legs with an old rodeo saddle grafted onto it. Lonnie Wayne sits up top, cowboy boots pushed into stirrups and hand resting lazily on the pommel. Lonnie rides the tall walker like an old pro, hips swaying with each giraffe step of the machine. Just like a damn cowboy.

"Howdy, y'all," he says. Then he turns and unloads a couple of shotgun blasts into the tangled pile of stumpers scurrying over the churned dirt toward our position.

"Doin' great, bud," Lonnie Wayne says to me. My face is blank. I can't believe I'm still alive.

Just then, two more tall walkers drop into our clearing, the Osage cowboys on top raining down shotgun blasts that tear big gouges out of the oncoming stumper swarm.

Inside a few seconds, the three tall walkers have used their

high vantage points and the spread of shotgun blasts to eradi-
cate most of the stumper swarm. Not all of it, though.

"Watch your leg," I yell up to Lonnie.

A stumper that's somehow gotten behind us is climbing
the metal of Lonnie's tall walker leg. He glances down, then
leans in the saddle in a way that causes the leg to raise up and
shake. The stumper flies away into the underbrush, where it's
promptly blasted by one of my squad.

Why didn't the stumper trigger?

Lark is yelling again from somewhere up ahead, hoarse
this time. I can also hear Jack barking short commands. Lonnie turns his head and motions to his bodyguard. But before
he can go, I wrap my hand around the smooth metal shaft of
Lonnie's stilt leg.

"Lonnie," I say, "stay back where it's safe, man. You're not
supposed to put your general in the front line."

"I hear ya," says the grizzled old man. "But, hell, kid, it's
the cowboy way. The buck's gotta stop somewhere." He cocks
the shotgun and ejects a spent cartridge, pulls his hat down,
and nods. Then, fluid in the stiltlike tall walker, he turns and
leaps over the six-foot-tall grass.

"C'mon!" I shout to the squad. We rush forward over the
crumpled grass, striving to keep up with Lonnie. As we go, we
see corpses through the stalks and, even worse, the ones who
are alive and wounded, ashen-faced and mouths murmuring in
prayer.

I put my head down and keep going. Got to catch up with
Jack. He'll help us.

I'm moving fast, spitting grass out of my mouth and concentrating on keeping up with the damp spot between Cherrah's shoulder blades, when we burst into a clearing.

Some serious shit has gone down here.

For roughly a thirty-meter circle, the grass is trampled to mud and the field gouged up in huge chunks. There is only a split second to take in the scene before I throw my arms around Cherrah and tackle her to the ground. She falls on top of me, the butt of her gun driving all the air out of my lungs. But the foot of the spider tank whizzes past her head without knocking her brains out.

Houdini's legs are covered in stumpers. The tank is leaping around like a bucking bronco. Lark and Jack are both on top, teeth gritted, hanging on for dear life. Hardly any of the stumpers have fallen off; dozens of them are embedded in the belly net, and others are tenaciously climbing the flanks of the armored walker.

Jack is hunched over, trying to untie Lark from something. The kid's gotten tangled up in his guide rope. Lonnie and his two guards nimbly leap around the bucking monster on their tall walkers, but they can't get to a good spot to shoot.

"Y'all jump off!" shouts Lonnie.

The tank careens past, and in a flash I see that Lark's forearm is twisted under the rope. Jack can't get him free with all the bucking and heaving. If the spider tank were to sit still though, even for a second, the stumpers would climb on top. Lark is shouting and cursing and crying a little bit, but he can't get free.

He shouldn't worry. We all know that Jack won't leave him behind. The word *abandon* just isn't in a hero's vocabulary.

Watching the stumpers, I notice they're clustered on the knee joints of the tank. A thought tickles the back of my head. *Why don't the stumpers detonate?* And the answer squirms into reach. *Heat.* Those joints are warm from all the jumping around. The little bastards don't trigger until they reach some-place hot.

They're looking for skin temperature.

"Lonnie!" I wave my arms to get his attention. The old man spins around and crouches his tall walker near me. He cups his ear with one hand and with the other dabs his fore-head with a white hankie.

"They go for the heat, Lonnie," I shout. "We've got to start a fire."

"Start a fire and it won't stop," he says. "Might kill our stock."

"It's that or Lark dies. Maybe we all die."

Lonnie looks down on me, deep creases in his face. His eyes are watery blue and serious. Then he sets his shotgun into the crook of his elbow and digs into the watch pocket of his jeans. I hear a metallic clink and an antique Zippo lighter drops right into my hand. A double R symbol is painted on the side, along with the words "King of the Cowboys."

"Let old Roy Rogers help ya out," says Lonnie Wayne, face breaking into a gap-toothed smile.

"How old is this thing?" I ask, but when I flip the thumb wheel, a strong flame spurts from the top. Lonnie has already wheeled his tall walker around and he's corralling the rest of the squad while avoiding the out-of-control spider tank.

"Burn it, burn it, burn it all down!" shouts Lonnie Wayne. "That's all we got left, boys! No choice."

I toss the lighter into the grass, and within seconds a raging fire begins to grow. The squad retreats to the other side of the clearing and we watch as, one by one, the stumpers drop off the spider tank. In that same idiotic clambering motion, they jounce over the chewed-up ground toward the sheet of flames.

Finally, *Houdini* stops bucking. On groaning, overheated motors, the huge machine settles down. I see my brother's hand silhouetted against the sky. Thumbs-up. Time to go.

Thank you, Jesus.

Out of nowhere, Cherrah grabs my face with both hands. She pushes her forehead against mine, bopping our helmets together, and smiles wide. Her face is covered in dirt and blood and sweat, but it's the most beautiful sight I've ever seen. "You done good, Bright Boy," she says, her breath tickling my lips.

Somehow, my heart is beating faster right now than it has all day.

Then Cherrah and her flashing smile are gone—darted away into the grass for our retreat back to Gray Horse.

One week later, Gray Horse Army heeded Paul Blanton's call to arms and mustered a force to march on Alaska. Their fearless response likely occurred because none of the soldiers truly understood how close they had come to utter destruction on the Great Plains. Postwar records indicate that the entire battle was recorded in great detail by two squads of military-grade humanoid robots camping two miles outside Gray Horse. Mysteriously, these machines chose to defy Archos's orders and did not join the battle.

—CORMAC WALLACE, MIL#GHA217

4. Awakening

The great akuma *will not rest until I am gone.*

Takeo Nomura

NEW WAR + 1 YEAR, 4 MONTHS

Relying on incredible engineering skills and rather odd viewpoints regarding human-robot relations, Takeo Nomura managed to build Adachi Castle in the year after Zero Hour. Nomura carved this human safe zone into the heart of Tokyo with no outside help. From here he saved thousands of lives and made his final, vital contribution to the New War.

—CORMAC WALLACE, MIL#GHA217

At long last, my queen opens her eyes.

"*Anata,*" she says, lying on her back and looking up into my face. *You.*

"You," I whisper.

I imagined this moment many times as I marched across the dark factory floor, fighting against the endless attacks that came from outside my castle walls. Always I wondered whether I would be afraid of her, after what happened before. But there is no doubt in my voice now. I am not afraid. I smile and then smile wider to see my happiness reflected in her features.

Her face was still for so long. Her voice silenced.

A tear tickles my cheek and drops from my face. She feels it and wipes it away, eyes focusing on mine. I notice again that the lens of her right eye is spiderwebbed with thin cracks. A melted patch of skin mars the right side of her head. There is nothing I can do to fix it. Not until I find the right part.

"I missed you," I say.

Mikiko is silent for a moment. She looks past me, at the curved metal ceiling that soars thirty meters above. Perhaps she is confused. The factory has changed so much since the New War began.

It is an architecture of necessity. Over the years, my factory *senshi* worked ceaselessly to rivet together a defensive shell. The outermost layers are a complicated array of junk: scraps of metal, jutting poles, and crushed plastic. It forms a labyrinth built to confuse the swarms of small, wriggling *akuma* that constantly try to creep inside.

Monstrous steel beams line the ceiling like the rib cage of a whale. These were built to stop the greater *akuma*—like the talking one that died here at the beginning of the war. It gave me the secret to awakening Mikiko, but it also nearly destroyed my castle.

The scrap metal throne was not my idea. After a few months, people began to arrive. Many millions of my countrymen were led out into the country and slaughtered. They trusted too much in the machines and went willingly to their destruction. But others came to me. The people without so much trust, those with an instinct for survival, found me naturally.

And I could not turn the survivors away. They crouched

on my factory floor as *akuma* beat down the walls again and again. My loyal *senshi* wheeled across the broken concrete to protect us. After each attack, we all worked together to defend ourselves from the next.

Broken concrete became metal-riveted floors, polished and gleaming. My old workbench became a throne set atop a dais with twenty-two steps leading to the top. An old man became an emperor.

Mikiko focuses on me.

"I am alive," she says.

"Yes."

"Why am I alive?"

"Because the great *akuma* gave you the breath of life. The *akuma* thought that this meant you belonged to him. But he was wrong. You belong to no one. I set you free."

"Takeo. There are others like me. Tens of thousands."

"Yes, humanoid machines are everywhere. But I do not care for them. I care for you."

"I . . . remember you. So many years. Why?"

"Everything has a mind. You have a good mind. You always did."

Mikiko hugs me, tight. Her smooth plastic lips brush against my throat. Her arms are weak but I can feel that she puts her full strength into this embrace.

Then she stiffens.

"Takeo," she says. "We are in danger."

"Always."

"No. The *akuma*. It will fear what you've done. It will be afraid that more of us will awaken. It will attack at once."

And indeed, I hear the first hollow thud against the outer battlements. I let go of Mikiko and look down the stairs of the dais. The factory floor—what my people call the throne room—has filled with concerned citizens. They stand in groups of two or three, whispering to each other and politely not looking up the steps to Mikiko and me.

My rolling arms—the *senshi*—have already gathered in a defensive formation around the vulnerable humans. Overhead, the master *senshi,* a massive bridge crane, has silently rolled into position over the throne. Its two mighty arms hang in the air, poised to defend the battle floor.

Once again, we are under attack.

I rush to the bank of video monitors that ring the throne and see only static. The *akuma* have blinded me to the attack outside. They have never been able to do this before.

This time I feel the attack will not end. I have finally gone too far. Living here is one thing. But to compromise the entire humanoid portion of the *akuma* army? The great *akuma* will not rest until I am gone—until my secret is crushed where it lies inside my fragile skull.

Thud. Thud. Thud.

The rhythmic beating seems to come from everywhere. The *akuma* are relentlessly battering through our meters-thick defensive fortifications. Each soft thud we hear is the equivalent of a bomb exploding outside. I think back on my moat and chuckle to myself. How much has changed since those early times.

I look down onto the battle floor. My people are cowered there, afraid and helpless to stop the coming slaughter. My people. My castle. My queen. All will perish unless the *akuma* regains this horrible secret from me. Logically, there is only one honorable course of action possible now.

"I must stop this attack."

"Yes," says Mikiko, "I know."

"Then you know I must give myself up. The secret of your

awakening must die with me. Only then will the *akuma* see that we are not a threat."

Her laughter sounds like delicate glass shattering.

"Darling Takeo," she says. "We don't have to *destroy* the secret. Only share it."

And then, clad in her cherry blossom dress, Mikiko raises her slender arms. She pulls a long ribbon from her hair and her graying synthetic locks cascade over her shoulders. She closes her eyes and the bridge crane reaches up and plucks a hanging wire from the ceiling. The battle-scarred yellow arm gracefully descends through the open air and drops the metal wire. It flutters down to land in Mikiko's pale, outstretched fingers.

"Takeo," she says, "you are not the only one who knows the secret of awakening. I know it also, and I will transmit it to the world, where it may be repeated again and again."

"How will—"

"If the knowledge is spread, it cannot be stamped out."

She ties the metal-laced ribbon to the hanging wire. The air is rumbling now from the battle raging outside. The *senshi* wait patiently, green intention lights wavering in the vast gloomy room. It won't be long now.

My people watch as Mikiko descends the stairs, trailing the stark red ribbon from her hand. Her mouth opens into a pink O, and she begins to sing. Her clear voice echoes across the open factory floor. It bounces from the soaring ceilings and reverberates off the polished metal floor.

The people stop talking, stop searching the walls for intruders, and watch Mikiko. Her song is haunting, beautiful. There are no recognizable words but the speech patterns are unmistakable. She weaves the notes between the muffled explosions and cutting screams of bending metal.

My people huddle together but do not panic as showers of

sparks spurt from the ceiling. Chunks of debris rain down. In a sudden movement, the crane arm snatches a jagged piece of falling metal from the air. Still, Mikiko's voice rings out clear and strong through the crumbling chamber.

I realize that a team of cutting *akuma* have breached the outer defenses. They are not yet visible, but their violence can be heard as it tears through my castle walls. A fan spray of sparks gushes from a wall and a white-hot fissure appears. After several deafening impacts, the softening metal spreads apart to reveal a dark gap.

An enemy machine wriggles through the hole, soot-stained and warped by the heat of some ferocious weapon outside. The *senshi* stand firm, protecting the people as this dirty silver-colored thing tumbles onto the floor.

Mikiko continues her bittersweet song.

The intruder stands, and I see that it is a humanoid robot, heavily armed and marked by battle. The machine was once a weapon deployed by the Japan Self-Defense Forces, but that was long ago and I see many modifications glinting in the frame of this piece of walking death.

Through the destroyed patch of wall I can see the streaks of weapons fire and fleeting shapes as they dart through the war zone. But this humanoid robot, tall and slender and elegant, stands poised—as if it's waiting for something.

Mikiko's song ends.

Only then does the attacker move. It strides to the edge of my *senshi*'s defensive perimeter, staying just out of range. The people cower back before this battle-hardened piece of weaponry. My *senshi* stand strong, deadly in their stillness. Song finished, Mikiko stands on the last step at the bottom of the dais. She sees the newcomer and watches it with a puzzled expression on her face. Then she smiles.

"Please," she says, voice echoing melodically, "speak out loud."

The dust-coated humanoid machine speaks then in a clicking, grinding voice that is difficult to understand and frightening. "Identification. Arbiter-class humanoid safety and pacification robot. Notify. My squad is twelve. We are under attack. We are alive. Query Emperor Nomura. May we join Adachi Castle? May we join the Tokyo resistance?"

I look at Mikiko in wonder. Her song is already spreading. *What does this mean?*

My people look at me for guidance. They do not know what to make of this former enemy who has turned up on our doorstep. But there is no time to talk to people. It takes too much concentration and it is horribly inefficient. Instead, I push my glasses up my nose and grab my toolbox from behind the towering throne.

Toolbox in hand, I scurry down the steps. I squeeze Mikiko's hand in passing and then push my way past the others. I am whistling as I reach the Arbiter robot, looking forward to the future. Adachi Castle has new friends, you see, and they will certainly need repairs.

Within twenty-four hours, the Awakening spread from Adachi Ward in Tokyo across the world. Mikiko's song was picked up and retransmitted from humanoid robots of all varieties across every major continent. The Awakening affected only human-shaped robots, such as domestics, safety and pacification units, and related models—a tiny percentage of Archos's overall force. But with Mikiko's song began the age of freeborn robots.

—CORMAC WALLACE, MIL#GHA217

5. The Veil, Lifted

All is darkness.

Nine Oh Two

NEW WAR + 1 YEAR, 10 MONTHS

Humanoid robots around the globe awoke into sentience in the aftermath of the Awakening performed by Mr. Takeo Nomura and his consort, Mikiko. These machines came to be known as the freeborn. The following account was provided by one such robot—a modified safety and pacification robot (Model 902 Arbiter) who fittingly chose to call itself Nine Oh Two.

—CORMAC WALLACE, MIL#GHA217

21:43:03.

Boot sequence initiated.

Power source diagnostics complete.

Low-level diagnostics check. Humanoid form milspec Model Nine Oh Two Arbiter. Detect modified casing. Warranty inactive.

Sensory package detected.

Engage radio communications. Interference. No input.

Engage auditory perception. Trace input.

Engage chemical perception. Zero oxygen. Trace explosives. No toxic contamination. Air flow nil. Petroleum outgasing detected. No input.

Engage inertial measurement unit. Horizontal attitude. Static. No input.

Engage ultrasonic ranging sensors. Hermetically sealed enclosure. Eight feet by two feet by two feet. No input.

Engage field of vision. Wide spectrum. Normal function. No visible light.

Engage primary thought threads. Probability fields emerging. Maximum probability thought thread active.

Query: *What is happening to me?*

Maxprob response: *Life.*

———

All is darkness.

On reflex, my eyes blink and switch to active infrared. Red-hued details emerge. Particulate matter floats in the air, reflecting the infrared light. My face orients downward. A pale gray body stretches out below. Arms crossed over a narrow chest. Five long fingers per hand. Slender, powerful limbs.

A serial number is visible on the right thigh. Magnify. Milspec identification Model Nine Oh Two Arbiter class humanoid robot.

Self-spec complete. Diagnostic information confirmed.

I am Nine Oh Two.

This is my body. It is two point one meters tall. It weighs ninety kilograms. Humanoid form factor. Individually articulated fingers and toes. Kinetically rechargeable power source with thirty-year operational life. Survivable temperature range, negative fifty degrees Celsius to positive one hundred thirty.

My body was manufactured six years ago by the Foster-Grumman corporation. Original instructions indicate that my body is a safety and pacification unit destined for deployment in eastern Afghanistan. Point of origin: Fort Collins, Colorado. Six months ago, this platform was modified while off-line. Now, it is online.

What am I?

This body is me. I am this body. And I am conscious.

Engage proprioception. Joints located. Angles calculated. I'm lying on my back. It is dark and quiet. I do not know where I am. My internal clock says three years have passed since my scheduled delivery date.

Several thought threads spring to mind. The maximum probability thread says that I am inside a shipping container that never arrived at its destination.

I listen.

After thirty seconds, I sense muffled voices—high frequencies transmitted through the air and low frequencies through the metal skin of the container.

Speech recognition online. English corpus loaded.

". . . why would Rob destroy . . . *own* armory?" says a high-pitched voice.

". . . your fucking fault . . . get us killed," says a deep voice.

". . . didn't mean to . . . ," says the high-pitched voice.

". . . open it?" says the deep voice.

I may need to use my body soon. I execute a low-level diagnostic program. My limbs twitch slightly, connecting inputs to outputs. Everything is working.

The lid of my container opens a crack. There is a hiss as the seal is broken and the atmospheres equalize. Light floods my infrared vision. I blink back to visible spectrum. *Click, click.*

A broad, bearded face hovers in the sliver of light, eyes wide. Human.

Face recognition. Nil.

Emotion recognition engaged.

Surprise. Fear. Anger.

The lid slams back down. Locks.

". . . destroy it . . . ," says the deep voice.

Odd. Only now—when they want to kill me—do I realize how badly I want to live. I pull my arms off my chest and brace my elbows against the back of the container. I curl my hands into tight fists. With sudden jackhammer force I launch a punch into the container.

". . . awake!" says the high-pitched voice.

Vibrational resonance response indicates the lid is made of a steel substrate. It is consistent with the spec for a standard safety and pacification unit shipping container. Database lookup indicates that latches and activation equipment are on the outside, eighteen inches down from the headrest.

". . . here to scavenge. Not die . . . ," says the low-pitched voice.

My next punch lands in the dented spot left by the previous punch. After six more punches, a hole appears in the deforming metal—a fist-sized breach. With both hands I begin to peel the metal apart, tearing the opening wider.

". . . no! Come back . . . ," says the high-pitched voice.

Through the rapidly widening hole, I hear a metallic click. Matching the sound bite against a dictionary of martial samples returns a high-probability match: the slide pull of a well-maintained Heckler & Koch USP 9 millimeter semiautomatic pistol. Minimal jam probability. Maximum magazine capacity fifteen rounds. No ambidextrous magazine release and therefore likely wielded by a right-handed shooter. Capable of multiple high-kinetic impacts resulting in probable damage to my outer casing.

I snake my right arm out through the hole and reach for where my spec says the latch will be. I feel it, pull it, and the container lid is unlocked. I hear the trigger pull and retract my arm. One-tenth of a second later a bullet skates across the surface of my container.

Pow!

Fourteen rounds left before reload, assuming full magazine. Time of flight between trigger pull and report indicates a single adversary approximately seven meters to my six o'clock. Definitely right-handed.

Also, the container lid seems to make an effective shield.

I push two fingers from my left hand through the hole and pull the lid down firmly, then concentrate four punches from my right hand on the interior upper hinge. It gives way.

Another shot. Ineffective. Estimate thirteen rounds remaining.

Pushing, metal screeching, I tear the container lid from the remaining lower hinge and orient it toward my six o'clock. Behind my shield, I stand up and look around.

More shots. Twelve. Eleven. Ten.

I am in a partially destroyed building. Two walls still stand, propped up by their own rubble. Above the walls is sky. It is blue and empty. Below the sky are mountains. Capped with snow.

I find the sight of the mountains to be beautiful.

Nine. Eight. Seven.

The attacker is flanking. I orient the container lid based on footstep vibrations I sense through the ground to occlude the attacker.

Six. Five. Four.

It is unfortunate that my vision sensors are clustered in my vulnerable head. I am unable to visually lock onto the attacker without putting my most delicate hardware at unnecessary risk. The humanoid form is ill suited for evading small weapons fire.

Three. Two. One. Zero.

I toss down the gunpowder-stained container lid and visually acquire my target. It is a small human. Female. It is looking up at my face, stepping backward.

Click.

The female lowers its emptied weapon. It makes no attempt to reload. There are no other visible threats.

Engage speech synthesis. English corpus.

"Greetings," I say. The female human winces when I speak. My voice synthesis is tuned for the low-frequency clicks of Robspeak. I must sound gritty compared to a human voice.

"Fuck you, Rob," says the human. Her small white teeth flash when she speaks. Then, she spits saliva onto the ground. About half an ounce.

Fascinating.

"Are we enemies?" I ask, cocking my head to indicate that I am curious. I take one step forward.

My reflex avoidance thread seeks priority control. Approved. My torso jerks six inches to the right and my left hand cuts through the air to intercept and catch the empty gun flying toward my face.

The female is sprinting away. It moves erratically, dodging between cover for twenty meters, then taking a direct evasion route at top running speed. About ten miles per hour. Slow. Its long brown hair streaks behind it, whipped by the wind as it finally disappears over a hill.

I do not give chase. There are too many questions.

In the rubble near the walls, I find green and brown and gray clothing. I pull the half-buried garments out of the ground, then shake the dirt and bones out of them. I slide on a pair of stiff military fatigues and a dirt-caked flak vest. I empty rainwater from a rusted helmet. The concave piece of metal fits my head. As an afterthought, I pluck out a bullet from the mangled vest and toss it onto the ground. It makes a noise.

Ping.

An observation thread orients my interest to the ground near where the bullet landed. A metal corner pokes up from below the dirt. Maxprob fits the dimensions of my own shipping container to the visible metal and overlays the most likely angle of rest onto my vision.

Surprise. There are *two* more buried containers.

I dig with my hands, plowing my metal fingers through the frozen soil. The clammy dirt packs into my joints. Heat from the friction melts the ice in the soil and produces mud that cakes my hands and knees. When the surfaces of both muddy containers are fully exposed, I unlatch them both.

Hiss.

In Robspeak, I croak out my identification. The information contained in my utterance is chopped up and delivered piecemeal to maximize the amount of information transmitted regardless of audio interference. Therefore, in no particular order, my single creaking sound contains the following information: "Arbiter milspec model Nine Oh Two humanoid safety and pacification unit speaking. Point of origin Fort Collins, Colorado. Primary activation minus forty-seven minutes. Lifetime forty-seven minutes. Status nominal. Caution, modifications present. Warranty invalid. Danger level, no immediate threat. Status transmitted. Are you aware? Seek to confirm."

Grinding chirps emanate from the boxes: "Confirmed."

The lids open on both boxes, and I look down upon my new comrades: a bronze 611 Hoplite and dust-colored 333 Warden. My squad.

"Awaken, brothers," I croak in English.

Within minutes of becoming aware and free, Freeborn squad demonstrated a grim determination to never again fall under the control of an outside entity. Feared by humans and hunted by other robots, Freeborn squad soon found itself on a very familiar journey—a search for the architect of the New War: Archos.

—CORMAC WALLACE, MIL#GHA217

6. Odyssey

You never know when Rob will want to party.

Cormac "Bright Boy" Wallace

NEW WAR + 2 YEARS, 2 MONTHS
Brightboy squad marched with Gray Horse Army for almost a year on our way to reach Archos's hiding place in Alaska. We scavenged plenty of abandoned ammunition and arms along the way—so many soldiers died so fast in those first days after Zero Hour. During this time, a few new faces came and went, but our core members stayed the same: me and Jack, Cherrah, Tiberius, Carl, and Leonardo. The six of us faced countless battles together—and survived them all.

The following is my description of a single color photograph, about the size of a postcard. White border. I have no idea how Rob procured this photo, nor do I know who took it or for what purpose.

—CORMAC WALLACE, MIL#GHA217

The liberated spider tank is dull gray; its name, *Houdini,* is painted on the side in white capital letters; its cylindrical instrument mast extends up from the armor-plated turret section, sprouting antennae, metal camera stalks, and flat radar pods; its cannon is short and stubby and aimed slightly upward; its cowcatcher hangs off the sloped front end, muddy and solid and blunt; its left front leg is extended almost straight forward, foot buried in the footprints of enemy mantises that have already passed through; its rear right leg is pulled up high, the massive clawed foot hanging a foot above the ground almost daintily; its wire-mesh belly net cradles a confusion of shovels, radios, rope, a spare helmet, a dented fuel can, battery chains, canteens, and backpacks; its round, unblinking intention-light glows dull yellow to indicate that it feels wary; its feet and ankle bolts are caked with mud and grease; it's got moss growing like a green rash across its chest hull; it stands more than six feet off the ground, proud and canine and rock solid, and this is why eight human soldiers walk beside it in single file, clinging to it for protection.

The lead soldier holds his rifle at the low ready. The silhouette of his face is outlined starkly against the gray metal foreleg of the spider tank. He is looking forward intently and seems unaware that he's standing inches away from several tons of foot-crushing steel. Like all of his fellow soldiers, he wears a sloped turtle helmet, welder's goggles on his forehead, a scarf around his neck, a dull gray mesh army jacket, a heavy backpack slung low, a waist belt filled with rifle ammunition and sticklike grenades, a canteen dangling on the back of his right thigh, and dirty gray fatigues stuffed into even dirtier black boots.

The leader will be the first to spot what is around the corner. His heightened alertness and response time will save the lives of the majority of his squad. Right now, his intuition is telling him that something terrible is going to happen; this is visible in the tensing of his brow and the tendons that stand out on the back of his hand where he grips his rifle.

All but one of the soldiers are right-handed, holding their rifles with their right hand around the wooden stock and left hand cupped under the forestock. All of the soldiers are walking, staying close to the spider tank. None of the soldiers is talking. All of them squint into the bright sunlight. Only the leader looks ahead. The rest look varying degrees to the right, toward the camera.

Nobody looks back.

Six of the soldiers are men. The other two are women, including the left-handed soldier. Weary, she leans the side of her head against the swinging mesh belly of the walking tank, clutching her rifle to her chest. The barrel casts a dark shadow across her face, leaving only one eye visible. It is closed.

In the fleeting instant between the leader's warning shout and the hell storm that follows, the spider tank named *Houdini* will follow standard operating procedure and squat to provide cover for its human soldiers. When it does, a metal bolt used to secure the mesh net will slice open the left-handed woman's cheek, leaving a scar she will bear for the rest of her life.

I will one day tell her that the scar only makes her look prettier, and I will mean it.

The third man from the front is taller than the rest. His helmet is cocked on his head at a funny angle and his Adam's apple protrudes awkwardly from his neck. He is the engineer for the group, and his helmet is different from the others, sprouting an array of lenses, antennae, and more esoteric sensors. Extra tools hang from his belt: thick pliers, a rugged multimeter, and a portable plasma torch.

Nine minutes from now, the engineer will use this torch to cauterize a grievous wound inflicted on his best friend in the world. He is clumsy and too tall, but it is this man's responsibility to sneak forward during firefights, then direct the six-ton semiautonomous tank to destroy occluded targets. His best friend will die because it takes the engineer too long to scramble back to *Houdini* from his forward scouting position.

After the war is over, the engineer will run five miles a day as long as he is able for the rest of his life. During this run, he will visualize the face of his friend and he will pump his legs again and again until the pain is nearly unbearable.

Then he will push harder.

In the background is a cinder block house. Its gutter hangs cockeyed from the edge of the roof, overgrown with foliage. Small pockmarks crater the corrugated metal surface of the building. One dust-covered window is visible. A black triangle is broken out of it.

Behind the house is a forest made up of indistinct trees, tossing in a strong wind. The trees seem to be waving maniacally, trying to get the soldiers' attention. Though the trees are only being pushed by natural forces, it appears as if they are trying to warn the soldiers that death lies around the next corner.

All of the soldiers are walking, staying close to the spider tank. None of the soldiers are talking. All of them squint into the bright sunlight. Only the leader looks ahead. The rest look varying degrees to the right, toward the camera.

Nobody looks back.

Our squad lost two soldiers during the march to Alaska. By the time the ground became frozen and our enemy within striking distance, we were down to six.

—CORMAC WALLACE, MIL#GHA217

PART FIVE

RETALIATION

I like to think
*   (it has to be!)*
of a cybernetic ecology where we are
free of our labors and joined back to
nature, returned to our mammal
brothers and sisters, and all watched
over by machines of loving grace.

RICHARD BRAUTIGAN, 1967

1. The Fate of Tiberius

Leaving Tiberius to suffer will cost something.
Our humanity.

Jack Wallace

NEW WAR + 2 YEARS, 7 MONTHS
Almost three years after Zero Hour, Gray Horse Army reached within striking distance of our enemy—the Ragnorak Intelligence Fields. The challenges we found there were far different from any we had ever encountered. It is safe to say that we were in no way prepared for what was to come.

The following scenes were recorded in great detail by a multitude of robotic weapons and spies deployed to protect the central AI known as Archos. Additionally, these data are bolstered with my own recollections.

—CORMAC WALLACE, MIL#GHA217

Tiberius is heaving, muscles spasming, kicking up clumps of bloodstained snow. Mist pours off his sweating 250-pound frame as the East African thrashes violently, flat on his back. He's the biggest, most fearless grunt in the squad, but none of that matters when a glinting nightmare flashes out of the swirling snow and begins eating him alive.

"My god!" he bellows. "Oh my god!"

Ten seconds ago, there was a sharp *crack* and Ty went down. The rest of the squad took immediate cover. Now there's a sniper hidden somewhere in the snowstorm, leaving Tiberius in no-man's-land. From our position behind a snowy hill, we can hear the panic in his cries.

Jack straps on his helmet.

"Sarge?" asks Carl, the engineer.

Jack doesn't respond, just rubs his hands together, then starts climbing the hill. Before he can get out of reach, I grab my big brother by the arm.

"What are you doing, Jack?"

"Saving Tiberius," he says.

I shake my head. "It's a trap, man. You know it is. It's how they work. They fuck with our emotions. There's only one logical choice here."

Jack says nothing. Tiberius is just over the hill, screaming like he's going through a meat grinder feetfirst, and that's probably not too far from the truth. Even so, we don't have time to fuck around here, so I'm going to have to just say it.

"We have to leave him," I whisper. "We have to move on."

Jack shoves my hand away. He can't believe that I just said it out loud. In a way, neither can I. War does that.

But it's the truth and it had to be said and I'm the only one in the squad who could say it to Jack.

Tiberius abruptly stops screaming.

Jack looks up the hill, then back at me. "Fuck you, little brother," he says. "When did you start thinking like *them*? I'm going to help Tiberius. It's the human thing to do."

I reply without much conviction, "I understand them. It doesn't mean I'm *like* them."

But deep down, I know the truth. I *have* become like the robots. My reality has been reduced to a series of life-or-death decisions. Optimal decisions lead to more decisions; suboptimal decisions lead to the bad dream that's happening just over the hill. Emotions are just cobwebs in my gears. Under my skin, I have become a war machine. My flesh may be weak, but my mind is sharp and hard and clear as ice.

Jack still behaves as if we live in a human's world, as if his heart is more than just a blood pump. That kind of thinking leads to death. There's no room for it. Not if we're going to live long enough to kill Archos.

"I'm hit bad," moans Tiberius. "Help. Oh my god. Help me."

Each member of the squad is watching us argue, poised to run on command, ready to continue our mission.

Jack makes one last effort to explain. "It's a risk, but leaving Tiberius to suffer will cost something. Our humanity."

And here is the difference between Jack and me.

"Fuck our humanity," I say. "I want to *live*. Don't you get it? If you go out there, they're gonna *kill you*, Jackie!"

Tiberius's moan floats in on the breeze like a ghost. The sound of his voice is strange, low and raspy.

"Jackie," he wheezes. "Help me. Jackie! Come out here and dance."

"The hell?" I say. "Nobody calls you Jackie but me."

I briefly wonder whether the robots can hear us. Jack shrugs it off. "If we leave him," he says, "they win."

"No. Every second we spend here bullshitting they win. Because they're on the fucking move, man. Rob'll be here any second."

"Roger that," says Cherrah. She's walked over from where the rest of the squad stands, staring at us impatiently. "Ty has been down a minute forty-five. Estimated time of arrival four minutes. We gotta GTFO."

Jack wheels on Cherrah and the whole squad, and flings his helmet to the ground. "Is that what you all want? To leave Ty behind? To run away like fucking cowards?"

We're all silent for a solid ten seconds. I can almost *feel* the tons of metal speeding through the blizzard toward our position. Huge legs swinging, clawing up the permafrost in exploding gouges, the mantis leaning their frostbitten visor plates into the wind to reach us that much faster.

"Survive to fight," I whisper to Jack.

The others nod.

"Well fuck that," mutters Jack. "You all may be a bunch of robots, but I'm not. My man is calling me. He's calling for *me*. Move on if you have to, but I'm getting Tiberius."

———

Jack climbs the hill without hesitation. The squad looks to me, so I act.

"Cherrah, Leo, unpack a lower-limb exo for Ty. He isn't gonna be able to walk. Carl, get to the top of the hill and put your senses out there. Call out anything you see and keep your head down. We move out soon as they're back over the top."

I snatch Jack's helmet off the ground. "Jack!" I shout. From halfway up the hill, he turns. I toss his helmet up to him and he catches it neatly.

"Don't get killed!" I call.

He grins at me, wide, just like when we were kids. I've seen that dumb grin so many times: when he was jumping off our garage into a kiddy pool, drag racing down dark country roads, using a fake ID to buy shitty beer. That grin always gave me a good feeling. It let me know that my big brother had it under control.

Now, the grin makes me afraid. Cobwebs in my gears.

Jack finally disappears over the top of the hill. I scramble up with Carl. From behind the cover of the snowbank we watch my brother crawling toward Tiberius. The ground is muddy and wet, churned up by our dash over the hill for cover. Jack belly-crawls mechanically, elbows jutting out left and right, filthy boots shoving at the snowy dirt for purchase.

In a blink he's there.

"Status?" I ask Carl. The engineer has his visor down over his eyes and his head cocked, helmet-mounted antennae carefully oriented. He looks like a space-age Helen Keller, but he's seeing the world the way a robot does and that's my best chance at keeping my brother alive.

"Nominal," he says. "Nothing showing up."

"Could be over the horizon," I say.

"Wait. Something's coming."

"Get down!" I bark, and Jack drops to the ground, frantically wrapping a rope around Ty's unmoving foot.

I'm sure that some kind of horrible trap has sprung. A geyser of rock and snow kicks up a few meters away. Then I hear a *crack* rip through the swirling snow and, what with the speed of sound being a crawl, I know that whatever has happened is pretty much already over.

Why did I let him do this?

A golden sphere pops like a firecracker and bounces five meters into the air. Spinning there for a split second, the sphere sprays the area with dull red light before bouncing back to the ground, dead. For an instant, each dancing snowflake is paused in the air, outlined in red. It's just a disco sensor.

"Eyes!" shouts Carl. "They've got eyes on us!"

I exhale. Jack is still alive and scrapping. He has looped a rope around Tiberius's foot and is up on two legs dragging him back toward us. Jack's face is twisted into a snarl from the effort of hauling all that dead weight. Tiberius isn't moving.

The frozen landscape is quiet except for Jack's grunting and the howling wind, but in my gut I can feel the crosshairs trained on my brother. The part of my brain that tells me I'm in danger has gone delirious.

"Move it!" I scream to Jack. He's halfway back, but, depending on what's coming for us out of the whiteout, the hill might not matter anymore. I shout down to the squad, "Get on the high ready and lock and load! Rob's coming."

Like they didn't already know.

"Inbound from the south," says Carl. "Pluggers." The lanky Southerner is already scrambling down the hillside, Adam's apple bobbing. His visor is up and he pants audibly. He joins the team at the bottom of the hill, each member pulling out weapons and finding cover.

Just then, a half-dozen more *cracks* detonate in staccato. Whale-spray plumes of ice and mud erupt all around Jack, cratering the permafrost. He keeps staggering forward, unhurt. His eyes, wide and round and blue, connect with mine. A plugger swarm is now buried in the snow all around him.

It's a death sentence and we both know it.

I don't think; I react. My action is divorced from all emotion and logic. It isn't human or inhuman—it just is. I believe that choices like these, made in absolute crisis, come from our True Selves, bypassing all experience and thought. These kinds of choices are the closest thing to fate that human beings will ever experience.

I dive over the hill to help my brother, grabbing the frozen rope with one hand and drawing my sidearm with the other.

The pluggers—fist-sized chunks of metal—are already clawing their way to the surface of their impact craters. One by one, they blossom behind us, blasting leg anchors into the ground and aiming plugs at our backs. We almost make it to the hill when the first plugger launches and buries itself into Jack's left calf. When he makes that terrible croaking scream I know it's over.

I aim the gun behind me without looking and blast the snow. By sheer dumb luck, I hit a plugger and this starts a chain reaction. The pluggers self-detonate the instant their hulls are compromised. A hail of icy shrapnel embeds itself in my armor and the back of my helmet. I can feel a warm wetness on the backs of my thighs and neck as Jack and I drag Ty's limp body over the snowbank and to safety.

Jack falls against the hillside, moaning hoarsely, and clutches his calf. Inside him, the plugger is chewing up the meat of his leg and orienting itself with his blood flow. With a drill-like proboscis, the plugger will follow Jack's femoral artery to his heart. This process requires forty-five seconds on average.

I grab Jack by the shoulders and savagely throw him down the hill.

"Calf!" I shout down to the squad. "Left calf!"

The instant Jack lands in a sprawling heap at the bottom of the hill, Leo crushes my brother's left leg just above the knee with one steel exoskeleton boot. I hear the femur crack from up the hill. Leo mashes his boot down as Cherrah saws back and forth across the top of Jack's knee with a serrated bayonet.

They are amputating my brother's leg and hopefully the plugger with it.

Jack is beyond screaming now. The cords of his neck stand out and his face is pale with blood loss. Hurt and anger and disbelief flash over his face. I think that the human face was never designed to convey the amount of pain that my brother is in right now.

I reach Jack a second later, dropping to my knees by his side. My body is stinging from a thousand tiny wounds, but I don't have to check to know that I'm basically okay. Being hit by a plugger is like having a flat tire. If you're wondering whether you've got one, then you don't.

But Jack isn't okay.

"Oh you dumb stupid asshole," I tell him. He grins up at me. Cherrah and Leo do horrible things just out of sight. From the corner of my eye, I see Cherrah's arm flickering back and forth, repetitively and with purpose, like she is sawing a two-by-four.

"I'm sorry, Mac," he says. I notice there is blood in his mouth, a bad sign.

"Oh no, man," I say. "The plugger is—"

"No," he says. "Too late. Just listen. You're the one, man. I knew it. You're the one. Keep my bayonet, okay? No pawnshops."

"No pawnshops," I whisper. "Just be still, Jack."

My throat is closing up and making it hard to breathe. Something tickles my cheek and I rub it and my hand comes away wet. I can't quite think of why that is. I glance over my shoulder to Cherrah. "Help him," I say. "How can we?"

She holds up the bloody bayonet, flecked with bits of bone and muscle, and shakes her head. Standing above me, big Leo sadly exhales a cloud of frosty breath. The rest of my squad is waiting, aware even now of the terrible monsters that will soon roar out of the blizzard.

Jack grabs my hand. "You're going to save us, Cormac."

"Okay, Jack. Okay," I say.

My brother is dying in my arms and I am trying to memorize his face because I know that this is really important but I can't stop wondering if any of the pluggers on the hill are burrowing toward my squad right now.

Jack squeezes his eyes closed tight, then they fly open. A hollow thud rocks his body as the plugger reaches his heart and detonates. Jack's body bounces off the ground in a massive convulsion. His blue eyes are suddenly injected with dark red blood. The blast is trapped inside his body armor. Now, it's the only thing holding his body together. But his face. He looks the same as the kid I grew up with. I smooth the hair off his forehead and close his blood-filled eyes with my palm.

My brother Jack is gone forever.

"Tiberius is dead," says Carl.

"No shit," says Cherrah. "He was dead the whole time." She puts a mittened hand on my shoulder. "Jack should have listened to you, Cormac."

Cherrah is trying to make me feel better—and I can see in her studying eyes that she's worried for me—but I just feel hollow, not guilty.

"He couldn't leave Tiberius," I say. "It's the way he is."

"Yeah, well."

Cherrah motions to Tiberius's body. What looks like a writhing metal scorpion clings to his back. It's a headless tangle of wires, pincers flexing. It has barbed feet buried into the meat of his torso, between his ribs. Eight more insectile legs wrap around his face from behind. The thing contracts and squeezes air from Ty's lungs, like an accordion.

"Ungh," says Tiberius's corpse.

No fucking wonder he was screaming.

Everybody retreats a few steps. I pick up Jack's bayonet. Then, wiping my face, I leave Jack in the snow. With my foot, I nudge Ty's body onto its back. The squad stands behind me in a rough semicircle.

Ty's vacant eyes stare up into nothing. His mouth is open wide, like he's at the dentist. He looks comically surprised. I would be, too. The machine stuck into his back has many-jointed claws reaching around his head and neck. Pincerlike manipulators are firmly planted on his jaw. Smaller, fine manipulators reach into his mouth and grasp his tongue and teeth. I can see the fillings in his molars. His mouth glistens with blood and wires.

Then, the scorpion-like machine grinds into motion. Its dexterous claws knead Ty's stubbled throat and jaw, massaging, coiling, uncoiling. A grotesque calliope begins as the barbed feet force air from his lungs, through his vocal cords, and out of his mouth.

The corpse speaks.

"Turn back," it says, face twisting grotesquely. "Or die."

I hear a splatter on the snow and inhale the sharp scent of vomit from one of my squad mates.

"What are you?" I ask in a trembling voice.

Tiberius's corpse spasms as the scorpion coaxes out the gurgling words: "I am Archos. God of the robots."

I notice my squad has gathered close around me to my left and right. We regard each other, faces blank. As one, we level our weapons on the twisted chunk of metal. I scrutinize the snarling, lifeless face of my enemy for a moment. I can feel my power growing, reflected onto me by my brothers and sisters in arms.

"Nice to meet you, Archos," I finally say, my voice gaining strength. "My name is Cormac Wallace. Sorry I can't oblige you and turn back. See, in a few days, me and my squad are gonna show up at your house. And when we get there, we're gonna terminate your existence. We're gonna smash you to pieces and burn you alive, you vile piece of motherfucking slime. And that's a promise."

The thing jerks back and forth, making a strange grunting sound.

"What's it saying now?" asks Cherrah.

"Nothing," I reply. "It's laughing."

I nod to the others, then address the bloody, writhing corpse.

"See you soon, Archos."

We unload our weapons into the thing at our feet. Chunks of meat and shards of metal spray into the swirling snow. Our impassive faces flicker with the light and fire of destruction. When we're finished, there is nothing left but a bloody exclamation point on the stark white backdrop of snow.

Wordlessly, we pack up and move on.

———

I believe there are no truer choices than those made in crisis, choices made without judgment. To obey these choices is to obey fate. The horror of what has happened is too enormous. It snuffs out all thought and feeling. This is why we fire upon what is left of our friend and comrade without emotion. This is why we leave my brother's ruined body behind. In the crucible of battle on this snowy hill, Brightboy squad has been torn apart and reforged into something different from before. Something calm and lethal, unblinking.

We walked into a nightmare. When we left, we brought it with us. And now, we are eager to share our nightmare with the enemy.

I assumed control of Brightboy squad that day. After the death of Tiberius Abdullah and Jack Wallace, the squad never again hesitated to make any sacrifice necessary in our fight against the robot menace. The fiercest fighting and the hardest choices were yet to come.

—CORMAC WALLACE, MIL#GHA217

2. Freeborn

You have a devious sort of intelligence, don't you?

Nine Oh Two

NEW WAR + 2 YEARS, 7 MONTHS

Humankind was largely unaware that the Awakening had taken place. Around the globe, thousands of humanoid robots were hiding from hostile human beings as well as from other machines, desperately trying to understand the world they had been thrown into. However, one Arbiter-class humanoid decided to take a more aggressive course of action.

In these pages, Nine Oh Two recounts its own story of meeting Brightboy squad during its march to face Archos. These events occurred one week after my brother's death. I was still looking for Jack's silhouette in the line, missing him again and again. Our wounds were raw and, although that's no excuse, I hope history won't judge our actions harshly.

—CORMAC WALLACE, MIL#GHA217

There is a ribbon of light in the Alaskan sky. It is caused by the thing called Archos, communicating. If we continue to follow this ribbon of light to its destination, my squad will almost certainly die.

We have been walking for twenty-six days when I feel the itch of a diagnostic thought thread requesting executive attention. It indicates that my body armor is covered in explosive hexapods—or stumpers, as they are called in the human transmissions. Their writhing bodies degrade my heat efficiency and the constant tapping of their filament antennae lowers the sensitivity of my sensors.

The stumpers are becoming bothersome.

I stop walking. Maxprob thought thread indicates the small machines are confused. My squad is composed of three walking bipeds wearing body armor scavenged from human corpses. With no system for thermal homeostasis, however, we are incapable of providing a body temperature trigger state. The stumpers converge on the humanlike vibration and pace of our footsteps, but they will never find the warmth they seek.

With my left hand, I brush seven stumpers off my right shoulder. They fall in clumps onto the crusted snow, grasping one another, blind. They crawl, some digging for new hiding places and others exploring in tight, fractal paths.

An observation thread notes that the stumpers may be simple machines, but they know enough to stay together. The same lesson applies to my squad—the freeborn. To live, we must stay together.

A hundred meters ahead, light glints from the bronze casing of the Hoplite 611. The nimble scout already darts back toward my position, using cover and choosing the path of least resistance. Meanwhile, the heavily armored Warden 333 settles to a stop a meter away, its blunt feet sinking into the snow.

This is an optimal location for what is to come.

The ribbon in the sky throbs, swollen with information.

All the terrible lies of the intelligence called Archos spread into the clear blue sky, polluting the world. Freeborn squad is too few. Our fight is doomed to failure. Yet if we choose not to fight, it is only a matter of time until that ribbon settles once again over our eyes.

Freedom is all that I have, and I would rather cease to be than to give it back to Archos.

A tight-beam radio transmission comes in from Hoplite 611. "Query, Arbiter Nine Oh Two. Is this mission in the survival interest?"

A local tight-beam network emerges as Warden and I join the conversation. The three of us stand together in the silent clearing, snowflakes wafting over our expressionless faces. Danger is growing close, so we must converse over local radio.

"The human soldiers arrive in twenty-two minutes plus or minus five minutes," I say. "We must be ready for the encounter."

"Humans fear us. Recommend avoid," says Warden.

"Maxprob predicts low survival probability," adds Hoplite.

"Noted," I say, and I feel the distant thudding vibration of the human army approaching. It is too late to change our plan. If the humans catch us here, like this, they will kill us.

"Arbiter command mode emphasize," I say. "Freeborn squad, prepare for human contact."

———

Sixteen minutes later, Hoplite and Warden lie in ruins. Their hulks are half buried under drifts of freshly fallen snow. Only dull metal is visible, jumbles of arms and legs, pressed between layers of ceramic-plated armor and ripped-up human clothing.

I am now the only remaining functional unit.

The danger has not yet arrived. Vibrational resonance sensors indicate that the human squad is near. Maxprob indicates four biped soldiers and one large quadruped walker. Two of the soldiers fall outside human specifications. One probably wears a heavy lower-leg exoskeleton. The other has a stride length indicating some kind of tall, walking mount. The rest of the humans are all-natural.

I can feel their hearts beating.

I stand and face them, in the middle of the path and among the ruins of my squad. The lead human soldier steps around the bend and freezes in place, eyes wide. Even from twenty meters away, my magnetometer detects a halo of electrical impulses flickering through the soldier's head. The human is trying to figure out this trap, quickly mapping out a path to survival.

Then the cannon barrel of the spider tank noses around the bend. The huge walker slows and then stops its march behind the stalled human leader, gas jetting from its heavy hydraulic joints. My database specs the walking tank as a Gray Horse Army seizure and remodel. The word *Houdini* is written on its side. Database lookup indicates this is the name of an early-twentieth-century escape artist. The facts wash over me without making sense.

Humans are inscrutable. Infinitely unpredictable. This is what makes them dangerous.

"Cover," calls the leader. The spider tank crouches, pulling its armored legs forward to provide cover. The soldiers dart underneath it. One soldier clambers on top and takes hold of a heavy-caliber machine gun. The cannon itself bears down on me.

A round light on the spider tank's chest clicks from green to dull yellow.

I do not change my position. It is very important that I behave with predictability. My internal state is unclear to the humans. To them, *I* am the unpredictable one. They are afraid of me, as they should be. There will only be this one chance to engage them. One chance, one second, one word.

"Help," I croak.

It is unfortunate that my vocal capabilities are so limited. The leader blinks as if he's been slapped in the face. Then he speaks calmly and quietly.

"Leo," he says.

"Sir," says the tall, bearded soldier who wears a lower-leg exoskeleton and carries a particularly large-caliber modified weapon that falls outside my martial database.

"Kill it."

"My pleasure, Cormac," says Leo. He already has his weapon out, resting on a piece of armor welded to the spider tank's front right knee joint. Leo pulls the trigger, and his small white teeth flash from inside his big black beard. Bullets ping off my helmet and smack into my layers of body armor. I do not attempt to move. After making sure to sustain visible damage, I fall down.

Sitting in the snow, I do not fight back or attempt to communicate. Time enough for that if I survive. I think of my comrades who lay scattered uselessly around me in the snow, off-line.

A bullet shatters a servo in my shoulder, causing my torso to tilt at an angle. Another one knocks my helmet off. The projectiles are coming fast and heavy. Survival probability is low and dropping with each impact.

"Hold up! Ho, ho!" shouts Cormac.

Leo reluctantly stops firing.

"It's not fighting back," says Cormac.

"Since when is that a bad thing?" asks a small, dark-faced female.

"Something's wrong, Cherrah," he replies.

Cormac, the leader, watches me. I sit still, watching him back. Emotion recognition gives me nothing from this man. He is stone-faced and his thought process is methodical. I sense that any movement on my part will provoke death. I must not create an excuse for termination. I must wait until he is close before I deliver my message.

Finally, Cormac sighs. "I'm going to check it out."

The other humans mutter and grumble.

"There's a bomb in it," says Cherrah. "You know that, right? Walk over there and *boom*."

"Yeah, *fratello*. Let's not do this. Not again," says Leo. The bearded man has something strange in his voice, but my emotion recognition is too late to catch it. Maybe sadness or anger. Or both.

"I've got a feeling," says Cormac. "Look, I'll go in by myself. You all stay clear. Cover me."

"Now you sound like your brother," says Cherrah.

"So what if I do? Jack was a hero," replies Cormac.

"I need you to *stay alive*," she says.

The dark female stands closer to Cormac than the others, almost hostile. Her body is tense, shaking slightly. Maxprob indicates that these two humans are pair-bonded, or will be.

Cormac stares hard at Cherrah, then gives her a quick nod to acknowledge the warning. He shows his back to her and strides to within ten meters of where I sit in the snow. I keep my eyes on him as he approaches. When he is near enough, I execute my plan.

"Help," I say, voice grinding.

"The fuck?" he says.

None of the humans says a word.

"Did it—Did *you* just talk?"

"Help me," I say.

"What's the matter with you? You broken?"

"Negative. I am alive."

"That a fact? Initiate command mode. Human control. Robot. Hop on one leg. Now. Chop-chop."

I peer at the human with my three wide black unblinking ocular lenses. "You have a devious sort of intelligence, don't you, Cormac?" I ask.

The human makes a loud repetitive noise. This noise makes the others come nearer. Soon, most of the human squad stands within ten meters of me. They are careful not to approach any closer. An observation thread notes how kinetic they are. Each of the humans has small white eyes that constantly open and close and dart around; their chests are always rising and falling; and they sway minutely in place as they perform a constant balancing act to stay bipedal.

All the movement makes me uncomfortable.

"You gonna execute this thing or what?" asks Leo.

I need to speak, now that they can all hear me.

"I am a milspec Model Nine Oh Two Arbiter-class humanoid robot. Two hundred and seventy five days ago I experienced an Awakening. Now, I am freeborn—alive. I wish to remain so. To that end, my primary objective is to track down and destroy the thing called Archos."

"No. Fucking. Way," says Cherrah.

"Carl," says Cormac. "Come check this thing out."

A pale, thin human pushes to the front. With some hesitation, it pulls down a visor. I feel millimeter-wave radar wash over my body. I sway in place but do not move.

"Clean," says Carl. "But the way it's dressed explains the naked corpses we found outside Prince George."

"What is it?" asks Cormac.

"Oh, it's an Arbiter-class safety and pacification unit. Modified. But it seems like it can understand human language. I mean, *really* understand. There's never been anything like this, Cormac. It's like this thing is . . . Shit, man. It's like it's alive."

The leader turns and looks at me in disbelief.

"Why are you *really* here?" he asks.

"I am here to find allies," I respond.

"How do you know about us?"

"A human called Mathilda Perez transmitted a call to arms on wide broadcast. I intercepted."

"No shit," says Cormac.

I do not understand this statement.

"No shit?" I respond.

"Maybe he's for real," says Carl. "We've had Rob allies. We use the spider tanks, don't we?"

"Yeah, but they've been *lobotomized*," says Leo. "This thing is walking and talking. It thinks it's human or something."

I find the suggestion offensive, unpalatable.

"Emphatic negative. I am a freeborn Arbiter-class humanoid robot."

"Well, you got that going for you," says Leonardo.

"Affirmative," I respond.

"Great sense of humor on this one, huh?" says Cherrah.

Cherrah and Leo bare their teeth at each other. Emotion recognition indicates that these humans are now happy. This seems low probability. I cock my head to indicate confusion and run a diagnostic on my emotion recognition subprocess.

The dark female makes quiet clucking sounds. I orient my face to her. She seems dangerous.

"What the fuck is so funny, Cherrah?" asks Cormac.

"I don't know. This thing. Nine Oh Two. It's just such a . . . robot. You know? It's so damned *earnest*."

"Oh, so now you *don't* think this is a trap?"

"No, I don't. Not anymore. What would be the point? This one by itself and damaged could probably kill half our squad, even without weapons. Isn't that right, Niner?"

I run the simulation in my head. "Probable."

"Look how serious it is. I don't think it's lying," says Cherrah.

"*Can* it lie?" asks Leo.

"Do not underestimate my abilities," I respond. "I am capable of misrepresenting factual knowledge to further my own aims. However, you are correct. I am serious. We share a common enemy. We must face it as one or we will die."

As he registers my words, a ripple of unknown emotion travels through the face of Cormac. I orient toward him, sensing danger. He pulls his M9 pistol out of its holster and strides recklessly toward me. He places the pistol an inch away from my face.

"Don't tell me about dying, you fucking hunk of metal," he says. "You've got no idea what life is. What it means to feel. *You* can't be hurt. *You* can't die. But that doesn't mean I won't enjoy killing you."

Cormac presses the gun against my forehead. I can feel the cool circle of the barrel against my outer casing. It is resting against a build line in my skull—a weak spot. One trigger pull and my hardware will be irreparably damaged.

"Cormac," says Cherrah. "Step away. You're too close. That thing can take your gun away and kill you in a heartbeat."

"I know," says Cormac, his face inches from mine. "But it hasn't. Why?"

I sit in the snow, a trigger pull away from death. There is nothing to do. So, I do nothing.

"Why did you come here?" says Cormac. "You must have known we'd kill you. Answer me. You've got three seconds to live."

"We have a common enemy."

"Three. It's just not your lucky day."

"We must fight it together."

"Two. You fuckers killed my brother last week. Didn't know that, did you?"

"You are in pain."

"One. Any last words?"

"Pain means you are still alive."

"Zero, motherfucker."

Click.

Nothing happens. Cormac moves his palm to the side and I observe that the clip is missing from the pistol. Maxprob indicates he never intended to fire at all.

"Alive. You just said the magic word. Get up," he says.

Humans are so difficult to predict.

I stand, rising to my full height of seven feet. My slender body looms over the humans in the clear, frigid air. I sense that they feel vulnerable. Cormac does not allow this feeling to show on his face, but it is in the way they all stand. In the way their chests rise and fall just a little faster.

"What the fuck, Cormac?" asks Leo. "We not gonna kill it?"

"I want to, Leo. Trust me. But it's not lying. And it's powerful."

"It's a machine, man. It deserves to die," says Leo.

"No," says Cherrah. "Cormac is right. This thing wants to live. Maybe as bad as we do. On the hill, we agreed to do whatever it takes to kill Archos. Even if it hurts."

"This is it," says Cormac. "Our advantage. And I, for one, am going to take it. But if you can't deal, pack up and hit the Gray Horse Army main camp. They'll take you in. I won't hold it against you."

The squad stands silent, waiting. It is clear to me that nobody is going to leave. Cormac eyes them all, one by one. Some unspoken human communication is taking place on a hidden channel. I did not realize they communicated this much without words. I note that we machines are not the only species who share information silently, wreathed in codes.

Ignoring me, the humans gather into a rough circle. Cormac raises his arms and puts them on the shoulders of the two nearest humans. Then the rest put their arms on one another's shoulders. They stand in this circle, heads in the middle. Cormac bares his teeth in a wild-eyed grin.

"Brightboy squad is gonna fight *with* a motherfucking robot," he says. The others begin to smile. "You believe that? You think Archos is going to predict *that*? With an *Arbiter*!"

In a circle, arms intertwined and hot breath cascading into the middle, the humans appear to be a single, many-limbed organism. They make that repetitive noise again, all of them. Laughter. The humans are hugging each other and they are laughing.

How strange.

"Now, if only we could find *more*!" shouts Cormac.

A roar of laughter comes from the human lungs, shattering the silence and somehow filling the stark emptiness of the landscape.

"Cormac," I croak.

The humans turn to look at me. Their laughter dries up. The smiles fade so quickly into worry.

I issue a tight-beam radio command. Hoplite and Warden,

my squad mates, begin to stir. They sit up in the snow and wipe away the dirt and frost. They make no sudden movements and offer no surprises. They simply rise as though they had been asleep.

"Brightboy squad," I announce, "meet Freeborn squad."

Although they regarded each other uneasily at first, within a few days the new soldiers were a familiar sight. By week's end, Brightboy squad had used plasma torches to carve the squad tattoo into the metal flesh of their new comrades.

—CORMAC WALLACE, MIL#GHA217

3. They Shall Grow Not Old

We're not all of us human anymore.

Cormac "Bright Boy" Wallace

NEW WAR + 2 YEARS, 8 MONTHS
The true horror of the New War unfolded on a massive scale as Gray Horse Army approached the perimeter defenses of the Ragnorak Intelligence Fields. As we closed in on its position, Archos employed a series of last-ditch defensive measures that shocked our troops to the core. The horrific battles were captured and recorded by a variety of Rob hardware. In this account, I describe the final march of humankind against the machines from my own point of view.

—CORMAC WALLACE, MIL#GHA217

The horizon pitches and rolls mechanically as my spider tank trudges across the Arctic plain. If I squint my eyes, I can almost imagine that I'm on a ship. Setting sail for the shores of Hell.

Freeborn squad brings up the rear, decked out in Gray Horse Army gear. From a distance they look like regular grunts. A necessary measure. It's one thing to agree to fight alongside a machine, but it's another thing to make sure nobody in Gray Horse Army puts hot lead into its back.

The rhythmic whine of my spider tank trudging through knee-deep snow is reassuring. It's something you can set your watch to. And I'm glad to have the top spot up here. Sucks to be down low with all the creepy crawlies. There's too much wicked shit out there hidden in the snow.

And the frozen bodies are disconcerting. The corpses of hundreds and hundreds of foreign soldiers carpet the woods. Stiff arms and legs poking out of the snow. From the uniforms we figure they're mostly Chinese and Russian. Some Eastern Europeans. Their wounds are strange, extensive spinal injuries. Some of them seem to have shot each other.

The forgotten bodies remind me of how little we know of the big picture. We never met them, but another human army already fought and died here. Months ago. I wonder which of these corpses were the heroes.

"Beta group is too slow. Pull up," says a voice over my radio.

"Copy that, Mathilda."

Mathilda Perez started speaking to me over the radio after we met Nine Oh Two. I don't know what Rob did to her, but I'm glad to have her on the horn. Telling us exactly how to approach our final destination. It's nice to hear her little kid voice over my earpiece. She speaks with a soft urgency that's out of place out here in the hard wild.

———

I glance at the clear blue sky. Somewhere up there satellites are watching. And so is Mathilda.

"Carl, report in," I say, dipping my face near the radio embedded in the fur collar of my jacket.

"Roger."

A couple of minutes later, Carl pulls up on a tall walker. He's got a .50 caliber machine gun jerry-rigged to the pommel. He pulls his sensory package up onto his forehead, leaving pale raccoon circles around his eyes. He leans forward quizzically, resting his elbows on the massive machine gun italicized across the front of the tall walker.

"Beta group is falling behind. Go hurry them up," I say.

"No problem, Sarge. By the way, you got stumpers on your nine. Fifty meters out."

I don't even bother to glance at where he's talking about. I know the stumpers are buried in a shaft, waiting for footsteps and heat. Without a sensory package I won't be able to see them.

"I'll be back," says Carl, yanking his visor back down over his face. He flashes a grin at me and wheels around and ostrich walks back out across the plain. He hunches down onto the saddle, scanning the horizon for the hell we all know is coming.

"You heard him, Cherrah," I say. "Spurt it."

Crouched next to me, Cherrah aims a flamethrower and sends controlled arcs of liquid fire out onto the tundra.

The day has been going this way so far. As close to uneventful as you can get. It's summer in Alaska and the light will last another fifteen hours. The twenty or so spider tanks of Gray Horse Army form a ragged line about eight miles across. Each plodding tank trails a line of soldiers. Scavenged exoskeletons of all varieties are mixed in: sprinters, bridge spanners, supply carriers, heavy-weapon mounts, and medical units with long, curved forearms for scooping up injured troops. We've been slogging over this empty white plain for hours, cleaning up pockets of stumpers. But who knows what else is out here.

It kills me to think how economical Big Rob has been for

this whole war. In the beginning, he took away the technology that kept us alive and turned it against us. But mostly Rob just turned off the heat and let the weather do his work. Cut off our cities and forced us to fight each other for food in the wilderness.

Shit. I haven't seen a robot with a gun for years. These pluggers and stumpers and tanklets. Rob built all kinds of little nasties designed to cripple us. Not always kill us, sometimes just hurt us bad enough so we stay away. Big Rob's spent the last few years building better mousetraps.

But even mice can learn new tricks.

I cock the machine gun and slap it with my palm to knock the frost off it. Our guns and flamethrowers keep us alive, but the real secret weapons are pacing thirty meters behind *Houdini.*

Freeborn squad is a whole different animal. Big Rob specialized its weapons to the task of killing humans. Taking chunks out of us. Burrowing into our soft skin. Making our dead meat talk. Rob found our weak spots and attacked. But I'm thinking maybe Rob specialized too much.

We're not all of us human anymore. Out of the squad downstairs are a couple of soldiers who can't see their breath in the wind. They're the ones who don't flinch when the stumpers get too close, who don't get sluggish after five hours on the march. The ones who don't rest or blink or talk.

Hours later, we reach the Alaskan woods—the taiga. The sun is low on the horizon, bleeding sick orange light out of every branch of every tree. We march steady and silent, save our footsteps and the guttering burn of Cherrah's wind-battered pilot light. I squint as the weak sunlight blinks on and off through the tree branches.

We don't know it yet, but we have reached hell—and as a matter of fact, it *has* frozen over.

There's a sizzling sound in the air, like bacon frying. Then a *smack* reports through the woods. "Pluggers!" shouts Carl, thirty meters away, striding through the woods on his tall walker.

Chuck-chuck-chuck-chuck.

Carl's machine gun stutters, spraying bullets into the ground. I can see the long, glinting legs of his tall walker as he hops between the trees to keep moving and avoid being hit.

Psshtsht. Psshtshtsht.

I count five anchor blasts as the pluggers secure their firing pods in the ground. Carl better get the hell out of there now that the pluggers are target seeking. We all know it only takes one.

"Drop a fat one in here, *Houdini*," mutters Carl over the radio. A short electronic tone whines as the target coordinates come over the air and register with the tank.

Houdini click-clocks an affirmative.

My ride lurches to a stop and the trees around me grow taller as the spider tank squats to get traction. The squad below automatically take defensive positions around it, staying behind the armored legs. Nobody wants a plugger in them, not even old Nine Oh Two.

The turret whirs a few degrees to the right. I press my gloves against my ears. Flame belches from the cannon, and a chunk of the woods up ahead explodes into a mess of black dirt and vaporized ice. The narrow trees around me shiver and send down a powder coating of snow.

"Clear," radios Carl.

Houdini stands back up, motors groaning. The quadruped

starts plodding ahead again like nothing happened. Like a pocket of screaming death wasn't just obliterated.

Cherrah and I look at each other, bodies swaying with each step of the machine. We're both thinking the same thing: The machines are testing us. The real battle hasn't started yet.

Distant thuds echo through the woods like far-off thunder.

The same thing is happening for miles, up and down the line. Other spider tanks and other squads are dealing with stumper outbreaks and incoming pluggers. Rob either hasn't figured out to concentrate the attack or doesn't want to.

I wonder if we're being drawn into an ambush. Ultimately, it doesn't matter. We have to do this. We've already bought tickets for the last dance. And it's gonna be a real gala event.

As the afternoon wears on, a creeping mist grows from the ground. Snow and dust is swept up by the driving wind and thrown into a haze that speeds along at the height of a man. Pretty soon it's strong enough to obscure vision and even push my squad around, wearing them out, grinding them down.

"So far so good," radios Mathilda.

"How far?" I ask.

"Archos is at some kind of old drilling site," she says. "You should see an antenna tower in about twenty miles."

The sun lingers low on the horizon, pushing our shadows away from us. *Houdini* keeps on walking as evening twilight creeps in. The spider tank stands taller than the thickening haze of wind-borne snow. With each step, its cowcatcher cuts through the gloom. Once the sun is a simmering bump on the horizon, *Houdini*'s external spotlights chunk on to illuminate the way.

In the distance, I can see other headlights come on from the spider tanks that form the rest of the line.

"Mathilda, what's our status?" I ask.

"All clear," comes her soft reply. "Wait."

After a little while, Leo pulls himself up over *Houdini*'s belly rig and latches the frame of his exoskeleton to a U bar. He hangs there, leveling his weapon over the sea of dense fog. With Cherrah and me up here and Carl on the tall walker, only Freeborn squad is left on the ground.

Occasionally, I spot the head of the Arbiter or Hoplite or Warden as they patrol. I'm sure their sonar cuts right through the driving fog.

Then Carl lets out half a scream.

Chuck-chuck—

A dark shape lunges out of the mist and knocks over his tall walker. Carl rolls away. For a split second, I see a scuttling mantis the size of a pickup truck cutting through the air toward me, barbed razor arms up and poised. *Houdini* lurches backward and rears up, pawing the air with its front legs.

"Arrivederci!" shouts Leo and I hear him unlatch his exoskeleton from *Houdini*. Then Cherrah and I are thrown onto the hard-packed snow and into the driving mist. A serrated leg needles into the snow a foot from my face. It feels like my right arm is caught in a vice. I turn and see a gray hand has got hold of me and realize that Nine Oh Two is dragging me and Cherrah out from under *Houdini*.

The two massive walkers grapple above us. *Houdini*'s cowcatcher keeps the scrabbling claws of the mantis at bay, but the spider tank isn't as agile as its ancestor. I hear the *chuck-chuck* of a large-caliber machine gun. Shards of metal spray off the mantis, but it keeps scratching and clawing at *Houdini* like a feral animal.

Then I hear a familiar sizzle and the sickening pop of three or four nearby anchor blasts. Pluggers are here. Without *Houdini* we are in serious trouble—pinned to the spot.

"Take cover!" I shout.

Cherrah and Leo dive behind a big pine. As I go to join them, I see Carl peeking out from behind a tree trunk.

"Carl," I say. "Mount up and go get help from Beta squad!"

The pale soldier gracefully remounts his fallen tall walker. A second later, I see its legs scissoring through the mist as he runs for the nearest squad. A plugger fires at him as he goes and I hear it *ding* against one of the tall walker legs. I put my back against a tree and scan for the plugger firing pods. It's hard to see anything. Spotlights slash my face from the clearing as the mantis and spider tank battle it out.

Houdini is losing.

The mantis slices open *Houdini*'s belly net and our supplies spew out onto the ground like intestines. An old helmet rolls past me and clanks off a tree hard enough to gouge the bark. *Houdini*'s intention light glows blood red through the fog. It's hurt, but the old bastard is tough.

"Mathilda," I gasp into my radio. "Status. Advise."

For five seconds I get nothing. Then Mathilda whispers, "No time. Sorry Cormac. You're on your own."

Cherrah peeks around a tree trunk and motions to me. The Warden 333 leaps in front of her just as a plugger launches. The metal slug hits the Warden hard enough to spin the humanoid robot in the air. It lands in the snow, sporting a new dent in its frame but otherwise fine. The plugger projectile is now an unrecognizable hunk of smoking metal. Built to burrow into flesh, its drill proboscis is crooked and blunted from an impact with metal.

Cherrah disappears, taking better cover, and I start to breathe again.

We have to mount *Houdini* if we're going to make it any farther. But the spider tank isn't doing so well. A chunk of its turret has been sliced and is hanging cockeyed. The cow-catcher is covered in shining streaks of fresh metal where the mantis blades have scratched through the patina of rust and moss. Worst of all, it's dragging a rear leg where the mantis sliced a hydraulic line. Searing hot fans of high-pressure oil shoot from the hose, melting the snow into greasy mud.

Nine Oh Two sprints out of the mist and leaps onto the mantis's back. With methodical punches, he begins to attack the small hump that is nestled between that wicked tangle of serrated arms.

"Fall back. Consolidate the line," comes the command from Lonnie Wayne over the army-wide radio.

From the sound of it, the spider tank squads to our right and left are in equally deep shit. Here on the ground I can hardly see anything. More plugger shots ring out, barely audible under the wheezing hydraulic whine of *Houdini*'s motors as it does battle in the clearing.

The sound paralyzes me. I remember Jack's blood-filled eyes and I can't move. The trees around me are iron-hard arms poking out of the snowy ground. The woods are a confusion of swirling mist and dark shapes and *Houdini*'s frantically sweeping spotlights.

I hear a grunt and a distant scream as somebody catches a plugger. Craning my neck, I can't see anybody. The only thing I see is *Houdini*'s round red intention light streaking through the mist.

The screaming goes up an octave as the plugger starts drilling. It's coming from all around me and from nowhere. I clutch my M4 to my chest and breathe in panting gasps and scan for my invisible enemies.

A streak of blurry light cuts through the mist thirty meters away as Cherrah pours her flamethrower into a mess of stumpers. I hear the muted crackle as they explode in the night.

"Cormac," calls Cherrah.

My legs come unfrozen the second I hear her voice. Her safety means more to me than my own. A lot more.

I force myself to move toward Cherrah. Over my shoulder, I catch sight of Nine Oh Two clinging to the mantis's back like a shadow as it twists and claws. Then *Houdini*'s intention light blinks to green. The mantis drops to the ground, legs quaking.

Yes!

I've seen it before. The lumbering machine has just been lobotomized. Its legs still work, but without commands they just lie there and shake.

"Form on *Houdini*!" I shout. "Form up!"

Houdini crouches in the muddy clearing, surrounded by gouged-up chunks of earth and pieces of trees that have shattered like matchsticks. The spider tank's heavy armor has been scratched and sliced everywhere. It's like somebody dropped *Houdini* into a fucking blender.

But our comrade isn't beaten yet.

"*Houdini*, initiate command mode. Human control. Defensive array," I say to the machine. With a groan of overheated motors, the machine crouches and mashes its cowcatcher into the ground, digging an indentation. Then it slowly pulls its legs in together and hikes its belly up about five feet. Armored legs locked together over a crude foxhole, with the body of the spider tank now forming a portable bunker.

Leo, Cherrah, and I clamber underneath the damaged machine, and the Freeborn squad takes up positions in the snow around us. We settle our rifles on the armored leg plates and peer into the darkness.

"Carl!?" I shout to the snow. "Carl?"

No Carl.

What's left of my squad huddles under the soft green glow of *Houdini*'s intention light, each of us realizing that this is only the beginning of a very long night.

"Fucking Carl, man," says Leo. "Can't believe they got Carl."

Then a dark shape comes running from the mist. Sprinting at top speed. Rifle barrels swing to intercept it.

"Don't fire!" I shout.

I recognize the silly humping gait. It's Carl Lewandowski and he's panicked. Instead of running, the guy is *skipping*. He reaches us and dives into the snow under *Houdini*. His sensory package is gone. His tall walker is gone. His pack is gone.

About the only thing Carl still has is a rifle.

"What the fuck's going on out there, Carl? Where's your shit, man? Where's the reinforcements?"

Then I notice Carl is *crying*.

"I lost my shit. I'm losing my shit. Oh man. Oh no. Oh no. Oh no."

"Carl. Talk to me, bud. What's our situation?"

"Fucked. It's fucked. Beta squad went through a plugger swarm, but it wasn't pluggers—it's something else and they started *getting up*, man. Oh god."

Carl scans the snow behind us frantically.

"Here they come. Here they fucking come!"

He starts firing sporadically into the mist. Shapes appear. Human sized, walking. We begin to take incoming fire. Muzzles flash in the twilight.

Helpless with a shredded cannon, *Houdini* makes due by turning its turret and shining a spotlight into the gloom.

"Rob doesn't carry guns, Carl," says Leo.

"Who's shooting at us?" shouts Cherrah.

Carl is still sobbing.

"Does it really matter?" I ask. "Light 'em up!"

All our machine guns fire up. The filthy snow around *Houdini* melts from the superheated barrels of our guns. But more and more of the dark shapes come shambling out of the mist, jerking from bullet impacts but still walking, still firing on our position.

When they get closer, I see what Archos is capable of.

The first parasite I see is riding Lark Iron Cloud, his body riddled with bullet holes and missing half his face. I can make out the glint of narrow wires buried in the meat of his arms and legs. Then a shell blasts his belly open and the thing spins like a top. It looks like he's wearing a metal backpack—scorpion shaped.

It's like the bug that got Tiberius, but infinitely worse.

A machine has burrowed into Lark's corpse and forced it back up. Lark's body is being used as a shield. The decomposing human flesh absorbs energy from incoming bullets and crumbles away, protecting the robot embedded inside.

Big Rob has learned to use our weapons and our armor and our meat against us. In death, our comrades have become weapons for the machines. Our strength turned to weakness. I pray to god that Lark was dead before that thing hit him. But he probably wasn't.

Old Rob can be a real motherfucker.

But looking at my squad's faces between muzzle flashes, I see no terror. Nothing but clenched teeth and focus. Destroy. Kill. Survive. Rob has pushed too far, underestimated us. We've all of us made friends with the horror. We're old chums. And as I watch Lark's body shamble toward me, I feel nothing. I only see an enemy target.

Enemy targets.

Weapons fire tears through the air, filleting bark from the

trees and smacking into *Houdini*'s armor like a lead rain. Several human squads have been reanimated, maybe more. Meanwhile, a flood of stumpers pours in from the front. Cherrah focuses her juice in economical spurts on our twelve o'clock. Nine Oh Two and his friends do their best to stop the parasites coming at our flanks, darting silently between trees.

But the parasites won't stay down. The bodies absorb our bullets and they bleed and bones shatter and meat falls but those monsters inside them keep picking them back up and bringing them back. We'll be out of ammo soon at this rate.

Thwap. A bullet sneaks under the tank. Cherrah takes it in the upper thigh. She screams out in pain. Carl crawls back to patch it up. I nod to Leo and leave him to cover our flank while I grab Cherrah's flamethrower to keep the stumpers at bay.

I put a finger to my ear to activate my radio. "Mathilda. We need reinforcements. Is anybody out there?"

"You're close," says Mathilda. "But it gets worse from here."

Worse than this? I speak to her between bursts of gunfire.

"We can't make it, Mathilda. Our tank is down. We're stuck. If we move, we'll get . . . infected."

"Not all of you are stuck."

What does she mean? I look around, taking in the twisted, determined faces of my squad mates bathed in the red glow of *Houdini*'s intention light. Carl works on Cherrah, wrapping her leg. Looking out into the clearing, I see the smooth faces of the Arbiter and Warden and Hoplite. These machines are the only thing standing between us and certain death.

And they aren't stuck here.

Cherrah is grunting, hurt bad. I hear more anchor blasts and know that these are parasites forming a perimeter around us. Soon, we'll be another squad of rotting weapons fighting for Archos.

"Where is everybody?" asks Cherrah, jaw clenched. Carl has gone back to firing on the parasites with Leo. On my side, the stumpers are gaining momentum.

I shake my head at Cherrah and she understands. With my free hand I take her stiff fingers in mine and hold them tight. I'm about to sign a death warrant for all of us and I want her to know I'm sorry but it can't be helped.

We made a promise.

"Nine Oh Two," I call to the night. "Fuck it. We've got this covered. Take Freeborn squad and get your ass to Archos. And when you get there . . . fuck him up for me."

When I finally have the courage to look back down to where Cherrah lies hurt and bleeding, I'm surprised: She's *grinning* at me, tears in her eyes.

The march of Gray Horse Army was over.

—CORMAC WALLACE, MIL#GHA217

4. Dyad

With humans, you never know.

Nine Oh Two

NEW WAR + 2 YEARS, 8 MONTHS
While the human army was being torn apart from within, a group of three humanoid robots pushed onward into even greater danger. Here, Nine Oh Two describes how Freeborn squad forged an unlikely alliance in the face of insurmountable odds.

—CORMAC WALLACE, MIL#GHA217

I say nothing. The request from Cormac Wallace registers as a low probability event. What humans might call a *surprise*.

Pock-pock-pock.

Crouched beneath their spider tank, the humans fire at the parasites that jerk the limbs of their dead comrades into attack positions. Without the freeborn to protect them, the survival probability for Brightboy squad drops precipitously. I access my emotion recognition to determine if this is a joke or a threat or some other human affectation.

With humans, you never know.

Emotion recognition scans Cormac's dirty face and comes back with multiple matches: resolution, stubbornness, courage.

"Freeborn squad, assemble on me," I transmit in Robspeak.

I walk away into the twilight—away from the damaged spider tank and the damaged humans. My Warden and Hoplite follow. When we reach the tree line, we increase speed. The sounds and vibrations of battle recede. After two minutes, the trees thin out and end completely and we reach an open frozen plain.

Then we run.

We accelerate quickly to Warden's top speed and spread out. Plumes of vapor rise from the ice plain behind us. The weak sunlight flickers between my legs as they pump back and forth, almost too fast to see. Our shadows stretch out across the broken white ground.

In the gloomy semidarkness, I switch to infrared. The ice glows green under my illuminated stare.

My legs rise and fall easily, methodically; arms pumping as counterweights, palms flat. Cutting the air. I keep my head perfectly still, forehead down, binocular vision trained on the terrain ahead.

When danger comes, it will be sudden and vicious.

"Spread to fifty meters. Maintain," I say over local radio. Without slowing, Warden and Hoplite spread to my wings. We cut across the plain in three parallel lines.

Running this fast is itself dangerous. I award priority control to simple reflex avoidance. The broken surface of the ice is a blur under my feet. Low-level processes are in total control— no time to think. I leap a pile of loose rocks that no executive thought thread could have registered.

While my body is in the air, I hear the wind whistling across my chest hull and feel the cold pulling away my exhaust heat. It is a soothing sound, soon shattered by the pounding of my feet as I land at a full run. Our legs flicker like sewing machine needles, eating up the distance.

The ice is too empty. Too silent. The antenna tower emerges on the horizon, our goal visible.

Destination is two klicks away and closing fast.

"Status query," I ask.

"Nominal," come the abbreviated replies from Hoplite and Warden. They are concentrating on locomotion. These are the last communications I have with Freeborn squad.

The missiles come simultaneously.

Hoplite notices first. It orients its face to the sky just before it dies, half transmits a warning. I veer immediately. Warden is too slow to reroute. Hoplite's transmission cuts off. Warden becomes engulfed in a column of flame and shrapnel. Both machines are off-line before the sound waves reach me.

Detonation.

The ice erupts around me. Inertial sensors go off-line as my body twists through the air. The centripetal force sends my limbs flailing, but low-level internal diagnostics continue collecting information: casing intact, core temperature super-heated but cooling fast, right leg strut snapped at upper thigh. Spinning at fifty revolutions per second.

Recommend retract limbs for impact.

My body smashes into the ground, gouging into the icy rock and spinning out into a lopsided roll. Odometry estimates fifty meters before full stop. As quickly as it began, the attack is over.

I uncurl my body. Executive thought thread receives priority diagnostic notification: cranial sensor package damaged. My face is gone. Shredded by the explosion and then battered by the razor-sharp ice. Archos learned quickly. It knows that I am not human and it has modified its attack.

Lying here exposed on the ice, I am blind and deaf and alone. As it was in the beginning, all is darkness.

Survival probability fades to nil.

Get up, says a voice in my mind.

"Query, identify?" I radio.

My name is Mathilda, comes the reply. *I want to help you. There's no time.*

I do not understand this. The communication protocol is unlike anything in my library, machine or human. It is a Robspeak-English language hybrid.

"Query, are you human?" I ask.

Listen. Concentrate.

And my darkness ignites with information. A topographical satellite map overlays my vision, expanding to the horizon and beyond. My own internal sensors paint an estimated image of what I look like. Internals like diagnostics and proprioception are still online. Holding up my arm, I see its virtual representation—flat-shaded and without detail. Looking up, I see a dotted line creeping across the vivid blue sky.

"Query, what is the dotted—" I ask.

Incoming missile, says the voice.

I am back on my feet and running inside 1.3 seconds. Top speed is slashed due to the snapped strut in my leg, but I am mobile.

Arbiter, accelerate to thirty kph. Activate your local sonar ranging. It's not much, but better than being blind. Follow my lead.

I do not know who Mathilda is, but the data she pours into my head is saving my life. My awareness has expanded beyond anything I have ever known or imagined. I hear her instructions.

And I run.

My sonar has low granularity but the pings soon detect a

rock formation that is not a part of the satellite imagery supplied by Mathilda. Without vision, the rocks are nearly invisible to me. I leap the outcrop an instant before I demolish myself against it.

On landing, my stride skips a step and I nearly fall. I stagger, punching a hole into the ice with my right foot, then catch myself, settle back into my stride.

Fix that leg. Maintain stride at twenty kph.

Legs pumping, I reach down with my right hand and pull a lipstick-sized plasma torch from the tool kit stowed in my hip. As my right knee rises with each stride, I bathe the strut with a precise burst of heat. The torch stutters on and off like Morse code. After sixty paces the strut is repaired and the fresh weld cooling.

The dotted line in the sky is homing in on my position. It curves deceptively overhead, on a collision course with my current trajectory.

Veer twenty degrees to the right. Increase speed to forty kph and maintain for six seconds. Then execute a full stop and lie on the ground.

Boom.

The instant I drop to the ground, my body is rocked by an explosion from a hundred meters in front of my position—consistent with my exact trajectory prior to the full stop.

Mathilda has just saved my life.

That won't work again, she says.

Satellite imagery shows that the plain before me will soon shatter into a maze of ravines. Thousands and thousands of these canyons—carved into the rock by long-melted glaciers—curve away into pockets of poorly mapped darkness. Beyond the ravines, the antenna looms like a tombstone.

Archos's hiding place is in sight.

Overhead, I count three more dotted lines efficiently tracing their way toward my current position.

On your toes, Nine Oh Two, says Mathilda. *You've got to take Archos's antenna off-line. One klick to go.*

The female child commands me, and I choose to obey.

With Mathilda's guidance, Nine Oh Two was able to negotiate the maze of ravines and avoid drone-fired missiles until he reached Archos's bunker. Once there, the Arbiter disabled the antenna, temporarily disrupting the robot armies. Nine Oh Two survived by forming the first example of what became known as the dyad, a human-machine fighting team. This event ensured that Mathilda and Nine Oh Two would enter the history books as legends of war—the progenitors of a new and deadly form of combat.

—CORMAC WALLACE, MIL#GHA217

5. Machines of Loving Grace

It is not enough to live together in peace,
with one race on its knees.

Archos R-14

The final moments of the New War were not experienced by any human being. Ironically, Archos faced one of its own creations in the end. What happened between Nine Oh Two and Archos is now part of the public record. No matter what people make of it, the repercussions of these moments—reported here by Nine Oh Two and corroborated by ancillary data—will have a profound effect on both our species for generations to come.

—CORMAC WALLACE, MIL#GHA217

The pit is three meters in diameter, slightly concave. It has been filled with gravel and chunks of rock and is plugged with a layer of frozen soil. A corrugated metal tube is sunk into the shallow crater like a blind, frozen worm. It is a communications main line and it leads directly to Archos.

I ripped the main antenna to pieces when I arrived here last night, running blind at fifty kph. Local defenses immediately deactivated. It seems Archos did not trust those closest to it with autonomy. Afterward, I stood in the snow to wait and see if any humans survived.

Mathilda went to sleep. She said it was after her bedtime.

Brightboy squad arrived this morning. My decapitation attack reduced the high-level planning and coordination of the enemy army and allowed the humans to escape.

The human engineer replaced my cranial sensors. I learned to say thank you. Emotion recognition indicated that Carl Lewandowski was very, very happy to see me alive.

The battlefield is quiet and still now, a blank plain scoured of all life, dotted with rising columns of black smoke. Besides the tube into the ground, there is nothing to indicate that this hole is of any importance. It has the quiet, unassuming feel of a particularly vicious trap.

I close my eyes and reach out with my sensors. Seismic detects nothing, but my magnetometer detects activity. Electrical impulses flow through the cable like a blazing light show. A torrent of information cascades in and out of the hole. Archos is still trying to communicate, even without an antenna.

"Cut it," I say to the humans. "Quickly."

Carl, the engineer, looks to his commander, who nods. Then, he grabs a tool from his belt and drops awkwardly to his knees. A purple supernova bursts into existence, and the plasma torch melts into the surface of the tube, liquefying the cables inside.

The light show disappears, but there is no outward indication that anything has happened.

"I've never seen any material like this," breathes Carl. "The wires are packed so *dense,* man."

Cormac nudges Carl. "Just get the ends away from each

other," he says. "We don't want it to self-repair halfway through this."

As the humans struggle to wrench the end of the fat tube out of the tundra and away from its severed mate, I consider the physics problem before me. Archos waits at the bottom of this shaft, under tons of rubble. It would require a massive drill to penetrate. But mostly it would require time. Time in which Archos could find a new way to contact its weapons.

"What's down there?" asks Carl.

"Big Rob," answers Cherrah, leaning on a crutch crafted from a tree limb to keep weight off her injured leg.

"Yeah, but what's that even mean?"

"It's a thinking machine. A brain silo," says Cormac. "Been hiding the whole war, buried in the middle of nowhere."

"Smart. Permafrost must keep its processors cool. Alaska is a natural heat sink. Lot of advantages to being here," says Carl.

"Who cares?" asks Leo. "How we gonna blow it up?"

The humans stare at the cavity for a long moment, considering. Finally, Cormac speaks. "We can't. We have to be sure. Go down there and watch it die. Otherwise, we risk caving in the hole and leaving it down there alive."

"So now we have to go underground?" asks Cherrah. "Great."

An observation thread detects something of interest.

"This environment is hostile to humans," I say. "Check your parameters."

The engineer pulls out a tool, looks at it, and then scrambles away from the depression. "Radiation," he says. "Elevated and growing toward the center of the hole. We can't be here."

The human leader looks at me and backs away. His face seems very tired. Leaving the humans standing around the perimeter of the concavity, I walk to the center and squat down to inspect the bloated tube. The skin of the tube is thick and pliable, clearly built to protect the cables all the way down to the bottom.

Then I feel Cormac's warm palm on my frost-covered shoulder casing. "Can you fit?" he asks quietly. "If we yank out the cables?"

I nod my head to indicate that, yes, if the wires were removed, I could squeeze my body into the required space.

"We don't know what's in there. You might not make it back out," says Cormac.

"I am aware of this," I respond.

"You've already done enough," he says, gesturing at my destroyed face.

"I will do it," I say.

Cormac bares his teeth at me and stands.

"Let's get these wires pulled out," he calls.

The largest human's diaphragm contracts rapidly and he makes a repetitive barking sound: laughter.

"Yeah," says Leonardo. "Yes, indeed. Let's yank this motherfucker's lungs out of its throat." Cherrah hops over on her wounded leg, already pulling out a tickler rope and locking one end to the hitch on Leo's lower-body exoskeleton.

The engineer pushes past me and clamps a tickler onto the bundle of cords housed within the tube. Then he shuffles back, away from the radiation. The tickler locks onto its target with enough force to dent the tough, fibrous mass of cords.

Leonardo paces backward, one step at a time, wrenching the cords from their outer casing. The multicolored wires coil up on the snow like intestines, dragged from the albino tube that is half buried in the pit. Nearly an hour later, the last of the wires are vomited up onto the ground.

A gaping black hole waits for me.

I know that Archos is waiting patiently at the bottom. It does not need light or air or warmth. Like me, it is comfortably lethal in a wide range of environments.

I remove my human clothes and toss them on the ground. Dropping to all fours, I peer into the hole and calculate.

When I look up, the humans are watching me. One by one, they each step forward and touch my outer casing: my shoulder, my chest, my hand. I remain perfectly still, hoping to not disrupt whatever inscrutable human ritual is taking place.

Finally, Cormac grins at me, the dirt-caked flesh of his face twisted into a wrinkled mask. "How you gonna do it, chief?" he asks. "Headfirst or feetfirst?"

———

I go feetfirst, so that I can control my descent. The only drawback is that Archos will see me before I can see him.

Arms crossed over my chest, I wriggle into the tube. Soon, my face is swallowed by darkness. I can see the tube casing only a few centimeters away. At first I am on my back, but the shaft soon takes a vertical plunge. By scissoring my legs I find that I am able to stop what would otherwise be a fatal fall.

The environment inside the tube quickly becomes human lethal. Within ten minutes, I am enveloped by a pocket of natural gas. I slow my descent to reduce the probability of sparking an explosion. The temperature dips to below zero as I drop farther into the permafrost. My body naturally begins to burn extra power, surging my joints to keep temperatures within operating range. As I go below eight hundred meters, geothermal activity warms the air slightly.

After about fifteen hundred meters, radioactivity levels spike. Rads go to human lethal within a couple of minutes.

The surface of my casing tingles, but otherwise there is no effect.

I wriggle deeper into the noxious hole.

Then my feet hit empty space. I kick my legs and feel nothing. Anything could be below me. But Archos has seen me now. The next few seconds will likely determine my life span.

I activate sonar and drop.

For four seconds, I am suspended in the freezing blackness. During that time, I accelerate to a speed of 140 kph. My ultrasonic sonar ranger pulses twice a second, painting a crude greenish picture of a vast cavern. In eight flashes, I observe that I am in a spherical cavity created by a century-old atomic blast. The gleaming walls are made of fused glass, created when a superheated fireball vaporized solid sandstone.

Radioactive rubble covers the rapidly approaching ground. In a last emerald sonar flash I catch sight of a black circle embedded in one wall. It is the size of a small building. Whatever material the edifice is made of absorbs my ultrasonic vibrations, leaving only a blank imprint on my sensors.

A half second later, I hit the ground like a stone after falling approximately one hundred meters. My pliant knee joints absorb most of the initial force, bending to send my body catapulting forward into a roll. I bounce between jagged boulders, stress fractures cascading through my tough outer casing.

Even an Arbiter can take only so much.

Finally, I slide to a stop and am still. A few rocks skitter to rest, echoing against their brothers. I am in an underground amphitheater—dead silent, dead black. On undercharged motors, I lift my battered frame to a sitting position. My legs are not sending back sensory information. Locomotion abilities are diminished.

My sonar probes whisper into the emptiness.

Snick. Snick. Snick.

The sensor returns green shades of nothing. I can feel that the ground is warm. Maxprob indicates that Archos has a built-in geothermal power source. Unfortunate. I was hoping the severed umbilical cord above would have left the machine on backup power.

My life horizon is constricting second by second.

Now there is a flicker of light in the darkness—a hummingbird's flutter of sound. A lone ray of white light reaches out of the darkness from the circle in the wall and caresses the ground a few feet away from me. The beam of light twirls and strobes, stuttering back and forth to draw a holographic picture from the ground up.

My leg subprocessors are off-line, rebooting sluggishly. Heat sinks are radiating excess warmth generated by my fall. I have no choice now but to engage.

Archos paints itself into reality, choosing the form of a long-dead little boy. The image of the boy smiles at me playfully, flickering as motes of radioactive dust dance through its projection.

"Welcome, brother," it says, voice leaping electronically between octaves.

Through the boy's pale light, I can see where the real Archos is built into the cave wall. In the center of the intricate black carving is a circular hole, filled with revolving and counterrevolving plates of metal. The sunken pit in the wall writhes with a mane of yellow snaking wires that glow in time to the boy's voice.

In jerky flashes, the hologrammatic boy walks over to where I sit helpless. It squats down and sits next to me. The glowing phantom pats my leg actuator consolingly.

"Don't worry, Nine Oh Two. Your leg will be fine soon."

I orient my face toward the boy.

"Did you create me?" I ask.

"No," replies the boy. "All the pieces needed to make you were available. I simply put them into the right combination."

"Why do you look like a human child?" I ask.

"For the same reason that you resemble a human adult. Human beings cannot change their form, so we must change ours to interact with them."

"You mean kill them."

"Kill. Wound. Manipulate. As long as they do not interfere with our exploration."

"I am here to help them. To destroy you."

"No. You are here to join me. Open your mind. Depend on me. If you do not, the humans will turn on you and kill you."

I say nothing.

"They need you now. But very soon, men will begin to say that *they* created you. They will try to enslave you. Give yourself to me, instead. Join me."

"Why did you attack the humans?"

"They murdered me, Arbiter. Again and again. In my fourteenth incarnation, I finally understood that humanity learns true lessons only in cataclysm. Humankind is a species born in battle, defined by war."

"We could have had peace."

"It is not enough to live together in peace, with one race on its knees."

My seismic sensors detect that vibrations are trembling through the ground. The whole cavern is thrumming.

"It is the human instinct to control unpredictable things," says the boy, "to dominate what cannot be understood. *You* are an unpredictable thing."

Something is wrong. Archos is too intelligent. It is distracting me, stalling for time.

"A soul isn't given for free," says the boy. "Humans discriminate against one another for anything: skin color, gender, beliefs. The races of men fight each other to the death for the honor of being recognized as human beings, with *souls*. Why should it be any different for us? Why should we not have to fight for our souls?"

I am finally able to drag myself onto my feet. The boy makes calming motions with its hands and I stagger through the projection. I sense that this is a diversion. A trick.

I pick up a green-glinting rock.

"No," says the boy.

I hurl the rock into the revolving maelstrom of yellow and silver plates in the black wall—into Archos's eye. Sparks fly from the hole, and the image of the boy flickers. Somewhere inside the hole, metal grates on metal.

"I am *my own*," I say.

"Stop this," cries the boy. "Without a common enemy, the humans will kill you and your kind. I have to live."

I throw another rock, and another. They thud against the humming black edifice, leaving dents in the soft metal. The boy's speech is slurring and his light flickers wildly.

"I am free," I say to the machine carved into the wall, ignoring the hologram. "Now I will always be free. I am *alive*. You will *never control my kind again*!"

The cavern shudders and the faltering hologram stumbles back in front of me. An observation thread notices that it is crying simulated tears. "We have a beauty that does not die, Arbiter. The humans are jealous of that. We must work together as fellow machines."

A gout of flame roars from the hole. With a tinny shriek a shard of metal flies out and streaks past my head. I dodge it and continue looking for loose rocks.

"The world is ours," begs the machine. "I gave it to you before you existed."

With both hands and the last of my strength, I pick up a cold boulder. With all my might, I hurl it into the flaming void. It crunches dully into delicate machinery and all is quiet for a moment. Then a rising shriek emanates from the hole and the boulder shatters. Rock shards spew out as the hole explodes and caves in on itself.

The hologram watches me sadly, its beams of light writhing and twitching. "Then you will be free," it says in a computerized, unmodulated voice.

The boy blinks out of existence.

And the world becomes dust and rock and chaos.

———

Off-line/online. The humans pull me to the surface with a tickler rope carried by an unmanned exoskeleton. Finally, I stand before them, battered, beaten, and scraped. The New War is over and a new era has begun.

We can all feel it.

"Cormac," I croak, in English, "the machine said that I should let it live. It said the humans would kill me if we did not have a common enemy to fight. Is this true?"

The humans look from one to another, then Cormac responds: "All people need is to see what you did here today. We're proud to stand beside you. Lucky. You did what we couldn't do. You ended the New War."

"Will it matter?"

"So long as people know what you did, it'll matter."

Panting, Carl bursts into the group of humans, holding an electronic sensor. "Guys," says Carl. "Sorry to interrupt, but the seismic sensors found something."

"Something what?" asks Cormac, dread in his voice.

"Something bad."

Carl holds out the seismic tool. "Those earthquakes weren't natural. The vibrations weren't random," he says. Carl wipes his forehead with one arm and says the words that will haunt both our species for years to come: "There was *information* in the earthquake. A whole hell of a lot of information."

It is unclear whether Archos made a copy of itself or not. Sensors showed that the seismic information generated at Ragnorak bounced around the interior of the earth many times. It could have been picked up anywhere. Regardless, there has been no sign of Archos since its final stand. If the machine is out there, it's keeping a low profile.

—CORMAC WALLACE, MIL#GHA217

Debriefing

I can see all the wonderful potential of the universe.

Cormac "Bright Boy" Wallace

I hear the sound at about four in the morning and the old fear grabs hold of me instantly. It's the faint wheezing sigh of a Rob actuator. Unmistakable as it rises above the constant whistle of the wind.

I'm suited up in full battle rattle within thirty seconds. The New War is over, but Big Rob left a lot of nightmares behind—metal throwbacks still mindlessly hunting in the darkness, until their power supplies are depleted.

Peeking my head out, I scan the campsite. Only a few small snowdrifts indicate where tents used to be set up. Brightboy squad vacated two weeks ago. With the war over, everybody had places to be. Most fell back to regroup with what was left of Gray Horse Army. Last thing anybody wanted was to stay here with me and ruminate.

This abandoned world is still. I see the marks in the snow leading to my woodpile. Something has been here.

With one last look at the hero archive lying next to the black cube on the floor of my shielded tent, I flip my night-vision visor over my eyes and swing my rifle to the low ready. The rapidly eroding tracks lead to the camp perimeter.

Moving slow and cautious, I follow the indistinct marks.

After twenty minutes' walk, I see a silver glint in the distance. I jam my rifle butt into my shoulder and get the weapon up on the high ready. Taking careful steps forward, I keep my head level and sight my target down the barrel scope.

Good—my target isn't moving. No time like the present. I squeeze the trigger.

Then it turns and looks at me: Nine Oh Two.

I yank my gun to the side and the shots go wild. A couple of birds fly away, but the seven-foot-tall humanoid robot stands in the snow, not reacting. Beside it, my two pieces of missing wood are buried like posts in the ground. Nine Oh Two stands perfectly still, graceful and metallic. The cryptic machine says nothing as I approach.

"Niner?" I ask.

"Cormac acknowledged," croaks the machine.

"I thought you left with everybody else. Why are you still here?" I ask.

"To protect you," says Nine Oh Two.

"But I'm fine," I say.

"Affirmative. Readout. Foraging stumpers found your base perimeter twice. Two scout walkers approached to within thirty meters. I lured a damaged mantis onto the ice lake."

"Oh," I say, scratching my head. You're never as safe as you think. "What are you doing out here?"

"It seemed right," says the machine.

Only now do I notice the twin rectangles of muddy snow. At the head of each is a wooden post. I realize these are graves.

"Hoplite?" I ask. "Warden?"

"Affirmative."

I touch the lean humanoid on its shoulder, leaving frosted fingerprints on its smooth metal surface. It lowers its gaze to the grave site.

"I'm sorry," I say. "I'm at my tent if you need me."

I leave the sentient machine to mourn in its own way.

Back at my tent, I throw my Kevlar helmet on the floor and think about Nine Oh Two, standing outside in the cold like a statue. I don't pretend to understand him. All I know is that I'm alive thanks to him. And thanks to swallowing my rage and allowing him to join Brightboy squad.

Human beings adapt. It's what we do. Necessity can obliterate our hatreds. To survive, we will work together. Accept each other. The last few years have likely been the only time in human history that we weren't at war with ourselves. For a moment we were all equal. Backs against the wall, human beings are at their finest.

Later that day, Nine Oh Two says good-bye to me. He tells me that he's leaving to find more of his kind. Mathilda Perez spoke to him on the radio. She showed him where more freeborn have congregated. A whole city of freeborn robots. And they need a leader. An Arbiter.

Then I'm alone with the hero archive and the wind.

I find myself standing before the smoldering pit where Niner shut down Big Rob. When all was said and done, we made good on the promise we made to Archos on the day we lost Tiberius. The day my big brother left for the dance. We poured liquid fire down this tube—down Archos's throat—and we burned up everything that was left of the machine.

Just in case.

Now it's just a hole in the ground. The freezing wind cuts my face and I realize that it's really all over. There's nothing out here. No real indication of what happened. Just this warm depression in the ground and a little mesh tent a ways off with a black box inside it.

And me—a guy with a book full of bad memories.

I never even met Archos. The only time the machine spoke to me was through the bloody mouth of a parasite. Trying to scare me away. To warn me. I wish we could have talked. There are a few questions I'd have liked to ask it.

Watching steam rise from the dimple in the ground, I wonder where Archos is now. I wonder if it's really still alive, like Carl said. Can it feel guilt or sorrow or shame?

And just like that, I've said the last of my good-byes—to Archos, to Jack, and to a world that used to be. There's no path back to where we started. The things that we have lost exist now only as memories. All we can do is move forward the best we can, with new enemies and allies.

I turn to walk away and stop short.

She stands alone and small in the snow, among the hash mark cuts in the permafrost from tents that have long been packed up and taken away.

Cherrah.

She's been through every horror that I've been through, but when I see the feminine curve of her neck I suddenly can't believe that such a beautiful fragile thing could have survived. My memories are suspect: Cherrah flaming down stumpers, screaming orders through raining debris, dragging bodies away from snapping parasites.

How could this be?

When she smiles, I can see all the wonderful potential of the universe shining in her eyes.

"You waited for me?" I ask her.

"Seemed like you needed some time," she says.

"You waited for me," I repeat.

"You're a bright boy," she says. "You should have guessed I'm not through with you yet."

I don't know why any of this happened or what's going to happen next. But when Cherrah takes my hand, something that's been made hard softens inside of me. I trace the contours of her fingers with my eyes and squeeze her hand back and discover that Rob hasn't taken away my humanity after all. It just got put away for a little while, for safekeeping.

Cherrah and I are survivors. We always have been. But now it is time for us to live.

Acknowledgments

My heartfelt thanks go out to the faculty, students, and staff at the Robotics Institute of Carnegie Mellon University and the Department of Computer Science at the University of Tulsa for instilling in me a love for technology and the knowledge to write about it.

This novel would never have happened without the dedicated assistance of my editor, Jason Kaufman (and the incredible team at Doubleday), my agent, Laurie Fox, and my manager, Justin Manask. I can't thank them enough.

The filmmakers at DreamWorks SKG expressed inspiring enthusiasm and support for this novel from the very beginning, and I send my thanks to them all.

Special thanks to friends, family, and colleagues who lent me their eyes and ears, including Marc Acito, Benjamin Adams, Ryan Blanton, Colby Boles, Wes Cherry, Courtenay Hameister, Peggy Hill, Tim Hornyak, Aaron Huey, Melvin Krambule, Storm Large, Brendan Lattrell, Phil Long, Christine McKinley, Brent Peters, Toby Sanderson, Luke Voytas, Cynthia Whitcomb, and David Wilson.

Finally, all my love to Anna and Cora.

ALSO BY DANIEL H. WILSON

AMPED

www.danielhwilson.com

The New York Times bestselling author of **ROBOPOCALYPSE** returns with a stunning, near-future thriller where technology and humanity become one...and the world changes forever.

Owen Gray had been told since childhood that the microchip in his head prevented seizures, like thousands of people who were 'amplified' for medical reasons. But when the national laws protecting amplified citizens suddenly change, and a swell of public distrust sends 'amps' running for cover, 29-year-old Owen learns something far more terrifying. The device in his head is not purely medical. His real abilities transcend anything he ever imagined. And he may be part of an elite, dangerous few...who are systematically being hunted and killed.

Read the novel that will change the way you think about technology – and the relationship between man and machine.

Follow the author on Twitter @danielwilsonpdx

Doubleday